A SELLSWORD'S WRATH

Book Two
of
The Seven Virtues
by
Jacob Peppers

A Sellsword's Wrath
Book two of the Seven Virtues

Visit the author website:
www.JacobPeppersAuthor.com

Dedicated to Olin Sidney Brown

One of the greatest men I've ever had the privilege to know

You have been well loved

And you will be missed

Sign up for the author's New Releases mailing list and get a copy of *The Silent Blade,* the prequel for The Seven Virtues, FREE for a Limited Time!

CHAPTER ONE

Adina frowned, watching the bout with an uneasiness she couldn't completely explain. Two men against one, and though the two had clearly been taught something of combat, their opponent always seemed to avoid their blows, dodging in and out of their attacks as if he knew where they were going to strike before they knew themselves. At least, *almost* always. Even as she watched, the man sidestepped out of the way of a wooden practice sword, but he stumbled and the second attack struck him in the shoulder. He grunted, losing his balance and falling to the ground.

Adina winced at the sound of wood striking flesh, fighting down the urge to call it off. Wood or not, the practice swords were capable of leaving deep, mottled bruises that were painful to the touch. Proof of this, if she'd needed any, was visible on the lone man's bared torso in the form of several large, dark purple blotches covering his skin.

The man grunted in frustration, struggling to his hands and knees, obviously in pain. "Are you alright?" Balen asked, stepping forward and removing his helmet, a look of concern on his sun-weathered face. He held out his hand. "Gods, I'm sorry—I didn't mean to hit so hard."

"I'm fine," Aaron said, ignoring the proffered hand and struggling to his feet. He could have made an excuse that, less than four days ago, he'd been poisoned and nearly killed, but Adina knew he wouldn't. Whatever else the sellsword was, he wasn't a fan of excuses. "It was a good hit."

The third man stepped forward, removing his own helmet and revealing a sweaty, grime-streaked face. "Are you sure, lad?" Herb, the tavernkeep, asked between gasping breaths.

"I'm sure."

"In that case," Balen said, grinning between his own ragged breaths, "a point for us."

Herb returned the grin, stretching and rubbing at his back. "Makes a man remember why he gave up fightin' in the first place, not that I was ever likely to forget. I swear my whole body ain't nothin' but one big bruise."

Aaron nodded, glancing between the two men. "Again?"

The two men looked at each other, red-faced and covered in sweat, their grins still in place, then they turned back to the sellsword. "You know what?" Balen said. "I'm thinking maybe it's time we had a break. I won't do you no good for practice, I'm lying passed out in the dirt."

Herb nodded, laughter dancing in his eyes. "Sounds good to me. Best quit while we're ahead. Besides, I'm fairly sure that Gryle should have the stew finished by now. And is the dead man going to eat, I wonder?"

Aaron smiled, and Adina thought she was the only one that noticed how forced it was, "Maybe later. I'm going to stay for a bit longer—you two enjoy."

"Oh, I'm not a man's ever been accused of passing up a good meal," Herb said. "We'll see you inside."

Adina watched them walk in, wondering if they'd even noticed that Aaron had been using his left hand. Then she turned back to see Aaron studying the wooden practice sword he held, a look in his eyes that was too close to desperation for her liking. Once the men had gone, he began his forms, pivoting his feet first one way and then the other, the blade following as a natural progression, a single part of some complex, often rehearsed dance.

If he noticed her watching him, he gave no sign, and Adina frowned. Three days ago, the sellsword had nearly been killed, yet here he was, taking on Herb and Balen every day that he could convince them to, pushing himself so hard it was a wonder he hadn't collapsed from exhaustion already.

She was so wrapped up in her own worries that she didn't notice that someone had walked up beside her until May spoke. "Ah, I thought I'd find you here."

Adina turned to the club owner, but the heavy-set woman was watching the sellsword as he practiced, a look of concern on her features that mirrored what Adina felt in her own heart. Unlike the first time Adina saw her, the club owner was dressed simply in a tunic and trousers, her long mane of bright red hair pulled back into a ponytail. "You worry for him," May said. It wasn't a question.

Adina turned back to Aaron. "Yes."

"Good," May said, "somebody has to. Still, I wouldn't worry overly much. If there's a tougher man out there than our Aaron, I've never met him."

"Three days, May," Adina said. "Three *days* since he nearly died, barely enough time for the poison to work its way out of his system and already he's killing himself training. I've tried to speak to him about it, to tell him to take it easy, but he won't meet my eyes, he only nods and says 'sure' and then goes right back to killing himself."

May sighed. "I know. He blames himself, you know. For letting Darrell be captured."

"That's ridiculous, May," Adina said, "What was he supposed to do? For the gods' sake, he was *unconscious* at the time."

"*I* know that, and *you* know that," the club owner said, looking back at Aaron, "but he doesn't. And once he's decided something...well, I've never met a more stubborn man, in my life. Still, it's his way. It's the reason he's the best at what he does; it's also what makes him the most infuriating man I've ever met."

"He needs to rest," Adina said, unable to keep the concern out of her voice. As soon as he'd been able to walk without assistance, Aaron had wanted to go into to the city to find out what he could about his old swordmaster, but Adina and the others had managed to convince him, *barely,* that many in the city would recognize him from the tournament, that it was too dangerous. Instead, Leomin, the Parnen captain, went out each night, questioning and finding out what he could about where Darrell was being held, but so far he had nothing to show for his efforts.

Since that first night, Aaron had spent nearly the entirety of each day training, pausing only to eat and get what Adina was increasingly sure couldn't be more than four hours of sleep before going back to it. "He needs to rest," she said again.

"Yes, he does," May said, "but I wouldn't waste my breath telling him that."

May said something else, but Adina didn't hear it. She was watching the sellsword, watching the way he moved. Each step was fluid, graceful and though his movements appeared more like a dance than anything that would be used in combat, she'd seen him fight enough to know that each movement was capable of leaving men dead or dying in its wake. Still, despite his skill, she noticed him wince regularly as his incompletely healed wounds pained him. Each time this happened, he'd frown, pressing harder and harder, his movements growing faster and faster until they were little more than a blur, the sweat flying off of him.

She wished that Leomin would find out *something* about the swordmaster. For now, Aaron had agreed to keep hidden but for how long? How many more days would he listen to Leomin explain in his sorrowful tone that he'd found out nothing about the old man's whereabouts? How long before he decided to go into the city himself, risky or not?

If Belgarin's men had taken the swordmaster—as they must have—they were keeping quiet about it, and the failed attempts and lack of news were even taking their toll on the usually obliviously optimistic Parnen. Each night, he returned later than the one before, exhausted, shaking his head sadly and going to bed only to wake up before the sun rose the next day and start again. Adina sighed. *Gods help us.*

***

Aaron spun, his wooden sword lashing out in a straight thrust. He held the pose until his left arm began to shake, then he held it longer, gritting his teeth. Finally, he hissed a curse and let the arm drop.

You push yourself too hard, Co spoke into his mind, her voice concerned. *She's worried about you. So am I.*

4

Aaron didn't turn to look where he knew Adina was standing, choosing instead to continue his forms. *I appreciate it, Firefly, but I'm fine. And while I sit here doing nothing, Darrell is probably being tortured—shit, for all we know he's dead already. I should be out there looking for him instead of sitting around waiting for news of his execution.*

They're doing everything they can; you know that.

What? Sending the Parnen out night after night? Gods, Co, who knows what the man's doing out there? I'll admit that he's proven himself to be a damn hard son of a bitch to kill escaping Aster like he did, but for all I know he's going out and drinking himself into a stupor each night.

You know better than that, Co said, her tone admonishing. *You're not being fair.*

Aaron paused, panting for breath, sweat pouring from him, and let the practice sword hang loosely at his side. *Maybe I'm not. But I can't help feeling like it's happening again. My parents...Owen...now Darrell.*

This is different.

Is it? He sighed and tossed the practice sword on the ground before turning and heading back into the mansion. He walked by Adina without speaking, could feel her wanting him to, feel her wanting something from him, but he found that he didn't have it to give. If he'd been faster, if he'd been better, then Adina and Gryle, her chamberlain, never would have been taken. Darrell never would have had to step in and sacrifice himself. He'd failed and, because of it, his master, the man who'd taken him in when he was an orphan living on the street, was going to die. *Everybody who gets close to me dies.*

Co didn't respond, and Aaron walked inside the mansion to find the others—Gryle, May, Herb, and Balen—standing near the front door. Herb had a pack slung over his shoulder, and the heavyweight innkeeper was shaking hands with the others, their expressions solemn.

They turned as they heard Aaron approach, and Herb's expression was almost one of shame. May was the first to speak. "Herb is going back to his family, Aaron. With winter coming in, each day that passes will make the trip more dangerous."

"Of course," Aaron said, nodding, and Herb seemed to wince as if struck.

He took a hesitant step forward, offering his hand tentatively, as if expecting Aaron to refuse it. "Aaron...I'm sorry. I want to stay but with the weather comin' on, and the missus and Paula to think about—"

Aaron forced a smile and shook the man's hand. "Don't say anymore, Herb. And thanks for everything you've done for us. We never would have made it here without you."

The innkeeper nodded, his expression tightly controlled. "Anytime," he said. Then he turned and headed for the door. Aaron stood with the others and watched him go, watched him climb onto the mule-drawn cart and start down the path toward the manor's gates.

May had sent Celes away the second day when it had become clear that Aaron was going to recover from his wounds. Ostensibly to watch after May's club, but, in truth, Aaron suspected the club owner just wanted her friend safely away from the city. Aaron understood the reasons for Celes and Herbert leaving, even agreed with them, but he couldn't help feeling that their chances of finding the swordmaster were getting less and less likely.

He was still standing there, staring out at the city through the doorway, when he felt a hand on his shoulder and turned to see May standing beside him. He glanced around and was surprised to see that the others had gone. "We'll find him, Aaron. If anyone can, Leomin can."

"Three days, May. Three days and nothing. He could already be dead by now."

She said nothing, giving his shoulder a squeeze before turning and disappearing up the stairs. Aaron stared out the door for another few moments, stared out into the night, thinking of what that darkness might conceal, of what mysteries it held, then he turned and made his way to his room in search of the sleep that, for the past three nights, had not come.

CHAPTER TWO

Aaron roused from the half-asleep, half-awake state that was the best he'd managed for the last several days to the sound of a knock at the mansion's front door. He dressed quickly, throwing on his shirt and boots, slinging his sheathed sword across his back before heading down the stairs. The knock came again, louder this time, an urgency to it that Aaron didn't like, and he found himself running down the stairs as he heard the sounds of the others stirring from their own beds. *Leomin. It has to be, and by the knock, he's found something.*

He made it to the door and hesitated before opening it, reminding himself that there was an entire city worth of soldiers that would be more than happy to kill him and the others and, if things had gone bad somehow for Leomin, they could very well be standing outside waiting for him to open it. The knock came again. Aaron did not move for several seconds, then his need for answers outweighing his caution, he drew his sword, slung the latch on the door, and threw it open.

He was surprised to find that the person standing on the manor's porch was neither Leomin nor a squad of soldiers hungry for blood. Instead, it was a kid of no more than twelve or thirteen and, judging by his clothes, a street urchin from one of the city's less reputable areas. The boy crouched with his hands on his knees, his breath coming in great heaving gasps.

I don't like this, Co said in his mind, and Aaron was forced to agree with the Virtue.

He frowned. "What is it, boy?"

The youth looked up, and his eyes went wide as he took in the naked steel in Aaron's hand. He held his own hands up, taking a quick step back. "I don't mean any harm, mister. Honest."

"Relax, kid," Aaron said, "I'm not going to hurt you. Now, what is it?"

"The...man," the kid gasped, then paused to take a breath. "He wrote a note, told me to bring it to this address. Paid me, and in real gold! He said it was urgent, told me not to dilly dally, had a funny way of talking. Mister, I'm not sure I know what dilly dallying is, anyhow, but he acted like it was real—"

"The note?" Aaron said, cutting off the boy's stammering, his eyes roaming the empty streets. The youth nodded, swallowing hard, and held up a crumpled parchment in his shaking hand.

The space between his shoulder blades itching as if someone were pointing a crossbow at it, Aaron took the note and nodded to the boy, tossing him a coin, "You've done well and my thanks. Now, I think it best you get out of here."

The street urchin nodded quickly and was off and running down the street without a word, disappearing into one of the nearby alleyways. A memory of his own time spent on the streets after his parents' murders came to Aaron's mind, time spent sneaking and hiding, begging when he could and stealing when he had to. The boy would be alright, whatever came. The orphans of any city, its poor and dirty children, learned early how to hide, how to disappear. When you were the weakest and the smallest, running was all you knew.

Holding his sword with one hand, he used the other to open the note.

They're coming.

-L

Aaron felt a cold shiver run down his spine. They'd been staying here on borrowed time, he knew that. If not for Darrell, he and the others would have no doubt left by now. In fact, he suspected by the looks he was beginning to see in the eyes of the others, more and more with each passing day, that were it not for him, they would have left regardless, counting the old swordmaster as the latest victim in Belgarin's bloody conquests. Aaron knew they were right, had known since Darrell was taken; a man who'd done the kind of things Belgarin had wouldn't be inclined to show any mercy to an old swordsman who'd helped his sister and the others escape his grasp.

Most likely, Darrell was dead already and staying around did nothing to change that—except for giving Belgarin a very real chance of finding them all, including Adina, and taking out several of his enemies at once. To stay had been stupid and reckless, he'd known that, but he'd not been able to find it in himself to leave his old master behind, not when there was a chance—however small—that they could save him. He owed Darrell that much for taking him in when he was a child, for training and teaching a stubborn, foolish boy who knew only anger at the world that had stolen everything from him, who felt only hate and hunger and little else. The truth was, he owed the old man a debt he could never repay—and now it looked like he never would.

But the *note*. The damned note changed everything. It wasn't just the meaning of the message, which was bad enough. It was the conciseness of it, the shortness of it. Aaron had come to like Leomin more than he ever thought he would—which meant that he only felt like murdering the man about half the time he was around him—and he'd come to realize that the Parnen captain possessed some very interesting talents, particularly an ability, it seemed, to talk himself into or out of anything. However, in all the time that he'd known the captain, the man had demonstrated an overwhelming incapacity to be brief and get to the point, often to have any point at all as far as that was concerned. The fact that the man would send a note with only two words—*they're coming*—and nothing else, spoke of a haste that demanded immediate attention.

Aaron dropped the note and the wind caught it, sent it fluttering down the street. He turned and was surprised to find the others watching him in the doorway. May, a heavy set woman, part club owner part rebellion leader; Balen, Leomin's first mate; Gryle, the chubby chamberlain of a royal household that no longer existed. And of course, Adina, the princess and one of the few remaining members of a rapidly shrinking royal family—all of them staring at him expectantly, waiting for news, waiting for him to tell them what to do. Not that he could blame them. May might be one of the cleverest people he'd ever met as well as the most powerful, in her subtle way, and Adina might be one of the remaining royal siblings, clever and resourceful and determined in her own right, but this was not their place. This was a question of fighting, of steel and blood, and with such questions, they looked to him for the answer.

What company we keep, Co spoke into his mind. *Still, there are more pressing matters.*

No doubt, Aaron thought back. He took a moment to steady himself and met the questioning eyes of the others. "They're coming." He gave them a moment to absorb the news, watched their faces go from shock to fear to uncertainty. He gave them only a moment, then he nodded. "Right. Two minutes. Grab anything that you can't live without with the understanding that if it slows you down you might die with it. Meet back here."

To their credit, they all scattered without protestation or complaint, hurrying to their rooms. Aaron went to his own room, pulled on his shirt and boots, tossed a change of clothes into a pack and slung the leather strap over his shoulder. That done, he glanced around the room and realized there was nothing else for him to take. No keepsakes, no priceless souvenirs or gifts from loved ones. All the things he'd once had, all the things he'd once loved, were gone, crumbled to ash and dust in a world of both. He wondered what it meant to be a man grown with nothing to show for the life he'd led, nothing to anchor him to it but the blade at his back and the memories of those things he'd lost. Hardly a man at all, really, but some dusty revenant wandering the world, good for the spilling of blood and little else.

There is time yet, Co said, *time to build a life.*

"That's the funny thing about time," Aaron muttered. "There always seems to be plenty of it—until there isn't." With that, he frowned and headed for the stairs.

The others met him at the door within the two minute window, each of them carrying a travel pack on their back and not much else—except for the heavy-set chamberlain who was carrying so many bags and satchels he looked in danger of toppling at any minute. "What's this?" Aaron said.

"I'm sorry, Mister Envelar," Gryle huffed, his face red and sweaty as he came to stand with the others. "I'm quite ready."

"No," Aaron said, "you're not."

Gryle followed his gaze to the many bags draped over him. "Ah, well, I can assure you, sir, that these are the *bare* necessities. After all, my lady must have attire for different occasions, and we have only just managed to begin rebuilding her wardrobe—as well as, of course, her collection of books." He grunted, shifting a strap back over his shoulder that had begun to fall. "A royal lady such as herself must always keep educated, and I find the best way—"

Aaron turned to Adina who stared at him with a pained expression on her face, clearly embarrassed, then he turned back to the chamberlain who was still speaking.

"—so, as you can see, it really is all vital to ensure—"

"Leave it."

The balding chamberlain cut off. "I'm sorry, sir?"

"I said, leave it."

A pained, desperate expression came over Gryle's face, and he sighed heavily. "Well, I suppose, I could find a way to consolidate some...perhaps, if I were to remove my own change of clothes, I could—"

"All of it."

A look of shocked horror came over the chamberlain's face, as if his number one concern was the breach in propriety of a princess traveling without her belongings and not the armed men who would soon be knocking at their door. "Sir, surely you can't be serious."

"There's a good chance we're going to be doing a lot of running in the very near future, chamberlain. Tell me, how well will you be able to run weighed down by dresses and books and the gods know what else?"

The chamberlain raised his chin haughtily in the air, the effect spoiled somewhat by the fact that he was nearly bent double under the weight of the packs. "I assure you, Mr. Envelar, that I will not slow you down. For my mistress, I will do what the situation demands, should that be walking or...running."

Aaron nodded. "Show me."

The chamberlain's eyes widened in surprise. "I'm sorry?"

Aaron drew his sword and pointed it at the chamberlain. "I'm one of Belgarin's men. I've been sent after a group of rebels by my master and—since they've spent all of their time jawing when they should have been running—I've managed to catch up with them."

He took a step toward the chubby man, meeting the man's eyes. "Now, let me see you run."

Gryle squeaked as Aaron took another menacing step toward him and turned to start down the hallway in a stumbling, awkward shuffle. He'd taken only a few steps when a large case slipped from his shoulder and fell to the floor. The chamberlain let out a squawk of surprise as he tripped over it and he—and the bags he carried— sprawled across the floor.

Aaron crouched beside the sweating, huffing chamberlain and held out his hand to help the man up. Once more on his feet, Gryle stared at the bags with something like shame before turning to the princess. "I'm sorry, my lady."

"Gryle," Adina said, stepping forward and putting a gentle hand on the chamberlain's shoulder, "it's fine. There's nothing there that cannot be replaced—they're only dresses and books."

Gryle's eyes grew wide. "Only dresses and..." He glanced at Aaron, swallowed once, and nodded. "Of course, my lady."

Aaron glanced around at the scattered bags. "Is there one of these that has food and traveling clothes?"

"Of course!" Gryle said, suddenly indignant. "I would not have my lady starve, Mister Enve—"

"Which one is it?"

Gryle hesitated, a confused expression on his face, then pointed. "That one there."

"Better grab it then."

The chamberlain walked over and lifted the pack then turned back to Aaron. "And the other bags?"

"Leave them."

"Leave them?" Gryle asked, his voice breaking, but already Aaron and the others were walking out the door and into the dark streets. He glanced back at the packs and bags scattered in the hallway and sighed before turning and following them out of the door.

CHAPTER THREE

The streets were crowded despite the late hour, and Aaron studied the people around them as they made their way through the city, watching for any sign of recognition or alarm. After his first night searching fruitlessly for any information about Darrell's whereabouts, Leomin had arrived back at the rented house with some flyers that he'd said had been posted throughout the city. The papers depicted Aaron and Adina in great detail, claiming that they were enemies of the crown and would most likely be traveling with several companions, a reward offered for any information that led to their capture.

Aaron kept the hood of his cloak thrown over his head, as did Adina, but that gave him little comfort. Such an odd group as they were couldn't help but draw attention. Telling himself there was no choice, the space between his shoulder blades itching, Aaron led the others through the crowded streets. Men and women who'd traveled to the city for the contest in which Aaron had nearly died made their way from shop to shop, from tavern to tavern, laughing and carousing, by appearances unmoved by the fact that their rightful ruler had been assassinated only a few short weeks ago and that the author of his death (who also happened to be his brother) had taken over the city.

Aaron had heard bits and pieces from Leomin about what had been happening in the city since Belgarin took over, but hearing about it and seeing it were two very different things. He wasn't surprised, exactly—growing up in the Downs, the poor, crime-riddled district of the city of Avarest, had quickly disabused him of any notions of human loyalty or kindness. Not surprised, but disappointed and angry. Not for himself, so much, but for Adina. Eladen, like Belgarin, had been her brother, but unlike Belgarin, the man had been known for being kind and compassionate, a man who had believed that the commoners should be looked after as much as the nobles themselves. A worthy ideal but, of course, it was also that ideal that had seen his second in command relinquish the city and its people over to Belgarin without so much as a hand raised in its defense.

Eladen had been, from all reports, a good man, though Aaron still had his doubts that there was such a thing. Either way, Adina had loved him, and the commoners had supposedly loved him as well. With each laughing, drunken soul they passed, he could see the princess's mood growing darker, saw the hurt grow in her eyes and, more than that, because of the bond between him and Co, the Virtue of Compassion, he could *feel* her anger, her disappointment. Eladen had given everything for his people—his very life, when it had come to it—yet they continued on after his murder as if nothing had happened.

Aaron fell back a step so that he was walking in line with the princess, the others lagging a few paces behind as they made their way through the city. "People are simple, selfish creatures, that's all."

She turned to him, tucking a loose strand of hair behind her ear and trying a smile that didn't come close to touching her eyes. "My brother wasn't. He was a good man, and it seems only weeks after he died they've forgotten all about him. It's as if they don't even care that the man who killed him is ruling their city."

Aaron shrugged. "You have to understand, Adina, such matters are far above the average man. He spends his time worrying about what his family will eat or how to keep his wife from discovering he has a mistress on the side, maybe wondering if the crops'll come in, or if he'll be able to pay when the tax collectors come a calling. Such things leave little room for worrying about who's sitting on a throne they've never seen and probably never will. Such things are too high up, too big. What's an ant care for the decisions of men?" He shrugged again, "A man takes a step to the left instead of the right, and the ant gets squished where he might not've, but there's no rhyme or reason to it—better to keep your head down and hope than to look up and see the boot coming."

"But surely you don't believe that," Adina said, "or else why are you here? Why come with us at all?"

Aaron met her bright blue eyes, the most beautiful he'd ever seen. "You know why."

A flush crept up her cheeks, and she smiled before turning back to the road. Aaron watched her for several seconds, the smooth line of her jaw, her long hair, the way it fell over her shoulders. A kindness there sure, but a hardness too, in the way her shoulders were set, in the way she faced the world head-on, never flinching away from something because she didn't want to see it, never acting like a thing didn't exist because it clashed with the way she wanted the world to be. Courage and kindness, hardness and determination. Things that, in his experience, rarely went together.

She's not bad to look at either, Co said, *or so I gather from the men we pass.*

Aaron frowned. He'd noticed the looks himself; they were the last thing they needed when they were trying to be discreet, to escape the city before their hunters found them. He told himself that was why he wanted to smash their faces in, to tell them to keep their fucking eyes where they belonged and to mind their own damned business unless they wanted him minding theirs. Only prudence, of course, only a caution any man in his circumstances might feel. Or so he told himself.

"What about the captain?" Balen asked for at least the fifth time, and Aaron bit back the urge to snap at the man. He was loyal to his captain, that was all, and there were plenty worse things than that.

"The captain's a...well, let's say he's a clever man. And the gods know he's a way of surviving when he's no right to. Besides," he said, turning a corner onto a side street, "he was able to write a note and send a runner; he'll be alright. A lot easier to blend in as one man than a group. If I were you, I'd be more worried about us than your captain."

"Well, 'spose you've a point there. The captain's a resourceful man and that's a fact."

"Aaron," May said, and there was something in her voice that brought him up short.

He turned and looked at the club owner and saw that she was pulling her long, fiery red hair into a pony tail and tying it with a ribbon, something Aaron had never seen before until these last few days. Her red hair, in many ways, was as much her calling card as the *Traveler's Rest,* the club that she owned and operated in the Downs. In truth, the club wasn't just a club at all, but a base of operations for an organization that, though it didn't rival the major crime bosses in brute strength, was possessed of a subtle power that was more difficult to define, one that whispered instead of shouted. A dagger instead of a broadsword, but no less deadly for all that. Aaron thought it more deadly in truth, for whatever else might be true of a broadsword, you usually saw it coming.

Aaron glanced around them at the worry in May's tone and realized that the street they were on was conspicuously empty. He cursed himself for his own carelessness, for allowing himself to get distracted by conversation and by thoughts of the others. An understandable enough mistake, maybe, for a man who'd spent the majority of his life alone with no one to call friend. Understandable, but that would be little comfort when the bleeding started.

He stopped and signaled for the others to halt, drawing the blade from across his back. The street was silent, too silent. *Idiot,* he thought. A lifetime learning hard lessons, hard yet true ones, and now in the space of a few days he'd let himself forget. His eyes locked on the road in front of him, Aaron motioned the others back, knowing it was too late even as he did it.

"What is it, Mr. Envelar?" Gryle asked. "Surely, this is the fastest way out of the c—"

"No questions now, Gryle," Aaron snapped, his heartbeat loud enough that he could hear it in his ears. Another lesson he'd learned was that no matter how many scrapes a man got in, no matter how many times the question of blood was raised and no matter how many times he answered it, each time felt like the first. Fear and self-doubt and wonder at the futility of it all. They were unwelcome companions, but they were, at least, familiar ones.

Aaron motioned for them to go back the way they'd come and wasn't surprised when two men emerged from the alley's entrance, wielding swords. Aaron gestured, indicating that the others should stop. The older of the two men ran a hand through his beard, shaking his head. "Well, looks like we've found us a group of fugitives. And Bert here thought we'd lose ya." He slapped the man beside him—Bert, apparently—on the shoulder and grinned. "Nah, but I told him. A group like that? Shit, we'd have to be blind to lose you, and it seems I was right enough. Gotta say, though," he went on, grinning at the princess, "the paintings don't hardly do you justice."

"You do a lot of talking," Aaron said, glancing behind him to see that two more armed men were making their way closer from the other end of the alley, in no hurry, confident that they knew how it was going to go.

The bearded man nodded as he and his partner started forward. "Yeah, I've been accused of it once or twice. Anyhow, I reckon we've got you well and proper. Any chance of you putting down that sticker? One sword against four...well, those are some pretty long odds, aye, fella?" He glanced at Adina as he and his partner stopped about ten feet away, his eyes tracing up and down her body. "My, but you're a fine thing. Curves in all the right places and that's a fact."

Adina's face grew red with anger and Aaron saw her tense beside him, but she said nothing.

"What do you say?" the man said, turning back to Aaron. "It'd be a damn shame for something to happen to a woman like that. Why don't you just put down your blade, and we can do this like civilized folks. Ain't no need for anybody to get dead over it."

"You're wrong." Before the man could respond, Aaron surged forward, drawing one of the knives he always kept secreted at his waist. To his credit, the bearded man reacted fast, knocking Aaron's sword aside with a two-handed strike that nearly made him lose his grip. Aaron used the momentum to spin his body around and bury the knife he'd drawn hilt-deep into the man's neck. The soldier's eyes went wide with shock and blood sluiced from his throat, staining his beard and tunic a deep crimson.

Behind you!

Through his bond with the virtue, Aaron felt the man coming, knew just how the strike would land, so he spun in a circle, toward his attacker. He grunted as the man's fist and the sword hilt he held struck him in the back and sent him stumbling, but not before his sword sliced deeply into the soldier's arm.

The man grunted in pain and his sword clattered to the ground, his wounded arm unable to hold it. Aaron managed to catch his feet and turn in time to see the man charging him. He grunted as he was slammed against the wall, the air knocked from his lungs. His own sword flew out of his hand from the impact, so he swung his elbow, striking the man in the face. The soldier's nose broke with a *crack*, but if it pained him he gave no sign. He punched Aaron in the face, and the sellsword's head whipped to the side, blood flying from his mouth.

He looked back in time to see a knife darting at his face. He caught the man's arm and jerked his head to the side but the blade traced a thin line of pain on the side of his neck. The man brought the knife back again, but Aaron latched on to his wrist with the blade only inches from his eye. The man gritted his teeth, hissing, spittle flying from his mouth as he bore down with both hands, forcing the blade closer, and Aaron strained with both hands to keep the knife's sharp point away.

He realized something as the blade inched its way closer and closer to his face: the man was stronger than him. In another second or two, the knife would find a home in his eye and then it would all be over. Desperate, Aaron brought his knee up as hard as he could, catching the man between the legs. His attacker let out a noise somewhere between a squeal and a grunt and his grip on the knife loosened. Aaron took the opportunity to tear it from his grasp and ram it into the man's stomach.

The soldier stumbled back, crimson blooming on his tunic in a spreading pattern, but Aaron followed him, tearing the knife free and ramming it in again. The man fell backward, and Aaron followed him down, stabbing all the while, spitting and hissing unintelligible sounds of rage and pain. By the fifth stab, the man's struggles had ceased, and Aaron crouched above him, gasping in an effort to get his air back.

The man's dead eyes stared up at him, an accusing expression on his face, as if Aaron had cheated somehow. Maybe hitting a man in the fruits was frowned on in official duels, but there were few things better for getting him to forget the knife he's holding. "Anyway," Aaron said, hacking and spitting out a gob of blood, "it's the ones that live who decide what's fair. Your boss knows that well enough."

He struggled to his feet, shuffling to his sword and stopping long enough to yank his knife out of the talkative soldier's throat before moving further down the alley. One of the soldiers had somehow managed to work his way around in fighting with the others so that his back was to Aaron. As he watched, the man moved toward Adina and May, the women backing away from him and circling as best they could in the narrow space the alleyway afforded.

Aaron moved up and rammed his sword through the man's back, the steel erupting from his chest in a shower of blood. The soldier screamed in pain and surprise, and Aaron jerked the blade free, letting the man crumple to the ground in a bloody, moaning heap before turning to check on the others.

Gryle lay in the alleyway a few feet away, a stillness to him that Aaron didn't like. He looked past him and saw that the first mate was facing off against the last soldier. One of Balen's arms bled freely from a deep cut, and he held a small, crude fishing knife clutched in his other hand. Aaron noted a pale waxiness to his skin, no doubt brought on by blood loss. Still, it hadn't all gone the soldier's way—the small knife Balen held was coated in blood.

Aaron flipped his own knife over in his hand, so that he was holding it by the blade, then hesitated. Darrell had tried to teach him the art of knife throwing but, truth to tell, he'd never been very good at it. To him, it had always seemed a terrible strategy, throwing away a perfectly good weapon. Still, he was too far away, and he knew by the way Balen was swaying on his feet that the man had little time left. The next time the soldier charged him would most likely be the last time.

So Aaron took a deep breath, raised his arm, and then in one motion flung his blade forward, pivoting his feet as he did. The knife flew end over end until it came to rest, blade first, in the back of the soldier's neck. The man dropped without a sound and Aaron allowed himself a grunt of surprise before he turned to May and Adina. "Are you okay?"

The two women nodded, clearly shaken up. "Good," he said, glancing at Gryle's still form. "See to Balen."

They hurried to the first mate, and Aaron shuffled toward where the chamberlain lay on his side, fearing what he'd discover. *Please not dead. Hurt or unconscious, fainted even. But not dead.* Aaron knelt down beside the chamberlain and put two fingers to his neck, breathing a sigh of relief as he felt the throb of the man's pulse. Then, grunting with the effort, he rolled the chamberlain onto his back, searching for a wound. He frowned, not seeing anything except for a dark red mark on the man's forehead where a bruise was already forming.

He slapped the chamberlain lightly on the cheek a few times, and the man's eyelids fluttered open. "M-Mr. Envelar. Is everything okay?"

"I'd say things are just about as far from okay as they can get," Aaron said, wiping an arm across his bloody mouth. "Still, we're alive and that's something. What happened to you?"

The chamberlain's chubby face went bright red. "I was...trying to help Mr. Balen and...well, gods forgive me, I tripped. I went stumbling into the wall and the next thing I knew...the next thing I knew you were shaking me awake."

Aaron grunted. "Well. The cobbles are slippery. Could've happened to anybody."

The chamberlain nodded, an ashamed expression on his face. "I'm sorry, Mr. Envelar. I really am worthless."

"Nah, not worthless," Aaron said. "If I end up going to any balls or fancy dinners, you'll be the first man I'll come to for advice." The chamberlain didn't smile, and Aaron sighed. "There's nothing to be ashamed of, Gryle. There's worse things than not being good at killing. Anyway, we're all still breathing, at least for the moment. I count that as a win." He held his hand out to help the chamberlain up and the man nodded gratefully, taking it.

They walked to where Balen sat propped against the alley wall, and Aaron saw that Adina had ripped off part of her sleeve, using it as a makeshift bandage for the man. "You alright there, first mate?"

The older man gave a weak smile. "Not the worst shape I've been in, but not the best either. Give me a pissed off ocean any day to a man with killin' on his mind. Anyway, I think I'll survive."

Aaron grinned. "And thank the gods for that. I don't want to have to be the one to explain to that crazy Parnen that we let his first mate get killed."

Balen grunted a pained laugh, shaking his head. "Just about exactly the opposite, to my reckonin'. You saved my life, Aaron. There's some port whores that'd thank you, if they could." He motioned to the man with the knife in the back of his neck. "One damn fine throw that. With us tangling like we was, just how did you know you wasn't gonna hit me, anyway?"

Aaron offered the man his hand. "I didn't."

The first mate laughed again and allowed himself to be pulled to his feet. Aaron shot a quick glance at the corpses littering the alleyway before turning back to look at the haggard, frightened faces of his companions. *So much for sneaking out of the city.* "Strip the bodies of weapons. We're leaving in one minute."

CHAPTER FOUR

"Hold it straight, damn you," Belgarin snapped, and the youth recoiled as if he'd been struck, nearly dropping the full-length mirror he held.

"Forgive me, Your Highness," the boy said, his eyes widening in fear as he strained to hold the heavy mirror upright.

Belgarin stared at his reflection, frowning at the man looking back at him. His once midnight black hair—fine enough that more than one blushing maiden had given up what virtue she possessed as she ran her hands through it—was now streaked with a gray as coarse and lifeless as slate. The eyes that looked back at him were cold and hard, and the face, once possessed of the fine chiseled features of royalty, had grown wrinkled and aged. He had not gone to fat as so many nobles did, but the black and gray beard he'd cultivated did little to hide a face that appeared wasted and emaciated no matter how much exercise he got or how much he ate.

He thought of his father—it seemed he did that more and more as the years went on. King Markus had been known as a kind and just ruler, a man who had led his people to prosperity. He'd been known in his youth as a warrior and leader of men and in his later years as a skilled diplomat and peacemaker. But to Belgarin, he had been more than that. He had been the world. Before Belgarin's brothers and sisters had come along, and it had been only him and his parents, his father had called him his "little laughing boy," had claimed, for anyone that would listen, that he was the happiest child he'd ever known, never crying or throwing tantrums like other children, but always smiling and laughing.

His little laughing boy. He wondered what his father would think of the man staring out of the mirror now, his blue eyes hard, sunken pits, an angry twist to his mouth that, try as he might, he never seemed able to banish completely. Belgarin frowned, turning to the sweating servant. "The glass is flawed. Leave and the next time you come, bring a proper looking glass instead of this poor quality craftsmanship, or it'll be your head as well as your master's, do you understand?"

"O-of course, Your Majesty," the boy stammered, ducking his head in apology before hurrying away and closing the door behind him.

Once he was gone, Belgarin sighed heavily. "That was wrong of me."

Caldwell stepped forward from where he stood in the corner of the room, his hands tucked in front of him in the long sleeves of his burgundy robe. "Forgive me, Your Highness, but a king is never wrong. Even I could see that the mirror was of poor quality. If Your Highness wishes, I will have a word with the boy's master."

"No," Belgarin snapped, "I do not wish it. It seems to me that most of those you have words with are never seen again."

Caldwell bowed his head. "As you say, Your Highness, though I beg you not to hold such against your loyal advisor. After all, I cannot help it if, when made to see the depth of their failures, men choose not to show their faces in your royal presence again."

Belgarin sighed and dismissed the matter with an annoyed wave of his hand. "Enough, Caldwell, I don't need any more royal ass kissing for today. Now, tell me," he said, strolling to the window of his richly appointed quarters and looking out onto the city, "what of the rebels? Have they been brought to heel?"

His advisor moved to stand beside him. "Regretfully, they have yet to be taken in hand, though it is only a matter of time, of course."

Belgarin turned to the man, frowning. He doubted there could ever have been a more nondescript man. Neither tall nor short, neither ugly nor handsome, his advisor was the type of man whose name you would forget a moment after meeting, and although the man's face rarely showed any emotion, Belgarin sometimes fancied that he could see disdain in the man's placid gaze. He slammed his fist against the wall. "You assured me that this would be taken care of, Caldwell. If, as you say, my sister really *is* with this group, they must not be allowed to run free in the city to turn the people against me. Unity. *That* is what we need now."

"Of course, Your Highness," Caldwell said, bowing his head deeply, and Belgarin wondered if he'd only imagined the hate that had flashed in the man's eyes. The truth was, the man had set him on edge since he'd become his advisor five years ago when he'd saved Belgarin from an assassination attempt made by one of his brothers, but there was no denying his effectiveness. It seemed to Belgarin, sometimes, that there was nothing the man did not know. Still...that look.

He narrowed his eyes. "Well? That's all you have to say? You told me that our men had found them not two hours gone!"

"And so they did, Your Highness," Caldwell said, "but those your sister travels with have proven...*difficult.* The fools that found them clearly underestimated them, and they died for their foolishness. Still, Your Highness need not worry—the same mistake will not be made again. Your sister and her companions will soon face the hangman."

"No, of course not," Belgarin sneered, "next time will be an altogether different mistake but, no doubt, with the same result. I tire of your pandering counsel, Caldwell. I go to see the Knower. Perhaps he will be able to give me something more than endless excuses. You will accompany me."

"Of course, Your Highness," the man said, and if being the subject of his king's ire bothered him, he gave no sign.

Belgarin scowled, his eyes narrowing. "Were I you, Caldwell, I would very much hope that news of the capture of my sister and her companions reaches us soon. I grow weary of your failures."

With that, he turned and strode from the room and so did not see the hate and disgust that flashed across the other man's face. In another instant, the expression was gone as if it had never been, the placid blank expression that gave away nothing back in place, and Caldwell looked thoughtfully out the window for a moment before turning and following his master.

***

Belgarin walked the opulent hallways of what was once his brother's castle, Caldwell, as always, at his back, his constant shadow. As he walked, he thought of his brother, Eladen. They had never been close—they saw the world too differently for that—but they had, at least, been family. He wondered when exactly that had stopped, wondered how disagreements had as children had turned into wars fought as men, but if there was a single moment at which to point, he did not know it. To him, it seemed that, as with most things, it had happened gradually, creeping up on them out of the night when they'd had their backs turned.

Thinking of his brother made his mood grow dark, so that his eyes did not see the beauty of the tapestries hanging along the walls, nor did his feet feel the soft plushness of the hallway's carpeted runners. He saw only the goal he'd set for himself so many years ago, felt only the memory of each sacrifice he'd made to get there. "We will be whole, Caldwell," he said. "The kingdom will be whole."

"Of course, sire."

"When?" Belgarin asked, and whether he asked the question of his advisor or himself, he could not have said.

Still, Caldwell answered, "Soon, Your Majesty. The pretenders grow weaker with each passing day while we grow stronger. Already our armies outnumber those of the pretenders two to one, if not more."

"*We*, you say," Belgarin said. "*Our*. But the men do not follow you, Caldwell. No royal blood runs in your veins, only that of some commoner whore, one who a drunken dockworker or some such spent a coin on to pass an idle hour, and yet you say *we*."

If his advisor took offense at the comment, he showed no sign, his face remaining expressionless. "As you say, Your Highness. A whore, no doubt, but one that I must be thankful for, none the less."

"Oh, and no doubt should we all," Belgarin sneered. "And anyway, those *pretenders* you speak of are my brothers. My sisters. Even at their worst, their darkest, their blood is a thousand times purer than yours. And hear me, Caldwell," he said, turning to face the robed man who stopped and met his eyes with that lifeless, reptilian gaze. "I will crush their armies, if I must. I will conquer their cities and put their fighting men to the sword, if it is the only way to bring the people of the kingdom together. These things, I will do. What I will *not* countenance is you speaking of them in that overly familiar tone as if you were good enough even to lick the dirt from their boots."

"Of course, my lord," the robed man said, bowing deeply. "Forgive me, for I misspoke. My wish is to serve you, nothing more."

The man's tone was all contrition and regret, but staring at his bent form, his bowed head, Belgarin thought he could almost hear something in it, could almost see something in that submissive posture that spoke not of anger, but a slow, deliberate plotting. He found that he was baring his teeth in rage, a low growl issuing from his throat, and he nearly reached out to strike the man. Perhaps then, he would show some human emotion, *something* other than that damned obeisance that always seemed wrong somehow. Finally, he mastered his anger and his hands unclenched at his sides. "Follow," he said then he turned and walked down the hallway.

Soon, they arrived at the rooms that were currently serving as the Knower's quarters and, as they drew closer, they came upon several pairs of guards standing on either end of the hall who bowed low as Belgarin passed, saying nothing. The guards seemed tame enough, but should any but Belgarin attempt access down this hall, the intruder would see just how well-trained they were. If any man or woman was foolish enough to persist in attempting to gain entry, the guards were under orders to stop them in whatever way they might, including killing them if they deemed it necessary. None were allowed passage into the Knower's quarters save Belgarin and Caldwell, and he only when in the presence of Belgarin himself.

Belgarin came to the set of guards nearest the Knower's rooms and nodded to them. The two men bowed low in return but did not speak. Not that they could have even had they wanted to. To guard the Knower's chambers was a great honor but there were certain sacrifices that had to be made for such glory. Namely, their tongues. Even these, the best of his guards, were not allowed to look into the room of the Knower but, in case they should happen to catch a glance in their duties, they'd been rendered mute.

The two men finished bowing and stepped to the side, the gleam of the fanatic in their eyes as they looked at Belgarin where he stood with Caldwell. *It's as if they think me a god,* Belgarin thought, careful to keep the disgust from his face. He had not wanted to mutilate the guards, had been sure that their loyalty would be enough to stay their tongues should they see anything they weren't supposed to, but Caldwell had insisted on the necessity and, eventually, Belgarin had realized he was right, had let go of his disdain for cruelty in the face of what was necessary. Sometimes, it seemed to him that it was all he ever did. After all, they all had their sacrifices to make.

He reached under his tunic and withdrew the key from where it hung around his neck. Already, the guards had knelt facing the opposite end of the hall, their heads down and their eyes closed. Belgarin took a deep, slow breath, steadying himself. He hesitated, as he always did, fear slithering up his spine like some icy serpent. Then, reluctantly, he unlocked the door and stepped inside.

The Knower did not look like much, swallowed as he was by the massive four post bed on which he lay. The bed's silk coverlet had been thrown aside, and as always, the man was dressed only in his night clothes. Through the thin fabric, Belgarin could see legs and arms that were no thicker than the fire pokers the servants used to coax a flame to life in the castle's great hall. The Virtue of Intelligence gave the man who possessed it many gifts but, as with the other Virtues, there was a price to be paid for such gifts.

The servant boy who'd been assigned to the Knower's rooms did not turn at the sound of the door closing, but of course that was no surprise. As the guards might be made mute for their own protection as well as the protection of others, so too was the boy who served the Knower deaf. A precaution as much for his own health as anyone else's. The first few had not been, and by the time the third servant, a young, pretty girl of no more than twelve years, had taken her own life like her predecessors, it had become clear that such precautions were necessary.

Belgarin watched for a moment as the youth, sitting on the bed beside the Knower, drew a spoon from a bowl of porridge and gently placed it in the Knower's mouth. If the man noticed, he gave little sign as a line of drool hung lazily from his mouth, and he stared out at the empty space of the room with eyes feverish with madness. The boy was forced to push the spoon further into the wasted man's mouth until finally he chewed on reflex, as much if not more of the honeyed oats falling onto the bib on his chest as made it down his throat.

It was a hard thing to watch, a hard room in which to stand, but then, like so many other things, it was necessary. Belgarin stood, waiting, reluctant to disturb the boy though he knew the business he had was best seen to as quickly as possible. Still, the sooner the boy finished, the sooner he would be forced to listen to the old man's words, words that could drive a weaker mind mad. Caldwell moved toward the boy to make him leave off feeding the wasted form in the bed, and it was all Belgarin could do not to reach out and stop him.

Caldwell put a hand on the boy's shoulder and the youth turned dully around. As he did, Belgarin wondered, not for the first time, where Caldwell acquired these servants. The boy's face was plain, his features the thick, ill-defined ones of a lowborn, and Belgarin noted that he had some sort of rash on the side of his face. The boy took note of Caldwell and Belgarin, and his eyes widened slightly, his face growing red and making the angry rash stand out all the more prominent for that. He dropped his head in a bow that Belgarin thought seemed directed more at Caldwell than Belgarin himself, then he took the bowl and hurried out the door.

Belgarin frowned after him for a moment, not liking the fact that the boy had seemed more terrified of an advisor in simple robes than his own king, but as he turned back to the bed the Knower's mad eyes were locked on his and all thoughts of the incident left him. Swallowing hard, Belgarin withdrew a silk kerchief from his tunic and held it to his nose and mouth before venturing closer toward the bed. The stink of the man grew stronger with each step he took, and it was all he could do to keep from gagging despite the perfumed kerchief. It was the smell of shit and rot and death, and it was one that he could not grow accustomed to no matter how many times he visited these chambers. For his part, Caldwell seemed unaffected, reason enough for Belgarin to hate the man had he no other.

"*My…King,*" the Knower grated in a raw whisper. His mad eyes met Belgarin's, and he smiled, revealing gums that held two remaining teeth, both black with rot. "*What an…honor.*"

Belgarin grunted, feeling somehow tainted by being so close to the man. He wanted nothing more than to get on with his business and be gone. But then, there were pleasantries to be observed. "How goes it with you, Knower?"

The man's grin widened, and he let out a series of choked wheezes that might have been laughter. "I'm dying. But then, aren't we all, Your Majesty? The boy is dying too, though he knows it not." He frowned. "I have tried to tell him as much."

He stared at Belgarin with eyes that knew too much, eyes made insane by the knowledge they carried. "As you said, we all are."

"Yes," the man said, grinning again, "but the boy's death will be a special one. Whore rot, they call it. You noticed, didn't you? His face?"

Belgarin fought back the urge to snap at the man. The Knower might have information he could use, but whether or not he chose to share it was up to him. After all, what could you threaten a man with who was already dying, whose every moment passed in excruciating agony as his body ate itself? "I noticed."

The man nodded, grinning. "There is a cure for the rot, of course. But it is known to only a very few, alas. The boy will become a man and that man will, perhaps, father sons and daughters. And they, too, will carry the rot, though theirs will be more severe, more …." He raised his withered shoulders in what might have been a shrug. "Pronounced. Those he fathers will not make it out of infancy."

It was Belgarin's time to frown. "And the cure?"

The Knower shrugged again. "Too late, I'm afraid. The boy will die, eventually. As will what children he has."

The withered husk watched Belgarin with obvious joy dancing in his crazed stare, enough to make it clear that he knew the cure and would not share it. Perhaps, if Belgarin pressed, the man might give it away, but there were more important things to concern himself with than one boy's life. *I do what is necessary.* "You've been apprised of the latest?"

"I was sent..." The man cut off, hacking a deep, wet cough that left bloody spittle on the front of his nightshirt. "I was sent documents," he said.

"Very well," Belgarin said, unable to keep the disgust from his voice. "Then you know that my sister and the man known as the Silent Blade are still eluding *Caldwell's* hunters," he continued, frowning at his advisor. "The man, in particular, has proven to be a great nuisance."

"Ah yes, I have been told of this man. A great nuisance, indeed." The man let out that withered laughter again, his emaciated frame shaking with the force of it until he once more fell into a fit of bloody, wracking coughs. Finally, he composed himself, wiping a shaking arm across his mouth, the sleeve of his shirt coming away red with blood. "He has led you a merry chase, that one. And, of course, there's your sister to worry about, isn't there? Sadly, they will be harder to catch now, as they will be leaving the city soon, if they haven't already.

Belgarin frowned. "Leaving the city? What makes you think so?"

The old man shook his head as if Belgarin was a fool. "Your sister and those with her have been discovered now. Their safety, here, was predicated on the fact that any reasonable man would have expected them to flee. Now that they're discovered, they've no choice but to flee in truth. You've of course sent your men to the docks?"

Belgarin glanced at his counselor who gave a slight shake of his head. "Do it," Belgarin growled, "now."

Caldwell bowed his head then vanished out the door. Belgarin watched the door close behind him then turned back to the wasted form lying in the bed. "What else?"

The Knower grinned again. "That you don't know? Oh so much, *My King.*"

Belgarin fought back the urge to throttle the man, though it did not go easy. "I meant about the situation at hand," he growled, "as you well know."

"Yes," the man said, "knowing is my business, after all. And what a profitable business it is, too. Do you know that I soil myself at least once a day? Oh yes," he added, at Belgarin's look of disgust, "my thoughts exactly. The mind may hold all of the knowledge the world has to offer, yet the body is a separate animal altogether, possessed of its own...truths. Still, do not think me ungrateful. I do so enjoy the oats the boy brings—what little of them my failing body manages to keep down."

"To be a Knower," Belgarin snapped, "is an honor—"

"Oh yes," the old man interrupted, his mad eyes dancing with anger, "an honor to feel each organ in my body shutting down, to know in no uncertain terms that I will die and do so horribly. An honor to know what is happening and to know, just as well, that there is no remedy. Give me no more honors, my king. I'm not sure that my heart could take it."

Belgarin sat in silence, watching the man. Finally, "I'm sorry for the suffering you must endure. Still, it is necessary."

"*Necessary*," the man hissed. "Oh, but how you love that word. It is not necessity but nature that drives, My King. House cats chase mice, toy with them, men cheat on their wives and wives on their husbands, men murder and steal and hate not because it is necessary but because it is in their nature. And keep your apologies—I care less for them than I do your honors."

Belgarin grunted and rose, tired of the man's games. He turned and started toward the door. "My King?"

He turned back at the sound of the man's voice, saw him watching him with that insane gaze. "Would you like to know how you will die?"

Belgarin sneered. "And are you some teller of fortunes, to see the future?"

The man wheezed laughter. "Oh, my *honor* is not to predict, but to understand, not to guess, but to *know*. Not that your fate requires much skill to foresee—it is writ plain for those who look closely enough."

"May Salen take you," Belgarin spat then turned for the door.

"Soon enough, My King," the man said behind him, "soon enough."

Belgarin grasped the door's handle and swung it open, but the Knower spoke one final time. "They will split up. This sellsword knows his business, knows that they will be too easy to track should they stay together."

Belgarin considered that, turning back. "And where will they go?"

"Where indeed," the man said, his voice a rasping whisper. "I think it is high time you sent a letter to your remaining siblings, the ones you've yet to murder. There are two, besides the one who now confounds you, are there not?"

Belgarin felt his face flush with anger and something like shame. "I did not *murder* them," he said, "they tried to kill *me*. Eladen and Geoffrey both, and Ophasia..." He shook his head. "She would not see reason. She did not understand what must be done, what I try to accomplish."

"Yes, of course," the creature in the bed said, smiling his ghastly grin. "You did only what was necessary."

Hissing a curse, Belgarin fled through the open doorway, the Knower laughing his wheezing laughter behind him. *Laugh if you will, foul creature,* he thought. *I leave you to your knowledge. To your death.* The thought was not as much of a comfort as it should have been.

CHAPTER FIVE

Aaron's gaze roamed the streets as they made their way through the city, the anxiety of his companions a palpable thing. Every drunken shout seemed to be a guard's cry of alarm, every rapid slapping of a child's running feet on the cobbles the hasty footsteps of their pursuers as they rushed to attack. "Just take it easy," he said to the others, and they nodded at him, though the fear remained, writ plain on their faces.

He, too, felt the sense of being hunted, of being watched. It was not a comforting feeling, but it was one that he was familiar with. It seemed to him that he'd been hunted by one person or another for most of his life.

And anyway, his thoughts were on other things. In particular, how they were going to make it out of a city full of men and women who wanted them dead. Stealth wasn't an option—they couldn't have been more conspicuous of a group if they'd tried at it. The guards at the gates were no doubt watching for them, and trying to leave by one would involve nothing but a long walk and a quick death.

Only one answer for it then, and not one that he liked. Nor, he suspected, would his companions. There was little talk as he led them in the direction of the docks, all of them thinking their own thoughts, entertaining their own fears. Finally, after what felt like an eternity, he saw the docks in the distance and the knot of tension that had been gathering in his shoulders eased a bit. Ships of all sorts and sizes lined the harbor. Most, he suspected, hired out by men and women who'd come to Baresh for the contest and decided to stay for a time.

He noted that, unsurprisingly, several guards moved back and forth along the docks, inspecting the ships and speaking with their captains. Could be they were just saying hello, maybe, or doing routine inspections. He didn't believe it, of course—wouldn't have believed it even if he hadn't seen the way the guards were so intent on checking each ship or the hard gazes they used as they questioned each captain. As if they thought the man had been sleeping with their wives or doing something else untoward, like maybe harboring and planning to aid in the escape of several criminals.

Aaron sighed and turned to his companions who were studying him with mirrored expressions of anxiety. "Balen, you're a sailor. Any of those ships down there ones you recognize?"

The first mate's skin was so pale as to be nearly white and sweat covered his forehead despite the chill northern air, but he seemed lucid enough. He turned to study the ships, shaking his head slowly. "No, I don't—" He paused. "Wait a minute. Well, gods be praised, that's the *Lady's Beauty,* there."

Aaron followed the man's gaze and took in a fine blue sailed ship, its curves and sweeps elegant and somehow contriving to make it almost appear as if it was moving despite the fact that it sat still at the dock. He knew little of ships, but this one looked as if would slice through the water at great speed and looked more like a piece of art to him than an actual ship. "Damn," he said, "I don't pretend to know much about them, but that's a damn fine ship."

Adina nodded beside him. "It's beautiful," she said.

"Eh?" Balen grunted. "Well, serviceable, aye, but I don't guess as I've ever heard anyone call the Lady beautiful before."

"Surely, you must be joking," Adina said, her eyes still roaming the gentle curves of the ship. "I've seen a lot of ships—my father had a special love for the sea—and that's one of the finest I've ever seen."

Balen frowned and looked back at the ships, then grunted a laugh. "Ah, yeah, so it is, so it is. A mighty fine ship, one any man or woman would be proud to serve on, if'n they didn't mind kissin' ass to some noble or another, listenin' to 'em play at barkin' orders when they couldn't be sea men if they grew fins like a fish." He paused then glanced at Adina, an ashamed expression on his face. "Err...that is, I mean no offense, Princess."

Adina glanced at Aaron and smiled. "None taken, first mate. We nobles do love to bark."

"Anyhow," the first mate continued, his face red, "I don't know a man rich enough or dumb enough to dye his sails. Ain't cheap, keepin' 'em that way, what with the sun havin' its way with 'em day in and day out. Pretty enough blue, I'll warrant, but the weight of all that dye will slow her down too. Not much mind, but not much can be the difference between kissin' your lady or a pirate's sabre, if you catch my meaning. Still,"—he shrugged, almost reluctantly—"a fine ship. I reckon with a good captain she'd be just about as fine of one as a man could want. Course, it ain't the *Lady*, and that's a fact. Naw, she's that one there."

Aaron followed the man's pointing finger and raised his eyebrows. "Ah," he said, frowning. The ship the first mate had indicated was about half as long as the other with a wide, flat bottom and one square sail. Barnacles covered much of its sides, and its wood surface was faded in places. The overall effect was such that he was surprised the thing floated at all. "*Lady's Beauty*, you say?" he asked, unable to keep the doubt from his voice.

Why do I get the feeling, Co said in his mind, *that this "lady" has a beard? And no doubt forgets to wash. Maybe has a—*

Alright, Firefly, I get the idea.

"Yeah, well," Balen said, "maybe it ain't the most accurate name, but I wouldn't say so to the captain. Festa's a good enough sort, but he's got a bit of a temper. Particularly when it comes to his ship."

Aaron sighed. "Do you think he'd take on some passengers?"

Balen frowned, as if just now realizing the direction of Aaron's thoughts. "Aye, I suppose he would. Festa's a good enough sort. Most times, anyway. There was one time he threw a feller overboard."

Aaron nodded slowly. "Well, I guess there's worse crimes that have been committed at sea than getting a man a little wet."

Like that ship, Co said, her tone in his mind filled with barely suppressed laughter.

"Aye, so there are." Balen nodded. "'Course the fella was dead before the captain took a mind to throw him overboard."

"Dead?" Gryle squeaked, shooting nervous glances around the alleyway as if the very word would draw Belgarin's troops down on them.

May patted the chamberlain on his shoulder. "Dead from natural causes, I'm sure, Master Gryle, there's no need to fret."

"Sure," Balen said, "natural enough, anyhow, when you're dealin' with Festa and the man was dead alright, you've no worry on that score. Few things that'll get it done quicker than a blade to the throat and that's a fact."

"Wait," Aaron said, frowning, "he was murdered?"

Balen shrugged, obviously uncomfortable. "Well, I don't suppose Festa would much agree with that phrasin'. He'd say the fella was rightly punished, so he would."

"Rightly pu—punished?" Gryle asked.

"Aye," Balen said. "Rumor was the poor bastard made comment on the *Lady's*...disposition, you might say. Nothin' others hadn't already said about her, I'm sure, but see, the thing was, he said it to the captain." Balen sighed regretfully. "Victor was a good enough sort, but the sea takes her due. Always has and always will."

"Wait a moment," Adina said, "are you saying that this captain killed a man, *killed* him, just because he said something bad about his ship?"

Balen nodded slowly. "Well, it don't sound real good, you say it like that. Anyhow, like I told you, Festa's got a bit of a temper on him. Friendly enough fella though. Until he ain't."

Aaron pinched the bridge of his nose between his thumb and forefinger and forced himself to take a couple of slow, deep breaths. "And this Festa, would you say he's your friend?"

Balen considered this for a moment. "Well, I don't know as Festa has *friends* as such. Got a crew, sure, but they ain't particularly talkative, that lot. Quietest group of seamen I ever met, truth be told."

"I wonder why," Aaron said dryly, and Co's laughter rang in his head. "Well, friend or not, we'd best see if the man has some spare room on his ship. It won't be long before the guards find us again." He glanced at Balen's wounded arm, "And we might not be as lucky the next time."

The first mate winced. "If this is luck, it's overrated I can tell you that. Still, you've a point. You all would be a whole lot safer on a ship, putting as many leagues between you and Baresh as ya can."

May stepped forward, frowning. "What do you mean, 'you all?'"

Balen tensed under the power of that gaze, but he forced his eyes to meet hers. "Beggin' your pardon, err...my lady, but I can't leave, not without the captain. Weren't for him, we'd all be dead. Why, if it weren't for him, I'd have rotted in a cage a long while back. No," he said, gaining courage as he spoke, "I don't mean to leave him—I won't is all."

May's eyes narrowed. "And just what do you think your captain would say to his fool first mate who plans on bleeding out hunting the streets for his captain—who was clearly well enough to send a *note* I might add—while soldiers are looking for him on every corner?"

Balen's eyes went wide at the woman's sharp tone, but he set his jaw, and Aaron saw the way it would go. "No point arguing over who's going and who's not," he cut in, "not, at least, until we know if this Festa will take us. Enough talking. Let's go."

To Aaron's immense relief, the others listened—proof enough, he supposed, that the gods were real—and in another moment they were all hurrying toward the docks, casting nervous glances behind them. By the time they finally made it to where the *Lady* was docked, the others were breathing hard, sweat beading their brows despite the near freezing temperature

Balen peered at the end of the dock where men were working, loading crated goods onto the *Lady.* He frowned for a moment then his eyes lit up, and he slapped his leg, shaking his head in wonder as he strode forward toward the working men. "Piss in a pot and call it stew," he called, "is that old Thom the Nose I see hoisting crates, doin' an honest man's work?"

One of the men rose from where he'd been squatted over a crate and turned, using his hand to shield his eyes from the sun. Judging by his lined, weathered face and gray hair, Aaron figured the man in his fifties, but the sleeveless shirt he wore showed arms that were gnarled and wiry with muscle. The man hurried forward at a jog when he saw Balen. "By the sea goddess's tits," he said as he approached, "if it ain't Balen Blunderfoot! And here I thought you found yourself a watery grave with that spot of trouble off the coast of that shitty little town...gods, what was its name again?"

"Taren, the locals called it," Balen said, "and it was a close one, that's a fact. Still, I'll make the goddess work for her reward as long as I'm able. And Blunderfoot..." He sighed. "I thought I'd left that name behind somewhere out near the western coast of Antaresh."

"Shit, *you* about got left behind, maybe, but a name's a name, Blunderfoot. You know that as well as I."

"Aye." Balen winced. "Supposin' I do. Anyhow, the deck was slippery as an eel. I swear to the gods one of them damn deckhands greased the thing, playin' at a joke, and if I ever find out who it was..."

The older man cackled laughter at that and clapped Balen on the back, "Good old Blunderfoot. Never met a ship he can stand on or a man he won't fight. The man's got him a knack for findin' trouble and that's the truth."

Balen sighed again, ignoring the amused, questioning glances from his companions. "Never seemed to me that I had to look real hard. Anyway, Thom, if it's all the same to you, I wonder if we can't have this conversation below decks," he said, shooting a nervous glance behind them at the docks where sailors went about the business of loading and unloading ships.

The old man cocked his head, thoughtful. "Hold on a damned minute, lad. Is that blood on your shirt?"

Balen looked at the wound sheepishly. "So it is."

The gray-haired man shook his head in wonder. "Same old Blunderfoot. Some things never change. Well, come on then," he said, ushering them forward and across the gangplank. "Go on up—I bet the captain'll be right excited to see ya when he gets back"

"Excited?" Balen said.

The older man grinned. "Well, leastways, he'll be interested."

Balen sighed. "I was afraid of as much."

CHAPTER SIX

The older man led them to the captain's cabin and sat them down at a beaten up wooden table, its surface dented and cracked from hard use. Aaron sat in what had to be the most uncomfortable chair he'd ever seen, made worse by the fact that its legs wobbled beneath him, threatening, at any moment, to crack and send him sprawling on the floor.

The man, Thom, walked to a cabinet and returned with a dusty bottle, an amber liquid sloshing inside, as well as several tin mugs. He glanced at them shifting uncomfortably in their chairs and nodded, "I apologize for the crudeness of the cabin, loves," he said. "The captain's a hard man and not given to soft things. And, as he'll no doubt tell ya once he returns from shore, the carpenter he hired for the chairs and table did a shit job of it. Naw," he said with what sounded to Aaron like a hint of pride, "ain't a chair on the ship that'll sit you straight, and it's a man takin' his life into his own hands to use one of the damn things."

Gryle squeaked as he nearly fell out of his own chair, grabbing desperately at the table and barely managing to keep himself upright. "What...what do you do, then?" he asked, clutching the table the way a drowning man might a rope.

"What do we do? Well, we do a lot of standin'," the old man said, throwin' him a wink. Then he set about pouring their drinks. When he was finished, he propped his back up against the cabin wall, grinning. "Nope," he said, "not a straight chair in the place. I figure if the captain ever catches that carpenter, Salen'll have another soul to lead across his fields before the day's out, and the carpenter'll be glad for the god's company, I expect. The God of Death's a cold bastard by all accounts, but the captain's just about hot enough to burn a man when he gets in his temper."

"Which he always is," Balen said.

"Aye, which he always is," the old man agreed, smiling.

Aaron listened to the back and forth with something like wonder and decided that, as a whole, sailors were unquestionably insane.

"Well, leastways," Balen said, "the chairs are the carpenter's fault, as is the table. Certainly not the captain's for throwin' 'em at whoever happens by when the mood's on him or beatin' on the table with anything he reckons fit for the job."

"Course not," the older man said with a wink. "Cap's got some real aim on him too lately, Blunderfoot. Why, he throwed one about half a year gone now, it was, hit Furley from damn near all the way across the ship."

"Gods," Adina said, "I hope the man is alright."

"Who, Furley?" the old man asked. "Oh, sure, he's right as weather. Just talks with a bit of a lisp is all on account of he lost a few teeth." He shrugged as if it was a small matter. "The way that chair hit? The man's a lucky bastard, I can tell ya that. I thought his damn head'd go flyin' off, the way the captain put his whole body behind it. Really sailed that one, he did."

Balen shook his head with a sigh. "Some things never change."

"Aye, true enough," the grizzled sailor said.

"While we're on that, where's the rest of the boys?" Balen asked. "I didn't see any of 'em when we was comin' aboard."

"Boys? Which boys is that now?"

"Well, all of 'em. How's ol' Handsome? Been a while since I seen that mug of his, and that's a fact." Balen grinned. "He still buryin' his oar in anythin' crosses his path?"

Thom nodded slowly. "Well, I don't think Handsome gets around as much as he once did. Truth to tell, I don't suppose he's been called by that name in a few years now."

"Is that so?" Balen asked. He shook his head. "Well, I suppose the man had a fair enough run anyhow. What, I don't suppose there's a man's daughter that's of age from here to Avarest ain't gave that man a bit of their virtue, so much as they have anyway.

What happened to him, anyhow? He catch somethin'?" Balen shook his head again. "Why, it's a wonder he made it this long, the way he'd carry on."

Thom shifted uncomfortably. "Aye, I suppose you could say he caught somethin'. Or maybe somethin' caught him, at any rate."

"How's that now?"

The old man rubbed a hand across his stubbly chin. "Well, you see that there?" he asked, nodding his head at a particularly large dent in the table's surface. "That there's where Handsome got introduced to the captain's table. Nah," he said, sighing, "he weren't so handsome after that. Ya see, this time it weren't a daughter, so much as it was a niece. Captain's own, if you'll believe it."

Balen whistled. "By the Fields, how'd the man get the notion in his head to do somethin' so damn foolish as that?"

"Weren't his head he was doin' his thinkin' with, I don't reckon." He glanced at Adina and May and his face turned a bright red. "Apologies, ladies."

May smiled a radiant smile and winked at the man. "That's quite alright, Thom. It is alright if I call you Thom, isn't it?"

If anything, the man looked even more uncomfortable, his expression one of a mouse finding itself cornered by a particularly hungry cat. "Yes ma'am," he mumbled, "if it pleases you."

"Oh, it does," May said, her voice silky, "it does indeed."

Aaron raised an eyebrow at Adina, but she only grinned and shrugged. "Anyhow," Balen said into the awkward silence, "that's a damn shame about Handsome. One of the best sailors I ever saw."

Thom nodded, apparently relieved at the excuse to look away from May's stare. "Sure enough. Still, it ain't all bad. The captain, see, he made 'em marry. If I've heard right, Handsome's set up somethin' pretty, workin' at a bank, makin' out like a pirate if what they say's true. Way I hear tell, most folks don't even mind that his face ain't exactly symmetrical anymore."

Balen nodded. "Well, I guess that's a good thing. Though I'd never have pegged Handsome for the bankin' type. I suppose some things do change, after all."

"True enough, true enough," Thom said. "Anyhow, enough of old times. Why don't you introduce me to your mates?"

Balen winced, glancing at Aaron. "It might be better if I don't, Thom, if it's all the same to you."

The older man glanced around at Aaron and the others before turning back to Balen, a gray eyebrow raised. "Like that, is it?"

"I think it's probably best if it is."

"Alright, well, if you think it best, Blunderfoot, then no doubt it is. Anyway, I take it you all are in a bit of a hurry."

Aaron frowned. "What makes you say that?"

Thom shrugged. "Nothin' particular, stranger. Just that it's cold enough to piss cubes and your man over there's sweatin' like Handsome was when the captain found out."

Even as Aaron glanced at Gryle, the short, chubby man ran a linen cloth over his sweaty forehead. Aaron looked back to the older man and met his eyes. "And if we are? Is that a problem?"

Thom shrugged again. "Ain't no problem to me, mister. If it was up to me, we'd take you all now and set sail this minute, leave the northmen to their snow and ice. So cold up here, a man wakes up to take a piss—" He cut off, glancing at May and Adina. "Err...that is, it's too cold for my likin'. Thing is, it ain't up to me, so if it's a hurry you're in, I'd best be on about findin' the captain."

Aaron frowned at the man's back as he started toward the door. All it would take would be for the sailor to decide he'd be better off telling some guards about the strangers on his ship, and Aaron and his companions would be dead long before the ship ever left. He took a step toward the man, but Balen stopped him with a hand on his shoulder. Aaron turned, frowning at the first mate, but Balen only nodded once.

"Well," Thom said, apparently having glanced back over his shoulder in time to see the exchange, "you've nothin' to worry about from me, mister. My head might not be a pretty one, but it's the only one I've got. I find it's a lot easier to keep it attached to my shoulders if'n I don't go poking it around in business that ain't none of my own."

"Oh, don't be modest," May said, smiling a somehow predatory smile, "I think it's a wonderful head."

The man seemed to shrink beneath the club owner's gaze, and he swallowed hard, nodding. "Well, I thank you for the kindness, ma'am. Now, if you all will just hang tight, I'll go find the captain and bring him back just as fast as I'm able."

May smiled. "Hurry back."

The man swallowed again then ducked his head and hurried out of the cabin, closing the door behind him.

Aaron turned to May. "Now, just what was all that about?"

The club owner met his gaze with an innocent, wide-eyed expression he'd never seen on her before. "I'm sure I don't know what you mean."

She likes him, Co said in his mind. *In fact, she is even now thinking about coupling with him. And she* does *have quite an imagination on her. The things she thinks about doing...I didn't even know human bodies could—*

Enough, Firefly, Aaron thought back, *keep it to yourself. She shouldn't be thinking such things anyway—*

Why not? You think them about Adina all the time. Why is it any diff—

"Enough," Aaron growled, and the others turned to stare at him.

Adina moved closer to him and put a hand on his arm. "What is it, Aaron? Are you okay?"

Aaron stared at her hand, at her bright eyes and long, dark hair, and he found himself thinking thoughts at odds with the danger they were in.

See? Co said. *Like just then—*

Aaron coughed loudly. "I'm fine," he gasped, "I'm fine." He took a slow, deep breath to get control of himself then turned to the first mate. "Are you sure we can trust him?"

"Who, Thom?" Balen asked, "Oh, sure. He's one of the best men I know. I'd trust him with my life."

"I hope you're right," Aaron said, "because you just did. And our lives in the bargain."

Balen swallowed hard, and they all shared uncertain looks before getting as comfortable as the chairs would allow, silent as they all thought their own thoughts, worried their own worries.

Co, Aaron thought, *back in Avarest when those men attacked us, you did something that let me know they were coming. What did you do?*

I did nothing, the Virtue said, *you did. It is Kevlane's Bond, remember? When a Virtue is paired with a mortal, they both begin to...change.*

Aaron frowned at that. *Change? Like weeping uncontrollably when I have to stick a knife in someone—because that's the sort of thing I'd like not to be repeated, if it's all the same to you. I can't afford to have that kind of weakness.*

It is no weakness, Co said in a long-suffering way, *to know compassion. Nevertheless, I will not argue it with you now. Any man or woman who possesses one of the Virtues will share certain similarities, such as what you so stubbornly refuse to see as anything but a weakness. After all, I am the embodiment of Compassion,* not *the embodiment of stabbing holes in people and laughing like a maniac while one does it.*

"Too bad," Aaron muttered, low enough so that the others couldn't hear, "I could use a good laugh."

The point, Co continued as if he hadn't spoken, *is that no one, not even me, knows exactly what shape the bond will take. After all, people's idea of what compassion is, as well as strength or intelligence, differs, having as many forms and shapes as there are leaves in the for—*

So you don't know how I did it, Aaron interrupted.

There was a pause then. *Correct,* Co said in a tight, clipped tone, *I do not know.*

Aaron fought back a sigh. Then a thought struck him and his eyes widened. *Wait a minute. You have no idea what will happen to me, yet you bonded with me just the same, without so much as asking my permission.*

Believe it or not, the Virtue said, her tone angry, *most people would be very pleased to be bonded with one of the Seven. They would think it a great honor. There are those out there—such as Aster Kalen—who search for us unceasingly.*

Aster Kalen. Aaron thought of the skinny man with the scar, of the way he'd thrown people into the ceiling as if they weighed no more than pebbles, of the sounds their bones had made when they'd struck the hard slate roof. The man was still out there, somewhere, and Aaron didn't think he was the type of guy to give up just because he'd failed to catch them once. As if they didn't already have enough people trying to kill them. *Never mind that for now, Co. I want to try something.*

CHAPTER SEVEN

The others sat in silence, their expressions troubled, and Adina knew well enough what they must be thinking. What would this captain turn out to be? The sword or the savior, death or deliverance? The thought that they might have come so far, have suffered so much, only to be cornered on this ship and murdered, was a dark one, one that made her skin grow cold.

She glanced at Aaron, looking for reassurance. The sellsword's gaze was unfocused as if he gazed at something only he could see, and his expression was grim, his jaw clenched as if straining under some great weight. She wondered what he planned. Even if, despite the danger, the captain did agree to take them with him—an outcome that seemed more and more unlikely with each passing moment—where did Aaron intend to take them? Where could they go that would be safe from a man who—if left unchallenged—would soon rule the entire kingdom? A man who, all knew, would stop at nothing to get what he wanted.

No, she knew Belgarin better than that—he was nothing if not thorough. No matter how well they hid, how fast they ran, he would find them. Sooner or later, he would find them. After all, as long as Adina drew breath, his rule would be in question. Not until all of the other royal seven were killed would he be able to claim the uncontested right to rule. Their only chance was to resist, to fight. She was just turning to Aaron to say as much when he suddenly stiffened, his hand going to the sword at his back. He took a step toward the door and turned to the others, "Get behind me. They're coming."

***

There was no sound to announce their approach, nothing to interrupt the normal sounds of sailors preparing to debark, and that was alright, for Aaron needed no sound. The door was closed, the walls of the ship blocking his sight, and that was alright too, for Aaron needed no sight. He did not see, nor hear, but *feel.* He *felt* each footstep on the dock, felt the intent with which they approached. One set of steps that must be the captain's, carrying in them a barely contained anger, yet a lust for life that bespoke a man of large appetites and large emotions, the second set hesitant, worried, and something about their feel was familiar. Aaron knew also to whom these must belong. Thom.

The cause of the worry the old man felt, that seemed to writhe and pulse in him like some foul, slithering creature, did not remain a mystery for long. Aaron strained his senses, sweat beading on his forehead despite the coolness of the cabin, the hand not holding his sword clenched into a fist at his side. Seven more sets of footsteps, seven more to feel, to understand. Six were easy enough to know, their hearts mostly filled with boredom, boredom covered with an anxiety risen not from fear, but of a readiness for action should the need arise. A soldier's readiness.

Aaron bared his teeth, closing his eyes and cocking his head to the side in an effort to feel the other stranger better. A man who was unsure of himself, but who hid his uncertainty even from his own thoughts, buried it beneath tasks that must be done, duties that must be accomplished, and overlaying it all a sense of arrogance that served less as a true part of his nature, but as a shield, one more barrier against the creeping doubt. Here, too, an anxiety, so deeply rooted that the man himself most likely did not know it was there. An anxiety that he would be found out, that he would find *himself* out.

Aaron released the bond, gasping for breath as sensations that had been dulled suddenly rushed back into him. He staggered on shaky legs, but a hand caught him, and he turned to see Adina staring at him with worried eyes. "Are you okay?"

Aaron took a deep, steadying breath, feeling somehow wrung out, used up, like a piece of fabric stretched to tearing, but he nodded slowly, meeting her eyes. "I'm alright," he said. He wanted to say more, to tell her how he felt so that, should things go badly, it would not have gone unsaid. But just then the door creaked, and he spun, his sword lashing out even as he pushed her behind him.

The man who opened the door was shorter than Aaron, about Adina's height. He seemed to be very wide and heavy-set, but Aaron couldn't be sure of that as the man wore what had to have been at least half a dozen shirts as well as a thick fur coat. His face was a bright red, matching the color of his unruly hair and the thick, unkempt beard that reached nearly to his waist. If he was frightened or alarmed by the tip of the sword that hovered only inches from his throat, he didn't show it. "By the gods, but it's as cold as Sheza's holy tits, and that's a fact!" He pushed the sword away with a bare hand as he stomped into the room, apparently oblivious of how close Aaron had come to killing him. "The northerners can have their fucking fairs and their contests all they want. As for me, I want to get out of this damned place while I can still feel my stones. Thom!

Damnit where is that useless son of a bitch, *Thom!*"

Thom, who'd followed the captain into the cabin and was even now standing right beside him ducked his head, clearing his throat, "I'm right here, Captain."

Festa turned to his side and narrowed his eyes at the gray-haired man. "Well just what in the fuck are you doing skulking around here anyway? You tryin' to make a fool of me, Thom? That it?"

The first mate was shaking his head before the captain was finished speaking. "No sir, wouldn't dream of it."

The captain studied him for a moment then grinned, his mood changing with incredible swiftness as he clapped his first mate on the back hard enough to send the other man staggering. "Old Thom!" he bellowed—it seemed to Aaron that this man did very little else. "Why, I don't know what I'd do without you. Well, go on then, friend, tell the boys to get the *Lady* ready, won't ya, before my rod freezes off, and we have to throw it over the side for fish food." He frowned. "Not that the missus would notice, the damned cold-hearted bitch. You'd think her clam was made of gold, the way she guards the thing."

Thom chose—wisely, Aaron thought—to ignore this last bit and nodded instead. "Yes, sir, Captain. I'll get them ready."

The first mate disappeared out of the door and, in another moment, two soldiers wearing Belgarin's colors walked in followed by a balding man so thin that Aaron thought if the man stepped wrong he'd fall through one of the cracks in the ship's floor and be taking a swim in the ocean. Aaron watched the two soldiers warily. Apparently, the other two had stayed on the deck to make sure the rest of the crew didn't cause any trouble. Something to be thankful for, at least.

The captain frowned at the thin man, his thick, pudgy hands on his hips. "Now, just what in the fuck are you doing stepping into my cabin? I thought I told you before, I ain't interested in paying no more taxes! Why, I've been paying the same docking and unloading fees for ten years now, and I don't aim to change it just because some sniveling little bastard—no offense meant—decides he wants to retire early. You get me?"

The man drew himself up as tall as he could, his nose tilted into the air. "Nevertheless, the taxes *will* be paid, Captain Festa. Or else, this ship—if you can call it that," he sneered, "as well as all of its contents, will be seized, and you—along with all of your crew..." He paused a moment, glancing around suspiciously at Aaron and his companions before continuing. You will all be arrested by order of His Majesty Belgarin himself. And you will *not* mock me again. You may call me 'Mr. Zake', and as secretary of shipping, it is my duty and right to oversee such transactions as well as taking the necessary steps to procure payment."

Aaron wouldn't have thought it possible a moment before, but the captain's face grew even redder at the other man's words. "What did you say about my ship?"

The thin man wasn't listening. Instead, he was staring at Aaron and his companions, a frown on his face. "You all seem familiar to me. Why might that be?"

Aaron's hand clenched tighter around the handle of his sword. He didn't expect the thin man would put up much of a fight, but the two soldiers—along with the other two currently up top—would be a problem in such close quarters. Still, he didn't have much choice. He was just about to bring his sword up to act when Festa stepped between him and the thin man. "Oh, don't mind him, that's just my nephew." He turned to Aaron, a scolding look on his face. "I told you, boy, to put that damned sword away and stop playing at being a pirate. My luck, you'll poke your damned eye out, and your mother'll kill me." He turned back to the thin man, sighing. "The boy's my nephew, and I love him as much as a man ought, but he's no scholar, if you catch my meanin'."

The thin man seemed to consider this for a moment then finally turned back to the captain. "Very well; now, as I was saying, Captain. I will have your taxes, or I will have your ship. Your ch—" He cut off, looking at May, his eyes narrowing. Then he glanced around at the rest of them. "Red hair..." He looked at Adina. "A young, pretty woman and three men..." Suddenly, his eyes went wide with realization. "*It's them! Kill the—*"

Aaron was moving before the man's words were out of his mouth. He rushed the closest soldier, barreling into him shoulder-first and slamming him against the wall. Then he lunged forward, lashing out with his sword at the next nearest soldier. The second man screamed as the blade cut a bloody path down his face, dropping his own sword, his hands going to the wound.

Before the man could recover, Aaron grabbed him by the shoulder and rammed his sword through the man's gut. The soldier let out a gasp that quickly turned into a bloody, angry snarl as his hands clamped around Aaron's throat and began to squeeze. Aaron gasped, struggling to rip the man's hands free with one hand even as the other plunged the sword into the man's stomach again, and again. Blood, warm and slick, coated Aaron's sword arm, yet still the man's grip didn't weaken.

Spots began to dance in the sellsword's eyes, and he could feel the strength leaving his limbs, but he gritted his teeth and rammed the blade into the man again, angling it up and into his chest. The man's eyes went wide as the sword struck home, and the grip around Aaron's neck finally loosened as the soldier stumbled backward and fell to the ground, dead.

Aaron's legs wobbled beneath him, and he fell to one knee, gasping for breath. He was still struggling to get his breathing under control past a throat that felt raw and chafed when a feeling of alarm sounded in his head. It wasn't just that he knew the strike was coming—although he did. It was that he knew exactly what shape it would take. In that instant, it seemed as if he knew everything there was to know about the remaining soldier. Knew, for instance, that when the soldier had been trained in the sword, he'd had a habit of holding the grip too tight. An affectation of many men when first learning to use a blade and one the guard captain who'd trained the man had—Aaron knew this, too—scolded the man about again and again.

It was a small thing, really. The type of thing that could be passed over nine out of ten times on the training ground, the type of thing that wouldn't keep a man from being a competent swordsman—although it would keep him from being a great one. A sword held too tightly loses its fluidity, its grace and, most importantly, its bearer loses much of his ability to react quickly.

Aaron felt the blade coming and ducked his head. Six inches, no more than that, enough that he could feel the wind of the blade's passing on the back of his neck then, half turning, his own sword struck, finding its home in the man's throat. The soldier let out a surprised gurgle before crumpling to the ground beside his dead companion. Each breath a torture, Aaron scanned the room and saw the others looking at him. Adina stood only a few steps away. She somehow had found a kitchen knife, and Aaron saw with surprise that there was blood on it, as well as on her mouth from where the soldier had apparently struck her.

Gryle stood holding the broken remains of a chair in his hands, his eyes wide with shock and surprise. May and Balen stood pressed against the door, their faces tight with strain, and for the first time Aaron noticed the shouts and thumps from the other side of the door as someone tried to force their way in.

In another moment, Adina was at his side, helping him to his feet. "By the gods, Aaron, are you okay?"

"Sure," he rasped, rubbing where the man's hands had been, "who needs a throat anyway?"

A loud *thump* from inside the cabin drew Aaron's attention, and he looked up to see Festa slamming the thin man's head into the pocked wooden surface of the table. *Ah,* he thought, *another dent to add to the collection.*

"*What. Did you say. About my* ship?" Festa roared as he brought the unfortunate man's head down again. Judging by the bloody mess of the man's face—barely a man's face at all now, really, but the broken, battered features of some cruel child's doll—the captain had been at it for a while.

"He's dead," Aaron wheezed.

Festa ignored him, growling like an animal as he brought the man's face down again and again, blood splattering with each impact. "*Talk about my ship, you sniveling, no good son of a bit—*"

"Festa, he's *dead,*" Aaron said, stepping forward and grabbing the man's wrists. The captain looked at him with wild eyes as if he planned on going for Aaron next. "What do you mean to do, kill him twice? If it's an answer you're looking for,"—he nodded his head at the man's ruined face still clutched in the captain's blood-soaked hands—"that's the only one you're likely to get. Unless you know some magic that'll make a dead man say sorry. If so, go on beating him, but otherwise..." He pointed at the door where May and Balen were barely managing to keep it shut, bouncing and stumbling with each loud impact from the other side. "We've got more important things to worry about just now."

The captain stared at Aaron for a second longer, then at the mangled features of the man he held. He recoiled as if just realizing what he'd done and let the man drop before turning back to Aaron, a grudgingly embarrassed expression on his face. "It's a good ship, that's all."

"Sure it is," Aaron said, feeling like a fool trying to talk a bear out of eating him. "I wonder who they'll give it to once Belgarin's headsman finishes with you. Someone like that one there, you think?" he asked, indicating the secretary.

Festa's eyes went wide with disbelief at that then his expression twisted with rage. "By the Pit they will," he growled. "I'll kill every whore's son among them before I'll let some bureaucratic piece of shit take the *Lady.*"

"Well," Aaron said in as reasonable of a tone as he could manage, "if we don't do something—and quick—I suspect that you'll have your chance. How long, do you think, before Belgarin's soldiers come in force? A scrap like this won't go unnoticed on the docks. Think, Captain, how long before the entire might of Belgarin's army is marching onto *this* ship?"

"And what do you think I'll do, leave? Sail away with my tail between my legs? And with a bunch of damned extra baggage," the captain said, gesturing to Aaron and his companions, "that for all I know, are spies of Belgarin himself, never mind what Thom says. Shit, could be, you deserve what's coming your way. "

"Oh, I do," Aaron said, "more than you could believe. But they don't." He stared at the man for another moment then turned, rubbing at his throat as he moved toward the door and the struggling May and Balen. "When I say, open it."

The two of them nodded, grunting as another blow struck the door. "One..." Aaron said, readying his sword, " two..." Before he could say "three," the knocks and shouts from the outside of the door abruptly cut off.

He frowned, waiting, then Thom spoke from the other side of the door. "Would it be too much trouble to ask one of you to kindly open the door?"

May smiled wide, swinging the door open before Aaron could so much as caution her against it. The gray-haired man stood outside of it with three other sailors, each with short, stout lengths of wood in their hands, the surfaces of which were red with blood. Two soldiers dressed the same as those inside the cabin lay on the ground unmoving. Before Thom could react, May pulled him into the room in a massive embrace and planted a kiss on him with such force that Aaron felt sure the man would have a sore neck in the morning.

Finally, May released him, and if the gray-haired man minded the club owner's attentions it didn't show as his smile stretched from ear to ear. "Well, I'll be damned..." he breathed.

"Not yet," the club owner said, winking, "but maybe later, if you're lucky." Thom's face went crimson at her words, and he ducked his head, but not so far that Aaron couldn't still see the smile well in place.

"That'll do," Festa said. "Thom, you do what you want with your own time, but for now we've got a ship to run."

The first mate cleared his throat and nodded. "Of course, sir."

Festa grunted, eyeing May and then Thom. "Alright. Show me the deck—let's check on the damage."

"Of course, sir." Thom nodded, leading the way.

Aaron and the others followed Thom and the captain up onto the deck where sailors were busy about their tasks, and Aaron glanced around, surprised not to see any signs that fighting had recently taken place. Two in the cabin, two more outside in the hall, meant that there were still two soldiers unaccounted for.

Festa, too, seemed taken aback. "Well?" he shouted. "Where are the soldiers? I know there had to be more of the sons of bitches. I want every last one of 'em dead, do you hear me?" The sailors worked on in silence until one's errands took him a bit too close, and Festa grabbed hold of his shirt. "Well, man? Where are they all?"

The man's eyes went wide, as if he were a rat caught underneath a cat's paw, but he motioned to the side of the ship with his head. Aaron and the others turned to where the man had indicated in time to see several of the sailors dumping the bodies of the soldiers from below decks over the side. Festa frowned and turned back to the man. "How many of them were there?"

"Four in all, Captain," Thom spoke from behind him, "but it's been dealt with."

Festa let the unfortunate sailor go and turned to Thom, frowning. "Well, shit. That's good then."

"Yes sir," Thom said, bowing his head.

Festa seemed to deflate, his expression one of something like disappointment as he glanced around the ship, his hands on his hips. "Alright then," he said, "that's that. Now..." He turned to Aaron and the others. "I think you'd all best follow me back to the cabin and tell me what it is you want of me. Thom, keep an eye on the docks, make sure no more bastards set foot on this ship without I give the okay."

"Yes, sir, Captain," Thom said, "no more bastard feet on deck."

Festa frowned, studying Thom for a moment as if trying to decide whether or not the first mate was mocking him. Then, finally, he grunted and headed back down the steps, motioning for Aaron and the others to follow.

CHAPTER EIGHT

Back in the captain's cabin, Festa sat down at the head of the table, the effect of his scowl diminished somewhat by the obvious concentration it took to keep from falling out of the wobbling chair. "Now then, why don't you all just tell me who in the Pit you are and what in the Pit you're doing on my ship?"

Aaron glanced at his companions and saw that they were looking at him, waiting for him to speak. He sighed and turned back to Festa. He considered lying to the man but decided against it and, before he knew it, he was recounting the events of the last few weeks to the scowling captain, leaving out anything about Co and the other Virtues. The captain listened without interruption until he was finished. Then Festa let out a whistle and rocked back in his chair—a move that very nearly caused him to spill out of it and onto the floor of the cabin. "Well, shit," he said.

Aaron nodded, "Yeah."

Festa shook his head in wonder, glancing at Adina. "A princess, huh? In my cabin?"

"Yes, Captain," Adina said.

"Well," Festa said, then paused to clear his throat, "ain't that something. And I suppose Belgarin's got quite a big sack of coin for any who brings you all in to him."

Aaron glanced at the others, met their anxious stares, then turned back to Festa. "No doubt."

"Belgarin," the captain went on, "who's, more likely than not, going to be the next king of Telrear, a man who—everyone knows—isn't exactly kind to those who go against him." He gestured to Adina. "Some of your royal sisters and brothers would no doubt say as much, were they able to speak. I suspect Prince Eladen would have a thing or two to say on the subject, if worm food could talk."

Adina's face turned crimson at that. "My brother was the noblest, kindest person I've ever known. He would have done anything for his people, for what was right and—"

"No doubt, no doubt," Festa said, interrupting, "and considering he died for them, I suppose he has. Still, there's nothin' evil in the saying of it, Princess. Men die, after all. It's the one thing even a fool can't fail at. A task made all the easier when you piss off a man like Belgarin. And by helping you, a man is pretty much volunteering his head to be next on the chopping block, ain't he? So a man is left to ask himself—does he cast his lot on the side that, so far as I can see, has already won? Or does he send his ship hurtling into a storm and hope the gods are kind—though I've never known them to be—on an errand that'll likely as not see him and his crew dead? And even if by some luck that's more than Inaden himself could provide, were he so inclined—and only a fool puts his trust on the God of Luck's whims—even *then* what could I expect in return?"

"Sir," Gryle spoke, his voice thready with anxiety, "my lady is quite kind and generous. For a man who would help her back to her rightful place, I'm sure—"

Festa waved his hand, dismissing it. "Oh, you can stow it, chamberlain," he said, not unkindly. "The gods know I've told my wife a lie or two when we're in the sack and I'm after a husband's wants—such lies were how my first son Wellum was born, after all. Aye, and the words are pretty enough, I'd say. Shit, when the mood's on me, I guess I'm just about the most poetic son of a bitch alive, as is every husband. Still, when we wake up the next day, our house still ain't a palace, and when washin' needs done, my wife still ain't got no servants to see to it, do you catch my meanin'?"

Aaron frowned. He didn't relish the idea of having to fight his way through a crew of sailors to make it back onto the dock. Such a battle would only end one way. Still, the alternative was letting him and the others be captured by Belgarin and what hope was there in that? Belgarin would kill them, though perhaps not right away. Probably, there would be the torture first, pain and humiliation. He glanced over at Adina and saw her staring at the captain with worried eyes.

No, he thought, *better to die here. Better for us all.*

He started to take a step toward the captain but hesitated as Co spoke in his mind. *Aaron, wait.*

There's no time to wait, Firefly, he thought back. *I won't let him take the others, take Adina. You know what Belgarin will do.*

I know, the Virtue said, a quiet confidence in her tone, *but wait.*

Aaron reluctantly subsided, watching the captain.

Festa gave him a wink, as if he knew the direction of his thoughts. "Anyway," the captain went on, "it seems to me that only a fool would put himself against Belgarin, seems to me that what the prince don't already own, he will soon. What hope is there, really? I don't mean to be rude, Princess," he said, glancing at Adina, "but your family tree's disappearin' so fast you'd think there was a team of woodcutters hired on for the job. You've got, what, two siblings left besides the one bent on murderin' ya? Prince Ellemont and Princess Isabelle, ain't it? Not exactly the pick of the litter, anyway, are they? Ellemont's a craven, spends his time hiding in his mountain castle like a mole. As for Isabelle...well, her army's pretty enough, I'll grant you. If war was won by the soldiers whose armor shined the most in the sunlight, then I suspect Belgarin would have already been defeated. Battles aren't fought with ornamentation and gilded helmets though, alas. They're fought with steel and arrow, and they're won with blood and pain. I wonder how pretty those legions of hers will be after Belgarin's troops start hacking into them. Not very, I expect."

Adina's hands knotted into fists at her side. "That is your prince and your princess that you speak of, Captain."

Festa grinned. "Not mine, Princess. Sheza is the only ruler I claim, and it don't stop me from knowin' that the Sea Goddess is a real bitch, anyway. Her storms kill those that follow her like anyone else, and I've never heard tell of a shark keeping his teeth in check for one of her own. The water takes what the water will, after all. It always has. She's much like mortal rulers, in that way, the old sea hag, but at least she's honest about it."

Adina met the man's eyes, and Aaron saw the courage there that was one of the many things he'd grown to love about her. "So you're saying you won't help us."

Festa barked a laugh. "Now, I didn't say that, did I? Oh, I'll you give what help I can. The *Lady's* seen better days, it's true, but she's still got some sailin' in her 'fore she's done. She and I are one and the same in that. I'll help, alright—the gods know I'm a fool, and my wife'd tell you as much if you but asked—but I don't expect to see nothin' out of it in the end but a headman's axe."

Adina frowned, curiosity and surprise mixing in her expression. "Surely you would want something for your help, though. Lands, of course. Some form of pay—"

The captain barked another harsh laugh. "Lands? And just what in the Pit do I know about tending lands, with peasants and the like? Shit, better that Salen take me to the Fields of the Dead than I end up cursed to watch turnips grow, or maybe listen to the fuckin' baying of sheep all day. No, Princess, don't do me any favors, thanks. The sea's my home, and not you nor anybody else can grant a piece of that. It's the one wild thing left to us, thank the gods, a wildness no man or woman can tame, nor should, even if they had the means." He grinned. "Maybe a gold statue then? Gods, my wife would never let me hear the end of it. 'Course, I always told her I had a golden c—" He hesitated, glancing at the princess and May. "Well, enough to say I don't need any reward—or none that you'd give, anyway. Enough to say that I'll help you."

Aaron frowned. "But why?"

Festa seemed to consider that for a moment, then he shrugged. "Because fuck Belgarin, that's all. Fuck him and that sniveling, shit-sucking advisor of his too—what, Caldwell's his name, isn't it? All of this killin' and all of this trouble and for what? So that one man's ass can sit in a chair instead of another? So he can look at a map and say 'that's mine'? I've traveled a lot, me and my crew. Been to Belgarin's lands, been just about anywhere you can find on a map and plenty of places you can't, and there's one thing I can tell you: when royals fight, it's the people that suffer."

His eyes took on a faraway cast then, as if seeing into the past. "People who, for those like Belgarin, are no more than figures on a map, their deaths as simple as removing a mark or two, an equation of blood and death and the smell of shit while royals look at their maps and play their games. No, I've got no use for the lot of it and him least of all. I've seen his people, seen the people here, in this city. Oh, they smile quick enough, make all the right faces and all the right noises. But their smiles are smiles of porcelain, ready to crack at any moment, their laughs too close to screams for my taste." He shook his head as if waking from a dream then grunted, "Anyway, you've my help—you would've anyway, had you but mentioned Leomin. That Parnen is one crazy bastard, but fact is I owe him. Now," he said, turning to Aaron, "what exactly do you need of me?"

Aaron glanced at the others, preparing himself for the tirade of disagreements that was no doubt coming and sighed. "I'd ask for safe passage for four people to Avarest."

Festa smiled widely. "Ah, Avarest. A city after my own heart—very well. We'll leave immediately."

"Four?" May asked, her tone dark and threatening. "Just wait a damned minute, Aaron—"

"What do you mean," Adina said, "only four? There are five of us—"

"Aye, lad," Balen began, "surely you don't mean—"

Aaron held up a hand, silencing them. "I won't be going with you."

May scoffed. "Don't be foolish. Of course, you'll be going with us. You said yourself, staying in Baresh is suicide. Belgarin's troops—"

"Will be looking for a group of people, not one man," Aaron interrupted. "Besides, May, Avarest has to be ready. I've got a feeling that Belgarin won't care much for claims of neutrality, once the real fighting starts. Anyway, your club—"

May scoffed again. "Celes can look after the club just fine, Aaron, and you know as well as I that Avarest's strength lies in its criminals, not in its rulers. And those pig-headed bastards Hale and Grinner won't listen to a thing I've got to say. Now, enough with this foolishness. You're coming back with us, and we can plan our next move together."

"There *is* no next move, May," Aaron said, and was surprised to find the words coming out in a shout that made the club owner recoil. "The next move is doing what we can to survive, to save as many as we can. I'm not asking you for permission—I'm telling you what's going to happen."

May opened her mouth to speak, but she must have seen something in his eyes, for she hesitated. Then, "Aaron...they won't listen..."

"Then you'll have to make them listen," he said, his tone ringing with finality, "there's no one else who can."

The club owner grew silent at that, her gaze veiled in thought, and Balen spoke. "That's all well enough for her, lad, but I don't intend on leavin' the captain to torture and torment, no matter what pretty words you say."

Aaron met the man's eyes, and through his bond with Co, he felt something of the man's own shame, his guilt in not being with Leomin, his captain, in not suffering with him in whatever fate had found him. *He grieves already,* Co said, *that poor, poor man. He loves him, you know. Loves him the way one might love his brother.*

I know, Aaron said, hating that he was about to have to make that guilt worse. It would help the man, save him, but Aaron doubted he'd thank him for it. "You won't do your captain any favors by staying here, Balen. Look at yourself," he said, motioning to the man's wounded arm, "what good would you be? Besides, with your accent, you'd be picked out of a crowd in no time. I will get the captain back myself. If you stay, you'll only damn us both and damn your captain in the bargain."

The first mate's face went pale at that, his mouth working with emotion, but Aaron only stared at him, his eyes hard, his expression unyielding. He'd seen a chink in the man's armor, the man's will, and he'd exploited it. Finally, Balen sighed, a quavering, watery thing. "You'll...you'll help him, though?" he asked, meeting Aaron's eyes.

Aaron nodded once. "I will. I'll save your captain, Balen, or I'll die trying."

"Then you'll die." Aaron turned to Adina and saw the anger flashing in her blue eyes, a storm in her gaze that spoke of powerful emotion. "And just when were you planning on telling us all that you intended to abandon us?"

"Abandon you?" Aaron asked, recoiling as if slapped. "Adina, I'd never abandon—"

59

"*Wouldn't you?*" she asked. "And for what, so you can commit suicide? I mean, that's what you're talking about, isn't it? Surely you don't think you'll be able to storm a castle and make your way to its dungeons alone. I guess the guards will just sit back and watch."

Aaron winced. "I'll figure out something. I'll save Parnen and Darrell both, if I can."

Adina hissed. "Then you'll *die,* Aaron. Do you hate your life so much that you wish to throw it all away, and for nothing?" she said, her voice breaking. "Does nothing else mean anything to you? Do *I* mean nothing—"

"Stop, please," Aaron said, emotions roiling in him like a storm as he moved toward her and grabbed her arms. "Adina, please. It's not like that," he said in a whisper only loud enough for them to hear. "Of course you mean something to me."

"Not enough, apparently," she said meeting his gaze with challenge in her eyes, "not enough to keep you from killing yourself."

"*Damnit,*" he said, forgetting to keep his voice low in his anger, "don't you get it? *Don't you?* You mean *everything* to me! I'm okay with dying, if that's what it takes—I've been okay with it for some time, I think. But not you," he said, his own voice raw and aching, "not you. I can't...*I won't* let anything happen to you. There's nothing else for me if it does, don't you understand that? *Don't you?*"

He only realized he'd been yelling when he finished and the final notes of his words hung in the silence of the cabin, the others staring at him with wide eyes. For her part, Adina studied him with tears winding their way down her cheeks, and he wanted nothing more but to reach out and wipe them away, to hold her and tell her that everything was going to be okay. But, then, it was not the time for it, and besides, he'd never been much of a liar. "*Words,*" she finally hissed, "*that's all.* The words of a dead man." She turned to Festa. "What cabin will I be staying in?" she demanded, and even the gruff captain looked taken aback.

"Third room on the left out of this cabin," he said. "It's the best—"

But Adina was already swinging the door open. She paused in the doorway, turning to meet Aaron's eyes. For all her anger and rage, Aaron could not avoid noticing the beauty of her standing there, her long dark hair falling around her shoulders, her blue eyes dancing with fury. *A woman to put even the gods to shame,* he thought. He wanted to say something, to make it okay between them, but there was nothing he could do, and so he said nothing, only watched as she wiped angrily at her tears and turned and walked away. He'd never been a praying man, but he said a prayer then, that he would see her again. Still, he didn't think it likely. The gods, like men, loved their tragedies.

Gryle stepped up to him, his head and shoulders scrunched like a turtle trying to hide in its shell. He took a deep breath as if to steady himself. "Mr. Envelar," he said, meeting Aaron's eyes with a visible effort, "are you quite sure—"

"I'm sure, chamberlain."

Gryle paused, then sighed, nodding slowly. "Very well. But please, be careful, I..." The man broke off, rubbing at his own eyes, unable to get the words out.

Aaron put a hand on his shoulder. "I don't have many friends, Gryle, but I would consider you one of them, for what it's worth. It's been my pleasure to know you."

The chamberlain's eyes went wide at that, and his lip started to quiver even more. "T-t-thank you, Mr. Envelar," he said. "It has been an honor."

The man still hesitated, and Aaron forced a smile past the lump in his throat. "Go on now, will you? Before we both start bawling."

The chamberlain nodded, wiping at his eyes with a handkerchief that he seemed to produce from nowhere, then turned and headed for the door. "And Gryle?" Aaron said.

The man turned back, a faint glimmer of hope in his eyes. "Take care of her."

The chamberlain nodded, squaring his shoulders. "If anyone wants to harm the princess, they will have to come through me first," he said, then he seemed to deflate in another moment before vanishing out the door.

Aaron sighed once the man had gone and turned back to Festa, offering his hand. "Thank you, Captain. For everything."

The man squirmed, obviously uncomfortable with gratitude, but he took Aaron's hand, giving it a firm shake. "Ah, shit, it's fine.

I've tired of Baresh anyway. I'll be happy for the excuse to get back to somewhere where I'm not waiting for some piece of me to fall off from the cold."

Aaron grinned. "Happy, huh?"

"Well, as happy as I get, anyway. "

Aaron nodded. "Safe travels."

The captain grunted. "Aye, to you as well."

Aaron turned and walked to Balen, offering his hand. "Don't worry, Balen. I'll do everything in my power to get your captain back to you."

"Aye, Mr. Envelar. I thank you for it. May the gods keep you safe."

"I'd rather they not get involved at all," Aaron said, "but I appreciate the thought."

"Well," Festa said, coming up and putting a hand on Balen's shoulder, "come on then, Balen. I'll get Frederic to see to that arm of yours."

In another moment, they were both gone, leaving Aaron alone in the cabin with May. "You're sure about this?" she asked.

Aaron shook his head slowly. "No, but it's the only option we have. I won't leave Darrell and Leomin."

She sighed. "I still think it's a mistake."

"I know."

"Well," she said, reaching into her purse and offering a hand full of coins, "I've said my piece. I won't belabor it."

"May," he said, staring at the gold, "I couldn't—"

"Oh, you *will*, Aaron Envelar," she said. "If you're to have a chance, you'll need some gold to buy the answers to your questions, or maybe for bribes. You will not defy me in this."

Aaron met her eyes, then finally sighed. "Alright," he said, taking the gold and pocketing it. "Thank you."

She nodded, her own eyes glistening with unshed tears. "You're welcome," she said, then she walked out the door, and Aaron was alone.

CHAPTER NINE

Aaron walked away from the docks, feeling a pang of sadness as he did. It was a strange thing, having people to care about and that cared about him, and not a thing he was used to. His thoughts kept swirling around Adina, around the anger that had flashed in her eyes as she'd walked out of Festa's cabin. Whatever had been growing between them, he had stolen its breath. It was a dark thought...but also a comforting one. She could hate him if she wanted—at least she would be alive to do it. It was the best gift that he could offer her. He'd acted calm enough when speaking to her and the others, acted as if he was confident in his chances. It wasn't the first lie he'd told in his life although, considering what was most likely in store for him once he started asking questions, it very well could be his last.

They could have helped you, Co said in his mind, a note of recrimination in her tone, *if only you would have let them.*

You mean they could have died with me, Firefly. And dying is one of the few things a man can do just fine on his own.

Aaron glanced at the sky where the moon gave out its cold light, unmoving and unmoved by the lives that were lived and lost beneath its pale gaze. The rush to the docks and dealing with Festa had taken up most of the night, but he still judged there were a couple of hours left before morning.

Anyway, Co said, apparently deciding to let the argument drop, *what's your plan? How do you intend to figure out where Leomin and Darrell are?*

"That's easy enough," Aaron muttered, as he ventured further into the city. "I'll ask."

At this time of the morning, most people—at least most honest ones—were asleep in their beds, and few shared the streets with him as he made his way through the city. He walked past the large, ostentatious shops of the richer quarter, past gilded signs of gold for this smith or that tailor, his senses alert for any sign of pursuit or recognition from the few he passed as he journeyed toward the poor district of the city.

He'd thrown the hood of his cloak up once again, obscuring most of his face, and he trusted to the near darkness to do the rest as he cut through alleyways and side streets, giving a wide berth to the few guards he saw patrolling the main avenues.

By the time he made it to the poor district, his nerves felt taut, frayed around the edges. He breathed a sigh of relief as he crossed into the city's version of the Downs. There were no obvious signs declaring it such, but they were there nevertheless, for one who knew what to look for. The first, of course, was always the smell. A stale, slightly rotten odor carried on the night's chill breeze, the smell of sweat and desperation, of hunger and thirst. It was one he recognized well. The distant peals of laughter, the far-off shouts of ecstasy, as whores plied their trade, faking their sounds of pleasure as ably as any mummer's troop.

And of course, there were the screams. A man, not knowing better, might take those barely audible screams as ones of joy or excitement, might lump them in with the whores and the sounds of their profession, but he would be wrong. They were sounds of anger and hate, of despair and pain as those others who lurked in the night went about their own professions, their own victims leaving just as coinless as those of the whores, though no doubt enjoying it less. That was, of course, for those who would live to see the sun again. There would be those, in a city this large, who would not. It was the way of things.

Most may not have found comfort in such sounds, such dark truths, but these were familiar to Aaron who knew well that those screams, those cries of pain and fear, were the heartbeat of this district, were the audible proof of its lifeblood pumping, of its existence carrying on from day to day. It was not a nice world, maybe, nor a kind one. But it was one he understood, so he wasn't particularly surprised when a shadow separated itself from one of the nearby alleys and kept pace some distance behind him.

Aaron took a moment to adjust his sword where it hung on his back, ensuring that the handle would be within easy reach should he need it. A situation that grew likelier and likelier with each step he took. The houses and shops on the border of the district to the rest of the city were reasonably nice, if simple and unadorned, but as he walked further, the houses on either end progressed into states of disrepair, as did those few people he passed on the street. They would not meet his eyes, not even so much as glance in his direction, but he knew that such things meant little. They were marking his passage just the same, deciding whether or not he was an easy target, trying to determine if this newcomer in their midst was predator or prey. Apparently, those eyes watching from the darkness decided he wasn't worth the trouble. Or—and this was more likely—they'd seen the shadow following him some twenty or thirty paces back, the shadow being casual enough about it but following him just the same.

Aaron wanted to believe that the man was out to mug him, maybe give him a toss and take everything he had. Wanted to believe it but did not. The night was dark, but not so dark that his face wouldn't have been visible in the lights spilling from the houses and shops he passed. Visible enough to be recognized, maybe, by someone who'd seen one of the flyers the prince's men had posted. Why mug a man and leave him knocked out or dead in some alleyway, after all, when you could turn him in and receive a small fortune and a prince's gratitude for your trouble?

He kept on, past the lurid shouts of women of the night as they hung out of windows, past clusters of shadows that congregated in the alleyways, watching with eyes veiled in darkness. Vultures circling, waiting for any sign of weakness, for any indication that the man who walked among them was a visitor who did not know the rules, who was unaware of the game.

Aaron considered as he walked. The man following him obviously wasn't a soldier or a guard—he'd have long since found himself surrounded, had that been the case. Which meant that his shadow intended to bring him to Belgarin himself, thereby ensuring one of the prince's men didn't make off with his reward. The fact that he hadn't already made his move meant he was waiting on something—friends, Aaron suspected. After all, better to split gold with friends than to have a coffin all to yourself. After walking for another fifteen minutes, Aaron came upon a tavern. The squat wooden building shone in the darkness like a beacon from the light of lamps within, and he could hear the shouts of anger and laughter coming from it. He went inside, pausing as he closed the door long enough to see his shadow hurrying away down the street and allowed himself a small smile. Not long, then.

Inside, the tavern was filled with pipe smoke so thick that it was nearly suffocating. A smell lingered in the air, a mélange of the bitter smell of ale, the sharp, acrid smell of vomit, and, of course, beneath it all, the vague, metallic scent of blood.

Is this wise, Co thought to him, *letting the man following us know exactly where we are so that he can bring his friends?*

They won't want to make a scene in a crowded common room, Firefly, Aaron thought back. *They'd be too scared some of these others might realize who I am—decide that the reward money would look better in their own coin purses.*

This place, Aaron, these people. They're full of greed and hate and anger. I can feel it.

Aaron smiled beneath his hood. *I know. Welcome home.* The common room was crowded, as he'd known it would be, and several people turned from their conversations to study him as he walked to the bar. "An ale," he said to the tavernkeep, sitting on one of the bar's empty stools.

The man—who was at least a head taller than Aaron and half again as wide at the shoulders—frowned at him for a moment, as if trying to decide if he was going to be a problem. Long thin scars traced the man's forearms, and his nose was little more than a lump of misbegotten flesh on his face, one that had long since lost its original shape. A fighter or a street thug then, but judging by the prodigious gut and the thin strands of gray hair on his head, one whose days of jumping people in dark alleys had long since passed.

After a moment, the big man nodded once and turned to pour the ale from a nearby cask. He thumped the glass down on the counter in front of Aaron, "Not a face I recognize." he said. "In town to watch the competition and decided to stay over a bit, eh? Make a trip of it?"

Aaron raised his head up from studying the ale and met the man's stare, giving him a small smile. "Something like that." He glanced over to where a youth, fourteen or fifteen years old at a guess, struggled under the weight of a cask of ale, lugging it behind the counter and setting it down. The youth was gasping for breath but still found the energy to scowl at Aaron before turning to the barkeep, a sullen question in his eyes.

"That's alright then, Janum," the tavernkeeper said. "Now, why don't you go on and see if Emma needs anything from ya—like as not, there's some linens need washin'."

The youth nodded, took the time to favor Aaron with another angry scowl, then stalked away. Aaron watched him disappear up the inn's stairs then turned to the barman, raising an eyebrow.

"Ah, don't mind Janum. My sister's boy. Been gettin' himself wrapped up in some trouble lately. Nothing big, mind, but got caught stealin' a time or two. Her husband's been dead goin' on three years now, and my poor sister don't know what to do with the boy, so I told her she could send 'em to me. Few things build character quicker than an honest day's work, I find."

Aaron gave the man a half-smile. "Seems like maybe he'd disagree with you. And what about that nose?" Aaron said, nodding at the man's face. "Get that through honest work, did you?"

The barkeep barked a laugh. "Well, now. There's honest and then there's *honest*, ain't there? Anyhow, I used to be a lot younger and a lot dumber. I learned my lessons, though it took me longer than it ought and that's for certain. My hope is the boy there'll learn his own without havin' to get the scars that came with mine."

Aaron considered that. "Some folks say it's our scars that make us who we are."

The man grunted. "Sure, they do. And some folks say that broke bones heal back stronger—sure do hurt like a bitch at the time though."

Aaron decided then that he liked the tavernkeeper. He hoped that he would be able to go on liking him, but then, there was still plenty of night left. "Fair enough."

The man grunted again. "Anyhow, seems like bout every swingin' dick on the continent came for that damn contest. Most of 'em don't make it into the city so far as this, though," he said, and it was clear by his tone that it was a question.

Aaron chose to ignore it and took a swig of the ale instead. "It's not the drink, surely?" he said.

The bartender crossed his massive arms across his chest, scowling. "I s'pose your business is your business."

Aaron nodded. "Yes, it is. I do have a question though. You say not many have made it this far into the city—though I can't see why, what with how great this ale is—but I'm sure some have, right?"

The bartender seemed somewhat appeased by that, and he let his arms drop, rubbing at the counter with a dirty rag. "Aye, I suppose we've had one or two."

Aaron nodded. "Any of these visitors happen to be Parnen? Long hair with bells in it, talks more than any man you've likely met before?"

The bartender frowned, considering. "Well, now. Thing is, I stay pretty busy here, as you can see," he said, gesturing out at the common room where people went about laughing and drinking and arguing. "Ain't such an easy thing to remember one face out of that many."

Aaron met the man's eyes as he tossed a gold coin—several times more than the drink was worth—onto the counter. "I understand well enough, I think. Still, anything you might remember could really be a help."

The big man considered again, glancing at the coin and back at Aaron. Finally, he sighed, a distinct note of regret in his tone. "Sorry, friend. Time was, I'd remember any face I passed in the street, could describe 'em to ya just as if they were standin' right in front of me. But then, time's a cruel bitch."

Aaron watched the man's face for a moment then finally shrugged. "Yeah, she is."

"Well," the tavernkeeper said, reaching for the coin, "give me a minute, I'll get you some change."

"Keep it," Aaron said, "I've got more."

The big man paused, raising an eyebrow at that. After a moment, he nodded and took the coin. "Well, I appreciate it, mister. I sure wish you luck in findin' the guy you're after."

Aaron nodded, grabbing his still half-full ale and starting to rise. "Just out of curiosity," the tavernkeeper said, his back to Aaron as he poured two more ales, "what do you aim to do with your man, should you find him?"

"Talk with him, that's all."

The man studied Aaron for a second, glancing at the sword handle protruding from the back of his hood. "You don't mind me sayin', strikes me you're the type of man folks don't necessarily enjoy talkin' to."

"See, now, that hurts," Aaron said. "And here I thought we were getting along so well. Anyway, I think I'll go have a seat at one of your tables. More room."

"Expecting some company, are you?"

Aaron smiled. "Something like that." He turned and left the island of relative calm the bar provided, wading through a sea of drunken shouts, drunken laughter, and of course, drunken threats. He passed a table where two men were arm wrestling, their faces red and covered in sweat—mostly sweat, anyway—as spittle flew from their straining mouths.

He passed another table where several kids of no more than twelve or thirteen sat gathered around an older man who spoke to them in low, harsh tones. A taskmaster, no doubt, apparently unhappy with the day's take. He ignored the sullen stares of men looking for a fight, making his way to an empty table in the corner that allowed him to see the tavern's entrance out of the corner of his eye. Then he relaxed into the seat and nursed his drink.

I thought, Co said, after no more than five minutes, *that you were going to ask questions. You've only questioned the tavernkeeper and, if you ask me, it seems like he knows more than he's saying.*

Sure he does, Aaron thought back, *but then, doesn't everyone? You don't need the bond of some long-dead magician to see that.*

Magician? Co demanded. *Kevlane and those of us who followed him were no street performers with colored ribbons up our sleeves and assistants in short skirts. You have no idea the amount of power he—we—wielded duri—*

Sure I do, Firefly. Enough to turn yourself into a floating ball of light—consider me impressed. My point is that we'll ask our

*questions soon enough. There's just something I have to deal with
first.*

Oh? Co asked. *Something more important than finding Leomin
and Darrell?*

Aaron saw the door to the tavern open out of the corner of his
eye and allowed himself a small smile as the woman from outside
sauntered in. She was thin—a bit too thin, really—but pretty
enough. She moved well, languidly and with an affected
carelessness that seemed to say she was comfortable with being
the object of men's desire and that—from time to time—she chose
to sate those desires. Some, no doubt most, noticed her flashing
eyes, the way they almost seemed to dance, and thought them
windows that looked on a woman rich with life's appetites. A
woman who a man might step out on his wife with and never see
again, a story for a young man to have for his friends the next day.
But Aaron knew such eyes, had seen them before, and he
suspected that few of those who dallied with such as this one ever
lived to tell their friends.

Patience, Firefly. The woman moved around the room with a
directionless grace, stopping here and there to speak to the more
forward men who tried their luck at winning her favor, rebuffing
them with words he couldn't hear that somehow left them smiling
even as she sauntered away from them and on to the next. *We're
about to have company.*

The woman continued on for another few minutes, stopping at
the bar to order two ales. Aaron waited, taking a drink out of his
own mug and fighting back the urge to yawn. Gods, he was tired.
He suspected she'd be at it for another few minutes and, if he'd
been a dumber man, he'd have given in to the nearly irresistible
urge to take a nap. Men rarely woke from naps in places such as
this. He was rubbing at his eyes beneath the hood of his cloak
when she finally made her appearance.

"Well, hello there," she said in a voice that tried for languid
sensuality and, if he was being honest, mostly made it.

"Hi."

"I know a lot of those who come in here," the woman said,
easing down into the seat across from him, and by some woman's
magic he'd never understood, managed to make the movement
alluring and evocative at the same time, "but I don't know you."

She set the two mugs of ale down on the table and leaned back, studying him.

"No," he said, trying—and not completely succeeding—in keeping his eyes off of the fair amount of cleavage her shirt displayed as she leaned over the table, "I'm not from around here."

"Oh, I didn't think you were," the woman said, smiling as if she'd scored a point. "Tell me," she said, leaning forward more and producing an even more irresistible view, "why do you wear your hood? You're inside, after all."

You know, Co said, anger clear in her tone, *it is considered polite, when speaking with someone, to look at their face.*

Aaron shrugged, forcing his eyes off the woman's chest and meeting her stare. "I guess I'm shy."

Co made a sound that was somewhere between a laugh and a snort, but Aaron ignored it.

She grinned. "Shy, is it? You don't strike me as shy." She leaned closer still, her hands reaching for his hood. He let her and, in another moment, she was sliding it back, her grin growing wider as she did. "My, but aren't you handsome. It's absolutely criminal of you to cover such a handsome face."

Aaron smiled. "Not the worst thing I'm guilty of," he said, then took another drink of his ale, emptying the mug.

"No," she said, her eyes dancing, "I doubt that it is." She ran a hand across his shoulder and his arm, making appreciative sounds in her throat. "I'd like to hear more about what you're guilty of, I think." She glanced down at his mug and noticed that it was empty. "It seems that you're out of drink," she said, smiling coyly. "Luckily for you, I brought an extra." She slid the mug of ale toward him, and he grabbed it.

"Ah," he said, "I'm thinking normally men are the ones buying drinks for you."

She shrugged as if it didn't matter, a motion that did some interesting things with her shirt. "Perhaps. But then, I know what I want and what I like and, right now, I like you."

"Lucky me."

"You have no idea."

Aaron met her sultry grin and smiled back. He decided that, objectively, the woman really wasn't bad looking at all. Quite good-looking, in fact. "I'm thinking maybe there's some men in this room that would be a bit jealous at that."

She shrugged again. "Let them." She winked, slipping a hand beneath the table and placing it on the inside of his thigh. "It makes it more fun, doesn't it?"

He nodded, not having to try very hard to seem interested. Not hard at all. "I guess it does."

She smiled at that and her hand moved further up his thigh. "I wonder, would you be so kind as to see a lady to her room?"

Co snorted. *Where's the lady?*

"Well," Aaron said, swallowing hard as the woman's hand traveled further up, "I think I could manage that."

"Oh, I'm sure I'll be amazed at all that you can manage," she said. She gave a squeeze hard enough that Aaron winced, then smiled and rose. "I'll be right back—you finish your drink."

Aaron grunted. "Okay." He watched her walk away, her hips swaying back and forth in a motion that was—he had to admit—more than a little distracting.

Surely you don't mean to...to bed *this harlot?* Co asked, her voice angry and shocked.

Relax, Firefly, he said, forcing his eyes away from the woman as she made her way to the bar and began speaking with the innkeeper, her back to him. Aaron rose, grabbing the drink the woman had brought him, and started toward the bar. "Lucky bastard," someone muttered from a table as he passed, and Aaron paused, turning to look.

There were three of them, the man who'd spoken and two of his companions, all in their early twenties, each obviously drunk and looking for someone to take it out on. *Sometimes,* he thought, *it really is just too easy.* "Ah, well, sorry for that, friend. Here, a drink on me." He set the beer down on the man's table then grabbed one of the empty ones. "I'll take this back for ya. Oh, and I'd go easy on that ale—it'll knock you on your ass, you're not careful." The man was frowning at the full glass of ale when Aaron resumed his walk to the bar.

The woman turned as he walked up beside her, cutting off her conversation with the innkeeper. She glanced at him, then at his empty drink, smiling wickedly. "Oh, but you are an impatient one, aren't you?"

"I've been called worse."

She smiled at that and turned back to take the key the tavern owner was holding out. She turned back to Aaron and winked. "Follow me."

Aaron was following the woman to the stairs when something crashed behind him, and they both turned to see the man he'd given the ale lying collapsed on the floor from where he'd fallen backward out of his chair. *I told him to take it easy,* he thought. He glanced back at the woman and shrugged. "I guess the man can't handle his drink."

She smiled. "I guess not," she said, then turned and led him up the stairs to the last room at the end of the hall. As soon as they were inside, she slammed the door closed and pressed into him until his back was against the wall. Then she began kissing him, her hands roaming over his chest and stomach in the dark of the room. In another moment, she'd stripped his shirt off and tossed it on the floor along with his sword and cloak. "Gods, but I bet you're a strong one," she said, breathless. "Show me."

Aaron hooked his hands under her and lifted her up. She gasped in pleasure at that, kissing him hard enough that his lips ached from it and wrapping her arms around him. He walked to where he saw the shadow of the bed in the dark room and laid her down. She smiled at him as she pulled her shirt off, displaying a pair of breasts that were just about as good as he'd thought they'd be. She pulled him down after her, and he paused, yawning.

"Oh, come now," she said, grabbing him, "don't tell me you're too tired."

"Of course not." He yawned again, blinking his eyes in an effort to keep them open. "I just ha—"

She pulled on his arm, flipping him onto his back and straddling him. "You just what?" she asked, pinning his arms on the bed and moving back and forth in a slow, rhythmic motion that made him realize with painful clarity just how long it had been.

"N...nothing," he said, letting his eyelids blink wearily, "I just...so tired..." He trailed off, letting his eyes close completely, his breathing go slow. The steady, easy breaths of a man sleeping. Considering that he'd spent the night before running and fighting for his life, it wasn't a particularly hard thing to do.

"Wait a minute, you're not sleeping are you?" the woman asked, whispering in his ear. "And here I thought we were going to have some fun."

He didn't answer, and she spoke again, this time her tone business-like. "Hello? Stranger?" He remained silent, keeping his body relaxed, his breathing even. A silent moment passed, then another, and the woman made a satisfied sound in her throat before climbing off of him, no sensuality to her movements now, only efficiency.

Aaron risked opening his eye a fraction and could just make out the shadowed form of her—still shirtless—as she pawed through his tunic. He took a moment, appreciating the silhouette she cut in the near dark, then reluctantly rose to a sitting position in the bed.

For her part, the woman was too engrossed in going through the pockets of his tunic and removing what coins he'd secreted there to notice. He watched the shape of her moving in the darkness for several moments—maybe a bit longer than was absolutely necessary. Then Co spoke in his mind. *Aaron,* she said, *do you think it's really necessary to—*

Aaron cleared his throat loudly and the woman spun, her eyes wide and shining in the dark. "And here I thought I wasn't supposed to pay until after."

Either the woman took issue with him being awake when he was supposed to be lying drugged and unconscious, or she had a problem with the implication that she was a whore. Either way, her eyes blazed with anger, and she made a furious sound in her throat—something similar to what a cat might make if a cat was a hundred pounds heavier and pissed-off enough to kill—then drew something thin and sharp from the waistband of her pants that shone in the poor light with a familiar, metallic gleam. Aaron was just about to ask where exactly she'd been hiding *that* when she rushed at him like some she-devil, swinging the blade in furious, if unpracticed, arcs.

Unpracticed or not, the blade was near impossible to follow in the darkness, and he took a cut on his forearm as she bore him back on the bed. In a moment, she was straddling him again, but a woman trying to kill you will take a lot of the fun out of such things. She raised the hand wielding the stiletto, intending to bring

74

it down and ruin what had already been a pretty shitty day, but Aaron managed to catch her wrist before she did. He shook it, hard, and the knife went clattering to the floor somewhere beside the bed. The woman hissed and spat, biting at him, and he flipped her over so that he was on top, pinning her arms to either side of her in an effort to keep from being scratched. It was then that he heard the sound of the door opening.

Damn it all, too soon, he thought. He'd expected the men, of course, but not yet. Not so quickly. He wanted to let the girl go, needed to be able to, but she was struggling viciously beneath him even then, and he knew that if he did, those teeth and nails would go to work, so he turned to look from his place atop her, wincing as his eyes, accustomed to the darkness, narrowed and pained him at the orange glow of the lantern the figure carried.

The figure let out a gasp, and he was surprised to find that it was a woman's voice. Not who he'd been expecting, then. "A-Aaron?" the figure asked in a voice that was very familiar. A voice that would have been a pleasure to hear on almost any occasion. The exception, of course, being while he was shirtless, lying in a bed atop a woman who was equally shirtless.

Gods be good. "Adina? What are you doing here?"

"What am *I* doing?" she demanded, and such was her tone that Aaron was glad she didn't have a blade handy. Otherwise, he'd have had a second woman running at him with a knife in as many minutes. "You ask me what *I'm* doing?"

His eyes had finally adjusted to the light, and he saw that she stood in the doorway with her mouth open, a tear running down her cheek. She'd dropped the lantern in her surprise and it lay on its side on the floor. "Look," he said, "it's not—" He cut off as the woman beneath him renewed her struggles, and he had to force her arms down on the bed again. "It's not what you think," he finished to Adina, out of breath from the struggle.

"Isn't it?"

Idiot, he thought to himself, *how do you get yourself into these kinds of situations?*

Practice, I'd say, the Virtue responded, a smug satisfaction in her tone, and he chose to ignore her.

"Look, Adina, it's not what it looks like. This woman—she was going to take all of my coin and more. She intended—"

"Oh, I think I know well enough what she intended," Adina said in a tone that dripped acid. "And all of your coin, was it? Well," she sniffed, "it seems excessive to me, but I suppose I'm not well-acquainted with the price of such things."

"No, damnit," he said, "it's not like that, don't you get it? And she isn't alone there's—"

"Not alone either?" Adina said in a tone that promised deadly retribution. "Well, I suppose her friend is around here somewhere then. Under the bed, is she? Or do they take turns? I confess I'm not sure how it all works."

"Adina, *listen* to me," he said, knowing that they were running out of time. Knowing that, any minute now, the woman's friends would come through that door to check on her and the fool who was supposed to be lying in the bed, drugged. In his need to make her understand, though, he'd let his grip on the woman's wrists slip, and he discovered his error as one of her arms broke free and her fingernails raked hot pain across his chest.

He cursed, managing to catch the woman's wrist again, slamming it back down on the bed. For her part, the woman laughed. "And this is what a princess looks like, is it? Cute enough, I guess, but probably not after my friends get done with her. Of course, I don't think Belgarin will care much, do you, *Your Highness?*"

Aaron knew he should question the woman, figure out how many were coming, but just then he was too angry. Instead, he let out a growl, grabbed the woman by the head and slammed it into the wall, hard. Her eyes rolled back in their sockets, and she went limp beneath him. Satisfied that there'd be no more problems from her, Aaron rose and crossed the room to where Adina stood, trembling with anger. "See, Adina? You heard her, it wasn't—"

She knocked his arms away then slapped him in the face hard enough to make his ears ring. "That doesn't explain why you're both *half-naked,* Aaron."

"Damnit, woman, just *wait,*" he said, the side of his face hot where she'd struck him, "there's no time for this now. Whatever you may think, that woman intended to turn me in to Belgarin, and she's not alone—her friends won't be far behind her." He sighed in frustration. "Salen take it, but you've the worst timing in the world, showing up now." He glanced around the room and saw that there was a wooden closet near the bed. It was of plain build, unadorned, with an eye toward functionality not beauty, but it would serve well enough.

"Look," he said, turning back to Adina, "I'm going to need you to get in that closet. Just for a mi—"

"I most certainly will *not,*" Adina interrupted. "I don't know what game you're playing, Aaron, but—"

Aaron heard what sounded like footsteps in the hallway, and he clamped his hand over her mouth to silence her. "*Five minutes,*" he hissed, "that's all I ask. Then I promise I'll explain everything."

She scowled at him, and knowing that they were running out of time, Aaron grabbed her and carried her across the room to the closet. He slung the door open and stuffed her inside. "Don't make a sound," he said, "*please.*" She stared at him angrily. *Thank the gods she doesn't have a blade on her,* he thought, then he closed the closet door. That done, he strode across the room and put out the lantern so that it was dark in the room once more.

The footsteps were closer now, only a few seconds before the men were inside. He bent and grabbed his sword from where the woman had tossed it, his cloak from the ground, retrieved also the stiletto the she'd carried, then stood behind the door so that he'd be covered by it when it was opened.

He'd just made it behind the door when it was eased open and three figures filed inside the room. They glanced around, noting his shirt lying on the floor and the disheveled state of the bed's covers, as well as the woman's figure lying there in the near darkness. "Well?" the one in front asked. "Is it done, Janet?"

She didn't answer, of course—being knocked unconscious had a way of killing any conversation before it really began—and the man took a step closer. "*Janet?* Where is he?"

The three men had their backs to Aaron, and he decided that he wasn't going to get a better chance than this. It would have been an easy enough thing to cut them down before they were aware of his presence, but he thought of Adina in the closet, knowing what he was but not having *seen* it before, not really. So, cursing himself silently for a fool, he stepped forward and slammed the handle of the stiletto into the back of the nearest man's head. The blade was simple, but the handle was made of solid wood and, when it met the man's skull, it was not the wood that gave. The man let out a sound somewhere between a grunt and a gasp then crumpled to the ground.

Aaron was already moving to the second man before the first one fell, but he turned quicker than Aaron anticipated, swinging the two-foot long club he carried in a wild arc. It struck Aaron in the arm, and he stumbled, cursing, his sword dropping out of fingers numb with pain. His attacker brought the club back to swing again, but before he could, Aaron lunged forward, his forehead slamming into the man's nose, and he felt more than heard it break. The man screamed, dropping the club he carried, his hands going to his face. Aaron reached down and scooped up the club, swinging it before the man could recover.

There was a meaty *thwack* as the stout length of wood struck the man in the temple, and he collapsed to the floor near his companion. Aaron was just turning to look for the third man when a length of rope was jerked around his neck from behind, making him stumble backward and nearly lose his feet. "*Bastard,*" the man spat from behind him, his breath sour and rank. "Damn bringing you in alive—the prince will just have to be satisfied in torturing a corpse."

Aaron gasped, struggling with the rope around his neck, but the man was strong and had all the leverage, and he couldn't get a breath. He felt himself weakening with each passing moment, knew that in seconds it would be over. He stomped on the man's foot, and his attacker cursed but only tightened his grip, pulling harder, and the rope sawed across Aaron's throat even as he pulled at it with his hands. *Should have killed the bastards,* he thought. Then, just when he felt the darkness overcoming his vision, the man choking him cried out in pain and his grip on the rope fell away.

Aaron fell too, landing on his hands and knees, hacking and gasping for air. It was an effort to turn his head, but when he did he saw that Adina was facing off against the man, holding Aaron's sword in front of her. The man was bleeding from a deep gash in his left arm, and he'd drawn a knife from somewhere. An ugly, crude looking blade that was at least a foot and a half long. "You'll die for that, bitch," he said. He swung the blade at her, but Adina knocked it aside with more skill than Aaron would have credited her. There was an opening then, where it would have been an easy enough thing for her to slide the length of steel through the man's chest, but she hesitated, glancing at Aaron, an uncertain look on her face.

"Kill the bastard," he tried to say past his aching throat, but what came out didn't sound like words so much as it did a gravelly, unintelligible wheeze.

The moment passed then, and the man didn't hesitate. He slapped the sword aside and rushed in, punching Adina in the stomach. The air left her in a gasp, and the sword clattered to the wooden floor as she fell to her knees. The man took a step forward, and Adina cried out in pain and surprise as he grabbed a handful of her hair and gave it a pull, jerking her head up and bringing the knife to her throat.

Through his bond with Co, Aaron could feel as well as see Adina's fear. In a split second moment of clarity, he knew it, understood it. Understood, too, the cruelty in the man's heart, knew that, if he thought it would benefit him, he would kill her with no more thought than he would give to swatting an annoying fly. And with this understanding came anger, an anger greater than anything he'd ever known, and not just anger, but fury. Rage.

It swept through him like a wave of fire, scouring all other thought from his mind. In that instant, there was no Belgarin, no Darrell or Leomin, not even an Adina. There was only the rage, the wrath that demanded release and that wrath's focus standing there in front of him. "*No,*" Aaron said, and the Virtue spoke with him with a fury to match his own, the two feeding each other until there was nothing in the world but that burning fire. The word was quiet as it issued from his injured throat, but it carried power and desire with it, and the man spun to look at Aaron, his eyes wide with fear, that single word, coupled with the bond, communicating something of the rage Aaron felt. He pulled Adina up, putting her between him and Aaron and held the knife at her neck. "D-don't," he said, "don't come one step closer, or I swear to the gods I'll carve up her fucking throat."

Aaron stood watching him, his breath coming in ragged gasps, his body shaking with anger and the need to make this man suffer. He should not have touched her—he should have known better. But he would learn. The man watched him with wide eyes, the hand holding the knife shaking with tremors. "J-just wait," the man said, and there was real fear in his voice now. "Just hold on a minute. We can work this out. Look, I'll let her go, okay? You can both go on about your day, and I'll forget I ever saw you, alright? What do I give a shit about whether Belgarin catches you or not? It doesn't make any difference to me."

Aaron stretched his neck and bared his teeth in a grin. "You're not leaving this room alive," he said, and they were not his words, but the words of the fire burning within him. "No, you will not leave alive," he said, and again three voices spoke as one. Aaron, Co, and the wrath, the last the greatest of the three. "It's too late for that. Far too late."

The man recoiled from him and suddenly he was pushing Adina toward Aaron, scrambling for the door. Aaron, smiling now, dodged out of the way, and the man had the door about halfway open before he was on him. He grabbed the man by the back of his head and slammed his face into the door frame, shattering his nose. The man screamed, and Aaron's grin widened as he reveled in that sound. Then he threw the man to the ground. The next moments came in flashes. Once, he was standing over the man, then he was straddling him, the woman's stiletto in his hand—though he didn't remember grabbing it.

The man whimpered and cried and that was good, was as it should be. He relished those cries, those whimpers, for they were his due. He plunged the steel in, and the man wasn't whimpering or crying then, but screaming and that, too, was good. The rage demanded its way and had its way, the blade going in and out, carving its due from the man's flesh.

When Aaron came to, he was panting hard, exhausted. He glanced around, confused, and saw that he was standing over the man—or what had been the man—blood coating his hands and bare chest. The stiletto still dangled from his right hand, and he stared at it with the bewildered expression of a man waking from a dream in a place he had not expected. He noted dully that the tip of the blade had broken off, its sides nicked and dulled. There was hair and blood and worse stuck to the blade, and he dropped it in revulsion.

"What...I don't understand..." Rational thought was slow in returning as he stared at the man's mutilated corpse, and he felt bile rise in his throat.

Aaron, Co said, sounding as confused and scared as he felt, *what happened?*

"I don't..." He raised his hands, looking at them. Calloused and bloody, several cuts and scratches on them that had not been there before, but they *were* his hands. Why, then, did they feel as if they belonged to a stranger? Why did he watch them uncertainly, as if he had no way of knowing what they might do at any moment?

Aaron, Co said, her voice still weak and afraid, *what...what did we do?*

I don't know.

He stood there, trembling, feeling lost, a ship come unmoored in the night with no idea where land might lay. Memory came in flashes, blood spurting, the knife going in, twisting and turning, and hands, *his* hands, stained crimson. Bile rose up in Aaron's throat again as the visions came faster, battering him, and he retched, bending over and gagging out spittle and blood—he'd bitten his tongue at some point, though he did not remember it.

He crouched there for some time, his hands on his knees, and then his thoughts drifted to Adina, and he jerked upright, spinning to look around the room, his heart hammering a thundering beat in his chest. He saw her then, lying on the ground unmoving, a slumped figure in the darkness, and he rushed to her, his fear for her making him forget the blood, pushing to the back of his mind what he'd done. He fell to his knees beside her and saw in the dim light that her eyes were closed. *"Please, no."* He pulled her to his chest with shaky arms, staining her clothes red where he touched them.

He sat there in silence for a moment, then another, then he felt the rise and fall of her chest, felt the fluttering, whisper-like touch of her breath on his neck, and he felt warm tears gliding down his cheeks, mixing with the blood on his face and falling onto her in crimson droplets. "Adina," he said, "Adina, are you okay?"

There was nothing at first, then she stirred slightly beneath him, and her eyes opened slowly, reluctantly, as if burdened by some great weight. "Aaron?" she said, her eyes narrowing to see him in the near-darkness of the room. "Is that you? What...what happened? The last thing I remember, that man threw me, and I fell. I think...I think my head must have hit the wall."

Aaron let out a slow breath that carried relief not just that she was okay, but that she had not seen what he had done, what *they* had done. *What is happening to us, Co?* he thought. *What are we becoming?*

I don't know, the Virtue said, and Aaron was so used to her sounding so certain, so sure, that the childlike confusion in her voice sent a shiver of fear down his spine. Still, there would be time for that later. He forced his fear down, the way he'd learned to do when he was a child living on the streets. There were things that must be done. "Listen," he said, "we have to get out of here. Someone will have heard"—*the screams, the screams how could they not?*—"the fighting. Someone will come looking to see what's happened. Can you get up?"

"Yes," she said, and he helped her to her feet. He hesitated for a moment, her hands in his, then he glanced down at his own, at those hands capable of such terrible, evil things, and let her hands drop. He walked to where his clothes lay by the doorway that he only just realized was open. Orange, ruddy light sliced into the room through the doorway, and he used it to find his clothes, bending to grab his shirt, cloak, and sword, and he heard Adina gasp behind him.

"Oh, gods be good, Aaron, you're covered in blood." She rushed to him, looking him over. "Where are you hurt?"

"I don't..." *It's not my blood. At least not most of it.* "Your arm and your poor hands," Adina said, looking him over. "Wait just a moment, and I'll grab something to bandage them."

"Adina," he said, "there's no..." He cut off as she was already moving toward the bed, ripping strips from the thin linen sheets. *My poor hands,* he thought as he watched her, wondering at that well of goodness and kindness that was in her, at that well of darkness and hate that was within himself. How deep did her well go? How deep did his?

"Alright," she said, her tone perfunctory and business-like, "stand still." She proceeded to clean what blood she could off of him—not all of it, of course, never all of it—then she bandaged his forearm and tightly wrapped thin strips around his hands. As she worked, it was all he could do to keep from screaming at her, to keep from grabbing her and shouting, *Can't you see? Can't you see that I'm a monster?* But he was too afraid of what she might think, too much a coward, and so he stood in silence as she went about her task.

"I don't know what happened here," she said as she worked, "but don't think that we're not going to talk about it—particularly about the half-dressed woman lying in the bed unconscious."

He almost laughed at that. As if that was the biggest problem they had. *A princess and a monster,* he thought, *it's the beginning of some children's tale. But this tale has no fairies and no sun, and it is not a tale for children at all.* "Okay," he said, "we'll talk about it."

She nodded, making a satisfied sound in her throat as she pulled the last bandage tight and tied it off. "Okay, what now?"

He went about the room, digging through the pockets of the woman and those others and taking their coins. "The way the day is going, we'll need all the coin we can get," he said, feeling the need to defend his actions despite the fact that she'd voiced no complaint. Then he grabbed the woman's shirt where it lay on the ground and tossed it to Adina. "Better put that on."

Adina frowned as she looked down, only now realizing that her own shirt was covered in blood, then glanced up at Aaron, her eyebrows raised.

Nodding, Aaron turned his back to her. A moment passed and she spoke, "Okay, you can turn around." He did, to see Adina frowning. "It's too tight. What, did the woman never eat?"

Aaron swallowed, staring at the shirt, much more attractive on Adina than it had ever been on the thin woman, tighter around her chest, too. "What now?" she asked.

"Hmm?" Aaron said, still looking at the shirt, the way it fit.

Adina cleared her throat, and he managed to pull his eyes away to see her scowling. "I *said,* what now?"

"Right," he said, shaking his head to clear it. He strapped his sword on his back and pulled his cloak over him, bringing the hood of it down to obscure as much of his face as he could. "Let's go."

They made their way down the steps and were walking past the bar toward the tavern's door, when the innkeeper gave a shout. "Hey there, stranger! Leavin' us so soon?"

Several of those seated in the common room turned to look, and Aaron bit back a curse as he turned toward the barman. "She's resting," he said, nodding his head toward the stairs. "I wouldn't disturb her just yet."

The barman grunted, glancing at Adina and leaning close. "You want my opinion, I wouldn't be steppin' out on such a one as you got here. Not many men so lucky as that, and they ain't a woman ever set foot in this bar good enough to speak to this one, you don't mind me sayin' so."

Aaron glanced at Adina, who smiled. "Thank you, Nathan, it's sweet of you to say so."

The ex-street thug blushed at that, rubbing at his scruffy chin. "Aw, just the truth as I see it, ma'am."

Aaron sighed. "You're right, of course." *Not that it's any of your damned business,* "I'll try my best to be better in the future."

The barman grunted, his eyes not leaving Adina's. "You just let me know if he don't straighten up, mistress. When I was young, I once hit an ornery horse and knocked 'em out. I'm older now, grayer and fatter too, but I don't think I'd have too much problem knockin' out a horse's ass, anyway."

Adina laughed at that, and those few men in the inn who weren't already staring turned at the melodic sound. The barkeeper slapped Aaron on the back, quite a bit harder than he thought was strictly necessary, then the big man seemed to remember something. "Oh, stranger, I don't guess you've seen Janum anywhere around here, have ya?"

"No," Aaron said, remembering the scowling youth, "why, is there something wrong?"

The barkeep rolled his eyes. "Wrong with my head, maybe, agreein' to look after the brat." He waved his hand dismissively. "Ah, I wouldn't worry about it none—the lad has a way of disappearin' sometimes, particularly when there's chores need doin'. I'm sure he'll turn up, as full of piss and vinegar as always."

Aaron nodded, not wanting to linger another moment in the inn. His cloak did much to hide the blood covering him, but its concealment would fail under close scrutiny. "Alright then," he said, turning, "I wish you luck with him."

CHAPTER TEN

The sun was just coming up as Aaron and Adina walked the streets, but it was a weak, pale thing, doing more to accentuate the shadows that clogged the alleyways than to banish them.

"Where are we going?" Adina asked.

Aaron frowned. He'd been considering that same thing and the truth was, he wasn't sure. When he'd been alone, the answer had been easy enough. He'd go from tavern to tavern in the poor district until he found out something about Leomin. Then, once he found Leomin, he would question the Parnen captain about everything he'd learned regarding Darrell and his imprisonment. It had been a simple enough plan, really.

Wouldn't it be better, Co said, *to check in the more...reputable parts of town? It seems to me that they would know more of what was going on in the palace than people who spend their days sleeping and their nights trying to rob, mug, or kill anyone they come across in the hopes of making a profit.*

I can see why you'd think that, Aaron responded. The Virtue made a satisfied sound, and he continued. *You're wrong, of course. You see, Firefly, you are right about one thing—the people that live in places like this are always in search of ways to make a profit. No surprise, really, considering the fact that many of them live in houses that stand a solid chance of falling in on them and don't know from day to day where their next meal is coming from.*

It's a terrible state of affairs, I'll admit, Co said, *but I don't see that it has any bearing on our current situation.*

Don't you? Aaron asked. *People who are watching their children or loved ones starve will sell just about anything they can, Firefly. Their bodies, their values, their services as street thugs. All of these things and more, yet none of them are as profitable as information. Knowledge, Firefly, knowing things that other people don't, that is one of the best ways to*—He cut off as a thought struck him, and he stopped in the street, turning to Adina.

"What happened with the ship, anyway? Did the soldiers board it? What about the others, are they—"

"Everyone's fine, Aaron," Adina interrupted. "The ship sailed without issue—I watched it go myself."

"And should have been *on it* yourself."

Adina frowned then, a princess in truth and one who would not be easily balked. "And just who do you think—" She hesitated and took a deep breath. "No, never mind that. I've forgiven you for that much, at least. You see, after you left, I sat in my cabin for several minutes, angry with you, so angry that I wanted to strangle..." She paused, glancing at his neck where it was still red and abraded from the rope. "Well, anyway, suffice to say that I was angry. I thought you had made a stupid decision for stupid reasons, and that you were going to get yourself killed for nothing."

She paused then, and Aaron raised an eyebrow. "And now..."

"And now, I still think you made a stupid decision for stupid reasons, but I understand that you did it because you wanted to keep us safe."

He nodded slowly. "That's right...but then, why didn't you stay on the ship? You could have been away from here, away from your brother and his men. It would have been the safest thing."

"But don't you get it, Aaron?" Adina said, grabbing his arms gently. "If my brother Belgarin has his way, *nowhere* will be safe. Especially not for me. What, you think that he'll just say, 'well, she left, so everything's okay'?" She shook her head, "Of course not. Whether now or later, my brother *will* come for me. He has to."

Aaron frowned at that, mostly because he knew she was right. "Still, later would have been better."

"Would it? Better that I run and hide in Avarest, a rabbit scurrying into its hole?" She met his eyes, challenging. "No. I won't live like that—I won't die like that. Not for anyone. Not even for you. If I have to die, I want to do it fighting for what I believe in—just like my brother Eladen did."

Aaron hissed in frustration. He'd lost too many in his life: Owen, his father, his mother. And here Adina was acting as if she was going to jump in front of her brother's sword. He pulled her close to him. "Sure, your brother died a noble death, and what's the difference in *that,* Princess? Help me here because I'm not understanding. Whether he died fighting or not, your brother is just as dead, and the worms will eat their fill regardless. What matters whether his end was noble or not, so long as it *was* an end? Who cares whether he died running or died fighting? Not the worms, I can promise you that."

She stood her ground under his anger and did not look away from him. A moment of silence passed once he'd finished, then another. Finally, she sighed. "Don't you understand, Aaron? *I'll* care. Besides, I believe that we can make a difference—we can help. Belgarin hasn't won yet."

"Hasn't he?" Aaron gestured around them with his hands. "Look around you, Princess. The Royal Seven, King Marcus's children, each with their own piece of the kingdom. And how many of you left now? Four?" He shook his head. "If your brother Belgarin hasn't won yet, he's damn sure winning. And what difference have we made? We've managed to get Darrell captured, and Leomin could be captured—killed for all we know—and for what? Belgarin took Eladen's kingdom *anyway.* We traveled all the way here, and *we did not make a difference.*"

It was Adina's turn to hiss in frustration. "So what, then, Aaron? You want to quit, is that it? You want us to run and hide with our tails between our legs, hoping that we can live a year, maybe two, before Belgarin's men find us? We're supposed to cower in some inn, afraid to walk out at night without covering our faces, and count down the time to our own execution? I'd be a coward."

"You'd be alive," Aaron said, and something of his feelings must have come out in his words because the anger left her expression in an instant, and she put a hand on his face. The tenderness of that touch, the kindness in her gaze, stirred something in Aaron, and he forced his own fears and uncertainties about what he was becoming down, burying them beneath his need to protect her, to keep her safe. He didn't know what was going to happen, or what he was becoming, but just then, it didn't seem to matter as much. If he was to be a monster, then he would be her monster. A monster to stand between her and all the other monsters in the world, one who would stand against any man, who would stand against the gods themselves, if that's what it took to keep her safe.

"Alright," he said in a voice little more than a whisper, then he cleared his throat and tried again. "Alright. I'll help you in whatever way I can, though I'd be lying if I said I thought there was much we could do against your brother and his armies."

"As for that," Adina said, "let's find Leomin and Darrell first. Then, I'll tell you my plan."

That sounded very much like trying to accomplish one impossible thing only to turn around and attempt another one to Aaron, but he didn't bother saying so. He expected Co to have something to say about the conversation, but she remained silent, and though she did not speak, Aaron thought he could feel her, pulsing with concern and confusion and more than a little fear as she no doubt recalled what had happened at the tavern, what he—what *they*—had done. Aaron wanted to say something to comfort her, to reassure her, but he had no comfort to give, so he led Adina further into the city in silence, questions of what had happened at the tavern and what would happen in the coming days pushed aside by the immediate concern of putting distance between them and the dead men. Murder might not draw guards, not in the poor district of the city, but even a fool knew that blood always drew predators, and he had no wish to confront anymore just now, not with Adina beside him.

Suspecting that the bodies had to have been found by now, Aaron's senses were keyed up, watching and listening for any hostile movement, any suspicious stares. It was an easy enough thing, then, to notice a shadow as it separated itself from the mouth of a side street they were walking past. Aaron had drawn his sword and lashed it out at an angle behind him, pausing inches from the figure's throat before it had taken three steps. "I wouldn't," he said.

"Aaron, what—"Adina began, but he held a hand up, asking for silence. For its part, the figure froze, and he could see even in the poor morning light a quiver to its stance. Not a professional then, not one used to having sharp steel held against it.

"Step into the light," Aaron said, motioning for the man to walk out of the shadowed alleyway and into the road. The few people in the street gave them a wide birth, moving to the other side as they made their way past, but Aaron noticed this only out of the corner of his vision as his gaze remained on the figure, waiting and watching for any sudden movement.

The figure did as it was told, stepping forward and into the light. For a moment, Aaron didn't recognize the youth standing before him, but he grunted in surprise as he recalled the boy from the tavern, the tavernkeep's nephew. "Joseph, wasn't it?"

Fear danced in the boy's eyes, but his scowl was still well in place, and his hands were buried in his tunic. "It's Janum," he said, his eyes studying the sword at his throat.

"Right. Well, Janum, I can see you don't like me very much and that's okay—truth is, I don't like myself very much. I've done a lot of things I'm not proud of, but if you pull that blade you've got hidden under your shirt, I'll be doing one more very soon, you understand?"

The boy swallowed hard, and he took his hands out of his tunic, holding them up high. Aaron grunted. "Put 'em down, boy. I'm not the constable, and I'm not here to arrest you. Now, what exactly did you aim to do with that blade, anyway?"

The boy let his hands drop to his side. "That's not...I mean, that's none of your business." Trying for tough but not quite making it.

Aaron tilted his head at the youth, studying him. "You sure that's the position you want to take here, son?"

"I'm not your son," the boy spat, his anger finally working its way past his fear.

"No," Aaron said, "and lucky me. The last thing I need is to be saddled with some ungrateful bastard thinks he's the only one in the world's got problems."

The youth sputtered at that. "Ungrateful *bastard*...if I had a sword of my own, you wouldn't *dare* to—"

Aaron cut the blade quickly to the left, so close that the youth had to have felt the wind of its passing, and Janum's words cut off. "I don't think a little shit like you could begin to comprehend the things I'd dare do," Aaron said. "And if you want a word of advice, I'd watch that tongue of yours. Not everybody's a troubled mother or a kind uncle trying to look after you—there's plenty enough people that would be willing to knock your teeth down your throat for you, that's what you're looking for. You hear me?"

The boy hesitated, glancing at the tip of the sword at his throat. Finally, "I hear you."

"Good," Aaron said. "Now then, why have you come after me?"

The boy hesitated still, rubbing his hands together anxiously, and Aaron sighed. "Look, Janum. It's been a long night with a long day coming, and I'm not the man you want to count on for patience right now. If I have to ask you again, your mother's going to have a very different problem than having a bastard for a son."

"*Aaron,*" Adina said, slapping him on the shoulder and moving to the boy before Aaron could grab her. "Look, Janum, we don't want to hurt you, okay?" she said in that soothing voice that Aaron suspected would take the fight out of a pissed-off bear. "Nobody's going to hurt you. Forgive my...friend. He wasn't lying when he said it's been a long day. Now, please, tell us why you were following us."

The youth stared at her with wide eyes, his mouth working. *Poor fool,* Aaron thought, *fallen already, and just how long was that? Five seconds? Ten?*

Not much more than you, as I recall, Co said, though the humor sounded forced. Still, Aaron was happy enough to hear the Virtue talk that he didn't bother with a retort.

"Yes ma'am," the boy said, looking at Adina. "It's just...at the bar," he continued, turning to Aaron, "I heard you talking to uncle about a man you were lookin' for, a Parnen fella, one with bells in his hair that—"

"Shut the fuck up," Aaron hissed, glancing around the street. The only people he saw were two women—whores, if their revealing clothes were any indication—making their stumbling, drunken way down the opposite end of the street, far enough away so that they couldn't have heard anything. Or so he hoped. "Get over here," he said, grabbing the boy by the shoulder and pulling him into the alley.

Aaron checked to make sure the alley was empty before turning back to the youth. He saw to his surprise that tears—no doubt borne of fear—were winding their way down Janum's cheeks. The youth must have seen him notice because he wiped at them angrily, clearly upset to be seen crying. He glanced at Adina and saw her scowling at him, an expression much more frightening than the youth's had been. *If looks could kill,* he thought, *Belgarin would have one less problem on his plate.* He sighed and turned back to the youth. "Tears aren't anything to be ashamed of, boy. It's when they stop coming that you should be concerned. Means you still feel something and that's a good thing. Now, tell me what you were saying."

"He's a nice man, mister," the youth said, his voice cracking, "was a lot nicer to me and my uncle than most, it's why my uncle didn't tell you anything. And he's got a way with words too, says things that I'm not sure what he means, but they sound nice, and I like them anyway. He made Uncle smile—seems to me sometimes that maybe he's forgotten how, but the Parnen made him. Anyway, I wouldn't see any harm come to him, neither would my uncle, that's why he kept the Parnen's secret."

Aaron felt his heart speed up in his chest. "His secret. Alright, lad, I can understand you and your uncle not wanting to tell me. I know Leomin well enough, and if the man can do anything, he can talk."

"But wait a minute," Adina said, "if you wanted to keep Leomin's secret, why did you follow us?"

"His reason," Aaron said, his eyes not leaving the youth, "is tucked into his tunic there. Isn't that right, Janum?"

The youth stared at his feet, his face growing red. "It's just..." He paused, withdrawing a small knife from his tunic. It was a crude, rusted thing with a worn, leather-wrapped handle, the blade dull with several notches in its edge from hard use. It reminded Aaron of the type of knife sailors sometimes carried for working on ships. Certainly not one that he'd want to have in a fight—or to shave with, as far as that went. Janum tossed the blade so that it landed at Aaron's feet. "Mister, I just didn't want anything to happen to the Parnen. He's...he's a good man."

Aaron considered that then reluctantly nodded. "Yeah," he said, "yeah, I think he is. But I need you to understand, Janum, that we mean the Parnen no harm. Just the opposite, in fact."

"Wait a minute," the youth said, staring at him with wide, hopeful eyes, "are you saying...is he a friend of yours?"

Aaron grimaced at that. "Well, thing is—"

"Yes, Janum," Adina said, shooting Aaron a look, "Leomin *is* our friend. You have my word, we don't want to hurt him. We want to help him."

The youth glanced back to Aaron, apparently having decided that, between him and Adina, Aaron would be the one most likely to hurt someone. Which, Aaron supposed, was fair. "Is...is that true?"

Aaron glanced at Adina's stern expression, then bit back another sigh. "Fine, he's our friend, damnit," he said, turning back to the youth but not quite fast enough to avoid seeing the smile on the princess's face. "Now, tell us what you know."

Janum glanced at them both once more, then came to a decision and nodded. "Alright. The Parnen came by the tavern early last night, just after sundown. He talked for a while—told some really great stories about how he used to captain a whole fleet of ships, the biggest pirating operation the world had ever seen, he said. Said that he was known throughout the world as the world's greatest smuggler and that in some places, kings and queens bowed to him. Said that—"

"Sure, sure, and in some places they worship him like a god and women beg him to bless their snot-nosed babies. Anyway, what happened then?"

"Well," the youth said, nodding, "he told quite a few stories, said some things that I wouldn't have believed coming from someone else—"

"Smartest thing you said yet," Aaron muttered, but cut off when Adina cuffed him on the shoulder.

"Anyway," Janum continued as if Aaron hadn't spoken, "he was so good at it—tellin' stories, I mean—that he had the whole place listenin'. So good that Uncle asked him if he wouldn't want to stay on, told him he'd pay him and everythin'. He said he couldn't just now, said there were some men lookin' for him, men with long swords and short tempers. Said that back when he was a captain of a pirate fleet, he'd always been charitable and that his soft heart caused him to rescue a great beauty, a singer, I think he said, and a homeless beggar who, he found out later, had a bounty on his head. The beggar, not the princess, of course. Said that, on account of his helpin' the leper—"

"Wait a minute," Aaron said, frowning as Adina giggled beside him, "was it a beggar or a leper?"

"Well..." The youth paused, thinking. "I'm pretty sure it was both, mister. Wait a minute," he said, his eyes widening as he turned to Adina, "you're the great beauty, ain't you?"

Adina started to speak, but Aaron cut her off. "Which makes me the leper beggar, yeah. Now go on. Tell me where he is."

"Well, that's the thing, mister," Janum said taking a step back from Aaron, "he's still at the tavern. Uncle took a likin' to him and told him he could have a room for so long as he needed one—no charge, he said."

Aaron shook his head in disbelief. "No charge? Do you mean to tell me that Leomin is back at the tavern we just came from?"

"Why, yes, sir," the youth said, nodding vigorously, "leastways, he was when I left."

Aaron glanced at Adina, and they both shared the same worry in their eyes. Leomin was back at the tavern—back where they'd left at least one corpse, and if the others weren't dead, they were damned sure pissed-off. If the tavernkeeper linked those to Leomin, the Parnen could be in real danger. The tavernkeeper was kind enough—truth was, Aaron found that he got along with most barmen, though he wondered if that had anything to do with the fact that they brought him ale—but corpses had a funny way of making people rethink their opinions. And, of course, there was always the chance that he'd call the guard. Poor district or not, sometimes the guard would get involved in such things, and if they did...

"We have to go," Adina said, echoing Aaron's thoughts. "Now."

Aaron nodded. "Right, let's go." He grabbed the youth's sleeve and then they were running.

CHAPTER ELEVEN

They made it back to the tavern in less than half an hour. Aaron knew it was foolish to rush inside without scouting the place, without taking precautions, but he kept thinking of Leomin being taken, of the guards torturing or killing him. The Parnen was clever enough, but even he couldn't talk his head back onto his shoulders if someone got it in their mind to swing a sword at it. The woman and her three companions had recognized Aaron, after all, and with his dark skin and long dark hair, bells hanging from it, Leomin wasn't exactly unobtrusive. So, instead of checking the perimeter, or waiting for any sign of something amiss—all the things that, generally speaking, kept a man breathing—Aaron and the others rushed into the tavern.

They went straight for the bar ignoring the curious glances they received for their haste. The barkeep scowled at the youth as they approached. "*Janum,* boy, just where in the name of the gods did you get to? We're damned near out of ale—much longer and our customers are gonna have to hope it starts rainin' if they want a drink. That or they can lick it off the tables, I guess—there's enough of it been spilled to get a horse drunk, I reckon."

"Yes sir," the youth said, nodding his head eagerly then he was off, rushing down the stairs behind the counter into the cellar.

The barman looked after him in wonder, "Sir, is it?" He said to no one in particular. Then he shook his head, turning back to Aaron and Adina, "Well if it ain't the stranger and his missus. Thought for sure I'd seen the last of you when you lit out of here."

"I thought you had too," Aaron said honestly, "but your nephew there," he said, nodding to the cellar, "he told me you might not have been completely truthful with me about the Parnen man I was looking for."

The barman scowled and folded his massive arms across his chest, "Said that, did he?"

"He did."

The two men studied each other for several seconds, and Adina rolled her eyes, stepping up to the counter, "Look, sir. I promise you, we mean Leomin no harm, and if what your nephew says is true, I don't think you'd like to see any harm come to him either. We're here to help."

The big man considered Adina for a moment then glanced around the common room as if checking that anyone was listening. Just then, Janum was working his way back up from the cellar, grunting with the effort of lifting the cask of ale. The three of them watched in silence as the youth removed the old one then hoisted the new one up into its place on the counter behind the bar. "There you are, uncle," he said, his eyes on the floor as if trying to avoid the tavernkeeper's gaze, "is there anything else I can do?"

The big man scowled for a second, his arms crossed. Finally, he sighed, "Yeah, lad, there is. Watch the bar for me for a few you minutes, will you? I've got some business with these two."

The youth nodded, "Yes sir."

The barman glanced at Aaron and raised an eyebrow, then motioned for him and Adina to follow. "*Sir,*" he said, incredulous as he led them up the stairs. Then he turned back to Aaron, "What did you say to him anyway?"

"I threatened to kill him."

The barman considered that for a minute then nodded, "I suppose that'd do it. Thanks." Then he turned back to the stairs, and Aaron and Adina shared a look before following after.

He led them to a room that was only two down from where Aaron had stayed, and Aaron stared at the door in wonder. The man had been right here, all along. The big innkeeper's knock was surprisingly gentle for such a massive fist, as if he didn't want to disturb the Parnen should he still be abed.

"As I told you before, Melinda," came the call from the other side of the door, "Melinda, whose face is like the sun and eyes like garnet rocks—wait, no gems? Is it a rock or a gem? Stones? Yes, yes, as I told you before Melinda, full of beauty and grace, I will most certainly call upon your person on the 'morrow, but for now, I'm afraid, there is not enough Leomin for the world. For the world has many hands and wants much, and I am spread then and wide upon it."

During this speech, Aaron and Adina met eyes, and Aaron felt himself growing more and more frustrated. The man didn't sound in imminent danger, that was for sure. Still, it was hard to tell with the Parnen. "It's Nathan, sir," the barman said, "they's some folks here would like a word."

"Ah, dear, Nathan, your noble voice does wonders for the constitution," the Parnen said, and it sounded to Aaron as if the man was out of breath, "and wonders are needed, I can assure you. Still, I've little words to spare just now, I'm afraid. Which, I assure you, is for the best. Words are dangerous things, after all, weapons in the hands of a man skilled with them."

Aaron considered that, trying to puzzle out what in the Pit the man was trying to say. Weapons, he'd said, and dangerous. The Parnen talked in circles, so there was no easy way to understand his meaning. Still, those two words seemed ominous enough to him, and it wouldn't be the first time the captain had warned him of danger in a particularly round about and—truth be told, infuriating—fashion. That, taken with the fact that the Parnen sounded not only out of breath, but strained somehow, decided him.

He motioned for the others to step back, and he drew his sword. Then, without a word, he pivoted and slammed his foot into the door jam. There was a sharp *crack* and the door swung open and into the room. Aaron rushed in behind it, scanning the room for soldiers until his eyes alighted on a figure on the bed. Not one, figure though, but four.

The Parnen captain lay in the bed shirtless, the bed's covers draped over his lower half. Three nude women lay around him, even now screaming and scrambling to cover themselves. Aaron took in the scene and let his sword drop to his side. "Son of a bitch." Three women and all of them pretty enough. No wonder the man sounded out of breath.

"It must just be my day," Adina said from beside him in a sardonic voice, "for catching half-naked men in bed."

"Perhaps not, fair lady," the Parnen said from his place on the bed, and if he was uncomfortable at the sudden appearance of the three, he did not show it. "After all, it may yet be your day, but your day for catching half-naked men? No, I think not, for half-naked is half-clothed, and I am neither."

"Which means—" Adina said.

"I find clothes so binding," Leomin said, "the wrappings and trappings with which we entrap and ... enwrap? Yes, and enwrap ourselves. Hiding our shame, we call it, yet a strange thing it is that such shame, when coupled with another's, can lead to some of the most joyous and entertaining diversions of which men and women are capable. Don't you think?"

Aaron rubbed at his temple, glancing at the three women, "Out. Now." To his surprise and more than a little consternation, the three women glanced to Leomin first, as if asking for his permission or, possibly, to see if he would protect them. Apparently, a man busting into their room holding a sword wasn't enough to put them off. But, then, Leomin and his inane chatter hadn't been enough to send them running either—Aaron was beginning to think he really didn't understand people.

"Ah, ladies," Leomin said, "it seems that we will have to continue our ... conversation at another date. My friends here seem to be in a bit of a hurry."

"Friends?" One of the women asked in a sultry voice that made Aaron decide that their screams and hurry to cover themselves when he and the others had come in had been nothing more than a show. The woman reached her hand beneath the covers, and Leomin's eyes went wide. "Are you *sure* we can't continue it now?" She asked, "I *was* so enjoying our ... chat."

Leomin glanced at Aaron, a question in his eyes, but he saw Aaron's frown and sighed. "Unfortunately, my beauty, I believe it best if you leave for now."

"My, but she's beautiful," another of the women said, glancing at Adina, "Wait, is she the one that you spoke of? The one you rescued?"

Leomin opened his mouth to speak, but the third started talking before he could get a word in, "My, she *must* be! Just look at that hair. He sang your praises," she said, glancing at Adina, "but even his serpent's tongue didn't do you justice."

Adina blushed at that, "Thank you."

"Wait a minute," the first who'd spoken said, "if she's the great beauty then that would make him..." she glanced at Aaron, her eyes going wide.

"Gods be good, it's the *leper,*" one of the others shouted and in a flurry of covers and clothes the women vanished through the doorway.

"Thank you for showing us here," Aaron said to the tavernkeeper through gritted teeth once the women were gone, "we'd like a moment or two alone with our *friend* here, if you don't mind."

He watched in annoyance as the big man also glanced to Leomin, as if to see if it was alright. The Parnen gave the slightest nod, obviously uncomfortable, and Aaron watched as the innkeeper left, closing the door as best he could with a broken latch. He decided that people were really beginning to lose respect for a drawn blade.

He glanced back at Leomin, and the Parnen must have seen something in his eyes because he cleared his throat loudly, refusing to meet Aaron's gaze.

"Beggar and leper then, is it?" Aaron asked.

Leomin fidgeted with his hands and nodded sheepishly, "Well, it seemed to me that it would be wise to hide our identities lest someone discover us, since discovery of our identities would no doubt lead to untimely deaths."

Aaron bared his teeth, "And leper and beggar was the best you could come up with?" Leomin opened his mouth to speak, thought better of it, and shut it again. "What's more," Aaron continued, "you considered it important enough to give us false identities, but not so important, I notice, to keep you from inviting *three women* into your room."

"Ah, yes, that," Leomin said, "well, to be fair I do not recall ever actually *telling* them they were invited. It was more of an understood, I think. Anyway, it wasn't what it looked like I assure you, Mr. Envelar. I was using them, you understand, for information. A man might go so far as to say I was questioning them."

Aaron opened his mouth to speak, but Adina talked over him, "Don't be overly concerned," she said, acid in her tone that Aaron felt sure was directed at him more than the captain, "Aaron here has done some of his own questioning tonight."

Oh, well done, Co said, and Aaron wondered why he'd ever been happy to hear her speaking again. Besides, it wasn't as if it had been the same—the woman had sought him out, not the other way around, and he'd only allowed himself to be led to her room so that he could control the situation.

Still, judging by the look on the princess's face, he decided that scolding Leomin for his foolishness with the women might wait for a better, more private time. "Anyway," he said, "we thought you were in danger—we came rushing back here and busting in the door like fools."

Leomin nodded in agreement, then saw Aaron's frown and held up his hands, "I, of course, appreciate the concern displayed—and it was quite marvelous, the way you kicked the door in. Very impressive to say the least. I only regret that you didn't try the latch first."

Adina let out a stifled giggle beside Aaron, and the sellsword closed his eyes, taking a slow, deep breath. "Do you mean to tell me that you were in here with three women, and you didn't even think to latch the door?"

"Ah," Leomin said, "well, if I had, I'm not sure how their friend would have gotten in—she was apparently tied up for a moment but was on her way. I suppose," he said, glancing at the room's small window, "she could have climbed the wall but—"

"*Four,*" Aaron said, "Gods man have you lost your damned mind?" He pinched the bridge of his nose between his thumb and forefinger, "You know what, don't answer that. I don't want to know. All *I* want to know is what have you discovered about Darrell? Is he still alive? Or were you too busy *questioning* these women here to ask?"

"Ah, yes, well, I suspect he is alive, and do not worry on that score, I know exactly where he is."

"You do?" Adina asked.

"Oh yes," Leomin said, "or, at least, I'm relatively certain of it."

"Well, where is he?" Aaron demanded, "Can we get to him?"

Leomin made an uncertain motion with his hand, "well, perhaps, though it would require a lot of work, and if you'll forgive me for saying so, I don't see that it is completely necessary. Truth be told, I couldn't tell you his *precise* location."

Aaron bit back a curse, barely. "Just how certain are you that you know where he is?"

"Well, as sure, I suppose, as men can be of anything in these times," Leomin said, shrugging, "I saw him, if it's of any concern."

"You *saw* him?" Aaron said incredulous, "well, then of *course* you know where he is."

"Too true, too true," Leomin agreed heartily, "only...." He paused, considering, "the last time I saw your friend, Darrell, he was getting on a ship."

"A ship?" Adina asked, surprised.

"Wait a minute," Aaron said, "why would he be getting on a ship? *Damnit,*" he hissed, "which ship?"

"Ah, well, the *Clandestine,* of course," Leomin said, a confused expression on his face as if he couldn't understand why Aaron would ask such a silly question.

"But the *Clandestine's your* ship," Adina said.

Leomin nodded happily, "So it is, if, that is, a ship is anybody's but its own. Of course," his brow drew down in concentration, "I am not on it. Is it still mine, do you think, if I am no longer on it? Or does it belong to those who sail it now? That is a question that requires some thought. After all, if a man takes another man's shoe and wears it, how long must he do so before it becomes his own? Or, perhaps, it's the distance traveled that matters. I wonder..."

"*Enough,*" Aaron said, cutting the man off. "*Why* would Darrell be on *your* ship?"

Leomin gave him that confused look again, "Well, setting the consideration of whether or not it actually is my ship aside—"

"That would be wise," Aaron growled.

"Then," Leomin said, clearing his throat, "I would be tempted to suspect that your friend, Darrell, is on my ship because I put him on it."

"You put him on it?" Adina asked, "I don't understand."

"Ah," Leomin said, nodding, "I see. Forgive me, 'put' is an awkward word, isn't it? I mean, it's not as if I carried him on the ship and sat him down—that would be ridiculous. Sometimes, I think that the gods—in their wisdom—created language as a way of confounding those who tried to communicate with each other. It can be truly vexing to one such as I who strives always for a clarity as pristine as ... glass. Wait, is glass pristine, would you say?"

"Well," Aaron said, "Since you *strive for clarity*, why don't you tell me how you managed to put—" Leomin raised a finger at that, as if to object to the usage of the word, and Aaron raised his sword in turn. The Parnen let his hand drop, and Aaron continued, "How you managed to *put* Darrell on your ship, considering that he is locked up in Belgarin's dungeon, no doubt chained and manacled to the *fucking floor.*"

"Ah, right," Leomin said, "well, to be fair there were no manacles—although he was chained," he said quickly as if Aaron was preparing to stab him which wasn't very far from the truth. "As for the chains, well, I found the key and took them off."

"You *found* the key? Where?"

Leomin shrugged, "It was actually fairly simple. It was on the same key ring as the key to his cell," he glanced at Adina, "not a particularly effective way of doing things, if you ask me. It would be better to have them separate and, in so doing, make it much more difficult to effect an escape."

Adina and Aaron shared a glance, "And, let me guess," Aaron said, "you, what? Found the keys lying under the bed maybe? Or in that drawer there, perhaps?" He said, nodding to the small nightstand beside the bed.

"Not in the night stand," Leomin said, "Although, I'll confess I didn't think to look. As for the bed, would you believe, I didn't even consider it. Wait," he said, frowning, "surely, you don't think—"

"*No,*" Aaron said, "I *don't* think. Where did you get the key ring?"

"Ah, that," Leomin said, nodding, "well, off of the fellow that runs the dungeons, of course. Nice enough man, smells a little rank, but then I suppose any man who spends his day in what amount to little more than caverns dealing with dirty, poorly fed prisoners all day has a right to smell a little ... shall we say, off-putting. Still all and all not a bad man, and we really can't hold his profession against him. He has a wife and two kids to provide for, after all, little Duncan and Sarah."

Aaron gritted his teeth in an effort to hold back a scream of frustration and Adina, apparently noticing his mood, took over. "But how did you get the keys from this ... family man?"

Leomin shrugged, "The way most people get most things—I asked for them. He was really quite accommodating after I spoke to him for a while. I suspect he gets lonely down in those dungeons with little to do but listen to people scream for help—prisoners really do carry on, let me tell you. Anyway, he invited me to dinner, in fact, though I'm afraid I won't be making that considering the hurry you both seem to be in. Not that I would have anyway," he said out of one side of his mouth, "He's an alright enough fellow, as I said, but I just don't think I could keep my appetite, what with the smell and all."

"Leomin," Aaron said, "it's been a long night, and I just want to warn you that I *have* stabbed men who got on my nerves a lot less than you. Now, simple yes or no, did you rescue Darrell?"

Leomin opened his mouth to speak, and Aaron raised a cautionary finger, "Once more, to be clear. A simple *yes* or *no.*"

The Parnen glanced at the finger then at the sword and nodded. "Yes."

Aaron released a breath he hadn't realized he'd been holding, "You put Darrell on your ship."

"Yes."

"And where, exactly, is that ship at now?"

"Well, I couldn't say for certain," Leomin said, "depending on the winds and how rough the seas—"

"Leomin," Aaron said, "where is the ship *heading?*"

"Ah, that," the Parnen said, "well, I've sent the ship along with my crew—minus Balen and myself, of course—to Avarest."

"That...." Aaron said, surprised, "That was actually smart."

Leomin beamed, "Well, I thought so, thank you, Mr. Envelar."

"Speaking of Balen," Leomin said, "where is my wandering first mate, anyway? The man talks too much for a certainty, a fan of many words when a few words would do, is Balen. Still, I've grown a certain attachment to him, and I would not see him harmed."

"He's safe," Aaron said, "Or as safe as anyone, the world being what it is. We've sent him and the others to Avarest."

"Ah," Leomin said nodding, "that is well. I had suspected you would, you know. It's the reason I sent Darrell. So. I suppose the question now must be—what is our next move? If move at all we make, that is. Sometimes, it is better to not move at all than to move incorrectly. Perhaps ... if we were to take a night to think on it...."

"Don't even think about it, Leomin," Aaron said, "I'm afraid those women will have to find someone else to occupy their time. As for what we do ...." He shrugged, glancing at Adina.

The princess nodded, "I've been thinking about that. We can't risk chartering another boat on the docks—if Belgarin doesn't know that his secretary of the docks and several of his men are dead he will before long and, besides, the others will be able to do what good may be done in Avarest without us. We'd be no help there."

Aaron nodded, "What then?"

"As I see it," Adina said, "there are four great powers left in Telrear. Belgarin—the greatest of the four, of course—the armies of my sister Isabelle and my brother Ellemont, and Avarest's own. While May and the others work on Avarest, I think it would be wise for us to try to win one of the other armies to our favor."

"What of your own kingdom, Princess?" Leomin asked, "Might not your people fight for you?"

A dark look came over Adina's face, "Perhaps they would, if they knew I was still alive. The nobles of my kingdom betrayed me to Belgarin. They came for me in the night, and I only just managed to escape thanks to Gryle. The last I heard before I left the capital, I'd been killed in an unfortunate riding accident." She frowned, her eyes dancing with anger, "Ridiculous, of course. I've been trained to sit a horse since I was a child—my father made sure of it, for all his children. But no, Leomin, to answer your question, I would not show up in the capital looking for an army—not with one already at my back, that is. Still," her eyes narrowed, "the traitors will be dealt with in time."

"That leaves us only two options," Aaron said, "and neither one that I much like from what I've heard of your remaining brother and sister."

Adina sighed, "Yes, Isabelle and Ellemont can be ... difficult, each in their own way, but they are not fools—I believe that they can be made to see reason, if given a chance."

Aaron nodded, "So ... it seems to me that our options are cowardice or vanity."

Adina sighed, "Festa was not wrong, unfortunately, in his assessment of my siblings. Still, I believe that our best chances lie with Isabelle. She has the greater army of the two, and I believe she would be easier to bring to our cause in any case. She, I know, will want Belgarin to rule Telrear no more than I. In fact, Eladen was in talks with her about an alliance."

Aaron raised an eyebrow, "Until he was murdered."

Adina shook her head, "Believe me, Aaron, Isabelle is many things, but she would not side with Belgarin and would certainly not betray Eladen. She is the second oldest, you know, next to only Belgarin himself, and they have quarreled since I can remember. No, she would rather watch the world burn than to see it fall in the hands of Belgarin."

"Right," Aaron said, "so keep her away from any torches."

"Aaron, I'm serious. This can work—it *has* to. With Avarest and Isabelle's kingdom Isalla behind us, we'll stand a real chance."

Sure, Aaron thought, *just so long as Belgarin can't add and see that he still has twice our numbers, at least.* But he nodded, "If you think this is the best way forward, then I'll go there with you, princess. You've no cause for worry on that front. "

Leomin nodded, "And I as well."

"Eh?" Aaron asked, unable to hide his grimace, "I'd thought you'd want to get back to the *Clandestine.*"

The Parnen captain shrugged, smiling, "And I do, Mr. Envelar. Every man has a place in this world, and this world has a place for every man. Mine, as you've surmised, is aboard the *Clandestine,* with Balen prattling in my ear and the sea rushing past us, the gulls cawing in the distance." He smiled wider, "Ah, but it is good even to think of it."

"Then why come?" Aaron asked, seeing a shred of hope.

"Because, Mr. Envelar," the captain said, his expression growing serious, "I have seen some of those things of which Belgarin is capable. Forgive me, princess," he said, nodding to Adina, "but such a man deserves no seat of power unless it lies beneath the headman's axe. Besides," he said, his smile returning, "I suspect you'll have need of me, before this is all done."

Aaron tried to think of a way that *that* could possibly be true, considered telling the Parnen that he needed him about as much as he needed a knife in the kidney. Less, really. A man could live with one kidney. Instead, he let it go. He was too elated by Darrell's rescue and too anxious of the trip ahead to think on it over much. "How far is it, would you say," he asked, turning to Adina, "to make it to Isalla? I've never been."

"Well, aboard ship—" Leomin began.

"We don't have a ship."

"Ah. Right."

"With horses?" Adina asked, "three weeks, maybe four."

A long way then, but it wasn't the journey itself, so much, that caused the headache to begin to form in Aaron's temple. It was the thought of being in close proximity to the Parnen captain for that long. Belgarin's executioner was beginning to look better and better.

Leomin smiled, oblivious of Aaron's thoughts, "Ah, but it is good to travel with friends. I, myself, am excited about the prospect of a journey with two such wonderful companions as yourselves. Now, might I suggest we all get a few hours of rest— after all, the road will be long and, I find, that anytime you set your feet on a path, there is no true telling where it might lead."

Most likely to a headman's axe, Aaron thought, *but at least we'll be moving.*

My bright and cheerful Aaron, Co said, the sarcasm practically oozing from her words, *always so ready to put a bold face on things.*

"Surely," Adina said, "it'd be better to leave now."

Leomin's mouth twisted into a pout, "But surely an hour—"

"Now," Aaron said, "your women will find someone else to keep them company, I do not doubt. The gods only know how you managed to find three of them willing to listen to your prattle—I would have suspected they were all deaf, if I hadn't seen it for myself. Anyway, you can console yourself with the fact that there will be more women where we're going."

"Four," Leomin mumbled, then he nodded slowly, his expression brightening, "Still, the women of the west ... I have heard some men say that they are the most beautiful women in the world."

"Have you?" Aaron asked.

"Well, of course," the Parnen said, grinning, "I said it, just now.
"

Aaron growled, "Come on." He and Adina headed for the door, the Parnen following after. Aaron hesitated and turned back to Leomin, "You'll want to put some clothes on first."

The Parnen captain looked down in surprise, as if only now noticing his nakedness, and Adina stared at the door, her body rigid. "Ah. Right," Leomin said, "I'll only be a moment."

**

Once Leomin was dressed, Aaron and the others made their way down to the common room of the tavern. Nathan, the barkeep, was standing at the counter, watching as they approached. "Leaving us so soon, are you?" He said, glancing at Leomin, "I wondered at seeing three very disappointed women walking down here not too long ago."

"Four," the Parnen mumbled again, glancing at Aaron before turning back to the bartender, "Yes, friend Nathan. It is unfortunately the way of the world that satisfaction so often remains within one's grasp, yet too slippery to the touch to be held for long. My friends and I must depart."

Nathan nodded and there was no missing the disappointment in his own gaze. "Well, if you really must leave, I understand. Still, it would have been a fine thing to have heard another story, before you left."

"Ah, but my friend," Leomin said, smiling, "where my friends and I go now, we will find many stories and many tales for the telling, not tall ones, though, only the … short, honest kind. I will, one day, return here to share them with you."

The man nodded and started to speak but the youth, Janum, rushed up before he could, giving Leomin a hug. "Are you sure you have to leave?"

Aaron and Adina shared an incredulous look, but Leomin didn't seem surprised by the boy's enthusiasm. "Alas, I must, young Janum," he said, patting the boy's head, "But I will always think of my time here fondly. I will return, if I'm able, of that I can assure you. You'll be good while I'm gone won't you? You'll stay out of trouble?"

Janum nodded, obviously disappointed. "Yes sir, I will. I promise."

The barkeep nodded and put an arm around his nephew's shoulders, "Oh, we'll be fine, don't worry on us any," he said, and Aaron stared at the man in shock. Were those *tears* in his eyes?

Leomin smiled, bowing his head, "As you say."

The barkeep and his nephew shared grins before seeming to notice Aaron and Adina for the first time. Nathan winked at Adina, "You keep him in line, won't you, mistress?" He said, glancing meaningfully at Aaron.

Adina's eyes went back and forth between the smiling Leomin and the two teary-eyed men, a youth that had been ready to commit murder, and a retired street thug. "Oh," she said finally, "you can be sure of that."

The big man nodded, apparently satisfied, and Janum took an obviously reluctant step toward Aaron, offering his hand. "Thanks for not killing me."

Aaron raised an eyebrow, taking the boy's hand and giving it a firm shake, "You're welcome. I won't tell you not to carry a blade, Janum, but I will tell you not to go looking for trouble. It'll find you, sooner or later—it always does. No sense in courting it. Just make sure that when it does, you've some real steel handy, will you? Not some fisherman's shiv."

"Y-yes sir," the boy said, wide eyed.

Nathan cleared his throat, patting the boy on the soldier, "Well, I guess you'd all best be on your way."

Aaron breathed a sigh of relief when they were finally outside the inn and on the move. A sense of urgency had been building in him since they'd found Leomin. A sense that time was running out, was already out, maybe. As far as he was concerned, they couldn't be quit of the city soon enough.

CHAPTER TWELVE

They stopped first at a tailor's shop, buying new clothes to replace the blood-covered ones Aaron and Adina wore as well as finding a hooded cloak for Leomin. The shop owner, a thin man with bad teeth, charged more than twice what the clothes were worth as far as Aaron was concerned, but they didn't have time negotiate, so he paid the man what he asked, whispering a silent thanks to May for the gold she'd given him.

As they made their way through the streets of the city—getting crowded now as the morning drew on and people went about their daily lives—Aaron glanced at Leomin. "Just what in Salen's Fields was all that about, back at the inn? You knew those people for a *day*. They gave *you* a place to hide, and you'd think that you were some king come to grace them with your presence."

"Yes," Adina said, staring at Leomin, "that was strange."

Leomin merely shrugged, "People are simple enough creatures, I think, and the heart knows what the heart knows."

Aaron grunted, "Meaning, you don't want to talk about it."

Leomin grinned displaying his almost too-white teeth, "Ah, Mr. Envelar, I have been told, from time to time, that I've a way with people."

"Really?" Aaron said, "I hadn't noticed."

The Parnen captain looked genuinely hurt, "Well, I'll admit that some hearts are more difficult to touch than others—your own being a prime example—but do not fret. I will find it, sooner or later."

"I doubt we've got that much time."

No one accosted them as they made their way down the city streets, due in large part, Aaron suspected, to the hooded cloak Leomin wore. With his long, bell-laden hair and distinct, dusky-skin, the man was by far the most conspicuous of the three of them. Still, a man might have thought the cloak was laced with poison the way Leomin had frowned at it when Aaron gave it to him, but he'd been persuaded to wear it nonetheless.

Soon, they arrived at the western gate and, by a bit of luck, found a horse trader nearby. In another stroke of luck, the man happened to have exactly three horses available, along with provisions for the journey. The problem, of course, was that Aaron didn't trust luck. The god of luck was a notoriously fickle bastard, and even a fool knew that luck always killed more than it saved. Luck, in Aaron's experience, was a sharp blade a drunk reached for in the dark. He was just as likely to get cut as find the handle.

Outside the stables, their business concluded, Adina took a moment to rub the side of her horse's face, muttering soft words before mounting it with a practiced grace. Aaron and Leomin glanced at each other then shrugged and mounted their own horses with considerably less skill. "Now," Adina said, "how do we get through the gate?"

Leomin smiled, "Leave that to me." Then, before Aaron could object, he was riding toward the gate, and Aaron and Adina were forced to follow.

Gods the man is gonna get us all killed.

Aaron, Co said, her tone curious, *do you feel something? It's as if something's … gathering. Growing.*

No, firefly, he said as he followed Leomin up to the gate, one hand on the reins and the other itching to reach for the handle of his sword. *I don't feel anything. Unless, of course, you mean the growing chance that we're going to get our fool heads lopped off.*

People attempting to leave the city were lined up at the gate, farmers and merchants mostly, gone to start their days, and Aaron frowned as he noticed that the guards were checking each person before they were allowed to leave, studying their faces and appearances, clearly looking for someone. *And I think I've a pretty good idea of who that might be.* He gritted his teeth, wanting to grab Leomin and get out of the line, but he knew that doing so would draw the attention of the guards.

It took about fifteen minutes to reach the front of the line, Leomin in the lead, and one of the four guards stationed at the gate walked up to the Parnen's horse. "Mornin'."

"Good morning, brave soldier," Leomin said, smiling as if he didn't have a care in the world. *A fool*, Aaron thought, *and soon to be a dead one.* He glanced at Adina and saw that her troubled expression mirrored his own thoughts. *And us along with him.*

The guard peered up at Leomin's face, struggling to see it past the hood that obscured most of his features. "Lose the hood, friend."

"Regretfully, sir, I must decline," Leomin said, "You see, business of the upmost importance forces my friends and I to regretfully depart your fine city. Alas, I am not used to the cold of the north and the hood—"

"I said lose the hood," the guard said, motioning one of his companions forward, and Aaron noted grimly that both of their hands were gripping the handles of the swords scabbarded at their sides.

With a sigh, Leomin lowered his hood revealing his dusk-colored face and his long dark hair, the many small bells still tied into it. It seemed, then, that everything happened at once. One of the guards gave a cry of surprise, and the other two, who'd been standing back, rushed forward, all of them drawing their swords. Several of those people in line behind them screamed, scattering in all directions. *Damn it all,* Aaron thought.

He drew his own sword and was just about to move forward, knowing he'd be too late to save the Parnen captain even as he did it. "Get down off the horses, now!" One of the guards shouted, "all three of you, and drop that blade!"

Aaron leaped from his horse, not trusting his ability to fight while mounted, but he did not drop his blade.

"*Wait*," Leomin said, and though he had not raised his voice, the word struck the air like a thunder crack, sending a shockwave of power radiating out from him. It struck the guards first, and their faces took on a vacant look as their arms went limp, their swords hanging loosely at their sides. The people in the street—who'd been running only moments before—froze in their tracks, their screams and shouts of surprise cutting off as if on cue. The guards and the people both turned to stare at Leomin, their eyes unfocused as if they'd been drugged. Even Adina, who'd been dismounting, paused hanging halfway off her horse to stare at the Parnen.

Aaron frowned glancing around himself. Thirty or forty people—thirty or forty, at least, and they were all staring at Leomin as if the man was a miracle worker, and they were waiting for his next act. That many people, and the street was as silent as a graveyard.

What the fu—

Sister? Co asked, her own voice full of hope and shock. Aaron felt part of himself—or part of Co, and it was really becoming harder to know the difference—quest outward, toward Leomin. Then there was a sensation, much of like having his hand slapped, and whatever sense had been reaching out toward the Parnen Captain recoiled and vanished altogether. Leomin turned and met Aaron's eyes, a serious, almost dark expression on his face, the first that Aaron could ever remember seeing on the normally jovial, if confounding Parnen. Never taking his gaze away from Aaron's own, Leomin held his index finger up to his lips in a quieting gesture.

Aaron frowned, but remained silent and, after a moment, Leomin turned back to the guard. *"We are friends,"* he said, his voice ringing with that same indescribable power, and Aaron could have sworn that he saw the people around him sway with the impact of those words. *"We are innocent travelers leaving this fine city. No one of note, or importance, and there is a really long day ahead of you. A long day and a drink of ale at the end of it. We need not make it longer than necessary. Let us all go on about our day."*

The guards seemed to flinch with each word as Leomin's gaze settled upon them, and, after a moment, Aaron was shocked to see them return their swords to their scabbards. The crystallized moment in time shattered then, and all of the people in the street went on about what they were doing, picking up conversations they'd left off midsentence as if nothing had occurred, and once more the sounds of laughter and shouts of merchants hawking their wares filled the street. "Alright, friend," the guard who'd challenged him said, "everything looks good. The gods' blessing on your journey."

Leomin smiled, "Thank you, and the gods' blessing on your own."

Aaron glanced at Adina and saw her shaking her head as if waking from a particularly deep, particularly *real* dream as she remounted her horse. He took the time to mount his own horse once more then, frowning, he followed behind her as Leomin led them out of the city.

Once they were away from the gate and on the dirt road leading west, Aaron rode up to Leomin, leaving Adina behind for the moment. "Seems to me like we have something we need to talk about."

The Parnen captain glanced over at him, his expression serious, "And talk we will, Mr. Envelar, but not now. Not here. We must put as much distance between ourselves and this city as possible. This thing that I have done ... there are those who know it for what it is, those to whom it is like a siren's call, beckoning them onward. They will come, looking for the source of that call. And the ones who come ... we are not ready. *You* are not ready."

Aaron started to ask him what he meant by *that*, but Leomin gave his horse's flanks a kick, and he was off, galloping down the road at full speed. Aaron stared after the man, a storm of emotions roiling within him. Confusion at what he'd seen, frustration at the Parnen's evasiveness but, most of all, worry. Leomin was not normally the type of man who took threats seriously. The man had somehow broken Darrell out of jail, had even suffered an assassination attempt by one of his crew shortly after Aaron had first met him, and he'd barely acted upset at all. The fact that he was so concerned now, that he was obviously afraid of whomever "they" were, those who would come hunting them for doing ... for doing *what,* exactly? Never mind. There would be time, he decided, to wonder over it all later. For now, he turned to Adina who was staring at the departing back of the Parnen in confusion. "Come on," he said, "let's go."

CHAPTER THIRTEEN

They rode the horses hard that night, pausing only in brief intervals to walk them and let them cool off before starting off again. During one of the few moments when they were walking the horses, Adina came up beside them. "Alright, now I need someone to explain to me what's happening," she said.

"Happening, my dear lady?" Leomin asked, his face one of picturesque innocence, "why, we are riding horses, of course. Or, perhaps, it can be said that they are walking us. Marvelous beasts, I must admit, easy of temperament, and their *speed!* Why, it is as if I ride on the wind itse—"

"No, Leomin," Adina said, "I will not be distracted. We'd barely left the city, and you and Aaron are riding as if there's a whole army chasing us. Did something happen at the gate?" She frowned, "It's the strangest thing. I'm having a hard time remembering how we made it through. Still, I've been checking behind us over every rise, and I don't see anyone following. Why, then, the haste? At this speed, we'll kill the horses long before we reach my sister's kingdom, let alone Perenia, the capital."

Aaron studied the Parnen, curious to see what he might say. Leomin stared at him, a world of meaning in his eyes, somehow communicating to Aaron the importance of Adina not knowing about what he'd seen. An easy enough thing, really, since he didn't understand it himself. Leomin turned back to Adina, smiling, "Ah, princess at the gate? Nothing of any import, really. Just a bribe to the guards to see us through. I've found in my experience that most men and women would rather be given a year's wages than fight for their lives. Of course," he smiled, glancing at Aaron, "men like dear Mr. Envelar here are the exception. Men who love to fight for the love of fighting and no more than that."

Adina frowned, "Aaron doesn't love to fight, Leomin. He did it for coin and now he's doing it for a kingdom."

Leomin acquiesced, bowing his head, "As you say, princess."

Aaron frowned, studying the Parnen. The man was clever, a master of avoiding saying anything he didn't want to say, and perhaps he was right in thinking that Adina didn't need to know the truth, but Aaron didn't like it. He was tempted to tell Adina the truth then and there, but he hesitated, not knowing the dangers involved. Besides, what would he say? Whatever had happened, he didn't understand it himself, so he decided he would speak to Leomin in private first to see what the man had to say.

They rode on through the day and into the night and the fields outside of the city slowly turned into woods until they were surrounded by a dense forest on either side. In the darkening night, Adina reigned up in front of them, blocking the trail. "We need to stop now. The horses need rest, and only a desperate fool rides at night."

Leomin glanced at the sky and then looked behind them, as if expecting to see someone there. It was a quick, furtive glance, but Aaron did not miss it. Nor did he miss the troubled expression on the captain's face. "Surely, my lady, we can make it a bit further tonight. Why, the moon is high and full, and the road is clear enough. A few more hours, I beg you."

"No, Leomin," the princess said, her voice stern. "I don't know what has you spooked, nor do I know why you won't share it with us, but I will tell you something I *do* know. Whatever it is you fear catching us will have an easy enough time doing it if we're forced to ride double because one of our horses steps into a hole it can't see and breaks an ankle. My father warned me often about riding at night, not just for my own safety but for the horse's as well, and I will *not* see a good horse suffer and die because you choose to keep your secrets close. We're stopping. Now."

Leomin glanced at Aaron as if for help, but the sellsword only nodded. "Whatever you say, princess. Lead on."

Adina nodded, leading them off the trail and into the woods for a short time before dismounting and tethering her horse to a nearby tree. Aaron and Leomin followed suit. "Now then," Leomin said, "what's for dinner? Perhaps, we could hunt some squirrel, a nicely cooked meal would sit well, I think." He smiled amiably, as if whatever worry he'd had was gone, but Aaron knew better. He could see it there still, dancing in the Parnen's gaze.

"No fire," Aaron said, "not here. May as well send invitations to anyone that might be chasing us."

Leomin sighed theatrically, "Very well, as you say."

They laid out their bedrolls and sat down, eating a meal of dried jerky and drinking water from one of the water skins they'd purchased for the journey. Once he'd eaten as much of the dried, tasteless meat as he could stomach, Aaron sighed, glancing around them at the gathering shadows clinging to the trees and undergrowth. "It's best if we keep a watch tonight, just in case. I'll take the first one. You two get some rest—we've got a long few weeks ahead of us."

The exhaustion was plain on his companion's faces and neither objected, instead unrolling their bedrolls in silence and lying down to sleep. Aaron made his way a little further into the woods to the top of a small rise he'd seen then sat in the shadow of a large oak's trunk, watching over the camp and listening to the sounds of the forest. *Alright, Co,* he said, *let's talk about what happened back at the gate. What did you mean when you said 'sister?'*

Very well. Do you remember when we spoke of the Seven Virtues, of how there was a mage for each of the Seven while Kevlane himself was meant to direct the gathered energies?

How could I forget? Aaron asked, *that was right around the time you made me weep like an old woman.*

Yes, well ... the point is, there were seven virtues and seven mages, a mage for each virtue. One, myself, for compassion, another, Melan, for strength and so on.

Right, Aaron thought back, *I remember. Now, what difference does that make?*

You have to understand, Aaron, the Virtue said, *being turned into ... what we were turned into ... being changed in that way ... it is a difficult thing. There is much that is forgotten in the changing, much that is lost.*

So what do you remember?

There was another of us, named Farah, and it was she who was tasked with the channeling of the virtue of charisma.

And she was your sister? Aaron asked.

No, the Virtue said, but there was uncertainty in her voice. *No, I do not believe so. Though, I believe we were all brothers and sisters in our way, we seven. And Kevlane and Caltriss our fathers.*

Wait a minute, Aaron said, *are you saying that Leomin is in possession of the Virtue of Charisma?*

Yes, Co said, *I believe he is.*

Son of a bitch. No wonder. That explains the women at the inn, as well as the fact that Nathan and Janum acted as if they were losing their best friend when he left. And, of course, it explains how we made it past the gate.

Yes, Co said, *but I am worried, Aaron. The captain was not wrong to show concern. The use of such power as Leomin displayed will act like a lodestone to those who have dedicated their lives to finding and uniting the Seven Virtues into one.*

You mean people like that Aster Kalen? The man who spends his spare time throwing people through walls?

Yes, and I do not believe Aster is the worst of it. There are other forces at work, Aaron. Darker forces. I do not know these things, but I feel them. I feel as if some serpent of darkness has twisted its way round in the night, has uncoiled and opened eyes long closed, that those amber orbs search, even now. For us.

Great, Aaron said, *many more people end up wanting us dead, they're going to have to form a line. Maybe have an auction.*

Not us, Co said, *they only want you dead. On me, they want to enact Kevlane's Bond. To be used by such a person ... trust me, Aaron. It's better to be dead.*

Aaron grunted, his mood growing sour as he considered. *Not making me feel any better, firefly. And as for better to be dead, I'm going to have to disagree with you. Where there is life, there is always the hope that things will get better again. False hope more often than not, but hope just the same. The world of the dead is bereft of such hope—the worms eat it and, believe me, they gorge their fill.*

There are worse things than death, Aaron.

Only a thing the living say; I think, perhaps, the dead would disagree. If they could. He stared up at the moon, a pale sphere in the darkness, looked at the stars overhead glittering and shining, and he felt at once both insignificant and overwhelmed. A year ago, his life had been so much simpler. Safer, too, and that was saying something for a man who'd spent his time selling his blade to the highest bidder, the majority of his days working with or against criminals and keeping an eye on his back, lest someone announce their presence with a knife to it.

True, being a sellsword wasn't glamorous, and it wasn't the type of thing that would get you famous—infamous, maybe. It was a job with a predictably short life span attached to it, one in which only the best made it more than a year or two and, of course, even they fell, sooner or later. It wasn't the type of job a man grew old in. A life fraught with dangers and betrayals, lies and plots, but it was one he understood, its dangers old, familiar acquaintances, if not exactly friends. Now, though, he found himself in a world he no longer understood. A world filled with creatures out of legend, with men and women hunting for him and those he cared about all, of course, while the ruler of the most powerful kingdom in the world did the same. It wasn't a question of whether or not someone would catch them. It was only a question of who it would be and what would happen when they did.

Thousands had already died in the wars between the Seven, and thousands more would die, he knew, before the thing was settled, one way or the other. Thousands of widows and widowers. Thousands of orphans, like he himself had been, he and his childhood best friend, Owen, up until the world did what it always did—used the skinny, kind boy up. Each life was a question, different in its own way, asked in its own way, and the world's answer was always the same. Death. Even Adina's late father, King Marcus, a ruler who'd been adored by commoners and nobles both, a man who was said to have been the wisest, kindest king Telrear had ever seen, still fell beneath the world's answer, succumbed to its terrible truth. *And yet the moon still makes its way across the sky and the stars, for all their beauty, for all that the poets might say of them, look on, unmoved and uncaring.*

If there was anything to be learned from life, Aaron thought it must be that. Let the philosophers debate and the scholars argue; ask a man who'd grown up poor, ask a man who'd watched his child starve or his wife die to an illness that was curable, if only he'd had the coin to pay for the medicine. The greatest truths, the most terrible ones, were not found in books, could not be discovered by endless debate and rhetoric. The greatest truths were not learned, they were felt. They were not understood—they were lived.

The end of the story, of *all* stories; he died, and he was forgotten. And the world moved on, didn't it? It was what it always did. The stage might change, the actors age and be replaced, and the audience none the wiser, for that was the greatest truth of the time—of any time. They lived. They died. They were forgotten.

You're wrong, Co said, *the world may move on, but the world can also be changed. It is a great wheel spinning, and any man or woman—king or peasant or slave—can alter its course. It is not about strength or power or even righteousness, only will and determination to see the thing done that alters the course of that wheel, that changes the lives of those who ride or will ride upon it. Every man can make a difference.*

A wheel, is it? Aaron thought, *fair enough, firefly. But you're wrong about one thing—men don't ride on the wheel. They're crushed beneath it. Leaving little more than bloodstains on its surface to ever show that they were there at all.* What was it the old headmaster at the orphanage had told him? Oh yes, *men weep, and men die, and the gods laugh.*

You're wrong, Aaron, and you will come to know it before—Co cut off as Aaron spun at the sound of footsteps in the darkness. He reached for his sword where it lay propped against the trunk of the tree and was rising to his feet when Leomin stepped out of the shadows and into the moonlight, his hands held up.

"It is only I, Mr. Envelar," the Parnen said. "There is no need for your blade to do its work just now."

"Isn't there?" Aaron asked with a grunt as he sat back down, leaning his back against the tree once more.

The Parnen didn't speak—a great surprise, that, considering that Aaron couldn't remember ever being in the man's company when he *wasn't* speaking. Still, it was just as well. Aaron's head was full of dark thoughts and dark premonitions, and just then he thought that anything coming out of his mouth would be poisoned, soured by the truths his mind held.

Instead of speaking, Leomin walked up and sat down beside Aaron, following his gaze to the moon and stars high overhead. Some time passed and finally the Parnen spoke, "Beautiful, isn't it?" he asked, "Ah, but the moon's beauty is a cold one, I think. Give me the stars, any day—or, I suppose, any night. The markers by which a man in troubled waters might find his way clear of the storm, the gods' gift to sailors and poets. The tapestry of creation, spread out above us each night, its meaning a mystery, yet there just the same."

Aaron shrugged in the darkness, "I've never been a big fan of art."

"No," Leomin said, and there was a sadness to his voice, "No, I don't suppose you have. You, my friend, are a man with devils at his sides and back, hanging on to him, pulling at him with each step he takes. And you will not beat them, you know, cannot, in fact. Not, that is, until you come to understand that you are those devils and that those devils are you."

Aaron scowled over at the man, "What in the name of the gods are you talking about?"

Leomin smiled a melancholy smile in the darkness, "I think you know well enough, Mr. Envelar. The push and pull of a man's soul is the cost—and the reward—for drawing breath. For each of us are possessed of light and darkness both, though you may not see it. It is, after all, difficult for a man to understand the workings of his own mind. The greatest lies are the ones we tell ourselves, after all, the strongest chains the ones we fashion link by link with each passing moment and the most impenetrable cage is the one that we build around ourselves, never seeing it for fear of opening our eyes."

They sat in silence for several seconds following that as Aaron considered the Parnen's words. "You know, Leomin, I don't have a fucking clue what you just said."

The Parnen laughed softly in the darkness, "Fair enough, Mr. Envelar. But know that I know, that you are not so foolish, nor so lacking in discernment as you would have people believe. A simple man looks out around himself and sees a simple world. A complex man, a complex one. So it is that we fashion our own lives, our own realities, build them up brick by brick or straw by straw, and what strength they have is a strength that we have given them in the making."

"Careful, Parnen," Aaron said, "you're starting to sound like a scholar, and I've little time for old men in old robes."

"Very well," Leomin said, nodding, "Some truths are more easily spoken and understood than others, but I see that the topic troubles you, and I will speak of it no more."

"If you want to speak about something," Aaron said, "why don't you tell me what exactly you did at the gatehouse and what—or who—you think is after us."

The Parnen took a deep breath and let it out. "Do you know, Mr. Envelar, that I was an only son?"

"Lucky for your parents," Aaron said, "maybe there are gods after all. But what does this have to do with the gate?"

"Everything and nothing, Mr. Envelar," Leomin said, "for our beginnings meld into our present, our present into our ending, and they all mean what they all mean. Still," he said smiling, "perhaps you are right. I would not truly know, one way or the other. I did not know my mother and father—or, at least, not in the way most children know their parents."

Aaron grunted, "Kicked you out at a young age did they? Couldn't stop you from talking?"

Aaron! Co scolded, but Leomin went on.

"Not ... exactly," the Parnen said. "Tell me, Mr. Envelar, what do you know of my people?"

Aaron shrugged, "Not much. A quiet lot, I know that much. Most live far to the south, beyond the reaches of Telrear in a country ... Shit, I forget its name...."

"Abalan," Leomin said, and there was something wistful in his voice when he said it. "Please, go on."

Aaron sighed, "I know that the Parnen are known in many circles for their wisdom, for their tolerance and patience. A careful lot too, I've heard. They say that a Parnen will not eat an egg unless he knows its origins and its history, will not slay a beast for food if it was the only surviving member of the birth."

Leomin nodded, "It is true enough, particularly about the only birth. You see, Mr. Envelar, among my people, an only child—

whether human or animal—is looked on as almost sacred, as blessed by the gods. For my people believe that each family is given the same amount of blessings from the gods as every other. Therefore, you see, an only child is revered, for he has no siblings with which to share his blessings."

Aaron grunted, absorbing that. "It seems to me, then, that all a family needs to do to gain esteem in your country is to only have one child. A simple enough thing, isn't it? After all, any village herb woman knows teas and brews that will make it impossible for a woman to get pregnant."

Leomin cringed, "We do not speak of such things as that, among my people," he said. "For among my people, such *measures* as those of which you speak are looked upon as the greatest of all sins and, if any should be caught partaking of such, the punishment is death."

Aaron stared at the man, shocked, "You must be kidding. *Death* because they don't want another child?"

Leomin nodded, "It is the way of my people, Mr. Envelar. You see, it is believed that every man and woman owe the gods a debt, a debt that they cannot nor ever will be able to repay and therefore one that must be passed on to their children, the same as any debt owed to a crediting house or bank in your own country. In this way, with time and generations, a man—or woman's—debt might be paid and it is only then that the individual's soul will enter into the afterlife and reside among our people and our gods."

"But that doesn't make any sense," Aaron said, "I mean ... with each generation, the overall debt just grows, doesn't it? So that you're always behind and always getting more behind. I mean ... you'd never be able to get caught up."

Leomin laughed his lilting, musical laugh, "And this, my friend, is one of the many differences between your people and my own. You see, I say debt, that you might understand, but it is more than that. The gods are no crediting house, no clerk to collect their interest and be on their way, and the debt is really not a debt at all, but a duty, an acknowledgment that we are beholden. It is called the *Fanea*, in my land."

"No offense, Leomin," Aaron said, "but I don't get it."

The Parnen grinned, "Nor would I expect you to, Mr. Envelar, for you are not Parnen. The same way that I do not understand the lighting of candles and the unified reciting of chants in your own religious establishments. As if the gods cannot hear us unless we are loud, cannot see us unless we guide their eyes to a beacon."

Aaron considered that then shrugged, "Okay, fair enough. Still, there must be a lot of only children, right? I mean, herbs or not, there are plenty of husbands whose wives refuse to take them to bed for days or weeks, sometimes years at a time. I've got to think its common enough."

"Not as common you might think," Leomin said. "You see, Aaron, among my people, a wife and a husband are not only beholden to the Fanea, but also to each other. A wife would not even consider begrudging a man's affections, as he would not consider begrudging hers. It would be looked at with much the same outrage as incest is in your country."

"Ah," Aaron said, "Well. I know some men that might just be moving to Abalan, if they heard you say as much."

Leomin grinned, "Yes, but the truth is that only children are very rare among my people. I myself was the only single child in my village. The holy women say that the gods blessed my people with great fertility, one not bestowed upon any other race of men as we are the chosen, the only ones given any chance of repaying their Fanea. It is not uncommon, among my people, to see families with eight or nine children, if not more."

"Must be crowded," Aaron said. "Anyway, do you believe all that—that your people are chosen?"

Leomin grinned, "I believe that, as you say, my people are a quiet, reserved race and not given to spending their time on idle chatter. This, then, frees up their time for more ... shall we say, physical endeavors."

"Not big talkers, yeah. I'd heard that," Aaron said, "so what happened to you?"

Leomin took a moment, thinking. Finally, "As I told you, I was the only single child of my village but not just my village, of all the surrounding ones as well and all the ones that surrounded *those*." He hesitated, rubbing a hand at his chin in thought. "I'm sorry, Mr. Envelar, but these truths are ones I have never shared with another—not even Balen. I find it difficult in the telling and, in truth, I do not know where to begin."

"That's easy," Aaron said, "you begin at the beginning."

Leomin nodded, "Let us say, then, that for as long as the history of my people has been recorded, we have held in trust a certain … truth. A certain power. One that, it is believed, was given to us that we might protect it. A thing which was entrusted into our care, it is said, by great Daonin herself, the Goddess of life and birth. A thing which my people believe, if possessed by the wrong person, could undo the fabric of existence itself, creating wars and strife until the world itself bled and burned and died."

"Sounds like a pain in the ass to me."

Leomin laughed, "As it did to me, too, at my first hearing of it, but let us leave that for now. Know, then, that this power was one entrusted into only the most holy of us and, in my culture, there is none holier than a child. It is believed that any man or woman of adult age who tried to bear this thing would be twisted and warped by the power it contained, the person they were burned to ashes and so much dust, and in their place would grow a monster with limitless power. The power to break the world."

"Damn," Aaron said. "Not exactly big on bed time stories your people."

"Not as much," Leomin agreed. "Though these things, these truths are taught to children from birth, so that all might know the danger and the honor of being Parnen."

"So what does this have to do with you?"

Leomin nodded, "As I said, there is none holier in the eyes of my people than a child and among them none more blessed than an only child of a wedded union. Such a child, it is believed, is the only one who might be given this thing, this power, and not be destroyed by it. Such a child is taken from his or her home at a young age to live under the tutelage of the holiest women, of those said to be the most blessed by the gods. Under them and among them. The child is not allowed any contact with his parents or the people he once knew, for he is chosen among all the chosen and therefore not considered to be, strictly speaking, human. Such a one as this, it is believed, cannot have his or her time squandered by such menial things as family and friends. They are, instead, given lives devoted to worship of the gods and to sit in prayer and worship and the rituals of it. Precautions which—it is believed— act as a shield against the power which will always try to corrupt and stain their souls."

Aaron let out a deep breath as he began to understand. "And you were such a child."

"So I was," Leomin said, and there was no mistaking the pain in the Parnen's voice. "For five years, I lived with my parents, Mr. Envelar. Five years with no brothers or sister—the time which my people believe a child is rightfully considered a single birth. Then I was taken by strange women that I did not know or understand to a place that I did not really belong to and that would never really belong to me. Among people who did not look at me as a person but as a vessel. A cup to be filled until rust and wear took their toll then discarded so that another might fill its place."

There was bitterness in the man's voice, something that Aaron had never heard from the Parnen, and he was taken aback by it. "But ... your parents," he said, "surely...."

"My parents," Leomin said, "did what any good Parnen does. Stand by and stay quiet. The truth, Mr. Envelar, is that I do not know them, and they do not know me. I cannot tell you even if they still live and, if they did, I would not know them upon meeting them. All I have are a few memories—the sound of my mother singing a lullaby of my people, her face blurred and faded with time in the memory like a letter looked at too often, until it is smudged and illegible."

Through his bond with Co, Aaron felt more than heard the Parnen's words, felt them as if he'd lived them himself. He saw himself dragged away from his parents, pulled into a world of prim and proper women, women who spent their days with him not in love but in duty. Devoting hours to examining and inspecting him the way a jeweler might some precious stone, searching for any weakness or flaw that might spread and corrupt the gem. He felt their words of scorn with each mistake he made, felt their silent displeasure as they watched him, believing him to not be taking his duty seriously enough, no matter how serious he took it, believing him to be ungrateful when the truth was he had nothing to be grateful for.

He could hear Co's voice, so soft as to be almost nothing, as she wept in his mind. What such a thing would do to a man, to a child, Aaron couldn't imagine. He cleared his throat finally, "I'm sorry, Leomin. It must have been terrible."

The Parnen turned, meeting his eyes in the darkness. "Yes," he said after several moments, "I believe you do know, Mr. Envelar. Still, it is not all so bad. There are many among my people—nearly all, in truth—who would have found it a great honor for their child to be chosen. It is a thing done only once a generation."

"Nearly all thought it a great honor," Aaron echoed, "sure. Except, maybe, the *children.*"

Leomin nodded, "So you have hit the truth of it, Mr. Envelar. As accurate in your understanding as you are with that blade you carry. To be an only child among my people is a blessing, and it is a curse. But a curse that's existence no child may ever speak, even to each other. Even when they are alone. For there are always those watching, in my country, wounding and drawing blood with their good intentions. "

He hesitated for a moment, and out of the corner of his gaze, Aaron saw the Parnen wiping at his eyes. "Still, I do not ask for pity, Mr. Envelar, nor do I want it. It was not all bad, and what bad there was came not from malice or hate, for my people are not good with such things as that. Our darkness comes from a very different place. It is the shadow we create when we light a taper to fend off the night. It is the words of kindness and love that remain unspoken for our silence. My most vivid memory of my childhood is of my mother and father standing at the door to our small hut, watching as the women took me away. "

Leomin laughed, but there was no humor in it, only bitterness and pain, "I remember crying out for my father to save me, to help me, but he did not, standing only in silence as I was taken. I know, at least, that he was a true Parnen then, though I cannot speak for times since. It is the only memory of him I have. My mother, though. I like to think that there was a certain ... *bend* to her as she watched me taken away. Not because I wish her pain, for I do not, but because it gives me the hope that my leaving weighed heavily upon her, at least for a time. That she *felt* my leaving, you see. My people, Mr. Envelar, are not very good at feeling. Such showing of emotions is a thing for children and heathens, not the chosen people of the gods. I like, too, to think that there were tears standing unshed in her eyes, that day, but there is no way for me to know, not truly. For the memory is little more than the ghost of a ghost, and it has had a lifetime to grow sour and wrong within me. Still. I like to believe as much." He paused, staring at the stars overhead, "She had such a sweet voice, my mother."

Aaron felt his face heat with shame. For years, he had carried around a hate for the world, a hate for an existence that would see his mother and father killed when he was a child himself, would see him orphaned and sent to a house of children where the headmaster beat and tortured them. Still, he could not imagine having lived with what the Parnen had. His parents, at least, had been taken from him. They had not stood by and watched as he was marched away, had not let him become dead in their minds even while he lived. Such a thing, he thought, would break most men. "I know that you do not look for pity, Leomin," Aaron said, "and so I will not give it." He grabbed the man's shoulder, "But I *am* sorry, and I know a fraction of what you feel. No child should have to lose their parents."

Leomin nodded, letting out a ragged sigh. "Thank you, Mr. Envelar," he said, wiping at his eyes again, "and forgive me my own emotions. It is an old wound, one that in forcing myself to forget, I foolishly thought healed. Instead, I find, that it has remained unchanged, as raw and sharp now as the day I received it. It's a funny thing, isn't it, that as I grew into a man, I thought I had left that bitterness, that anger behind me, but, in truth, it was there all along, within reach."

"As funny as a funeral," Aaron said, and for a time they were silent as Aaron sat and looked at the moon and the stars and listened to the sounds of a man—his friend—weeping beside him. He thought to comfort him, for through the bond he felt each fresh agony as Leomin ran the fingers of his mind over the wound, probing it, checking its size and texture and reliving each painful memory. But his was a voice that was not used to uttering words of comfort, did not know what they might be or what shape they might take. Besides, he thought that, for some things, the only comfort a man can offer is the comfort of companionship, for the other to know that their grief and their pain is not a thing they must stand up against alone, a load that—though it still must be carried—might be shared, if even only for a moment.

He did not know how much time passed but, after a while, the Parnen spoke, "I am sorry, Mr. Envelar, for putting all of my grief on you, as I have. I sought only to make you understand, to answer the question that you asked me." He paused to sniff then continued, "you have heard, I suspect, of the man, Aaron Caltriss, of the wizard Boyce Kevlane and the Seven?"

"I have heard of them," Aaron said, "though any child among my people could say as much. The story is a common one, grown old with the telling. And know, Leomin, that you have nothing for which you need apologize. A friend's job is to help with such burdens."

The Parnen smiled at that, "Friend, you say. Ah, you know not the kindness you do me, Mr. Envelar. But getting back to your original question, you have heard, then, of the Seven Virtues? Those beings created from the failed ritual of the ruler Caltriss and the wizard Kevlane?"

"I have."

Leomin smiled, "You see, it's funny, but that story, though common knowledge in your country of Telrear, is not known or spoken of in Abalan." He laughed, "I think that many of the holy women of my country would be paralyzed in terror at the thought of six more such powers existing in the world as the one over which my own people held dominion. I only heard the story upon coming to your country and realized that it is looked at as a fiction, a tale that parents tell their children."

"Yes," Aaron said, "it is looked at as a fairy tale, it's true. The Virtues as creatures of myth to cause wonder and delight in children, the barbarians monsters who will get them if they don't go to sleep when they should."

"Well then," Leomin said, holding his hand out in front of him with the palm up, "let me introduce you to a creature of myth." Several seconds passed and nothing happened. Finally, Leomin frowned and closed his eyes, "It is okay," he said in a whisper, and it was clear that he was not talking to Aaron. "There is no danger here."

After a moment, an orange orb flashed to light above the Parnen's palm. It flittered and danced, and there was something about its appearance that struck Aaron as nervous. "Forgive me, but Aliandra is not used to her presence being displayed to others and believes it to be a bad idea."

"Bad idea?" A voice demanded, and it seemed to Aaron as if it was a voice that might have belonged to a nineteen or twenty year

old woman. A noble's voice, if he'd ever heard one. *"No, Leomin,"* the voice continued, "a woman of station wearing trousers and a broad-brimmed hat, *that* is a bad idea. A holy woman in silks, *that* would be a bad idea. What you do now is not something so simple as 'bad,' nor is it even a simple lack of decorum or a youthful show of irresponsibility. What you do now is foolishness of the highest order. You are, you understand, confessing my existence—our *bond*—to a man who *kills people for money."*

"Well," Aaron said, deciding that maybe Co wasn't so bad after all, "the people I don't like anyway. The others I only rob and maim, if I can help it. Anyway, I haven't killed anybody for money in a while."

The glowing ball of orange light somehow contrived to snort, a trick that Aaron didn't care to delve too far into. "Rob and maim, is it? *Rob and maim?* Do you hear that, Leomin? If we're lucky, this ruffian might leave us enough fingers to fill out a nice glove between both hands. Yes," she said, and in her voice Aaron heard the distinct sneer that so many of the highborn shared, *"Quite* wise, Leomin. I do hope you are intelligent enough to appreciate your error before your neck departs your body, though I very much suspect—"

"Sister." Aaron's eyes widened in surprise as Co manifested hovering in the air in front of him.

"Co—" he began.

"It's alright, Aaron," the Virtue said, and though Aaron had still been undecided as to whether or not he would divulge the Virtue's existence, he had to admit that it had the beneficial effect of leaving Leomin's own silent for several moments.

The orange orb pulsed, somehow conveying surprise, then flitted away from Leomin's upraised hand to hover inches away from Co. "By the gods, can it be?" The orange virtue said, "Ev—"

"It is me, sister," Co interrupted.

"Oh, but it is good to see you!" Leomin's virtue exclaimed, flitting around in what Aaron took as excitement. "Why, you have no idea how *long* it has been since I've spoken with anyone of any intelligence. Do you know that I've spent what is nearly the last thousand years being equally feared and worshipped by these Parnen *savages?"* The orange light wavered in the air, seeming to turn in Leomin's direction, "No offense, of course, Leomin."

The Parnen captain gave a weary smile, and Aaron suspected that he must have had cause to hear such pronouncements before. "Of course, my dear, of course."

"Anyway," the Virtue said turning back to regard Co, "you've no idea what it's *been* like. I tell you, sister, it seems to me that all these 'holy' women do is sit around and chant and scowl at one another! And don't even get me started on the clothes. Why, they might as well be *naked* for as little as they wear, sister. I swear by all the gods, major and minor both, you wouldn't believe it unless you saw it."

Co laughed then, and Aaron heard something of a weary amusement in it, as if she had heard such talk before from the Virtue or, at least, from whom the Virtue had once been. "Ah, Aliandra, but it is good to see you. And I see that you have not changed, not in a thousand years and more."

"Well, sister," Aliandra said, a coyness in her voice, "Once you have found perfection, there is no reason to change it."

Co let out a noise somewhere between a grunt and a sigh, "Yes, well, I'm sure that there are plenty of suitors that would agree with you. Or were, at least. It has been a long time."

The orange Virtue let out a huff, "Long indeed. And you have no idea how difficult, sister. It is quite hard to make men fawn over the turn of your ankle when you don't *have* ankles."

"Yes," Co said, "A truly terrible conundrum. Why, if only I could question the gods, my first would be why they allow evil men to do as they do, but my second, of course, would be to ask them how they could see fit to get rid of such fine ankles as yours."

Aliandra glowed even brighter for a moment, "They *were* fine, weren't they, sister?"

"Of course."

Aliandra turned slowly, drifting along the air closer to Aaron, though not too close. Skittish, a dog afraid of being beaten begging for a meal. "And you are paired with this one, then?"

"So I am."

"Your ways are inscrutable as always, dear sister. I cannot imagine what would motivate you to choose such a ... *wild* pairing."

"I find him funny."

129

The orange Virtue drew closer to Aaron's face, so close that he had to shield his eyes with one hand. Scowling, he swatted at it with the other, and the Virtue flitted away. "Yes," she said doubtfully, "hilarious."

"He's an acquired taste," Co said, amused, "though I must confess that I am not entirely sure that I have yet acquired it, nor that I will, even given such time as I might have left to me."

Aaron grunted, "Just be glad I haven't yet acquired a muzzle that will work on floating balls of light, firefly."

"*Firefly?*" Aliandra said, her voice the perfect mimicry of an outraged noblewoman's, "I will have you know, sir, that you speak to—"

"None of that, sister," Co interrupted, "I am what I am, and nothing more. Not any longer."

The orange Virtue huffed again, "Still, it isn't right for him to speak to you so. Did you know," she said, turning, and somehow Aaron once more felt her regard, "that I was *worshipped* for nearly a thousand years?"

Aaron smiled, "You might have mentioned it."

"Yes, well," the Virtue said, as if thrown off by the lack of affect her words had, "It's true. Anyway, I wonder, sister, if we might not talk somewhere a little more ... private?"

"Oh, I would love to, of course, Aliandra. Only ..." She turned, and Aaron felt her regard. "I don't think it would be wise. Maybe another time or—"

"Oh, your Majesty, we'll be fine," Aaron said, not completely managing to hide his grin, "please, go and catch up with your friend. Take all the time you need." The magenta light of which Co was made grew noticeably darker at his words, a storm seeming to swirl inside of it.

"Better," Aliandra said, "though 'your Majesty' isn't technically—"

"*Very well,*" Co interrupted, "let us remove ourselves a bit, sister, so that we might talk. Do not fret, Aaron, Leomin. We will return soon."

Aaron grinned, "Oh, don't hurry on our account. Take your time. Catch up."

"Fine," Co snarled and then they were gone, two streaks of light vanishing into the dark forest.

"Ah, Leomin," Aaron said, "if your story didn't made me pity you, now I certainly do. I cannot imagine what tortures you must have gone through with that one."

The Parnen laughed, "Oh, Aliandra isn't so bad, Mr. Envelar. She is a character, that's certain. Though ... I wonder, can a character without a body still be called a character? I confess I'm not sure. Suffice to say, that though she might seem ... *difficult* at first, Aliandra has saved me and those I care about more times than I care to count. Indeed, if not for her I would have been dead and gone long before you and I ever met."

Aaron grunted, "Dead and gone, huh? That might be preferable."

Leomin laughed, and Aaron was glad to see that the dark mood that had overtaken the Parnen captain seemed nowhere in evidence. "Oh, Mr. Envelar, but I do enjoy your way of seeing the world."

Aaron shrugged, "The world is what the world is, Leomin. All I do is try to clear the dirt out of my eyes to see the truth of things. Anyway, what is she the Virtue of, exactly? All I can say is that, just now, I'm enjoying the virtue of her absence."

Leomin grinned, "Ah, yes. Well, Aliandra is, of course, the Virtue of Charisma."

"Charisma, huh?" Aaron asked, "So she's supposed to be able to make people like her? And you?"

Leomin frowned, "Well, there is, of course, more to it than that, but I suppose it is an accurate enough definition ... if a bit rough."

Aaron grunted, "I think she's broken."

Leomin shook his head, "I assure you that when Aliandra unleashes her charm, there are few men—or women, for that matter—who can resist it."

Aaron frowned at that, thinking. Then he scowled, "Do you mean to tell me ... the women at the tavern?"

Leomin coughed delicately, "Yes, well. The thing you have to understand, Mr. Envelar, is that I have been bonded with Aliandra since I was a child. Over such a great length of time, Kevlane's bond produces unexpected effects. One of the things the stories do not mention—I know, I've checked—is that through their bond, a man and a Virtue are both changed by the other. So that, after years of the bond strengthening, neither are what they once were."

"So what you're saying," Aaron said, "is that you used the Virtue of Charisma to seduce three women into your bed."

Leomin avoided his eyes, "It is not so simple a thing as 'using' anything, Mr. Envelar. What I'm trying to say is that, after so long, the bond has a pronounced effect. I am no longer the man I was before bonding Aliandra, nor, I suspect, is she the same as she was before bonding me."

"I wonder if that makes her more of a pain in the ass or less."

"Yes, well, my point is that the bond exerts itself even when I do not intend it, that even in normal conversation, my actions and words and, more importantly, the way people perceive those actions and words is changed because of the bond."

"Basically meaning that you can't help how charming you are."

Leomin opened his mouth as if to disagree then hesitated, finally sighing. "Crude, but true enough."

Aaron considered that. "Well, I suppose that might work on three women whose parents never taught them any better, but I have to be honest with you Leomin. The first time I met you I seriously considered turning myself into Belgarin. Figured there wasn't any torture he could inflict on me that would be any worse than what you were putting me through."

Leomin grinned, "No offense taken, of course. You see, I have long suspected that the bearing of a Virtue somewhat insulates the bonded from the effects of other Virtues. I had cause to believe this when that man, Aster, boarded my ship and your saying so only confirms my beliefs. And forgive me, though I think I know, I would like to confirm something. Which Virtue is it that you possess?"

Aaron sighed. "Well, Leomin, I've got the Virtue of getting weepy when I see a hungry dog in the street."

"Ah, Compassion, then."

Aaron shrugged, "A shorter name for it, anyway."

"Yes," Leomin said, a troubled expression on his face, "then there are two of us. Here. Together."

Aaron cocked his head, "Is there something on your mind, Leomin?"

The Parnen met Aaron's eyes, "As I told you, I have been bonded with Aliandra for most of my life, and I have had the unfortunate opportunity to learn a few things. Primarily, that there are those out there, Mr. Envelar, who seek the Virtues, who bend their will always toward finding them with the goal of uniting them together within themselves. It is believed that such a thing would create a warrior who was nigh on immortal. A man as above us as the gods themselves. Such a calling, it needn't be said, is not undertaken by those with altruistic intentions."

Aaron said, "Well, it's a big world, Leomin. I don't think there's too good a chance of the seven of us stumbling into each other."

"There you're wrong, Mr. Envelar," Leomin said, "though I wish you were not. You see, the Virtues, having been created within the same failed ritual, *call* to each other. It is not something they do intentionally, nor something that they can control. The truth is, it isn't even something as specific as being able to follow a trail to one another. However, if one bearing a Virtue were in the same city, say, as another? Then, were he trained in the use of his Virtue, he would know it and, most likely, he would come looking."

Aaron considered that. Co had never mentioned such a thing, but, he supposed, he hadn't asked. "So, then, you using your power on those people back at the gate...."

Leomin swallowed, nodding, "Was like lighting a beacon fire to any with the eyes to see it. Such a thing will lead those who follow it out of the western gate of Baresh in the direction through which we came. The truth is, Mr. Envelar, I am afraid."

Aaron sighed, "Well. What are a few more wanting to kill us when there's already an army in line? And speaking of truths, there's something I don't understand, Leomin."

"Then ask it, Mr. Envelar. I will answer you, if I can."

"From everything you've told me, your people went to great lengths to protect the world from the Virtue, believing it was their sacred duty to keep it out of the hands of those who might use it to cause harm."

Leomin nodded, "It is so."

Aaron met the Parnen's eyes, "Why, then, are you here with us and not sitting in some church with blisters on your ass and holy women praying and shaking beads around your head?"

An embarrassed look came over the Parnen's face, and he studied his feet. "Yes, that. Well ... you see ... I ran away."

Aaron nodded, "I figured as much."

"You must understand, Mr. Envelar," Leomin said, obviously anxious to defend his actions, "I knew the importance of what my people told me, of what I was chosen for but ... well, the bond grew stronger, and I grew less and less like myself. The Parnen are a quiet, conservative people, and, as a child, I was thought reserved even among my own kind. But the bond changed me. And, I must confess, it was not only that. After twelve years living among the holy women, looked at as little more than a vessel to be cleaned and kept safe, I just...." He paused, glancing at Aaron with something like desperation in his face, as if he needed to make Aaron understand. "It's only—"

"Look, Leomin," Aaron said, "you don't have to defend yourself to me. I wouldn't have made it twelve weeks, let alone twelve years. Shit, man, sitting around all day while women scowl at you and tell you how to behave? Gods, you might as well have been married."

Leomin let his breath out in a heavy sigh of relief. "Thank you, Mr. Envelar. For understanding."

Thinking of women and marriage, Aaron found his gaze drifting into the darkness where he knew, not far away, Adina lay down sleeping. *Don't be a fool,* he told himself. Still, his gaze lingered there even as he spoke. "How long do you think, Leomin, before these people you were talking about—these Virtue hunters—find the trail you left?"

Leomin considered that then finally shrugged, "There is no way to tell for sure. Much depends on how near or far they were when they felt it—and feel it they did, I assure you. That is one of the primary reasons I resist using my Virtue in such ways. My people had a saying—power calls to power—and, in my experience, it is one of the few things they got right. Those who come may be far away, and it may be many days before we see them, but they *will* come, Mr. Envelar. This I know."

"Alright," Aaron said, "well, the best we can do is be on the lookout for—" he cut off as the two Virtues came whisking through the air side by side.

They came to an abrupt stop a few feet in front of their respective Pairings, and Aaron raised an eyebrow. "What was that, a race?"

"Of course not," Co scoffed, "We are not children to go racing through the night without a care in the world."

"Don't be absurd," Aliandra put in, "Though if it *were* a race, clearly—"

"We came back," Co interrupted, "because, as I was telling Aliandra, there are more important things to be about then chatting. We can catch up on the last thousand years later."

"Yes, absolutely," Aliandra put in, "though you must not let me forget to tell you about the man's hands, sister. They were *so* big that—"

"Yes, yes, of course," Co said, and Aaron could hear the embarrassment in her voice, "we will speak of it later, Aliandra."

Aaron grinned, but he thought again of the forces arrayed against them, thought of Adina lying not far away, asleep, willing to take on the world despite an outcome that was obvious enough a blind man could see it, and the smile died on his face. "Well, you're right about one thing, firefly. We've more important things to do then chat." He turned to Leomin, "You need to get some sleep. It won't be any good for both of us to be exhausted."

The Parnen nodded and rose, the orange Virtue drifting inside of him until it was no longer visible. "Sleep well, Mr. Envelar."

Aaron nodded and watched the man go. *Sleep well?* He thought. *I'll be lucky to sleep at all.*

CHAPTER FOURTEEN

They woke early the next morning and spoke little as they prepared the horses and departed the campsite, heading back to the main road. Even without his bond with Co, Aaron could have felt the tension in the air; a palpable sense of danger that made each noise of the woods around them too sharp, too loud.

The night had been quiet after Leomin went to bed, and Aaron almost wished that it hadn't been. His life, he realized, had to this point been largely made up of situations in which he reacted instead of acted and rarely did he have time to think about the dangers of something before he was faced with it. Rarely had he had such an opportunity to consider all that he could lose. It would have been better, he decided, if something or someone *had* come in the night. At least then, he would have had something to fight against.

He found his mind wandering back to his time at the orphanage with Owen, his best and only friend. There had been a game they'd play where they would take turns walking into dark alleys at night, proving there were no monsters, until their courage abandoned them, and they came running back. A foolish game, Aaron knew now, for there *were* monsters waiting in the darkness. They might not have dagger-long fangs and scales, might wear the faces of men, even speak with a man's voice, but they were monsters just the same.

He did not remember ever even enjoying the game, but they had played it nevertheless; as, he thought, many children did. A game against one's self, a game that, in the end, you could only lose, but that you would play anyway. *Had* to play anyway. At least, that was, until the headmaster, Cyrille, had beaten Owen to death and disposed of the body, not even giving Aaron the opportunity to mourn his friend, saying only that he was gone, that he'd left in the night.

It had been a lie—everyone knew that—and it had been that lie that had led to Aaron murdering Cyrille and that killing, at least, he did not regret. One less monster in a world full of them.

The fear he felt now, though, was stronger even than he'd felt as a child, wandering into the darkness. Then, they had gone into the darkness on their own time, of their own minds. Now, he felt that the darkness was coming for them. *Felt* it coming, the way some men or women might smell a storm approaching, and so he rode in silence, looking behind them from time to time and finding no comfort in the fact that nothing was there. It would be, he knew, sooner or later.

A week passed, each day seeming harder than the last. Each near sleepless night leaving them wearier than the last. They spoke only when necessary and their voices seemed to carry a strain each time they did. It was as if they labored under some great, invisible weight that made talking difficult and all but pointless. Leomin tried to start conversations a few times, a forced joviality in his voice, but his words didn't sound like words at all to Aaron, but the sound of a child whistling in the darkness, telling himself the lie that everything was okay and that everything would be okay.

Adina too remained silent, clearly troubled, and Aaron wanted to speak to them, to tell them that it would all work out. The problem, of course, was that he'd lost the ability to lie to himself long ago, back when his father and mother had been murdered, when he'd stumbled wearily down the steps of his home until his bare feet came to rest in a pool of his parents' spreading blood. Since then, he'd only been able to see the world for what it was— dark and getting darker.

On the twelfth day, the woods that had surrounded them gave way to fields of grass as high as their ankles, the road cutting between them. The sun was setting when they stopped at an abandoned barn for the night, tethering their horses outside. "I'll take first watch," Leomin said once they'd finished.

Aaron turned to the Parnen, surprised at the weariness and resignation he heard in the man's tone. "You sure? I don't mind."

Leomin tried a smile, but the expression withered on his face and he let it drop, shrugging instead. "I'm not very tired."

Aaron studied the man, noting the circles under his eyes, the way his shoulders were slumped with exhaustion. A lie, then, but just because he could not comfort himself with little lies did not mean he would begrudge others theirs. "Alright," he said, "wake me when you're ready to switch."

"No, Leomin," Adina said, "it's my turn for first watch. You should get some rest."

The Parnen captain smiled, "Ah, princess, but you would be doing me a favor, truly. A long day's travel makes it difficult for me to sleep, and I would only lie awake, exhausted and unsleeping, until my turn at watch came. This way, when I *do* lie down, I will at least be able to get some rest."

Adina considered him for several seconds, "Are you sure?"

The Parnen nodded, "I'm sure. Only, I would like to have a talk with Mr. Envelar for a moment, if that's not too much to ask."

Adina frowned, "More secrets, Leomin?"

The Parnen held up his hands to his sides, "My secrets lay before you, princess. They are cheap and tawdry things, and I would not want you to soil your hands grasping them."

Adina sighed heavily, "Have it your way, Leomin. For now. Once we reach Isabelle's kingdom, I will ask you the truth of things, and I will expect an answer."

Leomin nodded his head, "And you will have it, princess. I promise you. I ask only that you forgive a strange man his strangeness, for it is all he has."

Adina glanced at Aaron, meeting his eyes, before taking her bedroll and disappearing into the barn.

Leomin turned to look back the way they'd come, over the miles of fields and into the distant woods, his expression troubled as if he'd forgotten he'd asked to speak with Aaron at all.

Aaron frowned and walked up to him, following his gaze. "You feel something."

Leomin frowned, "Perhaps. I cannot be certain, but I think that whoever, or *whatever* follows us draws near, Mr. Envelar."

Aaron sniffed and glanced up at the sky where he could see dark clouds gathering in the early night, promising the storm to come. "Tonight, do you think?"

Leomin shook his head slowly, "I don't know. I wish that I knew more, Mr. Envelar, but I only ... I do not feel good about the coming night. Not good at all. Tell me, did you see any honeysuckle as we rode?"

Aaron frowned at the abrupt change in topic, "No, I didn't."

Leomin nodded , still studying the woods, "And yet I smell it. Do you know, many people believe that the smell of honeysuckle means death is on its way."

"I had not heard that," Aaron said. *Though, in my experience, Leomin, death always is.*

The Parnen nodded, "Superstitious nonsense, I'm sure. A smell can no more predict death or pain than a sound or a taste—unless, I suppose, one tastes poison. In which case..."

Aaron rubbed a hand across his grainy eyes, "Leomin? Is there anything else?"

The Parnen finally turned to him then, meeting his gaze. "I only think we should be careful, Mr. Envelar. This night has a dark feel to it. It is as if I feel the breath of this thing on the back of my neck, can see its approach out of the corner of my eye. Yet each time I turn there is nothing there that should not be there. For it is always behind me, always just out of sight."

Aaron nodded. He'd been feeling much the same himself, though he'd wanted to pass it off as no more than a building of the jitters that had been working their way through him since they'd left Baresh. Now, though, with the Parnen's words, he knew them for what they were. He had felt such feelings before, had known such anxiety. First there was the feeling of something off, of somehow stepping outside one's self, watching one's movements as if they were the movements of a stranger. Then there was the anxiety, the kind one felt in a dream when everyone around him seemed to know everything there was to know, and he himself knew nothing. These things always came first, but they were not the end of it, only the beginning. The feeling. The anxiety. And then the blood. There was always the blood, a river of it, running just out of sight, the sound of it just beneath the threshold of human hearing. But there anyway, and Aaron was struck by the unexplainable feeling that the river would run a little higher before the night was through.

"I think that you must look after her, Mr. Envelar." Leomin said, pulling Aaron from his crimson thoughts. "I think that, tonight, we must all look after one another."

Aaron nodded, "Alright, Leomin. Stay close, and if you need anything, give a shout." He tipped his head, "However you may."

Leomin smiled and nodded, "So I will, Mr. Envelar. Good night, and may the morning find us safe and grumpy and feeling like fools."

"I hope that it does."

CHAPTER FIFTEEN

He stood in the barn's doorway, just able to make out her form there, in the darkness. She lay on her side, her back to the door and to him. He paused, wanting to say something, *needing* to say something, but the words didn't want to come. They were there, he thought, but buried, and he couldn't seem to get his hands on them. Buried beneath his own fears, his own worries—most of which revolved around Adina, one way or the other. So he only stood there instead, looking at the rise and fall of her breath, knowing that she was awake, knowing that she needed the words he would say and cursing himself for not being able to say them. Threats or angry words, sure, those came easy enough—they always did. As easy as the blood-letting that so often followed in the world he'd created around himself. But words of comfort, words of kindness and love ... those were alien things to him, tools of which he'd had no need and therefore of which he had no experience.

There was the fear of losing her, the fear of what might happen to her, of what he was becoming and, of course, there was the fear of the words she'd say in answer. It wasn't so much a fear of her rejecting him—though there was that, an image of her laughing and shaking her head, asking him was he serious and wondering how he could be—it was more a fear that she'd agree, that she'd accept his words, his thoughts, that she would utter her own. And what would follow, then? She would come to know him, in the days that followed, come to understand the weight and danger of the stone she'd tied around her neck. Who he was, what he was becoming, they would all be laid bare before her and then she would not deny, she would regret. She would not reject. She would condemn.

He knew too that, if he went to her, the darkness of the night would hide those flaws, tied inextricably about his person, woven in and out of his being, so that should a man grasp them and pull them out, there wouldn't be enough left of him to walk upright. If somehow he was to take away his hate, his anger, he wasn't sure what would be left—he wasn't sure if anything would. For he was made of blood and made for the drawing of it. He was nothing without that. Nothing and good for nothing. For no one.

The darkness could hide such truths for a night, maybe more than one, but the sun reveals. If it does nothing else, it does that. Sun and time. These two things would make her understand the pit into which she'd fallen, a pit that could be crawled out of only with great pain and suffering. He'd try to help, of course, but as his voice was not made to comfort, nor were his hands made to help. His was a voice made to shout, to threaten, his hands made not for holding but for hurting.

He turned away from her still form, feeling relief and shame both, somehow, the two mingled together inside of him so that he could not rightly separate one from the other, and made his way to the other side of the barn floor, setting about unrolling his bedroll. He lay down on his back, wishing to sleep and knowing he would not. Wishing, for a few hours, to let himself go into that abyss, to let all that he was, all that he'd made himself become, be washed away on the lolling waves of unconsciousness. But sleep did not come easy, nor had he expected it to. After all, nothing else ever had.

CHAPTER SIXTEEN

She came to him in the darkness, lying down next to him, the heat of her body almost a visible thing where it met his own. For a moment, neither of them spoke, only lay there in the darkness and the warmth that only two bodies so close can make. Her hair tickled his face, smelling of hay and flowers, and her breath was soft and warm against his neck.

After a time, her fingers quested out, interlacing with his own, and he was surprised by how soft they were, how delicate they felt in his own rough, calloused hands. She brought his hand up slowly and placed her lips on it in a soft, quiet kiss. "I'm scared," she said, her voice low and faint in the darkness.

"I know."

"I have a strange feeling," she said, "I can't really explain it. It's as if ... I feel like something's going to happen. Something bad."

He squeezed her hand a little, hoping it would transfer the comfort his words could not. "It almost always is."

She said nothing for a time, her breath slow and hot now against his neck. "I...." he started, and the words, the *damned words* fought against him. He cleared his throat and tried again, his body tensed like a man going through some great trial or pain. "I won't let anything happen to you if I can help it, Adina. I'll die first."

She leaned in close, her face, inches from his own, "That's what I'm afraid of." Then her lips were on his, and he forgot his objections, forgot the reasons that had been so clear and obvious moments ago. Under the weight of that kiss, he forgot, for a time, who he was, forgot those forces, understood and not understood, arrayed against them. It was only him and her, their bodies in the darkness, her lips against his, her hand reaching under his shirt, running across his stomach and chest.

He told himself he was being a fool, knew the truth of it, even as he pulled her closer, wanting more of her, wanting *all* of her. Her hair fell about his face in a curtain, and her hand quested lower, running over his trousers. An involuntary moan escaped him, and then she was straddling him, her hands locked in both of his own as she kissed him, their breath coming in short gasps between kissing.

She guided his hands to her breasts, and he felt the soft smoothness of them under her shirt, felt himself being pulled by an animalistic need greater than anything he'd known before. "Adina," he gasped, "I—"

"I know," she whispered, "me too."

He sat up, kissing her again then he turned and threw her on her back, his need a pressing, desperate thing now. He reached a hand down to her waist, felt the fabric of her trousers, started to pull them down then hesitated, staring at her outline in the darkness.

"It's okay, Aaron. Please."

He hesitated another moment, thinking. A princess. She was a princess, and he could have her, *would* have her in a barn that smelled of hay and old horse shit. And not just a princess, but the kindest, most perfect thing he'd ever seen in his life, and he would have her lying on a dirt floor with Leomin somewhere out in the darkness watching for a danger that moved toward them.

An image flashed in his mind, an image of hands stained crimson holding a dagger and digging into a man's guts, a man who'd come to rob them and carry them to Belgarin to be tortured and executed, but a man anyway. He saw the hands going about their grisly work, uncaring of the man's screams and choked pleas for mercy as they created their bloody art. Killer's hands. His hands. "No," he said, sitting up and jerking his hands away from her, "I can't—" he cut off, not knowing how to finish. He stumbled back and to his feet, the fear stronger than ever now, twisting and turning in his stomach like some fell creature newly born.

"Aaron?" She asked, "What's wrong? Please, it's okay. I want this. I need this."

Need. The way the hands had needed, had quested and tore and raked with the dagger's blade until there was little left. Want. The hands had wanted too, had rejoiced in the causing of pain, had drunk it in like some perverse dark priest that dined on blood. "No," he grated, "I'm sorry." Then he was grabbing his sheathed sword and slinging it over his back, putting his cloak back on and drawing down the hood, entering back into a world he knew and understood. "I'll go check on Leomin."

"Aaron, wait," she said, but he was already out the door, out of it and moving. Not so much toward Leomin as away from her, away from the pain that he would cause her.

CHAPTER SEVENTEEN

Balen stood on the deck watching Avarest appear on the horizon, the buildings only vague shapes at this distance. He took a puff from the pipe he held, breathing in the fumes deeply, wondering for what must have been the thousandth time what was happening with Leomin and Aaron and the princess. Wondering and worrying.

He sighed before taking another drag from the pipe, watching the smoke of it carried away on the wind. *They'll be alright,* he told himself. *Aaron can take care of himself, the gods know that, and Leomin and the princess are smart. They'll make it out okay.* It wasn't the first time he'd told himself as much and now, like all the others, it was of little comfort.

Looking for something to take his mind off of his worry, Balen glanced around the ship where Festa's sailors went about their given tasks in near silence. A quieter ship, he'd never seen. Safest, he supposed, unless they relished the idea of becoming another dent in the captain's table. He'd tried to help, at first, a way to take his mind off of things as much as anything else, but they'd rebuffed him in their silence, someone picking up a task even as he made his way to it and giving him looks that, though not hostile, were not humoring either.

He was just about to turn back to the city once more when he saw old Thom emerging from below decks. The man walked heavily, as if exhausted, and Balen couldn't help but smile as he watched his old friend head toward him. The gray-haired man took up a spot beside him, propping his arms on the ship's edge and gazing out into the ocean.

Balen grinned wider at the desperate look in the man's eyes, "Well?" He said. "How is it with you, Thom? You're lookin' a little stiff, you don't mind me sayin.'"

The older man slowly turned his head to study Balen. "Give me a pull of that herb you're smokin', why don't you?"

Balen grinned wider, passing the pipe to the first mate. Thom grunted, taking a drag before handing it back and turning to look at the ocean once more.

Balen waited several seconds then spoke, "You know, some of the lads have been speakin' of some squeals comin' from one of the cabins at night. Say they've been losin' sleep on account of it."

Thom grunted again, "Well. Ships sometimes get rats, you know that. It's natural enough."

"Aye," Balen said, nodding, "aye, rats. Thing is, they're sayin' this squealin' don't sound like that of a rat. Say it sounds more like that of a man, fightin' for his life maybe. Quiet enough lot, your men, but seems this has caused a bit of talk between 'em."

Thom frowned at him, "They'd do just as well to stay quiet."

Balen nodded, schooling his expression. "Well. You ain't heard any of the squealin' yourself, then?"

Festa's first mate sighed, "Alright, damnit. Alright. I'll just say as that woman is a handful and then some. She does some things ...." He hesitated, glancing at Balen, "I'll tell ya, Blunderfoot, I didn't know such things was possible. Why, I feel like I been beat every which a way a man can be. She'll be the death of me, for it's through."

Balen laughed, "I 'spose there's worse ways to go, if that's the case."

Thom studied him for a moment then his weary face showed a small smile, "Aye. I 'spose you're right. But the stamina on her...." He shook his head in something like wonder.

Balen stared off at the distant city, his smile fading. "In these times, I feel that a man has to get what joy as he may where he finds it, Thom. Sore bones and scratches are a small enough price to pay and less than most."

"Aye," Thom said, nodding, "you're right, of course, Blunderfoot."

"Won't be long now," Balen said to himself as much as his friend, "Soon, we'll reach the city. Then, I suppose, we'll see what we might see."

"Seems to me," Thom said, "you might do with a bit of joy of your own, lad. There's a dark cast to your features."

Balen closed his eyes for a moment, felt the cool sea breeze on his face, listened to the sound of the gulls cawing in the distance and the rush of the water beneath them. "You're right, old man. But I think I feel a storm comin' on. A bad one."

Festa's first mate glanced up at the blue sky, no cloud in sight, "The day's clear enough."

"Yeah," Balen said. He was a simple man, of simple pleasures, and he rarely expected much out of life. That, he'd always found, was the secret to happiness. His papa had once told him that a man expects a lot and gets a little is unhappy, but a man that expects nothing and gets a little is thankful for what he's given. He tried to tell himself that now, but, for the first time in his life, it didn't seem like enough. "But there's a storm comin' just the same, Thom. I can feel it as much as I can feel anything."

The gray-haired man grasped his shoulder, "Easy, lad. If a storm does come, it won't be the first blow you or I have suffered. Storms, after all, can be weathered."

"Aye," Balen said, studying the sky, "Most can."

They stood in silence for a few moments then, each with their own thoughts as the ship cut through the water, drawing them closer to the shore, closer to the future and whatever awaited them there.

"Master Thom."

They both turned at the sound of the voice to see May, the club owner, walking toward them, wearing some fancy green dress that looked to Balen like it belonged more in a ballroom than on a ship. Still, she wore it well. Her long bright red hair seemed almost on fire in the light of the sun. A thick woman, but one whose thickness only seemed to add to her beauty somehow, in Balen's eyes. And, apparently, in Thom's too, judging by the way the man was staring.

"I wonder," May said as she drew close, and Balen noted all of the sailors turning to glance at her as she passed, "if I might have a word with you before we reach Avarest." Her words and voice were casual enough, but there was something almost predatory in her green eyes, predatory and amused.

"Of course, my lady," Thom said, swallowing hard. "What can I help you with?"

"Oh," May said, "it's so loud out here, with the waves and the gulls. I wonder if we could speak below?" She nodded as if he'd agreed, "I'll expect you in a few minutes," she said, then turned and sauntered off, escorted by the eyes of every sailor on the ship until she disappeared below decks.

"Damn." Thom said, and Balen couldn't help but laugh.

"No worries, old man," he said, "as you say. All storms can be weathered."

"Aye," Thom said, running a hand through his graying hair, "Aye, as you say." Then he turned and started toward the cabins and despite all his complaints, Balen couldn't help but notice the eagerness in the old man's step. If that was a man walking to his own death, then he was doing it gladly.

Thom had only been gone for a minute or two when Balen saw the chamberlain, Gryle, making his way toward him. The short, balding man was wringing his hands as he approached. Balen tried to think of a time he'd seen the man where he hadn't been nervous and came up empty. "Chamberlain," he said, nodding, "how are things with you?"

The short man seemed surprised to have someone asking after himself, "Me? Oh, they're going well enough, Mr. Balen. Thank you for inquiring."

"Please, lad," Balen said, and there was such about the balding man's character that it felt right to call him so despite the fact that he was at least ten years Balen's senior, "as I've told you before, Balen will do. A man like me has no right to a mister."

"Of course, as you say, Mr. Balen," the chamberlain said nodding, his hands rubbing together in earnest now. "I apologize for my intrusion, of course, but I was wondering if I might ask you a question."

"Best go on ahead and ask it," Balen said, taking a puff of his pipe, "while you've still got any hands left."

The short man's face colored at that, and his hands dropped awkwardly to his sides as if he didn't know what to do with them. "Of course, sir, I'm sorry," he said, apologizing, though for what

Balen couldn't tell. "It's just ... the princess, you see ...." He took a moment, standing straighter and lifting his head slightly as he gathered his courage, "well, it's my duty, you understand, to keep her safe."

Balen nodded, studying the man. The chamberlain was a nervous sort by nature, ill at ease, but Balen liked him anyway. There was something about the man, an innocence, he guessed, that it was hard not to like. "No small task that, given what I've seen of her. The woman's got a mind of her own, that's for sure."

"Yes," Balen said in a relieved sigh then his eyes went wide as if he'd caught himself in some great sin, "I mean ... sir, that is to say that the princess is, of course, right to live her life the way she sees best. Only, as her protector, I find myself ... concerned."

Concerned was a vast understatement from what Balen saw on the man's face. Love, is what it was. Not the love a man has for a woman, but the love a father might have for a daughter, maybe. "Protector, is it?"

The chamberlain colored again as if he'd been mocked, "Sir, I know that I am not strong or clever, nor do I have skill with the blade, like Mr. Envelar, but—"

"Stow that, lad," Balen said, "I meant no offense. The way I see it, the princess is lucky to have a man as committed to her cause as you. All I meant was, do all chamberlains go as far? Would all of them be willin' to give their lives for their lords or ladies, as you are?"

Gryle sniffed, "I'm sure I don't know, sir, but my lady deserves the best. Unfortunately," he said, deflating, "she only has me."

Balen grinned, and it was his turn to offer comfort, patting the man on the shoulder, "Aye, well, I'm sure that'll be plenty, chamberlain. She's lucky to have you."

Gryle nodded slowly, "Thank you for your kind words, Mr. Balen. Only, I need to find the princess. I wonder, do you think Captain Festa would be kind enough to bring me back to Baresh after he drops you and the others off in Avarest?"

Balen studied the man in wonder. For a man who thought himself a weakling and useless, he was prepared to risk going back to a city where, if he was found, he would be tortured and killed. It wasn't the first time the man had asked the question either. Balen shook his head slowly, "Why don't you stay with us, Gryle. That

May seems to know what she's about—a clever woman in more ways than one from what I've heard. I'd think sticking with her would be the best thing. The safest thing."

Gryle hesitated then swallowed, "Forgive me, sir, and I understand, truly. But ... the princess, sir. It's my duty—"

Balen raised a hand, forestalling the man, "I understand, chamberlain, I do. I'll tell you what, Festa will want to stay in port for a week or two at least, gathering supplies and buyin' stock to trade to other cities for a profit. Why don't you give it a bit? See what happens and what we hear. Might be, we'll have news from your princess or one of the others before long."

The chamberlain considered this then gave a reluctant nod, "As you say, Master Balen. I will stay on with Miss May for a time, if she'll have me. It would be wise, I suppose, to get some supplies of my own for the trip back. I wonder, do you think that the shops here might sell cinnamon? It is the princess's favorite."

Balen raised an eyebrow. *Protector indeed,* he thought. "Well," he said, shrugging, "I guess we'll have to ask."

CHAPTER EIGHTEEN

"This had better be good, Caldwell," Belgarin said. "I've enough things to do without you wasting my time."

"Of course, my lord," the bald man said, bowing his head before turning and leading Belgarin on down the corridor, "I believe that you will find it most enlightening."

"I had better," Belgarin said, "but I warn you, Caldwell, my temper grows short, and I weary of your excuses. It is not enough that you could not find my wayward sister or her companions—not when I put the *entire* force of my command within the city at your disposal—no, what's more, you even managed to let the old swordmaster escape."

His advisor turned, his expression as lifeless as ever. "Your Majesty, surely, you must not think that I—"

"What I *think*, Caldwell, is that I have, perhaps, trusted the wrong person. What I *think* is that I have listened to your advice, and it has led us nowhere. Understand that though we might not have the old man, one head will work as well as another on the headsman's block. The executioner cares little and the axe less, whose life it takes."

"As you say, Your Majesty."

Belgarin studied the man's bland expression, a sneer rising on his own face. He had considered replacing Caldwell more times than he could count. The problem was that, until recent events, Caldwell had proved himself a capable and well-informed advisor. It had been him, after all, who'd warned Belgarin that Eladen planned to assassinate him under a veil of truce, allowing Belgarin to act first and beat his brother at his own game. It had also been Caldwell who'd known of Adina and her companions coming to Baresh in the first place. The man had proven his effectiveness on more than one occasion. Yet, perhaps, his effectiveness was coming to an end.

Belgarin waved the man on, frowning in disgust at the slime covered corridor walls on either side of them. Underground as they were, the dungeons were ever damp, and the walls would be cleaned one week only to be filthy the next. The man had better have a good reason for bringing him down here. "What of the guard who was on duty when the old man escaped? He's been questioned?"

"Thoroughly, Your Majesty."

The man said nothing else, and Belgarin frowned, "*And?*"

"The Parnen captain, my lord. The guard claimed that he remembered the man coming down into the dungeons, remembered challenging him, asking about his identity, and nothing after."

"He remembers *nothing?*"

"Yes, Your Majesty," Caldwell said, "so he claimed."

Belgarin barked a harsh laugh, "Truly, you are a fool, Caldwell. Am I to believe then that this guard had somehow lost his memory, coincidentally about the one occasion on which he was questioned? Do you not think it possibly, nay *likely* that the man lied? That you and your questions did nothing to uncover his secrets?"

"Forgive me, Majesty, but no. What secrets the man knew, he told. I made sure of it personally."

Belgarin frowned, "You speak of torture now," he said with disgust. "It is a filthy business, one that no man or woman of noble birth would participate in."

"Lucky then, your Majesty, that I am not of noble birth. And, if it pleases you, I do not speak of torture, but of serving my king in whatever way I might."

"Oh yes a loyal servant aren't you, Caldwell?" Belgarin asked, frowning at the man's back.

If the man heard the challenge in his king's tone, he gave no sign. "Of course, Your Majesty."

"Very well," Belgarin said, "You and I *will* talk about the guard later. Now, tell me about the woman."

Caldwell nodded, "Of course, my lord. She lives in the poor district. From what I gather, she ran with a small gang—petty crimes, mostly, robbing and mugging. She claims to have been having a drink at a local tavern when she saw the man and recognized him from one of the notices we put up throughout the city. Her and those with her attempted to detain him but failed."

"Failed?"

"Yes, Your Majesty. It seems that he resisted." Caldwell stopped and turned to Belgarin, the cell keys in his hand. A short distance up the hallway, two lanterns had been lit on either side of a cell, no doubt the woman's. "Your Majesty, forgive me but I must warn you. The woman is not ... in the best condition, now. It was felt that she might have been holding back some information so ... steps were taken."

Belgarin sneered, "I am no child to be hidden away and kept safe, fool. I am your king, and you would be wise to treat me as such." He snatched the keys from the bald man's hands and shouldered his way past, smiling a small smile as Caldwell bumped against the slimy wall in his haste to get out of the way.

Belgarin unlocked the cell door and stepped inside. The smell hit him immediately, and he barely managed to suppress a gag. He brought a silk kerchief from inside his tunic and covered his mouth and nose, looking at the figure lying hanging from manacles in the ceiling. Despite his words to Caldwell, he felt his stomach roil uncomfortably, and he had to struggle to keep his rising gorge in check.

The woman had once been beautiful, even in the fitful light of the lanterns he could see that. Of course, it had been a commoner's sort of beauty. The kind that would be pleasant enough for a roll in the hay, but lacking in the regal possession of a lady of higher station. Still, whatever beauty she'd once held was gone now, and the truth of what remained was made all the worse for knowing it had once existed. It put him in mind of when he'd been a child, laughing and running through his childhood castle.

He and a childhood friend had been playing at a game of chase, his father away visiting another part of the kingdom. He'd made his way through the castle, looking for a place to hide from his friend—a boy whose name he no longer remembered. He was running, his eyes searching frantically for some likely nook or cranny, when he came upon the formal dining room, a room his mother had told him was no place for children, forbidding him to go into it when not accompanied by an adult.

Of course, he *had* gone in, as children will when given such orders. His friend had found him there, and in his haste to get away, he'd knocked over an ornate porcelain vase, breaking it. Later, his mother had led him back to the room, made him study the broken pieces. "Irreplaceable," she'd said, her voice not scolding, only tired and resigned and all the worse for that, "A beauty from a kingdom that no longer exists, now broken and shattered." She'd turned to him then, and he thought it had been something like hate in her eyes when she spoke, "Why, Belgarin, must you always break things? Why must you always destroy?"

That had been all. No whippings or beatings—not for the firstborn prince. Not even any scolding, no more than that, at least. Only those words, said in a weary, tired tone, those eyes studying him. Only the words. But they'd stayed with him, always. *Why, Belgarin, must you always break things?* After that, he rarely played games with the other children. Instead, he'd put his effort and will toward being the prince he should be. He had watched with something like envy when he traveled the streets of the city with his family and seen common children playing games of chase, wanting to join in but knowing that such things were beneath a prince. *Why, Belgarin, do you always break things?*

Not this time, mother, he thought. *This time, I will unite us. I will put back together a kingdom that father, in his doddering old age destroyed. I will make it right.* He stared at the woman hanging there, thinking of that broken vase, the way it had looked lying shattered on the ground. "Gods be good," he said.

She was naked, her body covered in cuts and burns. Her face hung down in what could have been sleep or exhaustion, but he could see enough of it to see that it was covered in blood, making it appear as if she wore a crimson mask. The fingers of her hands were twisted and broken, hanging at unnatural angles. Belgarin forced himself to swallow the bile gathering in his throat as his advisor stepped into the room beside him.

"Tell the king what you told me," Caldwell said, and if he felt anything for the woman hanging there, he did not show it. There was no mercy or compassion in his words, only a cruel efficiency.

"My ... my lord?" The woman said, her voice low and raw and full of pain.

Belgarin opened his mouth to speak, to demand that Caldwell cut the woman down and put her out of her misery. She was obviously dying and in great pain. Still, he hesitated, the words coming to his mind, somehow helping to block out the pain and agony he saw in front of him. *We all do what is necessary.*

"Speak, woman," he said, "and I will see you released of you bonds and set free, your pain stopped."

With a great effort, she raised her head then. *"Promise?"* She said and a fresh wave of revulsion overcame Belgarin as he saw that all but two of her teeth had been pulled from her mouth and there was only a ragged hole where her left eye had been.

Belgarin forced his gaze away from her mouth, and the bloody ruin of her left eye and stared into the one remaining, the white of it all the brighter in that mask of blood. "I give you my word as king."

"The man," she said, pausing as she weakly spat a mouthful of blood onto her chin, "we tried to stop him. Wanted ... the reward. Knocked me out, but I woke and saw him and ... a woman."

"A woman?" Belgarin said, stepping forward despite the gruesome sight, "Are you sure?"

"Y-yes, my king."

"What did she look like?" Belgarin said, stepping closer so that his face was no more than a foot away from the woman's own. "Tell me."

"Brunette," the woman said, wincing at pain that could have come from any number of her wounds, "Pretty. I remember ... remember thinking she looked noble born. Something about the way she walked."

"And this woman," Belgarin said, "she was with the other? The man?"

"Not ... not at first," the woman gasped, "but later. In the room."

Belgarin turned to Caldwell, "I thought that Adina had left on the Parnen's ship. The *Clandestine.*"

The advisor nodded, "As did I, Your Majesty. Witnesses on the docks saw her board. Apparently, she must have gotten off of it at some point that we didn't see."

Belgarin frowned, "That means she's here."

"I do not know, Your Majesty."

Belgarin sighed. No, Caldwell did not know, nor did he himself. Still, there was someone who might. He rubbed a hand across his face, dreading the visit he knew he had to make. "See that she is freed, her pain stopped," he said, studying his advisor.

The bald man bowed his head, "Aye, Your Majesty. I'll have one of my men—"

"*No.* No, Caldwell," Belgarin said, "you will not have one of your men do it. You will do this thing yourself."

The advisor's brow creased, but he nodded. "Of course, My Lord."

Belgarin nodded then took one of the lanterns from the wall and started making his way out of the dungeon. He heard the woman scream behind him. *"You said you'd set me free!"* She yelled.

He winced at the words but walked on. *And so you will be set free,* he thought. *Of all pain. After all, we all do what is necessary.*

***

Belgarin would not have thought it possible, but the Knower looked even worse than he had on his last visit. The man's skin was paler now, so white that it looked as if it had never seen the sun, and his features were shrunken in his face. The boy left quickly enough when Belgarin motioned for him to go, obviously relieved at being sent away from this mockery of humanity for a few moments. Once the boy was gone, Belgarin turned and stared at the old man lying in the bed, unable to fully keep the disgust out of his expression. *How much ugliness,* he thought, *must one man endure to see things set right?*

However much is necessary, he answered himself, *no more than that.*

"Aaah," the Knower said, smiling his gap-toothed smile and displaying gums that were bleeding freely, no doubt what had caused the bib of blood staining the man's shirt. "Your Majesty," he said in a gurgling voice, "To what do I owe this unexpected pleasure? I have so few visitors of late."

Belgarin recounted the occurrence at the western gate to the man as well as his conversation with the woman in the dungeon. When he was finished, the old man licked his lips with a tongue that was gray and swollen. "Ah, tell me more of the woman. Tell me, how badly was she hurt? Was she in very much pain?"

Belgarin frowned in disgust, "Gods, man, have you no pity?"

The man laughed at that, a breathy cackle that sent blood and snot coming from his mouth and nose. "Pity? Pity, you ask? No, *my lord,*" he said, "I feel no pity. What pity once lived in me died long ago, withered and succumbed even as my body does now. Knowledge, after all, always has a price. Now, tell me more of this girl and her suffering. What little pleasure I now find can only be found in pain. Oh yes, Belgarin," he said at the king's disgusted look, "much pleasure can be found in pain."

Belgarin frowned, deciding to let pass the fact that the man had called him by his given name. "I will not feed your perversity, monster," he said. "Now, tell me, what is my sister's next move? Where will she, the sellsword, and the Parnen go?"

The old man's ruined mouth spread in a cruel grin, and he shook his head slowly. "All knowledge has a price, my king. Surely, you must know that. You need only look at the evidence of it lying in front of you in a pool of my own blood and shit. For small knowledge, the price is small. For great knowledge, knowledge that could decide the fate of kingdoms, the price must be greater still. Now, tell me of the woman."

"*I will not,*" Belgarin said, gripping the man by the front of his bloody shirt in his anger and shaking him. The man weighed nothing, and he laughed that evil, cruel laugh even as his head bounced around on his neck like a mistreated doll's.

"Oh, my king," the man said once Belgarin's anger was spent and he stood there panting. "What do you think you threaten? Pain? My *world* is pain. I wake to it in the morning, and I lie with it at night, a mistress that knows no mercy or surcease. A plague that continues to devour my flesh with each passing moment, yet leaves my mind clearer and clearer as the days go on. Do you think to threaten me with pain? Or is it death?" The man cackled again, "Oh, but I should be so lucky," he sneered. "Death is no torment to the tormented, *king*. It is only a stopping, an ending. *Oh, but blessed death.*"

Belgarin looked at his hands, filthy with the man's bile and blood and gagged. The sight of the woman, the sight of this man and his filth all over his hands was too much, and Belgarin rushed to the corner of the room, vomiting out his breakfast and listening to the ruined thing in the bed laugh as he did.

"Ah, let it loose, king," the creature said, "let it loose wherever thou will. It will likely not be noticed, not by me, at least. My nose has long since stopped its function—a small mercy, I suppose. A man can only smell his own urine and shit and blood for so long."

Belgarin's stomach heaved again at the man's words, and the creature laughed and laughed while he vomited. Finally, he was done, and Belgarin stood, weak and wavering, rubbing the sleeve of his fine robe across his mouth. "Gods be good," he said, his voice shaky, "what do you want from me?"

The creature smiled, "You know what it is I want, Belgarin. Pain. Knowledge *is* pain. I will sell the knowledge that you seek to you, but it is only right and just that I should have my *payment.*"

The last came out in a hiss, and Belgarin took an involuntary step back. "Fine," he said, "fine. The woman—"

"Oh no, my king," the thing said, smiling as blood leaked from its gums, "I find that the price has gone up while you dithered. Such things happen, of course. Fluctuations in the market, so many possible reasons. Even for me, it is no easy pattern to discern."

"*What do you want you foul creature?*" Belgarin said, "Why must you torment me so?"

The ruined, wasted thing laughed at that, "Torment, Belgarin? *Torment?* What do *you* know of torment? You wear your fine clothes, stick your cock in anything you'd like while they call you king and fawn and weep and laugh behind your back, and you would ask me of *torment?*"

Belgarin sank into the room's only chair, cupping his face in his hands, "Please," he said. "Please just tell me what you want."

"*Please,*" the creature mocked, "well, very well, Belgarin. How could I say no to such a request? What I want is a new one to look after me. One that speaks and hears and *knows.* Do you understand?"

Belgarin swallowed hard and when he spoke his voice came out lifeless and dull, "You want someone that you can murder."

"Murder?" The thing in the bed asked. "Oh, not murder, Belgarin. How might I do such a thing, when I've long since lost the ability even to wipe my own shit? No, it would not be murder. And if it were, I, certainly, would not be the killer. No, knowledge, perhaps. The gaining of it is never easy, as I think you now see."

"Fine," Belgarin rasped, "Fine, damn you. You'll have your victim."

"A girl," the creature said, cocking his head, "a young one."

"Gods be good but you're a monster."

"Oh, words that wound, my king," the thing said. "Not a monster, not me. But I *will* have my payment, or you will leave as you came—with nothing and understanding nothing."

We all do what is necessary. We all do what is necessary. Why must you always break things? "Alright," Belgarin said, his mouth unaccountably dry, "alright. You will have her. Now, tell me what I need to know."

"Of course, my king," the creature said, favoring him with another bloody grin. "It is easy enough to discern where she will go, though, is it not? The occurrence at the western gate is no coincidence—there *are* no coincidences, in fact, not truly. The universe, when it is boiled down to its basest elements, is all about cause and effect, purchase and price. You've learned, now, I think, judging by your grim expression, about the latter. The former should make the answer to your question simple enough. Where will your sister go? The only place she conceivably *can* go."

"Yes?" Belgarin said, "Well?"

Another breathy laugh. "West, you said. The same direction as your two other siblings, the coward and the fool. Oh, do not look so taken aback, it is what they are, you know it as well as I and dissembling changes nothing. So, let us think of it. The coward first, shall we? Your brother has the stronger position, it is true, his mountain fastness would prove a difficult nut to crack given as it would not allow the full bulk of your army to be brought to battle. A good place for sanctuary, for safety, if that is what your sister is after."

"Very well," Belgarin said, "then she has gone to Ellemont." He rose. "You will have your payment."

"Do not be hasty, *great* king," the thing in the bed said, "for is it truly sanctuary that your sister seeks? If so, why, then, come to Baresh at all, to the very place where she knew you and your armies were heading? Why be in Avarest at the time of your brother's ... unfortunate demise? No, she does not search for safety or security. She searches for an army."

Belgarin frowned and stopped, halfway to the door. He turned back to the man, "Would you not just *say* what you mean?"

"Not an easy thing to do, lord. Men have been killed, wars have been fought for the lack of a man or woman's ability to say what they truly mean. But fine, as I see your patience grows short, I will tell you. Your sister, Isabelle. The fool. Her armies are larger than your brother's, less than your own, of course, but not by so much, not even with those you have so recently added to its ranks. And she takes great pride in them, does she not? Her knights with their fine clothes, no dirt to mar those bright colors, no notches in those gleaming swords. A large army, a proud army, and one that, should she be allowed, your sister, Adina, will make her own. She travels there even now, my king, and with each night that passes, she grows closer to her goal."

"Very well." Belgarin turned and started away.

"My payment, my king—"

"*You will have it,*" Belgarin grated, then he was out the door, slamming it behind him and heading down the hall. Not running. Not exactly.

The thing in the bed watched him leave, a smile on its face, unknowing or uncaring about the blood that leaked from its open mouth and onto its shirt.

CHAPTER NINETEEN

Aaron started awake, casting his gaze around him for some sign of what had woken him. He looked at the sky and saw that it was still dark, though perhaps two or three hours had passed. *Fool,* he thought, *as if the odds aren't already bad enough, you let yourself fall asleep.*

He had told Adina he was going to Leomin, but that had not been true. He had only wanted to escape, to flee from truths about himself that he did not want to face. Instead of checking on the Parnen, he had made his way through the fields and back into the wood. He had kept going until the exhaustion of days spent on the road crept up on him, and he'd decided to sit down against a tree for a moment's rest.

Aaron, Co began in his mind, *there's—*

"Not now, firefly," he said, remembering the way Adina had looked lying there, remembering the betrayal and hurt he'd seen in her eyes as he'd left. "I don't want to talk about the princess."

It's not that, Aaron, Co said, and he realized that she sounded worried, *something's happened. Or is happening. I tried to wake you but—*

She cut off as the sound of a distant scream came to them. Aaron's heart leapt at the fear and anger in it, for he knew that scream, knew that voice. *Adina.* The thought had barely passed through his mind before he was moving, sprinting through the trees with reckless abandon, ignoring the scratches and cuts he received from the briars and bushes he charged through.

He ran as hard as he could, pushed himself forward faster and faster until he was careening between the trees. Still, he hadn't realized how deeply into the woods he'd went in his troubled state of mind, and it was at least half an hour before he made it to the edge of the fields. In the distance, he saw the barn, and his already galloping heart lurched in his chest.

The barn was on fire. A great blaze that sent smoke rising into the air in massive, undulating gray pillars. He forced his weary legs on, his breath coming in great, bellowing gasps as he charged for the barn.

He made it to the inferno a short time later. There was no movement, and he looked to where the horses had been only to see that they were gone. The heat on his skin was immense, but he held an arm over his mouth and forced his way forward. He kicked out at one of the blazing doors and it fell inside the barn in a shower of sparks and flame and smoke. "*Adina!*"

Aaron, you have to get out.

Ignoring the Virtue, Aaron held his other arm up in an effort to block his eyes from the smoke and flame as he swept his gaze around the barn. He could see nothing. No one. Only flame and ash and smoke. "*Adina!*" He shouted again, but the smoke was in his mouth, his throat, and his voice came out in little more than a croak.

Aaron, get out now.

The flame singing his clothes, his breath growing weak and labored, he stumbled his way out of the barn, collapsing to his knees a short distance away. "What have I done?" He said, feeling tears tracing their way down his painfully dry face.

Aaron—

"*No,*" he said, his voice coming out in a low growl, "do not speak to me, Virtue. Just leave me alone." He had been a fool. He'd let his emotions get the better of him, and he'd left her and the Parnen alone. While he was gone, someone had come, someone who'd brought fire and death, and he had not been here to protect her. He screamed then, a wordless, feral cry of rage and pain that went on until his voice grew hoarse and cracked and gave out.

Aaron—

"*Enough,*" he said, his words a harsh bark, and the Virtue went silent.

He turned back and stared at the blaze, feeling empty and cold despite the raging fire. She was in there, somewhere. Burning with all the rest. Had she cried out for him, when they'd come? Had she screamed for his help while he'd been dozing in the woods, too absorbed with his own problems to even know it? Too much. It was too much.

He hacked and coughed, his body trying to expel the smoke in his lungs until his eye caught on something a few feet away. It had never been harder to rise to his feet, but rise he did, shuffling wearily to what appeared to be a scrap of clothing that had been torn off somehow. He looked at it blankly for several seconds, his mind foggy and confused with grief. A light blue scrap of clothing. Belonging to one of the soldiers who'd come, perhaps, though they were Belgarin's colors. Frowning, feeling as if he was in a daze, he crouched down and grabbed the scrap of cloth, studying it.

Something tugged at the back of his mind and, at first, he didn't know what it was. Then, with a jolt, it came to him. The light blue. Adina always favored the color, *her* color, and wore it often. He thought back, casting his mind to when he'd been with her the day before, remembering riding behind her on the trail, remembering lying with her in the darkness of the barn. *Yes. Yes.* It was the same. The color was the same as the shirt she'd been wearing.

That meant that somehow it had been torn. This scrap had not been here when he'd gone into the barn or when he left it, of that he was fairly certain. But it was here now. Which meant ... which meant that *she* had been here. Or, at least, her shirt had. A fresh fear blossomed in his mind at that, but he forced it down. No. Adina *had* been here, he was sure of it. Which meant that she'd been taken from the barn, had been alive when it was set afire.

He thought of the Parnen captain who'd been set to watch and then his feet were moving, rushing to where the man had been up on a small hill a short way away from the barn. He ran to the place he thought Leomin had been, though in the darkness it was hard to tell for sure, but there was no sign of Leomin nor of any of his equipment. Cursing, feeling that time was running out, Aaron fell to his knees, frantically running his hands through the grass in search of anything that might help him determine what had happened to the Parnen.

He was beginning to despair when his hands ran over something wet, much wetter than the dew that covered the ground, and he frowned, bringing his hands up. In the light of the weak moon, the blood looked black. He stared at it for a moment, his jaw clenched, his hands knotting into fists in front of him. The Parnen had been here, but he was here no longer. Either the man was dead—in which case Aaron couldn't imagine why his attackers had taken the body with them—or he was still alive. Wounded but alive.

"Co," he said, rising, "I need you. Like the time when those men attacked us at the princess's hideout in Avarest, or the way we felt Festa and the others coming toward the ship."

Aaron, the Virtue said, her voice full of pain and doubt, *I don't know if we can. The bond may not be strong enough. The danger—*

"Damn the danger," he said, "Show me how."

Suddenly, an undefinable force exploded through him, and Aaron staggered, grunting in pain. He felt an immense *tug,* as if some giant had grabbed his insides and given them a hard yank, and he felt as if he'd be ripped apart from the pressure of it. He gasped, falling to his knees, his hands balled into fists in the grass, his back arched in agony as he gritted his teeth, spittle flying from his mouth.

Then, he felt something give, like a dam breaking under the strain of an unstoppable river and although the pain did not cease, it lessened, grew manageable. He opened his eyes from where they'd been squeezed shut and looked in the direction of the woods to the west. Faintly, so faintly as to be almost unnoticeable, he saw a light pink shimmer, little more than a speck of light in the darkness. He blinked his eyes, thinking he'd imagined it, but when he opened them again, the speck was still there, somewhere distant in the woods. Then there was another dot of light to match the first, then another, seven or eight in all, and Aaron stared at them, gasping for breath and easing himself to his feet.

There, Co said, and her voice sounded as weary and full of pain as he felt.

"Okay," Aaron breathed, rising with his hands on his knees, his breath a wheezing rattle in his chest. "Okay." Then he was running again, toward the lights in the darkness and what he would find there.

CHAPTER TWENTY

It was nearly an hour before he made his way to where the lights shone among the trees twenty or thirty yards off. They had resolved themselves into the shape of people, still shining that bright magenta, and he winced, shaking his head. This close, the figures blazed, blindingly bright, and he closed his eyes against it. *Okay, firefly,* he thought, shielding his eyes, *that's enough.*

He felt some of the strain leave his muscles and bones and opened his eyes to see only the darkness once more. The darkness and, somewhere in it, the shadows of figures moving. He waited for his eyes to adjust, narrowing them as much as possible as he scanned the woods in front of him. He saw, at the base of the hill on which he stood, a cart with two horses tethered to it. He also noted his and the others' horses staked to the ground beside it. Staring past the horses, he could see a tent that glowed in the darkness from some lantern or light within. He frowned, studying the cart and saw what he finally decided were several man-sized cages on the back of it. Slavers, then. Men who kidnapped and stole unsuspecting men, women, or children from their homes and sold their bodies to others for a profit. A good sign. They would have wanted Adina and Leomin alive. He only hoped they hadn't realized who it was they'd taken. So long as she was only a woman with a pretty face, she would be kept alive. But should they realize that she was a princess, one whose head Belgarin would pay a king's ransom for, she would not live long.

Aaron stared at the tent, at the vague outline of figures he could see in it by the lantern inside, and rage unlike anything he'd ever felt before built inside of him. Grew and grew, burning inside of him until he felt as if he would catch fire, a blazing beacon in the darkness. *These men.* These men had come and taken her, had stolen her from him, had taken Leomin too. *These men.*

The ache of his fire-chapped skin, the sharp pain in his side, the weariness from two weeks spent on the road vanished in an instant, swept away by the storm of his fury. He heard the sound of someone cough nearby, between him and the tent, and he turned his head, drawing his sword.

We need ... to stay calm, something said in his mind, a familiar voice, but just then it seemed distant to him, strange, unknown and insignificant. *Aaron, please—*

"Not Aaron," he said, but the words were spoken with three voices. His own, the feminine voice, and the anger's own. He bared his teeth in a grin, *not now.*

Then he was running, making no attempt to hide the sound of his approach, the dry leaves of the forest crackling beneath his feet as he ran. "What the f—"

The man's words turned into a scream as Aaron bowled into him, slamming him against the tree on which he'd been propped even as he drove his sword into the man's stomach with all the strength and momentum he could bring to bear.

The man dropped the crossbow he'd been holding, grabbing at the sword with both hands, oblivious of the sharp metal slicing through his flesh as he fought to get it out of his stomach. "*Who—*" He said, "*who the fuck—*"

"*Death,*" Aaron hissed, spittle flying from his mouth as he jerked the blade upward. The man screamed more as the steel cut through his organs, and Aaron smiled as a river of blood washed over his hand. Then, he felt something, a presence behind him and spun, jerking his sword free in a shower of blood and leaping to the side.

There was a sound of the crunching of dry leaves, and an arrow flashed by his shoulder in the darkness, burying itself in the man he'd been in front of only moments before. Aaron followed the course of its flight and saw a figure in the darkness, the man bent over, trying to reload a crossbow. It would be too slow. Much,

much too slow. "Heard you," Aaron said, but though the words came from his mouth, they were not in his voice and they were not his own. "Felt you." Some deep, dark part of him rejoiced, smiling at the man in front of him, rejoiced at the blood he would spill, at the art and the glory they would make together, and Aaron smiled with it.

He took his time, walking toward the man, reveling in each terrified glance the man cast up at him, the shadow in the darkness moving closer, a blade slick with his friend's blood at its side, the only sound the crunching of the leaves and the dripping of the blood on the forest floor. *Drip. Crunch. Drip.*

The man just managed to raise the crossbow when Aaron was on him, and he smiled wider at the sight of it, such a small, pitiful thing, really. Almost as weak, as frail as the hands that held it. But not quite. It was the reason the blade found the wrists, lopped them off, a bloody gruesome pair falling to the forest floor in fresh spurts of blood.

The man screamed, and Aaron screamed too, sharing in the man's pain, his soul feasting on it, glutting on it. *"My hands,"* the man said, his voice a wet gurgle as he stumbled backward, "Gods be good, *my hands."*

"Yes," the thing inside Aaron hissed, "Your hands. Beautiful, aren't they?"

The man cried and whimpered and started to fall to his knees, but Aaron caught him. "Oh," he said, grabbing the man by the back of the neck and bringing his face only inches away from his own, "Oh, you and I are going to make such beautiful art together."

The man screamed, but Aaron and the thing inside Aaron didn't mind. The screams were a part of it, and so they let him scream. And then they began their work.

CHAPTER TWENTY-ONE

Adina struggled against the ropes that bound her, feeling the skin of her wrists chafe and crack but not stopping, praying to the gods that the wooden stake to which her wrists had been bound would hide the motion from her captors. Her legs, too, had been bound, the knots tied tightly, but she thought she could untangle the binding quickly once her hands were free. She hoped.

The men had driven the two stakes in the ground when they'd brought her and Leomin in, though she'd been in and out of consciousness. One of them had struck her on the head, and she found that she couldn't remember much, the images of what had happened after Aaron left vague and distorted in her mind, coming to her in brief flashes, too quick and confusing to understand. Still, what the men intended was clear enough.

Leomin was tied to a stake of his own across the tent from her, though the Parnen had not stirred. A mask of blood covered one side of his face, and his head hung down on his chest, his arms bound to the stake behind him. She had tried to wake him without alerting the men who sat a few feet away, drinking ale and playing cards at a small table, but the Parnen had not moved or responded. Adina feared for him. It was obvious one of the men had struck him a blow to the head, as they had her, but she was afraid that they'd hit him too hard. She'd heard of such wounds before, bad head wounds from which men never truly recovered. Sometimes, such men didn't wake and then, often, when they did, they were no longer themselves, sometimes incapable of speech or rational thought. She'd seen such men before when she'd visited the healers' tents in her own kingdom.

The men, too, were no great mystery. Though she had never met slavers, she'd heard of them. Men who found their work in kidnapping others and selling them at underground slave markets, making of people possessions. Nothing more than items to be auctioned off to the highest bidder.

Adina had tried to speak to them when she'd first come to, but the men hadn't responded. Not, at least, until she'd kept on. Then, finally, one of them had risen, a thick, barrel-chested man with a dirty black beard down to his chest and breath that smelled of rot. The man had walked over to her silently and slapped her in the face hard, a full handed slap from which her lip was even now bleeding. Then he'd pawed at her breasts, ripping her tunic in the process, and even that hadn't been the most frightening thing.

The scariest thing had been the *way* he'd had done it. He'd pawed at her in a clinical, detached way, like a man checking on the health of a steer or mare before he takes it to the market to sell. She'd struggled against her bonds, spitting in his face, but he'd only smiled and tightened his grip on one of her breasts until she'd gasped in pain and stopped struggling. Then he'd continued pawing at her until one of the other two yelled at him to get back and take his turn.

The man had, but he'd winked at her first, a wink that carried in it a world of meaning, then he'd slowly risen and walked back to sit at the table. Adina felt real fear, then, not just for her, but for Leomin and Aaron too. Aaron was not here in the tent, so that could only mean one of two things. Either they hadn't captured him, or they'd killed him. That last thought sent a shiver of fear running up her spine. *No,* she told herself, *no. He can't be dead. He can't be.*

Still, as much as she told herself that Aaron wouldn't have let these men capture him, that he would have heard them coming, would have known, the image of him lying bloody on the ground in the forest would not leave her. She felt tears gathering in her eyes. *Damnit woman,* she thought, *get a hold of yourself. You can't do anything for him unless you get yourself free first.*

So she continued her work, thinking she was getting a little bit of slack in the tight ropes that bound her wrist, though she couldn't be sure. The image of Aaron lying bloody and broken on the ground fresh in her mind, she kept at it, struggling to keep a grimace of pain from her face even as her wrists grew slick with blood.

She was still working at her bonds, the men laughing at some joke they'd shared, when a scream sounded from somewhere out in the woods. It was a terrible, heart-wrenching scream that made gooseflesh pop out all over Adina's skin. It was the sound of a man in unbearable pain, a sound that didn't belong in the world at all, save only, perhaps, for the Fields of the Dead.

"What the fuck was that?" One of the men asked, stumbling out of his chair, the cards he'd been holding falling to the ground.

"Don't know," the bearded man said, rising himself, the three of them casting their eyes at the front of the tent as if they might see whatever apparition had voiced such a scream of suffering.

"Was that Malin?" The third and youngest of the three asked, his voice scared and uncertain. "Gods, that sounded like Malin."

"Doesn't make a difference whether it were or weren't," the first man said, "Whatever makes or causes a scream like that, you can bet your ass it ain't friendly. Get your weapons ready, boys."

The men did as ordered and, in another moment, they were all armed. One of them, the large bearded man, held a thick, wooden club, the others short, rusty swords that had been poorly maintained. "Alright," the apparent leader of the group said, "here's what we're gonna do. Rhett," he said, glancing at the bearded man, you—" he cut off as another scream came, this one even worse than the last. It went on for longer than Adina would have thought possible, not a man at all but some banshee of the damned voicing its pain and rage.

"*Fields take it,*" the youngest asked, his fear stealing away several of his years, making him no longer a nineteen or twenty year old youth, but a child, scared in the darkness, "Drost, what *is* that?"

"Whatever it is," the man named Drost said, "it'll bleed like anythin' else. Die the same too. Now come on. Me and you are goin' to go deal with this here and now. I can't stomach much more of that fuckin' screamin'."

Just then, the scream came again, this time with another scream, and where the first was full of pain and pleas, the second seemed somehow hungry, and in it, Adina thought she could hear pleasure. She felt a shiver of fear run up her spine.

The boy shook his head, "Drost, I ain't goin' out there. What, you lost your damned mind? A man steps out there's going to catch his death sure as anythin'."

Drost grabbed hold of the youth's dirty shirt and jerked him forward so that he slammed into the table then he put his rusty blade against the boy's throat. "You'll catch it in here, too, you don't mind what I'm tellin' you. You understand?"

The boy swallowed hard, nodding, "I ... I understand, Drost. Sure, I do. I was just scared, is all. I'll go out there, sure, that's what you want. Long as you come with me, course."

"I said I am, and I am, damnit," Drost said. "Now come on. Rhett," he said, turning to the bearded man, "You watch over the three we got here. Any of 'em gives you any trouble, slit their fuckin' throat and be done with it. We'll get our gold or we'll get our blood, one."

"Fine," the bearded man said, "that'll work."

For all his talk, Adina saw the leader, Drost, hesitate, staring at the tent flap. Then he finally screwed up his courage, "Alright, boy," he said, "let's go on and get it done." In another moment, they were gone, the tent flap falling closed behind them.

The screams finally cut off, and Adina swallowed hard. She didn't know what the men thought was out there, but she was afraid of it herself. Hadn't she felt as if something was coming? Aaron and Leomin too, whatever secret it was the Parnen had kept so close to his chest, it had been clear they'd both been troubled by something. Perhaps, it had been no more than the feeling of approaching danger she'd had herself that had driven the Parnen to want to gallop the horses in the night, a thing even the poorest horseman knew as foolishness.

What, then? Were her brother's men out there, in the darkness, working their way even now toward the tent? She wished she could reach the table, put out the candle the men had left—it might as well have been a beacon to whoever or whatever was out there, leading them directly to her and Leomin. And what would she do, when it came? She was bound and helpless. Whatever or whoever was out there, it need only kill the bearded man, Rhett, then it would be able to do with Leomin and her as it would, and she did not expect that it would show mercy or kindness. Kindness did not cause such screams as that, not ever in her knowing.

She redoubled her efforts at the ropes, rubbing her wrists together faster and faster, the friction causing the braided ropes to heat, and she was unable to repress a whimper as the coarse material scraped across her bloody wrists, hot lines of pain that only grew even as her efforts rose.

Something the men had said struck her then, and she paused, gasping and whimpering and glanced at the front of the tent near the opening where a tarp covered something. She'd taken it, at first, as a piece of furniture, a man-height chest, perhaps, though it had seemed strange to her that the slavers would make such an effort to carry along something that wasn't necessary. Now, she suspected it wasn't a chest at all, but a cage. And inside it, another person who'd fallen victim to her captors, no doubt some other innocent that had been going about his or her life only to be snatched away from their family and all they cared about in the night, destined to be sold into slavery or worse.

"Gods, help me please," she whispered, pleading not just for herself but for Leomin and the unidentified stranger too, as she started rubbing at the ropes once more. She'd been at it for no more than a few minutes when another scream came.

She turned to stare at the bearded man, still holding his club, still staring at the tent flap, and she felt a hate she'd rarely felt before. Whatever was out there, if it got her and Leomin, if it had *already* got Aaron, it would be this man's fault, his and those with him. They were the ones that had taken Adina and Leomin, *they* were the ones who had tied her and the Parnen to the ground, left them as helpless prey to whatever may come.

"What do you think, Rhett," she said once the screams had died down, "it is Rhett, isn't it? I don't know about you, but that sounded an awful lot like your young friend to me."

"Shut the fuck up," the big man growled, his eyes never leaving the tent flap.

"Why?" Adina asked, "What are you going to do, Rhett? Kill me? It seems to me that whatever is out there is doing plenty enough killing for all of us, don't you think?"

"I said shut your damned mouth," the bearded man growled, snatching a quick look back at her before turning back to the front of the tent.

There was another scream then, hoarse and loud, a man's scream. "And that one?" Adina asked, "Drost, wasn't it? I think, maybe, Drost's slaving days are over. If you ask me, I'm thinking you're all alone. Your best bet, the way I see it, is to let us all go. Whatever it is, it wouldn't be able to catch all of us, not if we were all running in opposite directions."

The bearded man didn't answer, but Adina saw his body tense.

"Or not," Adina said as the man, Drost's, screams died away. "How many men did you leave out there, Rhett? It's all a little foggy to me, what with the blow to the head, but there were three, weren't there? It seems like I remember three. All gone now, along with Drost and the boy, but I'm sure that's okay. Whatever is coming, I'm sure *you* can handle it where the five of them failed. I'm sure it'll be as scared of that club you're carrying as you are of it."

Rhett turned around then, his eyes wild, his teeth bared. "I told you to shut your fucking mouth, bitch. Whatever it is, you ain't goin to have to worry about it—you'll be dead 'fore it gets here." With that, he started toward her. He slapped her across the mouth again, and Adina cried out, her ears ringing, her eyes watering in pain.

Then he raised the club, and Adina lashed out with the one hand she'd managed to free in her struggles, striking him between the legs as hard as she could. It wasn't as hard as she would have liked, her position allowing her little leverage, but it was enough to hear a satisfying howl of pain from the bearded man as he stumbled back, his free hand going to his fruits. "You fucking bitch," he said.

Adina looked at him squirming and smiled past her bloody lip, "Yeah, you said that already."

While the man moaned, bent nearly double in his pain, Adina set about trying to free her other hand, pulling at the rope. It should have been an easy thing, accomplished in a matter of minutes, but she didn't *have* minutes, and the awkward angle coupled with the slick blood coating her wrist and the rope made it more difficult, and she watched, anxiously, as the man recovered and straightened once more.

"You're goin' to pay for that."

"Oh?" Adina asked, her mouth working before her mind caught up, wanting to say something, anything, to keep the man talking, "and here I thought we'd been getting along so well."

"Funny," the man said, stepping toward her once more and raising the club he carried, "wonder how funny you'll be when you're missing all your teeth."

"Funnier looking, I suspect," she said, working furiously at the rope, "still, you've nothing to worry about. I've a long way to go before I'm any competition for you. Tell me, is your nose *really* that big or is that some kind of disguise? And the smell," she said, shaking her head, struggling to keep her face calm while her heart galloped in her chest. "Well, I don't suppose the smell is funny, exactly. Scary though, I'll give you that."

The man growled and took a step closer.

""Wait," Adina said "hold on, Rhett. You can bash my teeth in in a minute, can't you? No need to be in a hurry about it. Tell me, I'm curious, what were you all planning to do with us? Where were you taking us anyway?"

"You think I don't know what you're doin'?" He asked with a smirk, "Oh, it's plain enough. You think to distract me, get me talkin' till maybe someone comes along to save you or that thing outside does your work for you. You might as well forget about it—I'm not as stupid as all that."

He started to raise the club again, "Don't sell yourself short, Rhett," she blurted, "If you ask me, you're the stupidest man I ever met." *What? Keep him talking woman don't make him angrier.* The man's expression drew down into a deep frown, "I mean to say," Adina said, her mind racing, "that is, except your friends that is. You are *much* smarter than them."

He cocked his head to the side, studying her, and she went on, "Well, I can't be certain about the owner of those screams we heard earlier, but I think you and I both are fairly sure. Considering that anything making a sound like that has to be dying, I'd say it's safe to assume that the others have went to meet Salen, are most likely even now being led across the Fields of the Dead. You see? They're dead, and you're alive—speaks a lot to you being the best of the lot in the intelligence department. And even if you weren't, well, at this point it's safe to assume you get the title by default, if nothing else."

"Enough talk," The man said, raising his club for the third time.

"Rhett, wait, let's—" but he *wasn't* waiting, that was sure. Instead, he grabbed her hair with his left hand and slammed the back of her head into the wooden stake hard enough to make Adina's teeth snap together.

Adina closed her eyes, praying for the gods to look after Aaron and Leomin, as well as the stranger in the covered cage. She winced, expecting a blow and then heard the man, Rhett, cry out in pain. Her eyes snapped open, and she looked up, a gasp of surprise escaping her at what she saw.

Aaron, or at least, she thought it was Aaron—in the shadows of the poorly illuminated tent and covered as he was in a hooded cloak it was hard to tell for sure—had lunged forward, his blade neatly piercing the bigger man's bicep. For a moment frozen in time, they stood there, the bearded man staring in shock at the steel impaling his arm. Then the figure—and surely it *had* to be Aaron, yet there was something about the way it stood, it moved, that reminded her of some animal, a wolf maybe—pulled the blade free in and, in one quick motion, his leg flew up, planting a kick in the big man's stomach that sent him stumbling backward until he tripped and fell to the ground.

The bearded man stared at the cloaked figure before him, its face in shadow. He took in the bloody sword it held. Then he screamed.

"Oh not yet," the figure said, "don't scream yet. We're just getting started." And although Adina could hear Aaron's voice in those words, she heard something else, too. It wasn't the familiar voice she knew—full of sarcasm and cleverness, confidence and fatalism. This voice, this one was different. It made her think of dark places and dark things, of blood pooling on slick cobbles, of people running and screaming, of children crying and looking for their parents. It was a voice devoid of mercy or kindness, the voice of a true killer, one who enjoyed his work.

The big man's eyes went wide at that, a feral fear coming in them as, Adina thought, he remembered the sounds his friends had made. He grabbed the club from where it had fallen near him and lurched to his feet, his eyes wild. "Come on then, you fucker," he said, "come on and let's get it done."

Adina could see little of Aaron's face with the hood that covered it and the ruddy, orange light, but she saw enough to see his mouth twist into a wide smile. He started forward then, and Adina watched the short exchange in amazement and something very much like horror. The bearded man swung his club wildly, shouting with the effort, and Aaron darted to the side, almost too fast to see, the club whistling by his face even as his blade reached out almost casually and slid through the flesh of the bigger man's calf.

Rhett screamed again, swinging his club again, desperate now, and Aaron was little more than a blur as he sidestepped, his foot lashing out and catching the bigger man in the midriff. Rhett fell backward, landing on his back on the small table. He tried to rise, but before he could move, Aaron was there. It seemed to Adina as if the bigger man was moving in slow motion, and he'd barely even begun to rise before Aaron was on him. Aaron punched him in the face, stunning him, as his other hand reached beneath his cloak and came out with a short, cruel-looking knife. Before the bearded man could recover, Aaron stretched one of the man's hands out so that it lay flat against the table and with one quick, savage motion, he drove the blade down into the flesh of the big man's palm, pinning it to the table.

Aaron's back was to Adina now, but he stared at the pinned hand for several seconds while Rhett screamed as if studying it and deciding whether or not it was to his satisfaction, oblivious or unmoved by the big man's distress. Finally, he nodded slowly then turned back to meet the big man's face.

"You and your friends, you took something that's mine," Aaron said in that not-Aaron voice again.

"M-mister," The bearded man stammered, and Adina saw that his lower lip was trembling as if at any moment he would break into weeping, "I'm ... I'm sorry, okay? Look man, we didn't *know*. Shit," he said, gasping in pain, "Gods, I'm hurtin' here, man."

Aaron cocked his head, turning it enough that Adina could see one side of his face. By some trick of the orange, flickering light, what bit of his face she could see seemed almost demonic, and she felt fear rising in her. Fear for herself but also fear for Aaron, for what he might do. "Hurting?" Aaron said in the voice that was not his own, "You think this is pain?" He shook his head slowly, "No. You know nothing of pain. But you will. Before we're done, you will."

The big man's face was a mask of terror, and he grunted as he swung his free arm at Aaron. Aaron didn't bother turning as he caught the arm and slammed it down on the table. He produced a second knife from behind his cloak and drove it into the man's hand, pinning it to the table as he had the first.

Then he took a step back, an artist examining his work. "Your friends," He said, oblivious of the bearded man's screams, "should have taken better care of their blades." He nodded his head at one of the knives. "The damp works on the blade, if it isn't cleaned and treated. Gets in to it, makes it lose its edge, makes it rust." He considered that for a moment then shrugged, "Doesn't matter. The blades are poor quality, but they will serve."

Adina found that she couldn't watch anymore. She opened her mouth to say something, to get Aaron's attention, but found, to her surprise, that for a moment words wouldn't come. It was as if she was scared to speak, scared to draw his attention. Stupid, of course. This was *Aaron,* after all. Whatever else they were to each other, they were friends, that at least. The man had saved her life on more occasions than she could easily count, had risked his own to do it, had *nearly* died doing it, in fact. Why, then, did she find it so hard to make the words come?

"Alright then," Aaron was saying. "Let's get started." Without any hesitation, his sword moved in a blur, too fast for Adina to follow, returning to hang down by his side so quickly that she was almost convinced that he hadn't moved at all.

At least, that was, until she heard the big man bellow in pain, her eyes going wide as she saw his dismembered foot lying on the ground. *Gods,* she thought, *that's not—how did he—*her thoughts cut off, her mind not knowing how to finish them. Rhett screamed, and Aaron laughed, loud, body-shaking laughs, and Adina stared in shock, her mouth moving soundlessly.

Then the sword flashed again, and the bearded man's other foot fell to the ground beside the first in a shower of blood. Spittle flew from Rhett's mouth as he screamed and whimpered, and Aaron glanced down, studying the two feet. "Going to make walking damn tough," Aaron said, a dark amusement in his tone. "Well, never mind. You won't be needing them anyway. See what you shouldn't have done, you shouldn't have taken them. They were mine, friend," he said, pacing back and forth in front of the bearded man, his hands clasped behind his back, his sword at an angle to the floor. "And you know as well as I, a man has to protect what's his. Doesn't he?"

Rhett, apparently too far gone in pain, gave no answer but his gasping, choked screams.

"Ah well," Aaron said, moving toward him once again and bringing his sword out from behind his back.

Adina knew she couldn't watch anymore, couldn't see this happen, and she managed to finally find her voice, *"Aaron, no,"* she said. It came out as little more than a croak, but he spun with incredible swiftness and, in an instant, he was looking down at her. Adina swallowed hard, suddenly wishing she'd said nothing as she stared at the cruelty, the hate that seemed big enough to encompass the entire world, swimming in his gaze. For a moment, she was sure that he was going to attack her, was going to do to her what he'd done to the bearded man.

Then, in an instant, the anger and hate left his eyes, the thing that had been lurking there vanishing or, at least, gone back into hiding, and Aaron was staring at her, a dawning shame and horror creeping onto his face as he stared at her then looked down at his bloody hands. He looked back up at her, an expression of confusion and fear on his face that she'd never seen on the usually self-assured, confident sellsword. "Adina?" He asked.

"Yes, Aaron," she said, swallowing hard as she looked up at him, "it's me."

"I'll get you out," he said, starting to bend down, but she shook her head.

"No, Aaron, please. Check Leomin first. He hasn't moved and I'm afraid...."

"Okay," he said, his voice shaky, "alright." He turned and made his way to the Parnen, putting two fingers to the man's throat. He waited for several moments then nodded, "He has a strong heartbeat," he said, turning back to Adina, "they must have just hit him a good one to the head. He'll be up and about before long."

179

Then he was down beside her, untying the rope, "Ah, gods, your wrists."

Adina, suddenly anxious to have Aaron so close to her, glanced at the man that still whimpered on the table, blood pouring freely from the two stumps where his feet had once been. "It ... could be worse."

Then he was helping her up, pulling her to her feet. Once there, his expression of relief vanished, turning into one of shame again, and he jerked his hands away from her. For a moment, they only stood staring at each other, neither sure of what to say.

But as Adina looked at him, she knew that *this*, for now, was the Aaron she knew. The one who'd been willing to give his life for her and others on so many occasions, the man whom she'd grown to care for. To care deeply for and, if she was being honest, quite a bit more than that. In another moment, she was wrapping her arms around him, holding him tight against her.

"Thank the gods you're okay," he said.

She laughed, a short, breathy, nervous laugh. "I thought you didn't like the gods."

"Well," he said, leaning his head against her shoulder, "Thank them anyway."

In that embrace, Adina could almost forget the sight of him standing over the helpless man, reveling in his pain and fear. Almost. She pulled him closer, as if by doing so she could somehow deny or forget the darkness she'd seen in his eyes. "*Rhett,*" a voice hissed, and suddenly the young man was pushing his way inside the tent, "we've got to get the fuck ou—" He cut off, noticing Aaron and Adina standing there. His eyes went wide and wild with terror as he glanced at his friend lying on the table, now dead, before looking back at Aaron. "Oh gods, no," he said, "no, no, please...."

Adina held her breath, glancing at Aaron, but he only stared at the boy, an amused expression on his face, as if he recognized him but couldn't remember from where.

Satisfied that Aaron remained Aaron, she turned back to the boy and gasped as she saw him more clearly in the candle light. He was shaking heavily as he stood staring at Aaron with wild eyes. The youth's shirt was ragged and torn, and he bled from several cuts, two of which looked dangerously deep.

Aaron continued to watch the youth with that confused expression on his face, the look of a man who'd just realized that what he'd taken for a dream was reality in truth. He didn't move even when the kid rushed forward and threw the tarp on the cage up, drawing a rusty knife and holding it against the throat of the figure inside. "Not one step closer. One step closer, and I'll slit her fuckin' throat, I swear by the gods I will, mister."

"Do I know you?" Aaron asked, and Adina felt her heart go out at the confusion and uncertainty in the sellsword's voice.

The youth looked close to tears, and he held the knife closer to the figure's throat, his hand shaking, "Don't, don't play with me, man. It was you did *this*," he said, glancing at the cuts all over his chest and arms, "now I swear it, come any closer and she dies."

"She?" Aaron asked, frowning as he stared past the youth to the figure in the cage. Adina followed his gaze, frowning herself. It took her a moment to be sure, the light as poor as it was, but there was no question that the figure inside of the cage wasn't a woman at all but a man. He was thin, nearly to the point of emaciation, and wore no shirt. He stared at the knife at his throat as if frozen, his blue eyes sparkling in the lantern light.

"*Wait,*" Aaron said, his words coming out in a whisper, "it can't be. Owen? Is that you?"

The youth, uncertain, turned and glanced back, recoiling and letting out a cry of surprise. "What the fuck? Who are you? What happened to the—" He would have no doubt said more but just then the man in the cage snatched the knife from his hand and buried it in the youth's neck.

The slaver grunted in surprise, stumbling away, his hands going to his neck where jets of crimson shot out in bursts. He tried to speak, but his words came out as wet, gurgling, unintelligible sounds and in another moment he crumpled to the ground and was still.

Adina stared in shock at the dead man then at the man inside of the cage who stared at her calmly, his hands gripping two of the bars, his dark brown eyes meeting her own before turning to Owen. *Wait a minute,* Adina thought, feeling confused and out of sorts herself now, the man's eyes had been blue. She'd been sure of it. Now, though, they appeared to be a brown so dark as to be almost black. She blinked, squinting in the candle light, but the man's eyes remained that dark shade of brown.

"Owen?" Aaron said again, and before she could catch him, he collapsed to his knees, his shoulders slumping. "It can't be."

Adina dropped down beside him, grabbing him in her arms, "Aaron, what's wrong?" She let out a gasp as she noted that the front of him was covered in blood. He'd been turned with his back to the light before, and she hadn't been able to see it. Now, though, she glanced down and saw a slender length of wood protruding from his stomach. It took her a moment, so unsuspected the sight was, before she realized that it must be an arrow, the end of which he'd broken off.

"Aaron," she said, "oh no, you've been shot."

Aaron glanced down at the arrow sticking out of him as if he had no idea of how it had gotten there. Then he met her eyes, his gaze troubled. "I ... I don't remember."

***

Aaron felt light headed, *wrong* somehow, as if he'd been used up, stretched thin. The last hour or two felt like a dream he'd had, one that he'd forgotten upon waking. He remembered finding what had been Leomin's guard post, remembered finding the blood from where the man had obviously been injured and that was all. The rest was nothing more than vague, confusing flashes of darkness and the shapes of the trees around him, of men brandishing weapons at him. Nothing that told him what had happened.

He glanced over at the man in the cage and felt goose bumps rise on his skin. "Owe—" he started, then the darkness that had been lurking at the corner of his vision surged forward, pushing its way into his thoughts and mind. He turned to Adina, knowing he had little time. He was either dying or losing consciousness and from the way he felt, it could go either way. "Horses ...." He said "Out back, behind the tent. Twenty yards, no more than thirty."

She nodded, swallowing hard, and he saw tears of concern and worry winding their way down her face. *No,* he thought, *don't cry. Not for me.* Still, there was something else in her blue eyed gaze too. Something, he thought, like fear. Fear of him, maybe. He turned once more to the man in the cage and saw the face of his friend from so many years ago, a friend he'd been sure had been killed. That face looked back at him, devoid of any expression, the eyes dark brown like he'd remembered, but giving nothing away. In his blurry vision and coupled with the poor light of the candle, the man's face almost seemed to writhe in the undulating shadows like a thing alive. It was a dark, disturbing image, and it was the one he carried with him, into the darkness.

CHAPTER TWENTY-TWO

"But the men, sire—"

"I will not hear another word about it, Caldwell," Belgarin said. "Or has your arrogance grown so great that you suppose you possess knowledge even *he* does not?" Belgarin immediately regretted the slip as those seated at the table shared curious glances. As powerful as those seated around him were, they knew nothing of the Knower, the creature who was no doubt even now poisoning and twisting the mind of the little girl tending to him, and Belgarin intended to keep it that way.

For his part, the advisor lowered his bald head, taking a moment to grab a silver pitcher from the table and refill Belgarin's wine cup. Belgarin frowned at the man, but he took a big drink of the wine anyway, liking the way the drink soothed his throat at first and his mind at last. He'd been drinking a lot of late and no true wonder, that. Even the best men could find themselves, at times, overwhelmed by such scheming and betrayal as he had been forced to endure over the last few years.

"I only seek to advise you, your Majesty," Caldwell said, "as is my duty."

Belgarin grunted at that and reclined back in his chair at the head of the dining table, taking another drink and glowering at those seated around him. Five men and a woman and not one he could trust.

To his right, Claudius, the highest ranking noble in Baresh and once regent until handing the kingdom over after Eladen's unfortunate accident, wiped pastry crumbs from his ample chin. "Your Majesty," he said, his voice a high shrill that always set Belgarin's teeth on edge, "I do not wish to overstep," *Yet you will,* Belgarin thought, "but I must admit that I find myself in agreement with your advisor."

That I do not doubt, Belgarin thought. Glancing between the fat man and Caldwell, *and just what was the cost of your agreement, I wonder?* "Oh?" He said aloud, and some of his buried anger must have come out in his tone for the others gathered at the table shared nervous looks, the fat man himself swallowing hard and refusing to meet Belgarin's angry stare. "Do tell, Claudius," he said, "I do *so* appreciate your counsel."

"Yes, well," the fat man said, rubbing his hands together, though whether in anxiety or an effort to rid himself of pastry crumbs, Belgarin could not have said for sure. "That is, I believe it may be wise for you to consolidate your position here in Baresh for a time. The guilds truly are quite remarkable, and I think there is much benefit and profit we can gain. I spoke to your brother, Eladen, about this once before, but he would not hear reason. If we were to take a year, perhaps two—"

"*Benefit,*" Belgarin spat, "*Profit.* You are a fat man, Claudius, and you have a fat man's thoughts. Wars are won with men and steel and courage. Not profit, and you will not speak of my brother again."

"Forgive me, my king," the only woman at the table said and all eyes turned to look at her—though most didn't have to turn far. Maladine Caulia was a beautiful woman; there was no denying that. "But as the representative of The Golden Oars bank, I feel that it is my duty to interject here, if I may."

Belgarin sighed heavily. *Representative, indeed,* he thought. Beautiful, alright. Beautiful and imperious and cold. He'd had occasion to learn as much the one time he'd bedded her. Not the most pleasant bedding he'd had despite the woman's beauty. She was all business, participating in the act of lovemaking like it was some transaction to be finished as efficiently and quickly as possible. A cold beauty, sure, as cold and hard as the coins her bank supplied and just as alluring. If he needed any proof of that, he could find it easily enough in the eyes of the men at the table as they watched her.

"Very well, Maladine," he said, "let us hear your side of it, though I think I might know it just as well without you speaking. As for being a representative," he grunted, "perhaps. Though I find it as likely that you own the damn bank, everyone in it too, no doubt."

The woman put a thin-fingered hand to her ample chest, shaking her head with a small smile, the kind of smile that always put Belgarin in the mind of some masterpiece. Not only that it was nice—though it was—but that it was cold and distant. A thing belonging to a painting, not a person. "My king does me too much service, I'm afraid," she said, "I am not worthy of such a post, of course, my masters far wiser and more intelligent than I."

Belgarin frowned, "Speaking of those masters," he said, "I have still not heard from them. Not one of them has so much as even deigned to *meet* their king. Were I a less patient man, Maladine, I might find myself offended."

The woman smiled, and unlike the others at the table, if she feared his displeasure, she did not show it. "My king, I understand that my masters' anonymity might seem ... strange, but know that they are fully dedicated to and invested in your victory. I do not mean to be crass, but the gold they have loaned you so far—"

"Enough," Belgarin said, waving the matter away angrily, "I know well enough what their *contribution* has been, woman. You need not remind me."

She bowed her head, "Of course, my lord."

By the look on her face, it was clear that she would speak further, so Belgarin waved her on. "Go on then. Out with it."

"Of course, my king. It is only ... though you were, of course, correct in your statement, that wars are won with soldiers and swords, I must remind the king that steel is not free, nor the armor for men or horses, nor the food they eat, even the water they drink has a cost. Wars might be won with soldiers, my king, but soldiers are fed and clothed and armed with coin."

Belgarin nodded, expecting something similar. "So you, too, then would caution patience? You would have me wait until my sister Adina has raised an army against me and only then set forth? Does that seem wise strategy to you?"

"Of course, my lord," she said, bowing her head, "I, as a woman, know little of such things—" *Bullshit,* Belgarin thought, "the art of warfare being a man's art. I do not claim to know the danger should your sister meet with your remaining brother Ellemont or your sister Isabelle. Military campaigns, strategy and tactics are, I'm afraid, too complex for a simple woman such as I am. Perhaps," she said, turning to General Fannen, "the general might be able to speak with more intelligence than I." *Not likely,* Belgarin thought.

The general was a little over fifty years old now, an age only reflected in the hard lines on his face, and the gray, short-cropped hair on his head. He sat erect in his seat, stiff and formal in his military dress uniform, his posture displaying, to Belgarin's mind, that strange breed of vanity of which only a lifelong military man seems capable. "My lady?" He asked, turning to her, his head seeming to swivel on his neck independently of the rest of his body. "Do you seek my opinion?"

Obviously, you pompous fool, Belgarin thought but held himself in check, barely.

"Indeed," Maladine purred, "Surely, one as experienced and knowledgeable about the art of warfare as yourself might have some opinion on the matter."

The general remained stiff, his expression impassive, but Belgarin saw the pleasure at the woman's compliment in his eyes clear enough. "Ah, my lady, I admit that I have some little knowledge on the subject."

"*Well?*" Belgarin demanded, "why don't you share what little knowledge that is, General Fannen, before we all die of old age?"

The general cleared his throat, straightening his tunic as if the damned thing wasn't already as straight and stiff as a board. "Forgive me, my king, only I had not expected for my opinion to be sought on the matter and had not thought to speak on it."

Then what the fuck are you doing here? "Well," Belgarin said, forcing himself to keep his temper. Fools or not, those seated around him were all powerful men and women in their own right, any one of which could cause him problems in the future, should they choose. "Let us acknowledge that you now *have* been asked for your opinion."

"Very well," the general said, nodding his head once. "On the matter of your sister, Adina, I cannot speak with any certitude, but as for the army, I think, perhaps, I might. We have arrived in

Baresh no more than a month gone. The men were long at sea on the journey here and some of them, I'll admit, fell victim to sickness on the long voyage."

As you yourself did, Belgarin thought, smiling as he remembered the sight of the normally so well-comported and polished general bent over the side of the flagship vomiting, his face a shade of green Belgarin hadn't known existed. "Yes," he said, still smiling, "some of the men had a hard time of it, didn't they?"

The general cleared his throat, his posture growing somehow even more stiff—an event Belgarin would have thought impossible. "Yes, my king. If asked for my opinion, I would say that the men might do well with some time to rest and gather themselves. It was an arduous journey and to set forth to battle again so soon ... it could affect morale."

"Time to rest and gather themselves," Belgarin said. "Time to whore and dice and drink, you mean. And do not think I haven't taken note of those young ladies—some barely of age at all, I've heard—who've graced your own chambers of late."

The general went crimson at that, his hands that had to this point been sat flat on the table, visibly tensed. Belgarin laughed, "Oh yes, Fannen, I know of your nightly interludes, and I do not begrudge you them. I wonder, though, how you manage to get your cock into anything and still maintain the creases of your pants, the part of your hair."

"My king," the general grated, "As your loyal servant, surely I do not deserve—"

Belgarin slammed his hand onto the table and several of the wine glasses tipped and spilled onto the white tablecloth. Servants rushed forward from the sides of the room and set about cleaning it, but Belgarin ignored them in his anger. "*Deserve? Deserve,* you say to me, general? As the firstborn, I do not *deserve* to have to fight a war for a kingdom that should rightfully be mine. As the heir to the throne of Telrear, I do not *deserve* to sit in this frozen fucking wasteland of a kingdom, freezing my ass off while I listen to a bunch of fools yammer on as if their opinions matter in the least."

The room grew quiet then, and the general stared at the tablecloth, sitting rigidly, not meeting the king's eyes. *Too far,* Belgarin thought wearily, wiping a hand through his hair, *too far.*

You need these men, you know that. Why do you always breaks things? He did not want to apologize to them—they *were* fools, after all—but he would. He would do much, if it was necessary. He sighed heavily, "Forgive me, gentlemen, lady," he said, nodding his head to each of them in turn. "My words were unfair and ill-spoken, and I ask that you forget them as quick as you may. It is only that I have found myself stressed of late. The rigors and troubles of being king sometimes are a heavy burden, indeed. Please," he said, motioning to the silver platters of food and pitchers of wine laid out before them, "eat your fill, drink and let us forget it. I value your counsel, one and all."

"Now, general," he said, once they'd started eating and drinking once more, "please, continue."

The general nodded, though the man was clearly still angry, "Of course, my king. It is my humble opinion that the men could use some time to rest and recuperate. Also, I would like time to work with the soldiers of Baresh as well, to incorporate them into the army, and such things take time. I would advise a march in two years' time."

"Two years," Belgarin said flatly.

"Yes, my lord," The general said, and Belgarin did not miss the glance he shot at Caldwell still standing at Belgarin's side, "Two years would be, in my estimation, the most propitious time. It would give the men much needed rest, and give us time to work with and train the Bareshian soldiers."

Belgarin grunted, "Thanks for your wisdom, general," he managed. "And you, High Priest? What are your thoughts on the matter?"

The High Priest, a doddering old man, seemed to start at the sound of Belgarin's voice as if he'd been sleeping with his eyes open—something that wouldn't have surprised Belgarin in the slightest. "I'm sorry forgive me," he said, "I had taken a moment to commune with the gods," he said in his holiest voice, though Belgarin didn't miss the yawn that was hidden beneath it, "they operate on their own time, of course, not that of us mortals."

"I'm sure," Belgarin said. He was also fairly sure that the High Priest communed with the gods about as much as fish communed with men—which was to say not at all. An old liar. Still, harmless enough, in his way. Just so long as the man wasn't trusted to make a decision about anything that mattered. "I was asking," Belgarin continued, reminding himself to be patient, "what your thoughts were on the army. Specifically, leading them against my sister Isabelle, the place where, my sources tell me, my wayward sister Adina travels even now, hoping to raise an army against me."

The old man's nod tried for sage and landed on vacuous. "Yes, yes," he said in what Belgarin suspected was an effort to buy time to work his way through what had been said. "I see. Well, urgency is a mortal affair, not of the gods and certainly not for them. The only right way to move is to move when it is right." He nodded deeply as if he'd just said something profound or, perhaps, as if he was growing sleepy once more.

"I see," Belgarin grated, "though I wonder if you couldn't be a little more specific. After all, not all of us are as close to the gods as you yourself and some of us, perhaps, might not fully understand the message left in their—and in *your*, of course—wisdom."

The High Priest shifted in his seat, obviously uncomfortable. "Ah, of course, your Majesty," he said, clearing his throat. "That is, it is my belief that the gods, in their might and wisdom, will show us a sign as to the best time of our moving but that such a time has not yet come."

Belgarin had to bite his tongue at that. So often holy men and holy women spoke of signs and wonders to be shown. What was a dead beetle to some was, to others, an omen of great portent—for ill or for good depending on who you spoke to. Signs, he thought, were an easy enough thing to find when you went looking. Made all the easier by the fact that people who disagreed were only not as holy as you yourself. He believed in the gods, of course. It was the right—mandated by the gods themselves in fact—that he fought for to earn his rightful inheritance. Still, he had little time for priests and all their words that meant nothing, words as insubstantial as air and of much less use.

"And what has the Merchant guild to say on the matter?" Belgarin asked, turning to Nigel, the guild's head. The man was young for such a post, not having seen his fourth decade, but he was said to have a skill with money. Almost, it was said, being able to create it out of thin air like some magician doing a show. "I suppose your opinion might mirror that of our dear Maladine?"

The young man smiled, taking a moment to enjoy the attention of everyone in the room, running a hand through his hair, the fingers so bedecked with heavy rings that Belgarin could hardly believe the man could lift it. He was the opposite of Maladine in so many ways. While she wore a simple, though elegant dress, her only adornment that of a fine, simple silver chain about her neck, Nigel wore the most ostentatious clothes Belgarin had ever seen outside, perhaps, of a mummer's show. Thickly ruffled white sleeves emerged from a rich, cream colored tunic, each finger bearing a ring with a separate colored stone. Enough wealth on his person to make Belgarin begin to believe that the rumors about his ability with coin must be true. Either way, he didn't like the man. You could dress snakes up in motley, if you chose, but snakes they remained. Or, maybe better to call the man a peacock and remove all doubt.

Nigel took his moment, nodding to each person at the table in turn like some magician in truth, warming up the crowd and acknowledging his audience. Belgarin was just about to lose his patience when the young man spoke, "I think," he said in a voice that was soft and cultured, "that such a decision is no easy one. I thank all that have spoken thus far—your wisdom and knowledge is humbling and, of course, I thank you, your Majesty for giving me the chance—"

"Yes, yes," Belgarin said, "get on with it."

The man smiled as if at a joke and nodded, "Of course, my king. It is my opinion that there are benefits to both courses of action. True, in a year, or two years' time, we would be better prepared, better equipped. But my life in the guild has always been one of taking chances, of weighing the risk against the reward, calculating the odds. We do not know where your sister Isabelle stands, currently. True, it is more than likely that she will raise her armies against us, but it is possible that she will bend the knee when we arrive at her castle gates. After all, from what I hear your sister is no fool—nor would I expect her to be," he added hurriedly, "being of such a fine and noble birth as she is. She has well seen, no doubt, what has befallen those who have opposed you. It would be quite surprising, I think, for her to offer resistance were you to be at her gates with an army behind you in a matter of weeks. But," he said, meeting each person's eyes in turn, his gaze seeming to linger on

Caldwell for a moment, "given time? Given two years to muster her forces, to recruit new soldiers and, of course, the whole while your sister whispering in her ear?" He shook his head, "that, my lords and ladies, seems to me an equation all too easy to solve."

Belgarin saw Caldwell frown the slightest bit and smiled in answer. *Ah, Caldwell. One opinion you could not buy, I suspect. What need a man of gold when he is already wealthier than most kingdoms?* Or, perhaps his advisor *had* paid the man. Yes, he preferred to think that was the way it had gone. *I could have told you, Caldwell,* he thought, *never trust a merchant once you open your purse strings.* "Your suggestion then?" Belgarin said, turning back to the head of the merchant's guild.

"For me," the man said, "and with all respect to those present, I find that the wisest course of action would be to act and act decisively, your Majesty. Do not give your sister time to work her wiles—for I have heard that she is adept at bringing people to her cause. As for the money?" He smiled at Maladine, the representative of the bank, but she would not meet his eyes. He shrugged finally, "Well. It will be found, of course."

Belgarin nodded, pretending to consider. "Very well," he said to the room at large, "that decides it. We will march in six months' time. Prepare, gentlemen and ladies. I want this war finished before two years have passed."

"Your Majesty, if I could have a chance to talk," said the one man Belgarin had not acknowledged. Belgarin glanced where Savrin sat. The man was thin—not the kind of thin that bespoke sickness or fragility, but the kind of whipcord leanness that seemed shared by all fencers and assassins. He was known to be a fencer—one of great renown, undefeated, in fact—and he was the current captain of Belgarin's household guard. A decision he had made on Caldwell's advice and insistence and one that Belgarin seemed to regret on a daily basis. Oh, the man was competent enough. His swordplay was quickly becoming legend, and he spoke with a surety and calmness that bespoke of complete confidence in his own ability. A good man to run the household guard, except for the problem that Belgarin was quite certain he was Caldwell's creature.

"The decision, I'm afraid, has already been made, Savrin, though I do appreciate you attending," Belgarin said. He nodded,

"Very well," he said by way of dismissal and those gathered rose, the fat Duke Claudius grabbing a handful of pastries as he did, "I'm sure we all have much that we should be about."

Belgarin watched them all file out, Caldwell included, then sat back and took another drink of wine. *Soon, mother,* he thought. *Soon, you will see—I do not always break things. Not always.*

CHAPTER TWENTY-THREE

Caldwell made sure he was the first out of the dining hall and stopped at the end of the castle hallway, watching the others file past. They each nodded to him in turn, troubled expressions in their eyes, and he wanted to scream at the fools for their transparency. The knowing nods were bad enough, the looks of defeat that they tried to share with him worse still. The king might have his suspicions—no, not might, the man was suspicious and that was a fact—but he didn't *know*. It had been a risk, so blatantly bribing and cajoling the members of the counsel to recommend waiting, but he'd had no choice. His master had spoken, and so he had obeyed. It was not his duty to question the wisdom of such a course of action. Still, he regretted that the king would now be suspicious. A pompous, self-absorbed fool and, lately, a drunken one too, but even a fool will understand much if given time and cause enough.

The head of the merchant's guild, Nigel, moved past, a smug smile on his face, casually waving a ring-bedecked hand at Caldwell as he went by. It was an effort to keep the mask of passivity in place, yet keep it he did. The boy seemed to think it all a game, to think that having a head for numbers, for bargains and sales could keep him safe, but he would learn differently and soon.

Behind Nigel came Savrin
, walking in that casual, almost lazy swagger that he had. He, too, was a fool, but that was alright. Fools could be used. A smith didn't wonder at the intelligence of the hammer when he used it,

didn't care for knowing its thoughts, only wanted to strike the metal, to shape it and form it. Such tools could be useful, so long as they were understood. Of course, this tool was not a hammer at all but a blade and few better. "Captain Savrin," Caldwell said, nodding his head. "I wonder if I might trouble you to walk with me for a moment."

The captain of the guard nodded his head as he approached, "Of course, Advisor. I'm to check on the guards' training, see that they've learned which end of the sword is the pointy one, that sort of thing, if you'd care to accompany me."

They made their way through the castle hallways talking about innocuous things: thoughts on the upcoming battles, the weather, the fine food that had been offered at the king's table. Inane chatter but necessary. The king had his own eyes and his own ears in the castle, though the fool didn't know Caldwell was aware of each of them. Had spent his time getting to know their strengths and their weaknesses, their vulnerabilities, for such time as his master gave him leave to have them silenced.

Eventually, they came upon the training grounds where mens' breath plumed in the air as they exchanged blows with practice swords, the edges of the blades dulled, most covered in sweat despite the cool air of the morning.

Between the shouts of men and the steady ring of dulled steel, the clearing was a raucous tumult of sound. Any ears that might be listening would have to be close indeed to hear over the cacophony. "What would you have of me, Advisor?" The captain of the guard asked, studying the movements of those arrayed before him with a slight expression of disdain on his face.

"Well," Caldwell said, "the king's decision is not the one I would have liked it to be, nor is it what our mutual acquaintance would have wanted."

"Yeah," Savrin said, "well, the drunken bastard wouldn't even let me speak. I'll tell you, I was tempted to carve a piece of his hide—"

"*Shut your mouth, fool*" Caldwell hissed, "Someone could hear you, even here."

The assassin turned casually, crooking an eyebrow at him.

"There are not many, advisor, who have called me fool to my face and lived to speak of it. A man in your position, unarmed as you are, might be wise to consider that the next time you open your mouth to chastise me. As for our mutual *acquaintance,* he isn't here, is he? And even if he were, what of it? With a blade in my hand, there is no man alive that I fear, Caldwell. Remember that."

Caldwell forced his expression back to its normal passivity. If he could deal with Belgarin's blather and mockery without losing his patience, surely he could deal with this ignorant wretch. "Threats?" He said, "Do you think to threaten me, Savrin? I will give my life, gladly, if it is what is required for our mutual *master.* And unarmed, am I?" He shrugged, "With blades, perhaps. I have never taken the time to learn the knowledge of them and care little for it. But I am not without my own weapons, Savrin. Yes, you strike an imposing figure there, with your sword at your waist so casually, as if born to it. The men, I hear, fear you. So much so that you must force them to practice with you. It is said that men who engage in such a bout walk away injured or not at all."

Savrin smiled a small smile, "It isn't my fault the bastards don't know how to fight. It's their *job* after all."

"Yes," Caldwell said, "you are quite fearless, that cannot be denied. Confident in your own skill and bladework to protect yourself and that, it seems, is justified. I wonder, though," he said, leaning in closer so that he was speaking into the man's ear, "Does your sister share such skill?"

The captain of the guard's body went rigid at that, and his jaw clenched. Caldwell allowed himself a small smile of his own. "Oh yes, captain, we know of her. Did you really think you might keep her secret by leaving her halfway across the world?" Caldwell chuckled. "There are very few things in this world our master does not know. I wonder, do you think your sister would be able to protect herself, should men come at her in the night? What of her child? A young boy, isn't it? Three now, maybe four years old? Does *he* possess his uncle's skill with a blade?"

"You'll leave them alone," the captain said, turning to him, "they've no part in this."

"That's where you're wrong, captain," Caldwell said matter of factly. "*You* have a part in this and so, then, do they. Understand that I would happily tear into your sister and the boy both, would hold their bleeding organs before them as they died if my master willed it, or if I so much as suspected you of not doing what you're told. And if you draw that blade at your side that your fingers seem tempted to, know that I will die if that is necessary, but that your sister and your nephew will bleed out their last in screams of terrible agony while men look on and laugh."

The captain's hand froze inches from the handle of his blade, and his jaw clenched. "One day, I will kill you."

Caldwell smiled, "Ah, captain, a pleasant enough fancy, I'm sure. A dream to keep your feet on the path and that's just as well. Only, see that it stays just a dream—all men have something to lose. You just like the rest. Now, our master requires your service."

The captain of the guard studied him for several seconds, making his way to understanding that he had no options. Then, finally, the truth of the thing settling in, he frowned, "What do you need me to do?"

Caldwell nodded, satisfied, "You will go and tell the master that Belgarin marches in six months' time—no other, *you.*"

"Very well," The captain said, "is there anything else?"

Caldwell smiled, "Yes, there is. Before you go, why not pay our dear friend, Nigel, a visit. Have a little talk with him. The man must learn a lesson that money given comes with certain expectations."

The captain winced, "The boy lover? What would I have to say to him?"

"You need not do any talking at all, dear captain." He glanced at the sword at the man's hip, "Play to your strengths in this. Do you understand?"

The captain grunted, "I understand."

"Finish here and be about it," Caldwell said, "I want you gone within the hour. I will find an explanation for the king."

Savrin nodded and started away, but Caldwell stopped him with a hand on his arm, "One more thing, captain. Have your fun as you will with our dear Nigel, but it must not link back to you or to us."

"Of course," the man hissed, "I'm no fool."

Caldwell nodded, "Then prove it."

CHAPTER TWENTY-FOUR

Aaron didn't wake so much as surface from the waters of unconsciousness, a scream on his lips that he only just managed to hold back. This scream was not of pain. Or, at least, not mostly of pain. It was a scream of fear, of some sort of knowing, of being brought face to face with a dark knowledge that things were not right, had never been right, and were too far gone for saving. He couldn't remember, as he laid there, his breath coming in gasps, the nature of his dream, his nightmare. He could only remember the feeling of fear, of being studied by an evil too vast and terrible to truly understand or comprehend. For a time, he only lay with his eyes closed, relieved to have escaped whatever dark specter had haunted his dreams.

Then, slowly, he opened them. Warm hands were on his face, and he saw Adina above him, her brow creased in worry. When she noticed Aaron rousing, she bent closer, studying him. "Aaron, thank the gods. Are you okay?"

"I'm alright," Aaron said, sitting up and wincing at the soreness in his side where the arrow'd gone in. It was morning now, and he held up a hand to block the bright sun. "Where are we?"

"Still headed west," Adina said, as she went about changing the bandage on his side, "We thought it best to leave the tent and those men as quickly as we could, so we were forced to carry you on one of the horses. We only just stopped. I was scared the jostling might have upset your wound, but Pellan said he had experience in such wounds, and that you'd be okay."

Aaron frowned, "Pellan, you said?"

Adina nodded, "That's right. The man that was in the cage in the tent, his name's Pellan. He's quiet, maybe a little strange and definitely shy, but he seems kind enough. He was the one that saw to your and Leomin's wounds."

Aaron's frown grew deeper, and he remembered, in fractured images, what had happened before he'd passed out. He remembered thinking of Owen and that was strange. He hadn't seen Owen since they'd been children in the orphanage, since Master Cyrille had taken him away and beaten him to death. Strange that he would have thought of him in the state he'd been in, before unconsciousness had claimed him. Strange that he'd think of him now. Still, *Pellan* she'd said. Not the rarest of names but rare enough that he'd only ever met one. His father. "Where is this Pellan now?"

Adina glanced around the woods, "I'm not sure. He said he was going to find us something to eat—said that you and Leomin would need cooked meat to heal the fastest, but that was an hour or so ago now."

Aaron nodded slowly, thinking of the man who'd been standing in the cage in the slaver's tent. He'd only seen him for an instant and that in poor, fitful light and shadow, but there had been something familiar about the man. Something in the shape of his face that had reminded him of Owen. "Alright," he said, "help me up, will you?"

"Pellan said that you should rest and that, should you wake up before he was back, to make sure you didn't get up."

"Well, help me up anyway, Adina," he said, and she must have caught something of his thoughts in his expression because she frowned, draping one of his arms across her shoulders and helping him to his feet.

"Is everything okay, Aaron?"

"I don't know," he said, wincing as he rose, blinking in an effort to clear his lightheadedness. "I'm sure it's fine, but I'd rather be safe than sorry. Where's Leomin?"

"Ah, Mr. Envelar, welcome back to the land of the living."

With Adina's help, Aaron turned and saw the Parnen sitting a short distance away. He was propped up against a tree, smoking a pipe and blowing great smoke rings into the forest air. Aaron noted that a bandage had been wrapped tightly around his head, no easy thing considering the man's long, thick hair. "Leomin," Aaron said, surprised at the amount of relief he felt at seeing the Parnen captain alive and well. "It's good to see you up and about. When I found the blood, I thought that maybe ...." He shrugged, "Well. It's just good to see you."

Leomin smiled, displaying his white teeth, "Well, Mr. Envelar, I am up, anyway. 'About', perhaps, is another few hours off, but I thank you for your concern. I woke only a short time ago myself— there are, I find, few things more effective than a club to the head to induce a man into a deep sleep. I hear that I have you to thank for saving us. I'm sorry that I missed it."

Aaron thought back to the night before, questing at the memories like a man searching blindly in the dark, and he recoiled at what he found there. Memories of blood and screams and pain and pleasure. *Co*, he thought, *what happened last night?*

I don't know, the Virtue said, sounding lost and scared, *I don't remember, Aaron. Only pieces. I remember being angry, angrier than I've ever been. I remember, screaming? Maybe? But not in pain ... I remember ... enjoying it. This never happened to me with Eladen, nor with all those that came before. I just ... don't know.*

Aaron grunted. Much the same as himself. Pleasure and blood. "I'm glad you're okay, Leomin," he said, wanting to close off that line of conversation, not sure he wanted to remember what he'd done.

He turned back to Adina there at his side, "Are you okay?" He said.

"I'm okay," she said, a sad smile on her face. "Last night, I was afraid. For you. And Aaron," she said, her voice low and troubled, "I was also afraid *of* you."

Aaron met her eyes, saw the worry in them and made a decision. "We need to talk," he said, "I'll tell you. Everything. If you don't want me around after that, I'll understand, but you need to know. About last night ... in the barn, before. And about what happened in the tent and the woods. I don't remember everything, but what I do remember, I'll tell you."

"Yes," Leomin said, rising unsteadily to his feet and putting his hand on either of their shoulders. "We will speak, all of *us*," he said, glancing meaningfully at the two of them, "but not now. Just now, I think I hear the sound of breakfast coming."

Aaron raised his eyebrow. He'd heard nothing, had been so focused on Adina, on what he would say, that he hadn't been paying attention and, sure enough, in another moment a man came out of the woods carrying two dead rabbits.

Aaron studied the figure as he approached, some instinct making him reach for his sword on his back only to find that it wasn't there. As the man drew closer, coming out of the shades of the trees and into the clearing, Aaron stumbled in shock and would have fallen had Adina not caught him. "*Owen?*" he said. "Is that you?"

The small man looked up from where he'd been watching his feet as if worried he'd step on a stone or snake, and he looked at Aaron with dark brown eyes that Aaron remembered well. Eyes that always seemed somehow sorrowful, even when he laughed that tittering, nervous laugh of his. The laugh that he gave now, "You're awake," he said.

"You're alive," Aaron said, stunned.

Owen—for it *was* Owen, he could see that in the way he stood, hear it in the way he spoke—smiled and held up the two rabbits. "And I have breakfast."

CHAPTER TWENTY-FIVE

Aaron and the others sat around the campfire, Owen—*gods, but he was alive*—stirring the rabbit meat into a stew, Aaron staring at him, speechless for possibly the first time in his life. Leomin and Adina, too, remained silent. They'd both heard him speak of Owen before, knew about the childhood friend he'd lost, and so they did not speak, letting him work through it on his own, and he was incredibly grateful to them for that. "I found the pot at the slaver's tent," Owen said in that nervous, self-deprecating way that was so familiar, "I didn't think ... well, they wouldn't need it anymore, I thought. Do you think it was wrong of me to take it?" He glanced at them, hunching his shoulders as if expecting to be hit for his troubles.

Aaron still found that he couldn't seem to make his voice work, so Adina smiled, patting Aaron on the hand from where she sat beside him even as she spoke, "I'm sure it's fine. As you say, they won't need it anymore. Besides, they *were* going to make us slaves."

"Right," Owen said, patting his forehead as if to show he was a fool, "You're right, of course. Still, it's a good pot, and I'm afraid I won't be able to blame it for the meal. I warn you all, I'm not much of a cook." He glanced down at the stew he was cooking, stirring it, "Not much of a hunter either, I'm afraid. I suspect we'll all get a belly of broth and little else."

Aaron shook his head slowly, still shocked to see this man he'd thought long dead, this *friend*, crouched before him stirring a pot of rabbit stew. It was surreal and strange and wonderful all at the same time. He glanced at Leomin and was surprised to find the Parnen captain studying Owen intently, as if he was a puzzle he was trying to piece together.

"So," Aaron said, finally managing to find his voice, "Pellan, is it?"

Owen looked up from where he stirred the pot, his eyes wide like a child caught doing something he shouldn't. "Ah, about that ... well, after I left the orphanage, I thought it would be the smartest thing to change my name. I remembered you talking about your father, once, and I had always liked the name, so I decided that it would do as well as any other." He started as if just realizing something, "I ... gods, Aaron, I hope you're not offended. I didn't mean—"

"It's fine," Aaron said, "really, Owen, it's fine. I'm just ... I can't believe that you're here. I thought ... shit, Owen, *everyone* thought you died."

Owen nodded, his expression growing troubled. "I almost did. It ... I don't remember all of it. I know that Cyrille was beating me, I remember that. I remember thinking he was going to kill me." He frowned, "I think maybe I passed out? Or he knocked me out, I'm not sure. All I remember is when I woke up I was in an alleyway in a part of the city I didn't know, hurt pretty bad, I guess. I couldn't move much—couldn't see much either, really. Some of his hits had got me in the face, so my eyes were mostly swollen shut." He paused, as if remembering, "Anyway," he said, smiling at Aaron, "I'm here now, so that's a good thing."

Aaron nodded, "Yes, it is a good thing. Whatever happened, Owen, I'm glad you're okay."

Adina was surprised to see Aaron get up and move toward the thin man. For his part, Owen seemed surprised too, taking an anxious step back until Aaron wrapped him into a tight hug. Adina smiled, never having seen this side of Aaron before, and she turned to Leomin, trying to meet his eye, but the Parnen captain was staring at Owen, a troubled expression on his face.

"It's good to have you back," Aaron said, with more emotion in his voice than the sellsword often showed. "And I'm glad you're okay. I'm glad, and I'm sorry."

"Sorry?" Owen asked, a surprised look still on his face, patting Aaron's back in an awkward, embarrassed way, "Why would you be sorry?"

"It was my fault," Aaron said, "my fault that Cyrille targeted you. They told me what happened—told me that you took the blame for what I'd done, tearing up his rooms."

"Yeah, well," Owen said, still patting Aaron's back awkwardly, "he was going to hurt you, Aaron, and you were my friend. Friends look after friends. Don't they?"

Aaron nodded, finally releasing the man from his embrace only to grab both the man's shoulders in his hands, "They're supposed to," he said, "but there are few enough people in the world who would go through what you did for their child or mother, let alone a friend."

"Ah," Owen said, rubbing the back of his neck, "it wasn't a big deal, Aaron, really..."

"No," Aaron said, "it *was* a big deal. You looked after me, and I intend to look after you. Though, I'll admit that you could have picked a safer time of showing up than you did. Still, we'll figure it out."

"Sounds good," Owen said, smiling in that shy way of his that Adina was beginning to see was a smile that was his alone. "Okay. Oh, and Aaron?"

"Yeah?"

"I think maybe the stew is burning."

Aaron laughed and let go of the thin man's shoulders, clapping him on the back. Then he moved and sat down beside Adina. She stared at him, thinking that he was happier now than anytime she'd ever seen him. *This,* she thought, *is the man he could have been. The man he* would *have been, had not the world stepped in with its own pains and its own tortures.*

"Still," Leomin said, "it's curious, isn't it? That you should just happen to be here, in these woods, miles away from any city and half a world away from where you and Aaron met?"

The joy faded from Aaron's face and his customary frown set in again. Adina scowled at the Parnen, tempted to grab a rock and throw it at him. Owen shrugged self-consciously, apparently not noticing her and Aaron's reaction, "Yeah, I guess headmaster

Cyrille was right about one thing wasn't he, Aaron? The gods have a sense of humor."

Aaron turned away from Leomin, his frown becoming a smile, "The bastard got that part right, anyway."

Owen went about stirring the stew, and they sat in a comfortable silence for a few minutes, Adina studying Aaron, the way he watched his old friend. Then she winced as Leomin spoke once more.

"And what exactly did you say brought you to this part of the world, Owen, if you don't mind me asking?"

Adina tried to meet the Parnen's eyes, willing him to leave it alone, but his eyes were locked on the thin man.

"I don't really think we need to be questioning him, Leomin," Aaron said, his voice cold and hard, "especially considering the fact that it was him who bandaged us both up, and is now cooking us *breakfast* do you?"

Owen's eyes went wide, somehow reminding Adina of an owl, "It's alright, Aaron, really," he said, "I don't mind, and it's a fair question." He turned to Leomin, "To answer, I'd heard about the tournament in Baresh, thought it might be interesting."

"So you're a swordsman, then?" Leomin said, and Owen shook his head. "No? Then, maybe, you had a friend who entered, is that it? And, if so, I wonder, where is that friend now? I would hate to think that those slavers hurt him."

"Oh, no, no," Owen said, smiling, shaking his head and not meeting anyone's eyes, "not a friend, not really. I just ...." He paused, sniffing, "Ah, I think the stew is done, such as it is." He went to the pot and began to dole out helpings of stew into tin cups, handing them out to each of the others in turn.

"I guess," Owen said, once he'd sat down with his own cup of stew, "that, since I was a kid, I don't really like to stay in one place for long. I get to feeling trapped, you know?" He said, looking at Aaron. "Gets to where I start to feel the walls closing in on me, no matter how big the city or nice its people."

Aaron nodded, "I understand that. Going through so much as a child," he said, turning and staring at Leomin with hard eyes, "sometimes, our troubles follow us into adulthood in ways we wouldn't guess. Such a thing is understandable."

"Absolutely," Leomin said, nodding. "Still, if you weren't going to fight in the tournament and you didn't have a friend fighting in it, then why—"

"*Enough,*" Aaron growled, "just leave him alone, Leomin. The man just got free of slavers, alright? He doesn't need any more of your damned questions. Just eat your stew, will you?"

Leomin nodded, but his eyes continued to study Owen as he ate. For his part, Aaron didn't notice, too preoccupied eating and watching Owen himself, as if afraid that the man would vanish at any moment, should he take his gaze away. Adina did though, and she patted Aaron on the knee. "I'll be right back," she said, "I'm going to speak to Leomin, see if something's bothering him."

She wasn't sure that Aaron even heard her, so engrossed in watching his long lost friend, but she rose anyway and went to sit down on the ground by Leomin. "And just what was all that about?" She said, her voice a near whisper.

The Parnen captain frowned, shaking his head slowly and wincing as the motion must have caused some pain in the wound in his head. "I'm not sure, princess, really. Only, if there is one thing that I know and know well, it is strangeness, being possessed of some humble degree of it myself. And there is something more than passing strange about this one and the story he tells—or, perhaps, more accurate to say the story he *doesn't* tell."

"He was captured, Leomin, that's all. Just like us. The world is a big place, yet it is small at the same time. This is not the first coincidence, nor will it be the last."

"Yes," Leomin said, "perhaps. Still, there is something more bothering me, princess, if you would hear it."

All Adina wanted to do was sit and eat her rabbit stew and let Aaron be happy that the world that had taken so much from him had finally given something back, but she sighed softly, nodding. "Okay, what is it?"

"When we were in the tent," Leomin said, "I admit that, for most of it, I was unconscious, so I do not remember all that transpired. However, I had come to a bit, there at the last, heard the guards words before that one," he motioned to Owen with his chin, the thin man's head hovering inches above his cup as he ate, "stabbed him in the neck. That itself is strange to me, for he does not seem the type to take such drastic action. I would not think him, had I not seen it, a man capable of killing."

"All men are capable of killing, Leomin," Adina said, "if given the right motivation. If the wars with my brother have taught me nothing else, they have taught me that. Belgarin wasn't always cruel, you know? Sure, he was always stiff and rigid, always wrapped up in the picture he painted for others of himself. So much sometimes that you could almost see him painting it, could see him working out each nuance of his speech and his words, so that they always rung false, somehow. Contrived. He was pompous, but he was not cruel. Not evil. At least, that is, until my father did not gift him the inheritance he thought he deserved as the firstborn. And now three of my brothers and sisters are dead by his word if not by his hand." She shook her head, "No, Leomin, the world can make murderers of us all."

Leomin nodded slowly, "Yet, do you remember the guard's words? Do you remember how surprised he seemed to find Owen there?"

"The man was in shock," Adina said, growing frustrated now, "he'd just nearly been killed and had seen or heard his friends all killed. It's no surprise that his mental faculties were somewhat ... confused."

"Confused," Leomin said, "yes, perhaps that's it. Still, the words are troubling to me. What was it, the man said again? 'I'll slit her fuckin' throat, I swear by the gods I will.'" He nodded, "Wasn't that it, princess? *Her* throat, the man said. And then, when he looked, he *asked* the man who he was? Was going to say something more, I think, before the knife took him in the throat. Does that not strike you as odd? Did you see nothing amiss yourself?"

Adina cast her mind back to that moment when she'd seen the man in the cage, remembered thinking that his eyes had been blue. A light blue, so light as to be almost white. Then, when she'd looked again, they'd been a dark brown. Strange, sure, but the young slaver wasn't the only one who'd been terrified or in shock. She'd been scared herself. Scared and knocked on the head in the bargain. "What difference does it make what the slaver said?" She asked. "Girl or guy, clearly he was confused. I mean just *look*, Leomin." She said, nodding her head at where Owen sat eating.

"There he is. A *he.* I suppose you could ask him to strip naked for you so that you could check his sex, but I'll be no part of that, I promise you. Or what do you think, exactly, that somehow this man has a way of changing from a man to a woman and back? And if so, why, Leomin, *why* by the gods, would he *do it?*"

The Parnen captain shrugged, "I don't know, princess. You're right, of course. There he sits, obviously a man. I need not check his parts to know that. Still," he said, his voice stubborn, "the guard said *her.*"

Adina took a slow, deep breath in an effort to calm herself, "Fine, Leomin. Think whatever you will, watch whatever you will. All I ask is that you don't upset, Aaron. The man's been through enough evil in his life—it would be a pleasant thing for him to get a little bit of good out of the world. I will not have you ruin this for him. Do you understand?"

Leomin nodded, "Of course, princess," he said, giving her a small smile, "I understand well enough and I, too, wish the sellsword happiness. I do not want to cause him pain or hurt."

"Then don't," Adina said, and with that she rose and made her way back to Aaron.

"I think Leomin's head just hurts him, that's all."

Aaron grunted, "It's the strangest thing, Adina, I swear. I never thought to see him again and now that he's sitting here before me, I almost don't know what to say."

"Tell him you missed him," Adina said, "that you care about him. That's all that you need say, Aaron. He is your friend—he will understand."

Aaron nodded, turning to her and giving her a smile that somehow made her heart race in her chest. "What would I do without you?" He said.

She smiled, "Only the gods know. Now go to your friend. It has been too long; don't make it be any longer."

Aaron kissed her on the cheek, and she still felt the warmth of it as he rose and made his way to sit beside Owen. Soon, they were talking and laughing, Aaron with his loud, somehow cynical laugh, and Owen with his own nervous, quiet titter. Watching them, Adina felt better than she remembered feeling in a very long time. At least, that was, until she glanced over at the Parnen and saw him watching them, a frown on his face.

Sighing heavily, Adina grabbed her cup and began to eat, praying to the gods for patience.

CHAPTER TWENTY-SIX

The brothel, like all other brothels, was also a tavern and, like all other brothels, it was packed at night by women seeking ways to make some coin and men seeking interesting ways to spend some. The ale here was some of the cheapest in the Downs, not that Celes expected any less. Gelsey, the owner and proprietor of *Mounted Nights,* was a very practical, shrewd woman. It was one of the reasons why her brothel was the most popular in the Downs.

A drunken man, after all, doesn't stop to count his coins like a sober one does. A man who's drunk enough wants a good meal and a good, soft bed, preferably with a good soft partner to share it with. All of which could be found in what most everyone in the city referred to as '*The Nights.*'

Celes made her way past tables of men playing at dice and cards, past groups of men standing around and pouring ale down their throats as if a crier had just announced that ale was a cure for any ill, and they all had diseases that needed curing. The drink wouldn't cure all their ills, of course, but it *would* help them forget about them for a time, and for most that was enough. A hand rubbed her leg beneath the short skirt she wore as she moved past a table, and she turned, arcing a perfectly shaped eyebrow at the offender.

"Sorry there, miss," he said, grinning stupidly, his eyes glazed over from the drink. "Didn't see you there."

Normally, Celes would have taken the time to correct the man, teach him in no uncertain terms that touching without an invitation was not alright—typically a kick to the fruits made the lesson sink in the best—but she didn't have time just now, so she only gave the man a small smile and walked past him and his sniggering friends toward the bar, taking a seat at the only empty stool. "What's a woman have to do to get a drink around here?"

The barkeep, a short old woman with gray hair, the type of woman who looked like she could be someone's favorite grandmother, turned and, seeing Celes sitting there, gave her a wide, kindly smile that only added to her grandmotherly charm. "Why, if it isn't Celes! How are you, my dear?"

Celes smiled back, "Hello Gelsey. I'm doing well, thank you. Yourself?"

The old woman gave her a wink, "Oh, I'm surviving, I suppose. The best any of us can hope for in such times." She filled an ale and sat it down in front of Celes, squinting at her. "Been a while since I've seen you around here. No time for your ol' friend Gelsey, I suppose."

Celes rolled her eyes, "Don't be silly, Gelsey. It's just that I've been fairly busy of late, to be honest."

The old woman nodded as she set about rubbing the already immaculate bar down with a rag. "Mmhmm. May keepin' you busy, I'm sure. When are you goin' to come on back and work for poor old Gelsey again? Why, I tell you, girl, we're busier than we've ever been. You'd think all the talks of wars and assassinations'd have folks hiding in their bedrooms. Instead, they decide to do their hiding here in *my* bedrooms, and I don't need to tell you that most all of 'em prefer to do their hidin' with a partner." She shook her head, "Figure if I laid out a board with a hole in it, maybe threw a dress over it, I'd make myself quite a few coppers."

Celes laughed, "Gelsey, you're as beautifully terrible as always."

The old woman cackled, "Well, I ain't been beautiful nothin' for a few years now, sweetling. My teats damn near hang to the floor, I don't keep 'em wrapped tight, and I got wrinkles so big one of these old fools'd likely fall in as not when he went to get his money's worth. Still," she said, her eyes getting a wistful look, "there was a time, girl, let me tell you, when folks'd travel from plum across the world to see your old mamma Gelsey."

Celes rolled her eyes, "As if they don't now. Don't think I didn't see that man—a tailor, wasn't he?—making eyes at you the last time I visited." She grinned, "As I recall, you ended up having some work you needed done that very night up in one of those rooms." She motioned with her head to the stairs leading to the second floor of the brothel.

The old lady grinned, "Well, I suppose I *might* remember who you're speakin' of. Good enough fella, I guess, a needle smaller than you might expect but, then, he knew how to use it well enough."

Celes laughed again, "You're terrible, Gelsey."

"Well. Tell me now, when you gonna come work for your poor momma Gelsey again? You were here, I reckon we'd have a line goin' all the way out to Nobles street. Those stuck up women with their noses so high in the air you'd think they'd just got uppercut would have a time wrangling their husbands together."

Celes shook her head, "Thank you, Gelsey, but the next man I have will win me with words and action, not coins."

Gelsey winked again, "Well, take it easy on the poor fool, whoever he is."

Just then, Celes felt a hand on her knee, and she turned to see the man that had felt her leg earlier smiling at her, his face only a few inches away. His breath stank of ale and unclean teeth, and the dirty linen shirt he wore was stained from where his drink had missed his mouth. "Hey there, beautiful, just how—" he paused to burp and shake his head, "I said just how much for a night of your company?

Celes frowned, "More than you can afford, I can promise you that."

"Aw, hey now," he said, his hand drifting further up her thigh, "you can't know that for sure, can ya? Might be I'm a prince, come here to make you a princess."

"*Might* be," The old woman said, "that you're a drunken fool, Radley Bohannon, and one that's soon had just about enough ale for one night. Now, you go on and get back home to Mildred for I let her know your hands have been travelin' places they don't belong."

"Aw, why don't you just shut up, you old hag," the man said, then he turned back to Celes, leaning in and trying to kiss her, so focused on his task that he didn't notice Gelsey's hands reach under the counter.

Gelsey moved with surprising speed for her age, and her hand came out with a length of stout wood. She swung once, much the way a woman might swat a fly, and the wood struck the man, Radley, in the forehead. He grunted, turning slowly to stare at her, and Celes saw a line of blood leaking from his scalp down his face. He opened his mouth to speak but never managed it before falling out of the stool and onto the floor, unconscious.

Suddenly, two large, thickly muscled men were standing on either side of the man, frowning down at him. "You remember Robert and Tilton don't you, sweetling?" Gelsey asked as if nothing unusual had occurred. "Couple of my grandsons."

Celes nodded to the men, smiling, "Yes I believe I do. Boys, how are you?"

The two men bowed their heads politely, "Ma'am."

"Well," Gelsey said, "why don't you boys take our poor friend Radley here home. Let him sleep it off."

"Yes ma'am," the two said, then they bent, one grabbing his legs and the other his arms and began making their way toward the door.

Gelsey nodded, turning back to Celes, "They're nice boys, if you're in the market for one. Not geniuses mind—nobody'll ever accuse them of bein' too smart, but what good is a smart man anyway? Fella that can sit around and think up ways to make a woman's life more of a trial than it already is. Nah," she said, "best just get you one that can follow orders, maybe dampen his wick when you're of the mind."

Celes laughed, "Thank you, Gelsey, but I think I'd rather wait and find the one for me the old fashioned way."

The old woman grunted, "As you wish, dear, but just be careful. You wait around too long for the old fashioned way, you're like as not to just be left with old. Now, if you didn't come for a job, and you didn't come to do me the favor of takin' one of my grandsons off my hands, what's got you out here this time of night? I know it ain't my company, no matter what you say."

"Well," Celes said, "to be honest, I'm looking for a man."

Gelsey scoffed, "I just told you I got two good men right there you could—"

"A *specific* man," Celes said. "Lucius."

Gelsey frowned, "Girl, you are far too pretty to go lookin' for that little bastard."

Celes laughed, "I'm not looking for Lucius for *that,* Gelsey. If it helps, I don't think he'll enjoy the conversation particularly."

Gelsey leaned forward, squinting her eyes, "Now, this wouldn't have anything to do with a certain red haired queen I saw gracing us all with her presence earlier, would it?"

Celes grinned, "Maybe."

***

"*I told you to come back later, damnit!*" A familiar man's voice came from the other side of the door, "*I'm busy just now.*"

Celes knocked again, louder, and she could hear the sounds of a man cursing from inside the room. Then, in another moment, the door opened and Lucius was standing in the doorway, a coverlet wrapped around his waist and nothing covering the skinny bare chest that would have been more at home on a twelve year old boy than a man grown.

He ran a hand over his attempt at a beard—grown no doubt in an effort to look more like a man, but one that failed considering that it only grew in patches. "Well, Celes," he said, his frown turning to a grin that displayed his crooked, pointy teeth. "Just what are you doing here?"

Celes glanced past him to the naked woman lying in the bed, now on her stomach, watching them with a bored gaze. "Sorry to interrupt," Celes said, but the woman only shrugged as if it didn't make any difference, then yawned heavily. "Anyway, Lucius," she said, smiling her best smile, "I heard that you were here, and I thought that maybe we could ... talk."

Lucius leered, studying her up and down, his gaze resting on her legs beneath the short skirt she wore. "Talk, is it? That all?"

"Well," she said, putting a finger under his chin and bringing his gaze back up to hers, "How about we start with talking, see where the night takes us?"

His grinned widened, as did his eyes, like a man who'd just found a bag of gold under his bed. Then, after a moment, his smile faltered. "Wait a minute. You ain't trying to get me wrapped up in nothin' with that miserable woman you work for, are you? Did she send you?"

Celes rolled her eyes, "I don't work for that red headed bitch anymore. Anyway," she said, leaning in and whispering in his ear, "Do you want to talk about May, or do you want to talk about me and you?"

He grinned, reaching a hand out toward one of her breasts, but she slapped it away. "Lucius," she scolded, "I can't believe you. If you want to talk, then we can at least, do it somewhere *private*," she said, glancing at the woman in the bed.

Lucius was nodding before she'd finished, "Of course, gods, what was I thinking? Hey, Nell," he said, turning to the woman in the bed, "I know I promised you a night you'd never forget, but ... do you mind, maybe I give you that night tomorrow?"

The woman in the bed rolled her eyes, "I'll try to manage without you."

Lucius nodded, apparently not hearing the sarcasm in her tone, then turned back to Celes. "So where do uh...."

"I have a room," Celes said, thinking that some things really were just too easy. "Come on, I'll show you."

"Sure, sure," Lucius said, smiling so wide she thought the man would be sore in the morning. "Oh, hold on," he said, "my clothes—"

"Oh," Celes said, grabbing his hand and barely managing to conceal a wince at the sweaty clamminess of it, "I don't think you'll be needing those."

"Well, alright," he said, "lead on."

Celes led him down the hall to her room then knocked on the door three times.

"Hey," Lucius said, confused, "why would you knock—"

His words turned into a yelp of surprise as the door opened and a thick-necked man with arms bigger than Lucius's legs drug him inside the room.

Celes glanced down the hallway then followed after, closing the door behind her.

"Aw, *shit,*" the weasel faced man, Lucius, said as he saw the woman sitting in the room's only chair. "I *knew* it." He turned to Celes, "You said you didn't work for this red headed bitch, no more."

"Red headed bitch, is it?" May said, glancing at Celes and raising an eyebrow.

Celes winced as she made her way over to stand by May, "Well, you do have red hair."

"Yes," the club owner said, "I suppose I do. And dear Lucius," she said, turning back to the thin man, still clothed in only a coverlet, "how are you?"

"How *am* I?" The skinny man asked, "I was just about to have a good night, and now I'm here, naked, with you two and this," he paused, glancing at the big man who now stood in the corner with his arms crossed frowning, "this uh ... gentleman here. So I'm not doin' great, I guess."

"Lucius," May said. "*Lucius,* look at me." The skinny man turned from where he'd been studying the big man anxiously to look at the club owner. "We've got some things to talk about."

The thin man swallowed, "Look, May, I swear I didn't know she wasn't for sale, alright? I didn't mean to cause any trouble at the *Rest,* I swear it. Anyway, she already gave me a black eye for my trouble. I mean, what, with all those skimpy clothes they wear now—"

"Lucius," May said, frowning, "what are you talking about?"

"Huh?" The thin man said, his eyes going wide, "err ... that is nothing. What are you talking about?"

May studied the man for several seconds while he fidgeted nervously under her stare. Then, "I want you to tell Grinner that I'd like to meet."

Lucius frowned, obviously confused, "Um ... you mean you ain't here to ... hurt me?"

May tilted her head, considering, "Well, we didn't come for that, but, I suppose, if it's so important to you—"

"Naw, naw," Lucius said, "anyway," he glanced at the big man in the corner again, "that is, I can try to talk to the boss, see if he'll meet with you."

"Try, Lucius?" May asked.

"That is," the thin man said, his eyes going wide, "Of course, I'll talk to the boss. I'm sure ... I'm sure he'd be happy to meet with such a ... pretty lady as yourself."

May smiled but there was little humor in it, "He had better be, Lucius. Or we'll have another talk, you and I. Maybe get around to the hurting bit."

The thin man nodded, "Um ... yes ma'am. I'll ... I'll tell him first thing tomorrow."

"Tonight, Lucius. You'll tell him tonight. At sunrise, the day after tomorrow, I desire his company and, that of a few others, at the *Rest.*"

"Others?" The weasel-faced man asked.

"Yes," May said, "*others.* Now, I think you'd best be on your way—if you hurry, you might even catch Hale before he's asleep. I think that would be best, don't you?"

Lucius swallowed hard and was out the door in a flurry of naked flesh and coverlet. When he was gone, the two women turned to look at each other. "Well," May said, "it's started."

Celes nodded, her expression grim, "Yes. For better or worse."

CHAPTER TWENTY-SEVEN

Aaron yawned in the saddle, shaking his head to wake himself. They'd traveled three days more since finding Owen and escaping the slavers, finding Owen a horse among the things they'd taken that first night. They'd decided to stick to the edge of the wood so far as they were able, none of them wanting to be out in the open at night after their experience with the slavers. Aaron tried to talk to his old friend often—and sometimes, he even did—but though they'd been close when they were little, he found that, now, many years separated the two of them from the friendship they'd once shared and from the children they'd once been. Still, Aaron'd had few enough friends in his life that he would not lose this one.

It was just a matter of catching up, that was all, of bridging the gulf created by the years. It wasn't as if he didn't still like Owen—the thin man was the type of guy it was about impossible not to like—the problem was that, often, he'd open his mouth to say something and find that damned lump of time between what he would say and the man he would say it to, a boulder of years blocking what should have been an easy path.

From what Owen had said about his past, Aaron took it that he'd traveled often, working his way from town to town or city to city, doing the odd job here or there to make his way. Such a man as that, such a man as the one that must grow from a child who'd been willing to give his life for a friend, what did such a one know about the life of a sellsword, a life spent in dealing with the worst the criminal underworld had to offer? No, it was more than that.

Not a life spent *dealing* with criminals, but a life spent *being* one. With two lives lived so very differently, it was no wonder that sometimes Aaron found he couldn't find words to say to the man.

He frowned over at Leomin riding beside him. It didn't help that the Parnen captain had, for some reason that Aaron couldn't comprehend, decided to take a dislike to Owen. Not that he was ever hostile or spoke out of turn, of course, that was not the Parnen's way. He spoke in riddles always, taking what to Aaron seemed the most circuitous route when a straight line would do and be faster besides. At least he hadn't asked anymore questions of Owen since the first night, but Aaron could see the questions just the same, hovering on the tip of the Parnen's tongue.

As far as Aaron was concerned, Owen's past could remain his and his alone for as long as he wished. After all, all men do things of which they are ashamed—Aaron knew that better than most— and if Owen didn't want to share the exact path that had led him to being in the middle of the wilderness, a victim to slavers, then that was his right. Aaron wasn't exactly excited at the prospect of sharing his own life's doings with Owen either. How could you say to the man who'd given his life for you that he had traded that which was most precious to him, had sacrificed it in a moment, thereby changing the entire course of his life, for a man who went on to rob and beat up and kill for a living?

It was a depressing thing, Aaron thought, for a man to have lived a life without one true thing of which he was proud. Without a single moment or instant he could point at and say, *Here. Here I was at my best, and I did my best and that cannot be lost or stolen. Here, in this moment, I was better than myself.* He thought surely most men must have such a moment, *had* to have one. Otherwise, what was the point of it all?

Adina called for them to camp. Aaron, thankful for the opportunity to rest and sort out some of the feelings that his friend's appearance had caused, led his horse to a nearby tree tied it with the others.

Once they'd all gathered their bedrolls and sat around a fire, Adina spoke, "Tomorrow, we'll have to leave the woods behind. Another few days' worth of travel, and we should reach Isalla's capital city, Perennia."

Owen nodded, handing out some of the hard biscuits and dried meat they'd scavenged from the slavers' supplies. "I just want to say, again, how much I appreciate you all letting me travel with you to the city. I'm not much of a warrior," he said, shrugging bashfully, "and should someone have come upon me out here in the wilderness, there would have been little I could have done."

Leomin met Aaron's eyes, but did not speak. The sellsword frowned. It wasn't as if the man actually needed to. What he would say, what he *thought* was clear enough. If Owen had known the danger of being out in the woods and the wilderness alone, then *why* had he come in the first place? Aaron turned away from the Parnen captain, doing his best to ignore the question in the man's gaze.

They sat in a circle, eating the dry, tasteless food and, for a time, no one spoke. *Not again,* Aaron thought. They'd spent the past several nights doing much the same, sitting in near silence, each of them speaking little, their faces dour or worried or downcast. It was a time that they should be celebrating. After all, how often did a man manage to run into a friend thought long dead? Not often. Now that he thought of it, even Co had been quiet for the past several days.

Co, he thought. Several seconds passed, and she did not answer, so he tried again, thinking the thought louder this time. *Co, are you there?*

I am here, Aaron, Co said into his mind, her voice quiet and small.

Then why have you been so quiet?

I ... do not know, Co said. *Only, I have felt ... strange, lately, Aaron. Or, at least, it is perhaps more accurate to say that I have felt it wise to remain quiet. Hidden.*

Aaron frowned, *Don't tell me you're worried about Owen as well?*

It is an unusual coincidence you must admit, the Virtue said, *to run into him out here, in the wilderness. That he just so happened to be taken captive by the same slavers who took Adina and Leomin.*

Aaron spat, *You're as bad as the Parnen. Any more of a coincidence than me running into one of the Seven Virtues? Creatures of myth and legend that almost everyone believes never existed at all? Or as coincidental as me meeting a princess and falli*—he cut off. *Ah, damnit, never mind.*

Still, Co said, *he does seem … unusual. There's something about him that seems somehow … off.*

You're a fucking floating ball of light, firefly, he said, *what by all the gods is more unusual than* that?

Aaron, the Virtue said, the concern obvious in her tone, *look.*

He glanced up then and was surprised to find Owen studying him, an intent look of concentration on his face. For a moment, Aaron was struck by the thought that the man sitting in front of him wasn't Owen at all, not with the way he sat so confidently, hunched slightly over his knees, his eyes—though they *were* Owen's—didn't seem like his just then. They seemed to be the eyes not of a nervous man, shy and bashful, but of a man with years of experience in the darker side of life, a man who had done things and saw things that most people only heard about in horror tales.

Then, Owen laughed and the image was gone, and he was Aaron's old friend again. "Sorry," Owen said, "I don't mean to stare. It's just … it's been a really long time, hasn't it?"

Aaron nodded, "It has, Owen. Too long."

It's almost as if he saw us speaking, Co said, her voice so quiet in his head that he could barely hear it, *or that he was listening, somehow.*

Ridiculous, Aaron thought, but he glanced back at Owen anyway, only to find that his old friend was staring at the fire, the image of it dancing in his eyes. *You just imagined it, Co. Relax. You can trust Owen completely. The man sacrificed himself for me by the gods. What more could you ask?*

I understand, the Virtue said, *I just … I don't know, Aaron. There's something … odd about him. Besides, that was a long time ago. People change.*

Aaron let out a growl of frustration. He'd been considering something for some time now and the way Co and Leomin were acting had decided him. "I've got something to say," he said, and the others looked up from their meals.

Aaron, Co said, *I know what you're planning, but I don't think—*

"You have all been good to me," he said, glancing between his companions, "better than I deserve, in truth. Without the three of you, I wouldn't be sitting here today, one way or the other, so I want to say thank you."

He hesitated, unsure of how to go on, but held up a hand, asking for silence, for a moment to gather his thoughts. He turned to Adina, sitting there watching him with questioning eyes, questioning but trusting and that hurt the worst. "You've all been honest with me, and it is only right that I should be honest with you." He glanced at Leomin to see how he'd be taking it, but the Parnen was looking off into the woods, his head cocked as if listening to a sound only he could hear. Aaron was sure he was speaking with his Virtue, no doubt a frantic conversation about what Aaron was likely about to divulge.

As Aaron watched, the Parnen removed a flask of liquor from his tunic—yet another prize from the slavers—and took a long drink. *Alright then*, Aaron thought, deciding there'd be no argument from that quarter, as much as he had expected one. "If I have been acting strangely lately," he said, glancing at Adina, his eyes studying her, "If, perhaps, I have seemed ... difficult or confused, there's a reason."

He sighed heavily. "Ah, shit. I'm not good at this kind of thing so bear with me. Point is, I wouldn't consider myself a good man. I've been called a bastard, a murderer, a thief, a monster, and I'm all of those. You see," he said, staring at Adina, "I've done things...."

He shook himself, forcing his eyes away from the princess to take in Owen who watched him with an expectant expression. "I've done things I'm not proud of, always telling myself that a man had to look after his own interests. That in a world of blood and steel and fire, a man had to find what joy he could, anyway he could find it. Thing is," he rubbed a hand through his hair, "the thing is, I was wrong. I wasn't a monster. Or, at least, no more than many men. Now, though ... now, I think, I am becoming a monster in truth."

"What do you mean, Aaron?" Adina said, "What's wrong?"

Aaron gritted his teeth, "Damnit, this isn't coming out right."

Aaron, please—

"What I'm trying to say," he said, "is that ... I have something, inside of me. I don't really understand it, but ... it's changing me. I know that. You see, not too long ago, I took a job where I found a man," he turned to Adina, hating the thought of bringing up an old memory and the old pain that came along with it, "your brother, dying. By all rights, the man should have already been dead when I found him—he'd been through a lot, but he took it as well as any man can, that I saw with my own eyes. He was brave, your brother," Aaron said, and Adina nodded softly, a tear coming from the corner of her eyes.

"Damnit," Aaron said, "even that's not the point. Thing is, when your brother passed ... something happened to me. Something found me ... or maybe *I* found it, I'm still not really sure. Anyway, this thing—"

"A heart," Leomin said, taking another pull from the flask he carried and stumbling to Aaron, putting a hand on his shoulder, "You found a heart, Mr. Envelar, I understand. It was there all along, you know. A bit unhealthy maybe, a bit *unwise,* but there anyway. Still, I'm glad to hear—"

"*No,* damnit," Aaron said, "not that. It's—" He cut off as Leomin suddenly tripped, stumbling toward him. The Parnen's arms pinwheeled, sending liquor spilling all over the front of Aaron, and Adina let out a gasp of surprise as she too, was splashed with alcohol.

"Leomin, what the fuck?" Aaron said, grabbing the man's shoulders and righting him.

"Oh, gods be good, I'm sorry, Mr. Envelar, Adina," he said, nodding his head, "I must have drunk more than I'd realized. It's the funny thing about it; it seems that the more I drink, the thirstier I get. Thirstier and more foolish. Please, forgive me."

"It's fine," Adina said, looking at the front of her shirt that was now covered in liquor, clinging to her breasts in a way that Aaron found distracting.

"Yeah," he said, unable to peel his eyes away, "It's fine. Just ... be more careful, will you?"

"Of course, Mr. Envelar, of course" Leomin said, stumbling back on unsteady feet, "*Careful* is the word, as you say. It always proves most ... wise to be careful." Then he stumbled another step back and sat down heavily, propping his head against a tree trunk. In another moment, the man was snoring.

Aaron watched him with annoyance and more than a little fascination. "Oh my," Owen said, moving forward with the same urgency most men would have shown if they'd just seen someone stabbed, "are you alright?" He brought out a kerchief from his pocket and began rubbing at the front of Aaron's shirt.

Aaron grunted, catching his hand, "It's fine, Owen, really."

"I think I saw a stream not far from here," Adina said, standing and rooting in her pack for a change of clothes. "I'm going to go get cleaned up." She turned to look at Aaron then and something in her eyes made his pulse quicken. "I can show you where it is, if you'd like."

Aaron nodded slowly, unable to help himself. "Alright." He turned back to Owen, "You'll be okay here, with him?"

Owen glanced between the two of them for a moment then coughed politely. He looked at the Parnen for a moment then back to Aaron, a shy smile on his face. "I think we will be fine. I'll make sure he doesn't roll into the fire."

Aaron nodded, "Thanks," he said, "we won't be long."

He glanced at Adina, and she raised an eyebrow as if to ask whether or not he was sure about the time it would take.

Aaron cleared his throat and drew a change of clothes from his own pack, grabbing his cloak and sword from where they lay by the fire. "Ready when you are."

She nodded, smiling, and started off into the woods.

The stream was no more than fifteen minutes away from their camp. It was a small forest stream, the water not deep enough for swimming but deep enough to wade in. Adina stopped at the water's edge, turning to him. The moonlight seemed to glisten in her hair, and her eyes danced. He drew closer to her so that they were only a few feet away. She met his eyes, unflinching and unafraid. "What you were saying before at the camp. You're wrong, you know. You're not a monster."

"Adina...." He started, but she stepped forward, putting a finger to his lips.

"No," she said, "I've listened to you speak on it enough, now it's time that you listened to me. You're not a monster, Aaron, no matter what you may think. You forget, I grew up in my father's kingdom, in my father's castle. I've been betrayed by my own nobles, and I've a brother who has murdered three of my siblings already and will murder the rest if he has his way. I understand something about monsters, and I know you're not one."

"But Adina," he said, thinking of the slavers, of the blood on his hands, the blood that he could almost see there no matter how many times he washed them. "The things I've done...."

"Are no more than that," she said, her voice low and soft, "nothing more than things you've done. And speaking of things you've done, what about saving my life? You've done that too. What about saving Gryle?" She shook her head, "No, Aaron. You're not evil, no matter what you think. You've made mistakes but what of it? If there's one thing I've learned about life, it's that no one gets through it without scars. But it's those scars, Aaron, that make us who we are."

"It's more than that, Adina," he said, "the thing, I was talking about before?" He hesitated, not wanting to tell her the truth about what he was, about what he was becoming, but knowing he had to anyway. Better her reject the truth than accept the lie. "Have you ever heard of the Seven Virtues? Of Aaron Caltriss and Boyce Kevlane and all the rest?"

"Of course," she said, clearly puzzled by the abrupt change in topic, "everyone's heard the tales. Seven virtues an old king and his wizard made to create the perfect warrior. What were they ... strength, intelligence, speed..."

"Compassion," Aaron said.

"Yes, that's right. Compassion ... I forget the others."

"Charisma, for one," Aaron said, "the others are perception and adaptability. Anyway," he said, waving a hand, "the point is, Adina ...." Hesitating again, scared of what she would say, of what she would think. A funny thing, really. He could face down men bent on killing him, could even deal with whatever was coming after them now—both things caused fear, sure, but it was a known fear, one he understood. An old acquaintance. One you wouldn't invite to dinner exactly, but, then, you wouldn't be all that surprised when he showed up, either. No, this was a new worry, a new fear. It wasn't something he'd done much of in his life, worrying about what other people thought, but it seemed to him that, at that moment, it was all that mattered.

"The thing is ... well. They're not just fairy tales, Adina. Not just stories that parents tell their children before bed. The Virtues are real." He held out his hand and, on cue, Co appeared hovering above it, a magenta ball of light floating in the air. "And I have one."

Adina let out a startled yelp and took a step back. Then, when nothing happened, she eased closer, her eyes wide in surprise. "I can't ... Aaron ... it's ... it's beautiful."

"Thank you," Co said, and Adina jumped again, her hand shooting to her mouth.

"Oh gods watch over us, it can talk!"

"*She*, dear," Co admonished, but Aaron could hear the amusement in her tone, "*she* can talk."

"Oh," Adina said, "I'm ... sorry about that. Ma'am?"

Co laughed then, bouncing up and down in the air. "Oh, Co will do," she said.

"Or firefly or lightning bug," Aaron added, "She loves those."

Adina laughed then, something of wonder and amazement in her face and, in that moment, Aaron thought he could see what she'd looked like as a child. The innocence she'd had before the world did what it does best and stripped it away. "It's amazing," Adina said shaking her head, "You're amazing. Both of you."

"Well, thank you," Co said, as if it was her due, "I do like to think—"

"Adina," Aaron said, hating that he had to take it a step further, to make her understand. "You still don't get it."

But, if she heard, Adina wasn't paying any attention. "So which one?" She said, "Which are you?"

"I am the Virtue of Compassion," Co answered.

Adina glanced between the ball of light and Aaron's face then let out a laugh, "Compassion? And you're with *him?*"

"Yes, well," Co said, "let us say it's a work in progress."

Adina laughed again and Co joined her. Aaron frowned, "If there's a joke, I don't see it."

"Oh, come on, Aaron," Adina said, "surely you have to see the humor in it. You, of all people, are the one that gets the Virtue of Compassion? The Virtue of Grunting and Cursing a lot sure, but *compassion?*" She laughed again, "It's just not the one I would have guessed, that's all."

"Well," Aaron said sourly amid their laughter, "you're not any more surprised than I was, I guarantee you that."

"But ... how?" Adina said finally, "how did it happen?"

"Your brother," Aaron said. "When I showed up and took care of those holding him, he was still alive. Barely. When he ... when he died, Co passed on to me. The only thing I can figure is she's lazy and didn't feel like searching around for a better option."

"Eladen, was bonded with the Virtue of Compassion?" Adina said, then she slapped a hand to her forehead, "Of course. That would explain how, years ago, he started acting so differently. He was always kind, sure, always concerned with other people's feelings, but even I noticed a dramatic difference in the way he treated everyone. In the way he spent so much time focused on bettering the lives of the commoners despite the fact that it was the nobles who held all the power. It all makes sense now."

Co bobbed slowly forward, coming to rest only inches from Adina's face where, even now, a tear traced its way down her cheek. "Your brother was a good man, and he taught me much. I have never met one finer than him, and I doubt very much that I ever shall. Know that, when I was bonded to him, I knew your brother, knew him as well as he knew himself. He loved you, Adina. He spent much time worrying for you, for all of Telrear. He rarely slept for his worry."

Adina swallowed, wiping at her face, "Thank you, for that, Co. It means a lot."

Co bobbed once, as if in agreement, then came back to float above Aaron's shoulder.

"So you see the problem, Adina. As much as I would want to ... as much as I like you, I can't ... *we* can't."

Adina frowned at him, "Why?"

Aaron ran a hand through his hair, "I just told you. I have one of the Virtues. I'm bonded to her."

"So?"

"Damnit, Adina, I don't want to hurt you," he said, "don't you get it? Those men I killed, those slavers? I *don't remember it.* Something's happening. With me, with Co. I just ... when I saw they took you, I got so angry. I killed those men, Adina," he said, "I killed them badly. I remember enough to know that. I *enjoyed* it. Don't you see? I *am* a monster."

"No," Adina said, coming up and grabbing his hands in hers, stepping close and holding his gaze in her own. "You're not a monster, Aaron. What you did, you saved us. Me and Leomin and Owen. *You* did that. Just as you saved me and Gryle by getting us out of Avarest when Belgarin's men were chasing us. Whatever is happening, you don't have to face it alone."

"Adina..."

"*No.* Whatever is happening to you, Aaron, you *won't* face it alone. We will figure it out together. You didn't abandon me, and I won't abandon you. You got it?"

Aaron nodded slowly, overcome by the intensity in her eyes, her words. "I got it."

"Good," she said. "I'd hate to have to try to knock some sense into that thick skull of yours. Now," she glanced at the stream gurgling softly behind them then back at Aaron and Co floating over his shoulder. "Co, I wonder ... would you mind terribly...."

"I think I'll go check back at camp," Co said, "see how Leomin and Owen are doing." Then she was gone, a magenta ball of light streaking through the darkness, growing dimmer as she went until, in another moment, she was gone. Aaron watched her vanish then turned back to find Adina standing naked before him, her skin smooth and silky and pearlescent in the moonlight.

"Gods," He said, "but you are beautiful."

She smiled, cocking her head slightly, her long dark hair falling over her shoulders, "You talk about the gods an awful lot for someone who doesn't believe in them."

He studied her, standing there. The most beautiful thing he'd ever seen, so vulnerable and so strong all at the same time, and he smiled, "I'm starting to."

She smiled then stepped forward, pulling his cloak off and tossing it on the ground, then his shirt and the rest of it. She studied him, whistling appreciatively, and he felt his face heat in the darkness. "Sword fighting does all that, does it?" She said.

"The scars, anyway," Aaron said, then he pulled her to him, their lips met, and for the first time in a long time, he wasn't worried about the things he'd done, wasn't scared of what he was or what he was becoming. His only thoughts were of her, of the heat of her pressed against him, of her smooth flesh against his own, the way her hair glided over his fingers as he ran his hand through it. He felt like a man who had finally set down a heavy burden, knowing he would have to pick it up again, but knowing, too, that that would be okay. That he could do it now, could carry it so long as he was required to. So long as there were moments like this in the world it wasn't all bad—it couldn't be all bad.

"Come on," she said, a moonlight nymph of impossible beauty and grace standing there in the darkness. "Follow me." She turned and made her way into the water, and Aaron did the only thing he could do. He followed her.

For a time, they left the world behind them. Left all their troubles and all their worries, their only thoughts of flesh and heat and the rhythm they made together so that nothing else existed at all but the two of them. So focused were they on one another that they did not notice the shadow that shifted by a nearby tree. Shifted and waited and watched before, finally, floating away back into the darkness.

CHAPTER TWENTY-EIGHT

They arrived at Perennia two days later. Aaron, like the others, was weary from the road. That, coupled with the fact that he and Adina would sneak away at any free moment had left him little time for sleep. Not that he was complaining.

"Are you as tired as I am?" Adina asked beside him as they made their way through the city gate. The guards looked at them with frowns that seemed the sole property of men who spent long hours guarding buildings or gates, but they did not stop them.

"Tired, sure," Aaron said, "the kind of tired I could get used to though."

She grinned at that, blushing in the sunlight, and he glanced at Leomin and Owen riding behind them, neither speaking. If either man had noticed his and Adina's nightly meetings, they had made no comment. In fact, neither of the two had said much of anything the past couple of nights, the majority of the talk belonging to Aaron and Adina but that was understandable, really. Weeks spent in the wilderness had a way of working on a man, making him feel disconnected, alone, making him really understand just how small he was and just how big the world is.

"What do you want to do?" Aaron said.

Adina glanced at her own clothes and at Aaron's frowning, "Isabelle can be somewhat ... influenced by appearances."

"She should love you then."

She smiled, tucking a strand of loose hair behind her ear, "While I appreciate the compliment, I think that we need a bath."

Aaron grinned back, "Sounds good to me."

"I *mean*," she said, her blush deepening, "a bath where the focus is on *washing* not on … well, anything else. No matter how … diverting."

Aaron nodded, "Diverting, huh?"

She winked, "Very."

"Alright," he said, "A bath it is. Though, I'll admit, I was just getting used to the smell of dirt and grass."

"No doubt," she said, and Aaron saw a mischievous glint in her eyes that he liked. Liked very much. "And to a certain type of bath too. Anyway, we need to get cleaned up, and we need some new clothes too." She frowned, thinking, "What gold we have, coupled with that we got from the slavers, should be enough to get us what we need."

"*Should* be?" Aaron asked, "gods woman we've got enough gold to live comfortably for a year in the Downs."

"Yes," Adina sad, "I believe you. The problem, of course, is that we're not *in* the Downs. Isabelle will expect a certain level of … sophistication. Anything less, and I doubt we'll make it past the castle door, let alone into a private audience with her."

"Seriously?" Aaron said, "You're her sister."

"Yes," Adina said, "but I will be her *well-dressed* sister. Not *too* well dressed, mind, not enough to be seen as competition to her, not enough to cast her in a poor light. Only enough that she can claim me without feeling as if she's losing face."

Aaron sighed, "Nobles and their games."

She met his eyes, "Yes, nobles and their games. But this is a game we have to play, and one we must not just play but *win* if we're to have any hope of convincing Isabelle to ally with Ellemont against Belgarin." They'd spoken about this on the road, deciding that Isabelle's army would not be enough to stand against Belgarin, that they would need Ellemont's as well. Adina had seemed hopeful enough, but Aaron couldn't help remembering what Festa had said. *A craven*, he'd called him.

"Anyway," Adina said, "Isabelle might hate my older brother, but she has little love for Ellemont either. It will take some convincing to get her to see reason, and I would like us all to look our best. Besides, it's late in the day. I would prefer to show up in the morning when Isabelle—and we—are fresh."

"An inn, then."

"Yes. And a bath."

Aaron glanced over at her, raising an eyebrow, "You keep saying that."

CHAPTER TWENTY-NINE

Aaron relaxed in the warm water of a bath the inn's serving girl had prepared and, despite what he'd said to Adina, he was glad for the moment to rub some of the soreness out of his muscles. Remembering the cause of some of that soreness was fun enough, but he was just as ready to lose it just the same.

She loves you, you know. The gods alone know why, but she does.

Aaron sighed, "Can't you let a man enjoy a simple bath, firefly? Besides, it doesn't seem exactly proper, you hanging around while I'm naked. What would Aliandra think?"

Nothing much, is my guess, Co said in an obviously satisfied tone, *she's had occasion to see such things before, more often than most. I do not expect she would be unduly alarmed ... or impressed.*

"Damn, firefly. Well, the water's cold anyway."

"That," Co said, speaking aloud and coming to hover inches from his face, "is not what you were thinking a moment ago."

He frowned, "Never mind what I was thinking a moment ago. A man's thoughts are his own, firefly. Or should be, at least."

"I only say this, Aaron. I like you—truly, I do, though even I do not understand the reason. You are an insufferable, disagreeable, man, and possibly the most overtly hostile person I have ever met."

"Eh ... thanks?"

"My point" Co went on as if he hadn't spoken, "is that, despite all of your flaws—and, believe me, there are many—I enjoy your company. It seems that the princess does too, though in a very different way."

"In quite a few ways, as I recall" Aaron said, leaning against the tub and letting his eyes close. The water really was warm and never mind the damn lightning bug and her jibes.

"*Lightning bug?*" She asked. "I'll let that pass for now, but only because I want to explain something to you. The princess is a good person, a kind person. I do not know what strange twist of fate has brought you two together, but I promise you this; if you break her heart, I will make you suffer for it. Do not think that my lack of arms or legs means that I cannot administer a proper beating, a proper *spanking* when the need arises. You will treat her with respect and kindness, as she deserves."

"As she *deserves?*" Aaron grunted a laugh, "Firefly, she deserves to live in a castle and be married to a prince. Problem is, princes have a way of getting killed of late and castles are faring little better. If we all got what we deserved, I would have died a long time ago. Adina deserves a lot better than me, and that's a fact."

"I'm glad to hear you say so," Co said, "if you are not what she deserves then you must strive to become it. Do not let her down, Aaron Envelar. And tell me. Do you love her?"

Aaron scratched the side of his neck, shifting in the tub. The water felt a little cooler now after all, and his position in the tub was not as comfortable as he'd thought it. "That's none of your business, firefly. Shit, you're ruining a perfectly good soak. Isn't there somewhere you need to be—like checking on Leomin, maybe? I know the man said he'd find us the right clothes, but forgive me for doubting the judgment of a man that walks around with bells in his hair."

Just then, as if he'd been waiting for his name to be called, the door opened and the Parnen captain strutted in, a shirt and pants slung over one arm. He closed the door behind him, whistling as he did and laid the clothes on the bed. Aaron, surprised, had half risen out of the tub, the sword in his hand, before he realized who it was.

Leomin glanced over at him and raised an eyebrow in question, as if *he* was the one doing something strange. "Leomin," Aaron said, "I'm certain that I locked the door when I came in."

The Parnen captain nodded, "You did, Mr. Envelar, indeed. That's why I had to ask the innkeeper for a key. Really a very nice lady," he said, and if he noticed Aaron's annoyance, he didn't show it as he went about lying the shirt and trousers down on the bed, fussing at them to keep them straight, "Has *eight* grandkids, if you can believe that. The oldest—Tommy, I believe it was—married now for ten years." He shook his head, "The world, Mr. Envelar, is truly full of remarkable people."

"And rude ones," Aaron said, "the kind that'll walk in on a man in his bath."

"Yes and those too," Leomin said, clucking his tongue, "still," he said, shrugging, "there is no accounting for what people might do. They are more vast than the stars and just as complex."

"You're right," Aaron said, frowning, "like, sometimes, people beat the shit out of each other for no good reason. Of course, sometimes they beat the shit out of each other for *perfectly* good reasons."

Leomin seemed to finally notice something in Aaron's tone, for he turned, glancing at Aaron who still stood half out of the tub, the sword in his hand. "Ah. I am only here to deliver your clothes, as the princess asked. You will not need your blade, Mr. Envelar."

"I haven't decided that yet."

The Parnen swallowed, "Right. Well, I suppose I'll be going then. Is there anything else you need from me, Mr. Envelar?"

"Just the one thing."

Leomin paused for a moment then nodded, "Ah, yes, I see." He headed toward the door and hesitated, his hand on the knob. Aaron had just settled back into the tub when Leomin turned. "A curious thing, Mr. Envelar. I saw your friend, Master Owen earlier."

"Yeah?" Aaron said, "Well, you would, Leomin. Considering the fact that he's staying in the same inn as us—only two doors down from my own room, in fact." His eyebrows furrowed in thought, "I wonder if that's close enough that he'd hear the screams."

The Parnen's eyes widened, but he nodded again, slowly. "You're right, of course. Still, I saw him a few streets over, speaking with a man I haven't met before. The sort of man that seems dangerous."

"Oh?" Aaron said, rolling his eyes, "And what exactly seemed dangerous about him? Was he screaming and running around with a bloody sword, maybe?"

Leomin shook his head, "Nothing so obvious as that, I'm afraid. There was just something in the way he moved, the way he walked. A thin man, though not overly so. He seemed fit enough and something about the way he moved reminded me well ... of you, Mr. Envelar. I wouldn't bet my life on it, but if I had to hazard a guess, I'd say the man was a fighter of some kind."

"What gave it away?" Aaron asked, suddenly more exhausted than he had been after listening to the Parnen's prattle. "Have a knife scar across his face? Punching someone when you seen him, was he?"

"No and no, alas," Leomin said, "for either of those would, perhaps, help put to bed my confusion. He was only talking, though quietly, to our young friend, Owen. I could not tell you, with any certainty, what was said, of course, me not being the type to spy on people without their consent."

Aaron wondered what exactly it meant to spy on someone *with* their consent but said instead, "No, you? Of course not. Anyway, why are you telling me about this? Owen is his own man and welcome to speak to whomever he chooses."

"Of course, of course," Leomin said, nodding, "still. I found it passing strange that he and this man spoke with such familiarity. Almost as if they knew each other and, this could be my imagination, but it seemed to me as if the man was subservient to our friend."

"Subservient?" Aaron said, "So something about this stranger screamed fighter and subservient to you?"

"Indeed. I only found it mildly curious since Owen explained that he'd never been to Isalla before. How strange, then, to happen across someone he knows, wouldn't you say?"

Aaron frowned, "No stranger than a man wears bells in his hair," he muttered, then said aloud, "Is there anything else, Leomin?"

"No," the Parnen said, "not especially."

The two stared at each other for a moment, and Aaron said, "Well?"

Leomin started, "Ah, yes, of course. My apologies, Mr. Envelar. Please, do enjoy your bath."

Too late for that. "Oh, and Leomin?" He asked as the Parnen opened the door.

"Yes, Mr. Envelar?"

Aaron glanced at the clothes on the bed, "They don't have a lot of frills do they? Tassels and what not?"

Leomin smiled, but it was a smile that did little to put Aaron at ease about what he would soon be expected to wear. "No more than necessary, Mr. Envelar. No more than necessary."

CHAPTER THIRTY

They approached the castle gates early the next morning, Aaron frowning for what had to have been the hundredth time at his shirt and trousers. The midnight black trousers fit well enough, though they were too tight. The shirt, though, was of a sky blue color and had long puffy sleeves at the end of which were frills like some noble dandy might wear. As far as Aaron could see, there wasn't any practical use for the damn things except for getting in a man's way when he tried to take a leak. *Damn Parnen.* At least the man had bought him a new hooded sable cloak of much finer make than his old tattered cloak had been even when it had been new.

He glanced over at Leomin now as they waited in line for entrance to the castle behind about a dozen people. All, it seemed, seeking audience with their queen. The captain had assured Aaron that the billowing sleeves were the height of fashion, though the sellsword couldn't help but notice that the Parnen's own orange shirt had no such adornments. A simple long-sleeved tunic, though of fine material and richly made. His own tan trousers leaving enough room, Aaron thought, so that the man, unlike himself, probably didn't feel as if his legs were going numb if he stood still for too long.

Owen, at least, seemed as uncomfortable in his fine attire as Aaron felt, his body too long in places and seemingly too short in others, so that the green shirt he wore looked hung awkwardly on his lank frame.

Adina though … Aaron stared at her back—and the rest of her—appreciating Leomin's choice in dresses, at least. The light blue dress she wore—a color that mirrored Aaron's shirt, and he wondered if that wasn't' Leomin's roundabout way of saying their association wasn't as secret as they might have hoped—clung to her in ways that Aaron found most distracting. If her hope had been to not eclipse her sister in beauty, Aaron thought she would be disappointed. Even were the Goddess of Love sitting in her sister's throne, she couldn't help but look plain in comparison.

Finally, it was their turn at the gate, and it was just as well. Aaron was beginning to sweat in his clothes and cloak, his body used to the colder temperatures of Baresh. Still, he was loath to take the cloak off. It did a passable job of concealing the ridiculous shirt he wore underneath.

Adina stepped up to the two guards at the gate, taking the lead as she'd said she would before they'd left the inn. They were dressed in spotless white uniforms, their breastplates and helmets gleaming in the morning sun. The visors of their helmets were thrown open now, and Aaron could see that they were young men, both, the type that he thought most women would find attractive. No scars or wounds to mar those raised cheekbones and sharp, pointed noses. He didn't think he'd ever seen soldiers look so pretty. Or so stupid.

"Good morning, gentlemen," Adina was saying.

The first guard's eyes roamed up and down Adina's form, and he smiled, "Good mornin' to you too," he said, bowing his head.

"Just so," the second said, sharing a grin with the first, "though it could be a better morning for us both, I think, you meet me at an inn I know later, lass."

"Or the both of us," the other guard said, "we're not against sharing, if sharing's called for."

Adina smiled slowly, and Aaron resisted the urge to grab the two fools and slam their faces together. He wondered how pretty they'd be with broken noses. He had just about decided there was only one way to find out when Adina glanced back at him, a warning in her eyes, and he sighed and watched in silence.

"A tempting offer," she said, "unfortunately, I've other business I must attend to. Perhaps another time. I must speak with your queen."

"You sure?" The first asked, his eyes roaming over the princess's body in a way that had Aaron thinking he'd be surprised she didn't come out of this pregnant just from the man's look. "See, thing is, it's a long line of folks that wait to speak with Her Majesty."

"So it is," the other guard said, "why, I've seen people wait a week for an audience and still not get so much as a glance at her Royal Highness. Maybe," he said, grinning again, "if you could see your way to doing *us* a favor, such as it is, we might find a spot for you and your," he glanced at Aaron and the others then seemed to dismiss them immediately, "servants here, closer to the front. The queen, after all, is only one person, no matter how wise and beautiful, and it's a big city. A bigger kingdom. She can't be expected to see every farmer or shop owner comes calling."

"Oh, I think she'll see me," Adina said, her smile still well in place. "And might I just add that those really *are* fine uniforms. Quite pretty." The two men smiled at that, but she went on, "I wonder how it is that the two of you manage to keep the filth that comes out of your mouth from staining them. It must cost a fortune in laundering."

Aaron grunted a laugh at that and turned to see Leomin grinning back at him. The two guards' smiles were slow in fading as they began to understand that they'd been mocked. "Well," the first said, "there's no cause to be a bitch, lady."

"Yes," the other said, "no cause at all. And, as it turns out, it seems that the queen has stopped taking audiences for the day. Maybe you should come back tomorrow. Might be, you'll be in a more amicable mood then."

"Amicable?" Adina said, "I'm impressed. Come up with that one all on your own, did you?"

The man let out a growl, "Get your ass out of here and take this trash with you," he said, motioning at Aaron and the others, "before we find you an unoccupied cell in the dungeon."

Adina nodded slowly, "Well, I certainly don't want to remain where I'm not wanted. Only ... perhaps we'd better check with your queen first, just to be sure. Why don't you tell her the ... what was it you said? Oh yes, the bitch, her sister, Adina, has come to visit."

The two guards' eyes went wide at that, and they stared at each other in shock. Then, finally, one of them smiled slowly, turning back. "Adina, is it? Well, you're pretty enough, lass, good enough for a roll in the hay, maybe more than one."

"I wouldn't kick you out of bed," the other agreed.

"Thing is," the first one who'd spoken said, "the princess Adina is said to be—or, I should say, said to have *been*—one of the most beautiful women in the world, and I don't know that you quite make the cut on that score."

"Though," the other said, "I don't guess we could really say for sure, could we? Not until we'd seen you dressed as the gods clothed you, anyway."

"He means naked," the first said. "Still, I say *been* on account of word reached the capital weeks ago now of trouble in Adina's kingdom. Tale is, the princess's beauty—though great it surely was—wasn't enough to keep her horse from throwing her and trampling her under it."

"He means she's dead," the second guard supplied.

"And yet," Adina said, her smile still well in place, and Aaron was struck again by the woman's patience, "here I am. And as for being good enough for a roll in the hay, I'm sure I'll have to let my sister know of the graciousness of her guards, once I speak with her."

"Let it go already," one said, "gods, woman, it was a clever enough joke, but you'd best drop it now and be on about your way. Unless," he said, taking a step closer to her, "you've reconsidered our offer?"

"I think," Adina said, standing her ground, "I'd like to counter with an offer of my own. You go in and tell my sister that I've come to visit her *now,* and maybe I'll forget about the crassness and foolishness of her guards when we speak. I do not think she would like to hear that her younger sister had been kept waiting at the gate to be ogled and propositioned by her guards. If proof is needed of my identity, ask her if she remembers the name Sophie. Sophie Ravenhair."

The two guards turned to each other, "Surely, you don't think..."

The other shook his head, a man whose warning had went unheeded, "Best send a runner to tell the queen." He turned back to Adina as the other guard motioned a man forward, whispering into his ear, "I don't think you've any idea how much trouble you're going to be in, miss, once the man comes back and says the queen doesn't know you from anybody. I were you, I'd get gone before he does."

Adina smiled, "I think I'll wait just the same."

The man shrugged, "Have it your way."

They stepped to the side of the line by the gate, and Leomin smiled, bowing his head to Adina as if in acknowledgment. "Handled most deftly, my princess. Truly, it is a joy to watch you."

Adina rolled her eyes, "They aren't the first fools I've had to deal with, and I don't suspect they'll be the last, but thank you just the same."

They waited, Aaron fidgeting and wiping the sweat from his brow, for what must have been close to an hour, until even Adina was visibly losing her patience. Then, finally, the runner came back and spoke some hurried words in the guards' ears, glancing at Adina and the others.

The two men paled visibly, and Aaron couldn't help but smile at their obvious discomfort as they made their way over to him and the others. "Princess," One said, bowing his head so low that Aaron thought the man would tip over, "I ask that you please forgive us our ... jokes. It can sometimes become ... tedious standing and watching a gate all day."

Adina stared at the man, no smile in evidence now, her nose slightly up, her face regal and impatient, a princess in truth. "As tedious, I suspect, as standing in line for nearly an hour only to be spoken to like some tavern harlot by two guardsmen that should know better. As tedious, no doubt, as what most suffer each day, waiting in line for hours on end to see the queen only to be met with two fools such as yourselves."

The other guard swallowed, "Princess," he said hurriedly, "we didn't mean--"

"Never mind what you meant," Adina said, "for I know it well enough as do these with me," she said, gesturing at Aaron and the others, "my *companions* who I expect will be treated with the respect you would show me."

"Of course, of course," the first said, "Please, sirs, forgive us our jests. They were not given with ill will. Princess," he said, turning back to Adina, "the Queen will see you now, if you and your companions are ready."

Aaron snorted, "Ready? Well, we were just now thinking about hanging around out here until the pool of sweat beneath our feet got big enough to swim in, but I suppose if you insist."

Adina smiled at him then turned back to the captain. "You see, guardsman? Jokes are supposed to be funny. Now, lead us to my sister and be quick about it—I've little patience left."

CHAPTER THIRTY-ONE

Aaron stifled a yawn, shifting in his chair to try to find a more comfortable position. They'd waited for nearly two hours outside the Queen's audience chamber, and he wasn't a man used to waiting around unless he was getting paid to do it.

She intends to show Adina who rules here and who does not, Co said, a sneer in her voice, *it is the way of nobles.*

I detect a bit of hostility there, firefly. Anyway, she makes us wait much longer, they'll open the doors to a snoring sellsword. Or skeletons, maybe, depending on how much this Isabelle has to prove.

He glanced at Leomin and noted that the Parnen's head hung loosely on his chest, and though his long dark, braided hair obscured his features, it was easy enough to tell by the steady rise and fall of the Parnen's chest that the man was asleep. As for Owen, the thin man sat nervously, his hands, when they weren't fidgeting at his shirt in a failed attempt to make it fit better, clasped tightly in his lap like a child who'd been up to mischief waiting for his punishment.

Adina, on the other hand, grew angrier and angrier as Aaron watched, her frown a slight thing at first, now a steady scowl in truth as she got up for what must have been the tenth time and moved to the officious looking older woman sitting behind the desk by the door. "How much longer until we are allowed to see the queen?" Adina said, her exasperation evident in her tone, "The news we carry is urgent."

The old woman glanced up from some papers she'd been looking over and shook her head slowly, apologetically, though Aaron thought he could detect a certain satisfaction in her eyes, "I'm afraid I'm not sure, princess. The Queen does not see fit to divulge her schedule to one as lowly as I, after all. Still, I was told she was very excited at the prospect of your visit and, no doubt, you will be allowed in shortly."

"That's what you said an hour ago."

The woman didn't answer, only smiled benignly at Adina. Finally, Adina let out a huff and walked back to sit down beside Aaron. "This is ridiculous," she said.

"Well," he said, wincing at the soreness as he adjusted his seat in the straight-backed wooden chair, "at least the chairs are nice."

"You would think," she said, apparently not having heard, "that she would be, oh, I don't know *excited* to see her sister who'd she thought was dead. Instead, it is the same games as always, the same stupid demonstrations of power. All nobles play the game to a degree, I suppose, but Isabelle has always been the worst—or best—at it, depending on your view. Still, I would have thought she'd grown out of it, changed by now. It has been many years since I've seen or spoken to her."

"My experience," Aaron said, "People don't change unless they're made to, and I don't think there's too many around here that are going to make your sister do anything except what she wants to do."

Adina still didn't seem to be hearing him, too busy being angry, feeling the urgency just like Aaron himself did, feeling like every minute counted, including the last hundred or so they'd spent sitting in contraptions that he could only assume were overflow from the torture room. After all, it wouldn't be long until Belgarin decided to bring his army to bear against Isabelle or his brother Ellemont. With Avarest, they were the only powers of any size worth mentioning, the only armies that could possibly have a chance of standing against him and even still he'd have the greater numbers—assuming Adina's own troops threw in with him as well, which seemed likely. If Belgarin's wasn't on its way already, it would be soon.

As if her thoughts had been running a similar course, Adina rose up out of her chair again, stomping toward the door.

"Princess, I'm sorry—" the woman began, but Adina ignored her, banging on the wooden door as loud as she could, slamming her fist against it.

Aaron raised an eyebrow and stood, making his way to her. They'd taken his sword from him when he'd come into the castle which was too bad. He had the feeling that if Adina's anger didn't cool—and it showed no signs of that—he might have need of it before long.

Finally, just about the time Aaron was getting ready to tell Adina she'd better hold off before she broke her hand, the door swung open and two frowning guards, their swords drawn, stared back at her. "We have journeyed a long way," Adina told the men, "and I do not intend to be kept waiting all day when I've important news for my sister. Now, get out of our way."

The two guards glanced at each other then moved forward, intending, it seemed, to grab Adina and force her out. Before they could, a voice rang out from back further in the hall, "*Adina?*" Came the woman's voice, filled with pleasant surprise, "is that you? Well, men put those swords away please before you hurt someone. That's my royal *sister* you have before you."

The two guards did as they'd been ordered, scowling as they moved to either side of the door, and Aaron and Leomin followed after. Owen trailed behind them, his head bowed low as if he expected to feel the bite of the headman's axe at any moment.

The woman seated on the throne was, if not as fat as the Duke Claudius had been, a close second, Aaron thought. She wore a fine ostentatious dress—far more frills and embroidery than Aaron's own shirt, thank the gods—and her long hair fell in lazy blonde curls about a face that was nearly as round as a dolls, bloated and pink with over indulgence and excess.

The fabric of the white, orange, and gold dress, Aaron thought, would have been enough to fit Adina four times over with some to spare. Three tables formed a U-shape on a level below the queen's throne and in the center of them stood three men with dueling rapiers in their hands.

Two of the men were dressed in the simple, ragged browns of commoners, and they held the dueling blades awkwardly, clearly not trained in their use. The third wore a uniform of white, gold, and orange that was nearly as ornate in its embroidery and finery as the Queen's own, and held the blade at his side, a small confident smile on his face.

The finely dressed man turned to them, and his smile faded to a look of slight disgust as his gaze seemed to settle on Aaron, choosing him out of the lot as the one at which to direct his ire. No surprise, really. Aaron knew such men—had had occasion to deal with them in the past. Men who always felt they had something to prove and looked for someone easy enough to prove it. Evidence of that stood in the dueling circle with him, the two commoners, no doubt farmers or sailors, who were breathing heavily, the man himself composed and relaxed, enjoying the game he'd been playing and angry at its interruption.

"Adina, but it is a pleasure to see you," Isabelle said in a cooing sort of way that Aaron found strange, as if she was speaking to a child.

"I had wondered about that," Adina said, and Aaron could hear her forcing civility into her tone, "as we have been kept waiting for near on two hours. Forgive me, sister, but I had almost begun to think that you had forgotten about us. That, or, perhaps, that we'd been made to wait intentionally for some reason, though I cannot imagine what such a reason might be."

The queen laughed softly, waving fingers as thick as sausages, "Oh, of course not, dear sister. Forgive me, it's only that we were in the middle of a show, you see. The captain of my guard here," she said, nodding at the uniformed scowling man, "Francis, has been putting on *quite* a display for us, hasn't he, my lords and ladies?" The dozen or so noblemen and women seated at the tables smiled and murmured their agreement. "*Quite* a show," the queen continued, eyeing the captain the way a starving mongrel might eye a steak. Truly, an impressive demonstration of skill and valor."

The scowling man smile deeply, bowing his head low to her, "Ah, my queen is far too kind, and it is my honor to show what small skill I have for the entertainment of her and such lords and ladies as are gathered here." He turned back to look at Aaron when he'd finished speaking, the look in his gaze making Aaron suspect that, just maybe, he wasn't included in that group.

The queen's mouth opened in a pleasured cooing sound again, and she motioned with a finger, a pretty young girl hurrying forward in servant's garb to set about fanning her face. *Gods,*

Aaron thought, *what a job, keeping that cool. Might as well try to take the heat out of a fire.* "My, but dear Francis you *do* have a pleasant way with words, don't you? *Quite* a speaker."

The man bowed his head again, "I strive to be whatever my Queen requires, of course, your Majesty."

The queen let out a titter at that, "Please, Adina," she said, motioning to a few empty seats at the end of the table farthest from her, "have a seat, you and your companions. You have arrived just in time for, what I suspect," she said, eyeing the two obviously weary commoners, "will be the end of our little show."

Aaron glanced at Adina as she visibly gathered herself, pushing her anger down. "This, I'm afraid, is not a social visit, sister. I have matters of some import I would like to discuss with you."

The queen made a pouty face, "Oh, Adina, please. Not during the feast," she said, motioning at the heaping piles of meats and pies and pastries littered on the tables, "surely, it can wait until after."

"It has waited already, sister," Adina said, "Two weeks hard travel in the woods, an hour at your gates, and another two in your room there," she said, motioning stiffly with her head, "I do not think it wise that it should wait any longer."

"Yes, yes," the queen said in a pouty, put upon voice, "I see that you feel it is important, whatever it is. And we will hear the reason of your coming soon enough, once the show and feast are done. So please, sister, do sit. Have something to eat—there are all matters of delights and delicacies laid before you."

Aaron noticed, as she said this, that her eyes were locked on the captain of the guard, Francis, the man smiling a small, knowing smile at her. He glanced at Adina and, judging by her expression, she had not missed it either. "Truly," the queen went on, studying Leomin, "I would be very much interested to hear what you've been up to of late and how, exactly, you came by such ... exotic companions," she said. Then she turned to Aaron, "Exotic and pleasing to the eye as well. A formidable group indeed. I am most excited to hear your news. *After* the show and dinner."

Aaron did not need to turn to look to know that the captain was staring at him angrily and wished for the hundredth time that the damned pants weren't so damned tight, but he forced himself to stand steady under what could only be the queen's lecherous gaze. "Very well," Adina said stiffly, obviously angry but deciding it was best to let the matter go. She walked stiffly to a nearby chair and sat, Aaron and the others following her lead.

Once they were seated, the queen smiled beneficently over her gathered guests then back to the man, Francis. "Now, captain," she said, "if you and your ... opponents, are ready?"

The commoners, wincing and obviously reluctant to end their short reprieve, stood from where they'd sat crouched, holding their dueling steels the way a man might hold a stick. *A farce,* Aaron thought, *no fair competition this, never mind that there are two of them. There could be half a dozen, and the outcome would be the same.*

Oh, but the nobles do love their shows, Co said, and there was that bitterness again, something Aaron intended to ask her about when they had the time.

The captain waited, motioning with his rapier for the two commoners to approach, and they did so reluctantly, knowing it was expected of them. Their swipes with the dueling steels were wide and telegraphed, and the captain of the guard sidestepped or parried them easily, doing nothing to hide his disdain for their lack of skill, not just batting their attacks aside, but embarrassing them, tripping them where he could, or sending their dueling steels knocking into each other, so they got tangled up more than once. The nobles, for their part, watched on, laughing and whispering at the show, as if those two men down there were not men at all but animals performing for their entertainment, and the captain the beast master, showing what tricks he'd taught them.

Aaron felt the familiar anger that he'd held for so long at nobles rise in him as he watched the mockery of a duel, watched the commoners pick themselves up off the ground after each embarrassment only to wade head first into the next. Finally, after having drawn it out as much as possible, the captain tripped one man, sending him to the ground and slapping his rapier across his opponent's face, leaving a welt and drawing blood. The commoner cried out in surprised pain, but the queen and nobles laughed and clapped their hands.

The second man let out a growl and came on, swinging wildly for all that he was obviously exhausted, and the captain batted his attack aside, pushed him off balance and sent him stumbling past, smacking him on the backside as he did. The man tripped and fell, climbing to his feet with a curse, but he'd taken no more than a step when the captain's blade was at his throat, pressed just hard enough to draw a dot of blood.

"Bravo, bravo!" The queen exclaimed, and she and the nobles clapped their hands again, laughing and bragging about the display to each other as if they'd been the ones to do it, as if it the outcome hadn't been a foregone conclusion from the beginning.

The man, Francis, pulled his rapier away from the commoner's throat then gave it a flourish before bringing it down to his side, soaking in the applause as a guard came forward and escorted the two exhausted commoners from the hall.

Aaron watched them go, defeated and limping, their postures slumped in a way he'd had cause to see plenty of times before. This wasn't the first cruelty they'd experienced, and they knew enough about the world, he suspected, to know it wouldn't be the last. They'd no doubt take some small bit of coin—enough to help them feed their families for a time—and it cost them nothing but a little bit of their dignity, something that was no doubt already in short supply.

"Oh, but my dear Francis," the queen said, a poutiness in her voice again, "you've finished the show too quickly. Now, what will my lords and ladies have to keep them entertained while they finish their meals?"

The sight of you in that chair ought to be enough, Aaron thought.

"Forgive me, my queen," the man said solemnly, bowing low, and Aaron had to struggle to keep back a snort of disgust, "I did not mean to finish so quickly."

"Oh, well," Isabelle said, "I forgive you, of course," her voice again taking on the tone of one talking to a child, "still, I do wish there was *someone* else here that might offer you a fair competition. Some spectacle for my lords and ladies to enjoy. I, myself, do so get *invigorated* by such displays of manly skill."

Aaron sighed inwardly, knowing what was coming even before the guard captain turned to look at him, running a hand through his perfectly styled hair. "What about one of your sister's men?" He said, as if the thought had just occurred. "As my queen has said, they do seem most formidable. Perhaps one of them would be so kind as to help me entertain these fine lords and ladies."

"You, sir?" He said, looking directly at Aaron, "have you any experience with a blade?"

Aaron sighed, glancing at Adina, waiting for her to give him a slight nod before turning back to the man. "Some."

"Some indeed!" The man exclaimed, grinning, playing to the crowd as he held his hands out, "Why, I bet you are *most* ferocious, sir. You strike me as, perhaps, one with great experience in such things, never mind your humbleness."

Aaron rubbed a hand across his jaw, but did not speak. Finally, the guard captain's smile faded some, "Well?"

"Sorry?" Aaron said, "There was a question in that?"

"My question, sir," the guard captain said, "is if you have participated in such a contest, man against man, blade against blade, as this?"

"Like the one I just watched?" Aaron said. "No, not like that, I haven't."

The captain grinned again, looking around at the table of noblemen and women who laughed and tittered behind their hands as if at some joke. "No, truly?"

"Truly," Aaron said, "generally the … *contests* did you call it? Generally the contests that I participate in have a lot more blood and the losers aren't often able to walk away after. Still, I suppose the show was diverting enough, though I'd just as soon watch mean-hearted children chase a mongrel dog in the street. At least the dog has a chance."

The man's smile vanished. "Mean-hearted children, you say?"

Aaron nodded, "That's right. Anyway, the kind of scraps I've been in, people have a tendency to walk away with a bit more blood on 'em. If they walk away at all, that is, and it's not treated like some cheap street show, folks pay a copper and get to see men make fools of themselves."

"Fools, is it?" The captain said, his face turning a deep shade of crimson. "I wonder, sir, are you all talk?" He turned, addressing Aaron but taking in the noblemen and ladies and, of course, the queen, "It's an easy enough thing, I suppose, to sit in your chair, comfortable and at ease, and criticize better men."

"Better men?" Aaron said, "I'm not sure. Let me know when the better men get here, I'll tell you if it's easy or not."

"A challenge!" One of the noblemen shouted gleefully, clapping his hands together.

Soon, the other nobles were clapping as well, the queen looking on with a look that Aaron could only think of as hungry. Of course, judging by the size of her, he wasn't sure that the woman had many others. "What of it, boy?" The handsome captain said, smiling and running a hand through his hair. He lifted one of the rapiers from the ground where the commoners had dropped them and held it up, hilt first to Aaron, "Why not show us this contest of yours that always ends in blood. I'm sure myself and those gathered here would love to see it."

"*Challenge,*" one of the nobles, a balding, thick-jowled man shouted around a mouthful of cake then the others took it up, chanting it. Aaron sighed and glanced at Adina again. She looked around the room and shrugged, "There's not a lot of options," she said in a voice low enough that only he could hear, "just make it fast, will you? We've wasted enough time already."

Aaron nodded, rising, "I'll see what I can do."

He started away, but she caught his hand, halting him, "Aaron," she said, "don't kill him, okay?"

Aaron gave her a small smile, "I'll see what I can do."

He walked to the center of the floor, between the tables, and took the thin dueling steel the man offered. He tested it with a couple of swipes and shook his head. The damned thing might as well have been a toy. No real way to hurt a man, not with such a flimsy, light thing. Unless maybe you stuck him in the eye, he supposed. If such a blade was the only thing between him and death, a man would be better to drop the thing and run like Salen himself was after him. Hope his opponent tripped and broke his neck, maybe.

"I think it would only be fair to warn you," the handsome guard captain said, "that I have been trained for ten years by some of the best duelists in the city. I have spent the better part of my life learning the art of the blade."

Aaron grunted, "With a name like Francis, I guess you'd have to, wouldn't you?"

The man hissed in anger at that, "My queen," he said, turning, "we are prepared when you are."

The queen smiled, glancing around at the gathered nobles, "Well, my lords and ladies, shall we have us a show?"

The nobles clapped and gave cheers as if on cue, puppets knowing what was expected of them when their strings were pulled.

"Very well," the queen said, "but try not to hurt your sister's companion too much, please captain. And let us make it interesting. The man who draws first blood will be considered the winner." Then she clapped her hands, her chins shaking with her laughter, "Begin!"

And begin he did, the captain hurtling forward, his attacks swift and confident. Aaron backpedaled, moving in a circle in the relatively small space the room afforded him, taking the man's measure. The captain was fast, that was true, his strikes sure, but he was angry now and that, coupled with the fact that he'd never fought for his life, never had the real fear of death to spur his actions, meant that he paid little attention to his own defense, sending in strike after strike with no care for what his opponent might counter with.

Aaron let himself be pushed back and back, always circling so that he didn't fetch up against one of the tables—this crowd, he didn't know if he'd ever be forgiven for disrupting the pastries. The captain grew more confident with each backward step Aaron took and soon there was a smile on his face, a smile saying he already knew how the thing would end, it was just a matter of getting there.

Aaron's blade seemed to barely parry each attack, saving him at the last instant each time, and the captain's smile grew wider still. The nobles and the queen clapped on, leaning forward in their seats in expectation. Then, judging when the time was right, Aaron stopped backpedaling under the man's assault, instead stepping forward and swinging his thin blade at the man's own as it darted forward, knocking it wide.

In another moment, the tip of his dueling steel was at the man's throat, a small drop of blood gathering there. The guard captain stared at it in shock, as if it was some strange creature that he'd never seen before and had not thought existed. "Ten years of training, you say?" Aaron said. "I've been training my entire life."

"I … captain," the queen began, her voice suddenly unsure and confused, but the young handsome man wasn't listening. He growled and knocked Aaron's blade aside with his own as he began his assault again.

Aaron had expected as much from the man, a man not used to being matched against someone with any skill with a blade, and he allowed himself to be pushed back under the assault once again. Closer and closer they drew to the tables, Aaron not circling this time but moving straight back as the young man hissed and cursed and swung his blade in ferocious arcs, charging forward, his anger controlling him now.

Aaron gave the queen what time he could, time to get her man in check, to call him down for having lost, but she said nothing and a stolen glance showed her leaning forward eagerly, licking her lips in anticipation. *Alright then.* Aaron waited until he judged the tables a couple of feet behind him, no more, then he stepped out of the way of one of the young captain's lunges and, instead of bringing his own blade to bear, he knotted his free hand into a fist and hammered it into the captain's stomach.

The captain's breath left him in a pained gust, but Aaron wasn't finished. He stepped forward, grabbing the man by the back of the head, and slamming his face down into one of the tables, the noble sitting across giving a shout of surprise as he did. The captain's head rebounded off the table, and his steel fell to the ground as he dropped backward onto his ass.

Aaron stared down at the whimpering man, a hand over his freshly broken nose, blood running from it onto his face and his fine white clothes. "Y-you … bwoke my nose." The young captain stammered, his eyes staring at Aaron in shock.

Aaron nodded, shrugging, "I warned you," he said, tossing his own steel to land at the young man's feet, "where I come from, there's always a lot more blood."

The dining hall grew completely silent then, a stunned, shocked silence. Then, a single set of hands began clapping, and Aaron turned to see a guard extricate himself from the side of the room where he and others soldiers had been stationed. He was an older man, in his fifties, maybe, short cropped gray hair, and a coarse growth of beard and moustache, as if he hadn't shaved in a few days. The stubble did little to hide a scar that ran down one side of his face, no doubt the reason for the patch covering his left eye. "Well done," he said.

Aaron stared at the man. Not as pretty as the youth, maybe, not an ornament to be fancied up and go well with a certain dress or to pander to the nobles, but a man who clearly knew his business. Aaron nodded to him, dipping his head low, and the man grinned before turning to the queen, "Your Majesty," he said, "With your permission, I'd better get the captain here to a healer, see what can be done about the nose."

The queen sat frozen for a second, then her face slowly twisted into that of a petulant child, a spoiled one who'd just been told 'no' for the first time in her life. "Very well, sergeant," she spat, "take him and see to it that he gets the best of care."

The man bowed, "Of course, my queen."

He walked toward where the young captain still sat on the ground, his broken nose cradled now in two bloody hands. "Alright, captain," he said, putting his hands under the man's arms and hoisting him up, "Up you get."

"*He bwoke my nose,*" the young captain said again, slobber and blood coming out as he did.

"Yes sir," the older man said, glancing at Aaron, his eyes dancing in amusement, "A clean break." He got the man upright and slung one of the young captain's arms over his own and turned to start toward the door but paused at the sound of the queen's voice.

"Sergeant?" The queen said.

"Yes, your Majesty?"

"We will speak with you alone, after. Perhaps, it would be wise to see that you are taught something of decorum and manners."

The sergeant bowed his head as well as he could under the weight of the young man, but Aaron could see the laughter still lurking in his eyes, "Of course, your Majesty. As you will."

"Sergeant is it?" Aaron asked as the man walked past, thinking that, from what he'd seen, the man should have been captain. Knew enough to know that the man would have made a good one.

The older man didn't speak, his only answer a wink with his one good eye as he made his way toward the door.

"Well,' the queen said, her voice petulant and annoyed, once the sergeant had led the bleeding, slobbering captain from the hall. "I don't know how you do things where *you* come from, sir," she said, turning to Aaron, "but here in Isalla, we do not *assault* men who we are dueling for sport. We are not *savages,"* she said, glancing at Leomin, "after all."

Aaron didn't know how to respond to that. Sure, he could mention the fact that he *had* drawn first blood, the queen's own rule, but that the man had kept at him anyway, and he'd only been defending himself, but why bother? It was clear enough how it was going to go, so he said nothing instead.

"And now you do not speak?" Isabelle said, shaking her head in disgust and turning to Adina, "I do not know *where* you find such creatures as this, dear sister, but I am of a mind to throw him in a cage until you leave. Who knows what such a one will do next?"

Adina turned away from staring at Aaron to look at the queen and sighed. "Sister, you know as well as I that Aaron drew first blood. Your captain is the one—"

"My *captain* is now injured, *sister,"* the queen hissed, "and his nose might never set right again after your," she hesitated, waving her chubby fingers at Aaron, "your *thug* there so cruelly broke it." Adina started to speak again, but the queen held up an angry hand, forestalling her, "Know also, *younger sister,* that I will not be lectured in my own halls."

"Very well," Adina said, with an obvious effort, "I apologize, sister. If there's anything we can do to help with your man's recovery—"

"*Such as?"* Isabelle spat, "what, will your pet Parnen cast some witchery on him, sister? No, I think not. My own personal healers will see to Francis, thank you."

"These men," Adina said, "are the most trustworthy I have ever known, sister. I would trust any one of them with my life and more but as you will. Anyway, it's important that I talk to you about why we've come. You see—"

"No, no, *no,"* The queen said, "I will not speak to you of whatever business has brought you to my door step now, for I am too upset. I know some bit of your own troubles, sister, and I'd think that a princess without a kingdom would be wise to show more courtesy upon visiting others. Think of that, while you wait in your rooms." She waved a hand and several guards stepped forward to escort Adina and the others out. "Show my sister and her ... *associates* to their rooms. I will call for them later, once I have had some time to reflect."

Adina looked like she wanted to say something but thought better of it, turning stiffly and following the guards out. Aaron started to follow then glanced at the blood staining the perfectly white floor. "Does anybody have a napkin?" He said, glancing at the nobles at the tables who stared at him as if they didn't speak his language.

"Get *out!*" The queen screeched, and Aaron nodded, turning and following after Adina and the rest.

CHAPTER THIRTY-TWO

They'd all been shown to separate rooms on one wing of the castle and guards were posted at the end, ostensibly to keep them safe, but Aaron suspected the men were really there to keep an eye on them. He'd been in his room for no more than half an hour before Adina came to get him, leading him into her own room where—he was disappointed to see—the others waited. "Well" she said once they were all settled, "that maybe could have went better."

"Still," Leomin said, grinning at Aaron, "it was fun to watch. Mr. Envelar, if you ever decide to change professions, I confess that I believe you would excel in the theater."

Adina laughed, "I'll admit that I did enjoy watching that pompous bastard be taught a lesson. But...." She glanced at Aaron, "did you have to break his nose?"

"No. I didn't have to. But, then, he didn't have to embarrass those men, either."

Leomin laughed at that, and even Owen gave a tentative smile. "A room full of fools," the Parnen said, "It would have done them well, I think, had they all received similar treatment as our poor young captain." He glanced at Adina, "No offense, of course, to your sister, princess."

"Never mind that, Leomin," Adina said, "She's the biggest fool of the lot, at least. I still can't believe it. Isabelle always had a touch of vanity, sure, but ... what we saw in there?" She shook her head, "I almost didn't even recognize her and not just from the way she looked. My sister has always been vain, but she's never been cruel before, watching and laughing while Captain Francis did that."

"A room full of fools, maybe," Aaron said, "but I wonder about that one man. The older guy, one your sister called sergeant. He seemed to know what he was about."

"And that's another thing that troubles me," Adina said. "The man you're speaking of? His name is Brandon Gant. He once served under my father, a good soldier, a good man. The last I heard, he was serving as my sister's captain of the guard. To be replaced by that pompous bastard Francis...." She shook her head, "It's troubling."

"Not pretty enough, maybe," Aaron said, "what with the missing eye and all."

"Perhaps," Adina said, "but I think it's more than that. Did you see the way my sister spoke to the young captain?"

"Sure," Aaron said, "like he was the biggest pastry she'd ever seen, and she couldn't wait to get her hands on him."

Adina slapped his hand, *"Aaron,"* she scolded, but there was laughter in her voice. "Still, it's true enough. Something's going on here, and I don't like it. I think it would be wise if we were all very careful with what we did and said moving forward." She glanced at Aaron, "And try not to break anymore noses will you?"

Aaron nodded, "I'll do my best."

Adina sighed, "I get the feeling we need to be very careful in who we trust here."

Leomin glanced at Owen, an almost imperceptible look, but Aaron caught it. He considered saying something but let it pass instead. They had enough going on without him worrying about Leomin's mistrust. "Well. What do we do now?"

Adina shrugged, "There's not much we can do but wait until Isabelle calls us." She shook her head in anger, "It's foolish; we travel all this way, and then we're sent to our rooms like children up past their bedtime."

"Maybe," Aaron said, "but I wouldn't mind a little bit of sleep myself."

Owen nodded, yawning, then looking around sheepishly, "Sorry. I agree with Aaron though—I didn't sleep particularly well last night." He let out one of his self-deprecating laughs, "Nerves, I guess."

"Yes," Leomin said, studying him, "nerves, I'm sure."

CHAPTER THIRTY-THREE

Aaron had only just closed his eyes when there was a loud knock at the door, jarring him from sleep. He rose and moved toward it, reaching for his blade instinctively only to remember at the last moment that he'd been forced to leave it with the guards before entering the castle. Biting back a curse, he threw the latch on the door and opened it slowly, half expecting to see the young captain on the other side, a bandage on his nose and a blade in his hand.

The man who stood on the other end did have a blade, though it remained in the scabbard at his side. Aaron was surprised to find it was the older man from before, the one who Adina had spoken of, Brandon Gant. "Alright son," the older man said, turning to a young guard standing beside him, one Aaron recognized as one of the men who'd been set to watch on their hall, "you go on back to your station."

"But Sergeant...." The man began, hesitating at a look from the older man. He swallowed hard and nodded instead, "Yes, Sergeant," he said, then turned and was gone.

The sergeant glanced around the room, still standing in the doorway, noted the messy covers on the bed. "Getting any sleep?"

"Trying to," Aaron said, smiling slowly, "till a knock like thunder came at my door, anyway. What do you have hands made of iron or something?"

The older man laughed, a warm, true laugh, and Aaron found himself grinning. "Sorry about that. Occupational hazard, I guess.

Sometimes, only way to get some of these louts to hear you is to be louder than everythin' else."

"By louts," Aaron said, "I'm assuming you mean the other guards and soldiers."

The older man grunted, "Sure, if you want to call them that." He offered his hand, and Aaron took it, giving it a firm shake. "The name's Brandon Gant," the man said, "sergeant of the queen's guard and of her armies, such as they are."

Aaron grinned, "Aaron Envelar, and I know your name. The princess told me."

The sergeant's grin grew wide, a grandfather hearing about a favored granddaughter, "and how is the princess? Lady Adina," he shook his head, "a strange thing, seein' her all grown up." He sobered then, "I was glad to see that the rumors of her death were a lie, but sad for what it means." He snorted, "Riding accident. That girl's been on a horse since she was a child, and if there's a better rider in the world, I've never seen him."

Aaron, Co said, *maybe you should ask the gentleman inside.*

And put my virtue at risk?

"Please," Aaron said, stepping to the side and motioning, "Come in."

The sergeant did, closing the door behind him. "Don't worry," he said, "I won't be long. Let you get back to your sleep."

Aaron shrugged, "However. I wasn't getting much of it anyway—the bed's so damned soft I thought I was going to sink right through the thing."

The sergeant grunted a laugh, but his eyes studied Aaron sharply, "Not used to such luxuries then? Better a cot on the floor for you?"

Aaron shrugged, suddenly feeling like he was being interrogated, "I guess."

The older man nodded as if he'd just had some suspicion confirmed. "It was good blade work you showed in the dining hall," the man said, "It's not often I've seen such skill."

Aaron grunted, "Comes from a lot of practice trying not to get stabbed, I guess."

The sergeant nodded, his eyes narrowing, "Which begs the question. How did you end up with the princess, Aaron Envelar? A man like you ... forgive me for sayin' so, and I don't mean any offense, but seems to me that a man like yourself don't spend a lot of time around royalty. If you did, I suspect there'd be a lot more people with broken noses."

Aaron hesitated, unsure of how to answer the man. "I'm a friend of the princess's," he said finally, hating himself for how lame it sounded.

The sergeant was slow in answering, studying him, "Do you know, Mr. Envelar, I used to serve Lady Adina's father, King Marcus."

"So I've heard," Aaron said.

"Yes, well, I say that to say that I've known Adina since she was a little girl, since the Queen—gods rest her soul—gave birth to her." He shook his head, his gaze lost in memory, "A sweet child, the sweetest you'd ever meet. Showed kindness even to a simple, common man like me, though the gods know I didn't deserve it. I was younger then, though not anymore handsome, alas," he said, winking and grinning.

Something about the man's grin was infectious, and Aaron soon found himself grinning too. "Anyway," the sergeant continued, his grin vanishing, leaving Aaron feeling off balance, "point is, I never had any children or grandchildren of my own. My wife couldn't have kids, you see, and after a while that didn't matter either because she got sick of a fool husband spent all his time worrying about guarding other people instead of her and then off she went. What I'm tryin' to say, Mr. Envelar, is that the princess ... well, maybe I'm overstepping my bounds here, but I've always sort of looked at her like the daughter or granddaughter I never had. Like family. You understand?"

Aaron nodded slowly, meeting the man's gaze, "I understand."

"And any man worth the skin coverin' him, well, he *protects* his family. Such a man, well, I guess he'd do just about anythin' to just about anyone," he said, leaning close to Aaron, not overly threatening but making his point clear, making sure they understood each other. "Man like that, felt somethin' or someone was puttin' his family in danger ... well, a little blood wouldn't stop 'em, if that's what was called for."

"I hear you," Aaron said, "and I wouldn't expect it to."

The sergeant nodded, seeing that they understood each other. "Anyway," he said, and suddenly the menace and atmosphere of tension that had been filling the room vanished. "I didn't come here to talk about history and old times. I came here as more of a warnin' for ya."

"That so?" Aaron said, "I'm feeling fairly warned."

The sergeant laughed, "Oh, not about that. No, I mean about young Captain Francis. Far as I could see, he took a dislike to you soon as you and the others stepped in the dining hall, and you breakin' his nose hasn't helped matters."

"What can I say?" Aaron said, "I've got a way with people."

"Sure, you do," the older man nodded, "just a real people pleaser. Anyway, I thought as I'd come warn you that the captain, he'll be lookin' for payback. The man isn't the kind to let a slight go, and he'll be after you sure as shit out of a bird's ass. Won't even be for the nose or not especially, but for the way you made a fool of 'em in front of all those lords and ladies, in front of the queen too, in the bargain. He'll be lookin' for an excuse, waitin' for you to mess up, give him reason."

"How in the name of the gods did that fool get made captain, anyway?" Aaron said, "I heard you filled that role and not too long ago. What, didn't put enough grease in your hair? Not enough sequins on your clothes?"

The older man gave a small smile, but he shrugged, "I'm sure I don't know the mind of the queen, and I wouldn't think to question her judgment. I'm a simple man, Mr. Envelar, and the truth is, I'm glad. If somebody's ass has to be parked in a chair going over troop reports and listenin' to the queen's staff prattle on and on about security and costs and all, well, I'd just as soon it not be me. I'm gettin' on in years, and I find that sittin' for any amount of time wreaks havoc on my back. No, sergeant's plenty good and more than a common man like me can usually hope for."

"And the shows?" Aaron asked, "The *sport,* where your captain fights two men that'd be more at home with a shovel in their hands than a blade?"

The older man frowned at that, "There's always a cost, Mr. Envelar. One thing I've learned with my years; there's always a cost. Speakin' of, I were you? I'd get your friend not to wander around, he can help it. The captain's after you, but I don't suppose he'd be much opposed to makin' do with your friend, in a pinch."

Aaron frowned, not sure what the man was talking about, "My friend?"

"Sure," the sergeant said, "thin fella, looks like he's set to break into a run somebody so much as looks at him sideways? Anyhow, Just a suggestion. Now, I'll leave ya to it," he said, starting toward the door. Then he turned back, his hand on the latch, "and Mr. Envelar? Don't forget my advice, will ya? I'm no prophet or scholar, but a man don't have to be able to see the future to know there's a shit storm comin' your way."

"I got it," Aaron said, "don't fuck up. Thanks."

The sergeant grinned, winking with his one good eye, "Don't mention it."

***

Aaron was still sitting on the edge of the bed thinking about the sergeant's warning, thinking about what reason Owen would have for 'wandering' as the older man had put it, when there came another knock at his door.

He rose and opened it, saw Adina standing there with the two guards that had been watching the end of the hall, their expressions not hostile, not really, but definitely not friendly. Serious and officious. "It's time," Adina said.

"Can it wait half an hour?" Aaron said, "I was just now getting a really good nap in."

One of the two guards opened his mouth to speak, no doubt to spit some officious threat, but Aaron held a hand up, "Just kidding, fellas. Relax." He followed them out to the hall to Leomin's room next, the guards having to damn near break the door down before the Parnen—who they could hear snoring from the other side of the wall—woke up and answered. They went to Owen's room last, and there was a startled yelp from inside as they knocked. Owen appeared a moment later, his clothes disheveled and wrinkled. Which, was to say, the man looked the same as he always did.

As the guards led them down the hall, Aaron dropped back to where Owen was walking. "Might not be such a good idea to go

265

wandering just now," he said, "we're not exactly loved here, if you hadn't noticed."

"Wondering?" The thin man said, "I haven't done any wondering, Aaron. I was asleep when you all came—and gave me quite a fright I might add," he smiled his shy smile, shaking his head at his own foolishness.

"Really?" Aaron said, frowning, "One of the guards told me you'd been out. That's strange."

Owen frowned at that for a moment then nodded his head, "Aaah," he said in realization, "yes, well, I see what it must have been. I had to visit the privy. When I get nervous," he shrugged, embarrassed, "well. Anyway, that's where I went."

Aaron nodded satisfied, "Alright. Well, just be careful."

"Of course," Owen said, "but ... we're not in *danger* are we, Aaron?"

Always, Aaron thought, but he shook his head, "No, it's fine. Just, if it comes up, hold it if you can, okay?"

Owen nodded, his eyes going wide in that owl-like expression again, "Okay, Aaron."

"Good," Aaron said, and then they had no more time to speak as they were led into a room of the castle, the guards posting up on either side of the door as Aaron and the others followed Adina inside.

A long table stood in the center of the room, two servants dressed in white tunics and trousers on either side. The queen sat at the table along with three others. One of them was familiar, though the young captain's face could hardly be seen for the bandage on his nose, but the other two were strangers to Aaron. The first was an old man in gray robes, in his seventies or eighties at least, his head nearly bald, only wisps of pale white hair left, and the second was a man that, from what Aaron saw, could have been the young captain Francis's twin, if he was ten years younger. And had a broken nose, of course.

One glance at this man, seated in his immaculate military dress uniform, his long dark hair going to his shoulders, sipping wine from a silver cup and glancing around the room as if everyone gathered were little more than bugs he'd deigned to show favor with his appearance, told Aaron all he needed to know.

"Your sister really goes for a certain type, doesn't she?" He whispered to Adina who nodded in turn.

The most interesting one to him was the old man seated at the table, and though his age would have made some think him infirm, there was a sharpness in his gaze, an intelligence, that couldn't be found among the others. "Ah, sister," Isabelle said, a slight frown on her face, "I am so pleased that you have been kind enough to grace us with your presence, if somewhat later than we had hoped."

Adina frowned, "We came as soon as we were told you wanted us, your Majesty."

Isabelle waved a hand dismissively, a forgiving monarch accepting the faults of those beneath her as expected. "Let us forget it. Now, that you *are* here, I think we had best hear what you have to say. You and your companions may sit. *Though,*" she said as they began moving toward chairs, "I wish it to be known that I will not countenance another such show of ... of *barbarism* as we witnessed earlier this morning. Is that understood?"

The words were clearly meant for Aaron, but Isabelle was staring at Adina as she said it, apparently deciding Aaron wasn't worth her attention—something he wouldn't lose any sleep over. "Of course not, your Majesty," Adina said, and Aaron and the others followed her lead, sitting down at the table.

"Now," the queen said, "it appears that introductions are in order." She held up a thick hand toward the captain, "Francis, of course, you've already met," she said, and Aaron thought he detected the slightest bit of recrimination in her tone. Apparently, getting a broken nose and ruining the show she'd intended for her nobles wasn't something the man would get a free pass on, inappropriate liaisons or not. For his part, the young man felt the disapproval too and though he nodded his head, what parts of his face the bandage did not cover grew a deeper shade of red.

"This," the queen continued, her voice much noticeably sweeter as she turned to the man in the dress uniform, "is our wonderful and esteemed General Vander, a man," she said with a withering glance at Francis whose shoulders seemed to hunch further, "who is known for not just his skill with a blade—although it *is* legendary—but also for possessing one of the most profound military minds in the whole of Telrear, possibly the greatest tactical genius of our age."

The man gave the squirming Francis a smug grin before bowing his head low to Isabelle, "My queen, you are far too kind and, might I say, you are as radiant as the sun this day. I only regret that the observance of my duties did not allow me to attend the demonstration this morning. I heard," he said, glancing at Francis again, "that it was *quite* elucidating."

The queen beamed, "Oh, Vander, you speak like a poet," she said, favoring him with a smile that held a promise. *Gods help them both,* Aaron thought, glancing between Francis and the general. Clearly, the two men were in competition for the queen's affection, and he suspected that Francis had been held in higher favor until the incident earlier in the day.

Nobles always love to play their games, Co said in his mind.

Like watching two ham bones fight to be eaten first, Aaron said, shaking his head in wonder.

"And your third guest?" Adina asked.

Isabelle turned away from studying the handsome general with obvious reluctance, "Ah, yes," she said, with none of the excitement in her voice that she'd shown when speaking of the general, "is Headmaster Mirmanon, a reputable scholar and the man in charge of running the university here."

Not exactly a glowing introduction, Aaron thought, *not when compared to the one given the others. Maybe not enough hair to warrant a better one.*

"Gentlemen," the queen went on, "this is my sister, Adina, and her ... companions, such as they are."

The captain and the general didn't so much as nod in their direction, but the older man smiled, bowing his head, "Princess," he said, his voice surprisingly strong for such a frail frame, "it is a great honor to meet you and your compatriots." He nodded to each of them in turn as if they were distinguished guests.

"And you, sir," Adina said smiling, "I have often heard the name of the scholar Mirmanon—my tutors made sure of it when I was a child."

"Ah, forgive them, I beg, princess," the older man said, smiling, "I'm sure they meant well."

"There is nothing to forgive," the princess said, "It is a truly hopeful thing to have such a wise and knowledgeable man as you among us, sir."

"Yes, well," the general said, rolling his eyes, "I'm sure that there are more important things to discu—"

"Forgive me," Leomin said, staring at the older man with something like awe, "but Mirmanon, you say? As in, Fendar Mirmanon, the historian who wrote *The Forming of Telrear* and *The Making of the Seven,* the history of Aaron Caltriss?"

The old man smiled, "I'm afraid so, young man. I hope that you didn't find them *too* boring."

"*Boring?*" Leomin shook his head, "Mr. Mirmanon, I thought it was amazing. The best history of the time of Caltriss and the barbarian kings I've ever read—not that there are many, of course."

The old man's smile widened, "Well, sir, I do thank you very much for the compliment, though I suspect your enjoyment has little to do with my own poor skill and much more with the subject matter. They were exciting times."

"Fairy tales," The general sniffed, "stories for children to put them to bed at night."

"I would think you'd enjoy them then," the young captain said in a nasally, squeaking voice.

The general frowned at that and soon the two men were scowling at each other, the queen glancing between them, a smile on her round face, clearly pleased at watching the two men compete for her attention. "Putting all of that aside," Adina said, "I wonder if we could get to the reason for my visit."

The queen sighed, "Very well, sister," she said, "but might I recommend that, in future, you learn patience. It is very crass to demonstrate such haste."

"Forgive me my crassness," Adina said, her voice flat, "but I would think you and those others gathered here would be as interested as I—considering that the news I bring could very well see them all dead by the end of the year."

That got their attention, each head swiveling to Adina. The queen, of course, sighed again, shaking her head, "Oh, sister, but it seems you did not lose your penchant for exaggeration when you lost your kingdom. Pity."

"I do not believe it exaggeration," Adina said through gritted teeth, "to say that Belgarin and his men will soon be marching, bringing an army several times larger than your own against you or Ellemont. For my part, I suspect he will come here first as Ellemont's mountain presents its own challenges for any conqueror."

The general let out a laugh, draping one of his legs over the arm of his chair, his posture a studied one of casual disregard. "Belgarin, is it? Forgive me, Adina—if I may call you Adina—but we are not overly concerned with that oaf and his machinations."

"You may call me princess," Adina said, meeting the man's gaze, and Aaron couldn't help but notice the way the general's eyes took the opportunity to wander over her. "And perhaps you should be concerned, general. My sister Ophasia, and my brother Geoffrey did not take Belgarin's *machinations* as you call them seriously either—they're both dead now, of course. As is my brother Eladen," she said, and Aaron could hear the emotion in her voice, tightly controlled, "though he did take them seriously, he is dead anyway."

The general sighed as if bored, "Yes, well," he said, looking to the queen, "it is truly a pity that your brothers and sister were slain and, had I been there, I would have ensured their safety. Alas, I was not. Still," he said, turning back to Adina, "it must be said that they did not have the power that my queen does. Isalla boasts the most powerful army in all the world, *princess*. I only hope that Belgarin *is* foolish enough to come and meet us in the open field. His rabble will be cut down by our soldiers, and we will end whatever threat he poses once and for all."

"Rabble?" Adina said, incredulous, "Is that what you think of them? Understand," she said, turning to her sister, "that Belgarin's troops are not to be underestimated. These men have fought in battles against Eladen's army as well as my own. They are battle hardened with more practical combat experience than any other fighting force that currently exists. *Including*," she said, turning back to the captain, "your own."

The captain scoffed, turning to the queen, "My queen, I assure you there is no cause for fear here. Your mighty legions would deal with Belgarin's own in short order, I assure you, should he be so foolish."

"Well," Aaron said, unable to help himself, "they're certainly shiny enough. If it turns out to be a fashion contest, I'm confident that Belgarin will slink away with his head between his legs."

"And your name, peasant?" The general sneered.

"Aaron. Aaron Envelar, but we can introduce ourselves properly later, if you'd like." He nodded his head at the bandaged guard captain, "Francis and I have already met."

"Perhaps I'll take you up on that," the general said, "until then, why not mind your betters—"

"*Enough*," The queen bellowed, "Enough. You explain to your man, sister, that I will not tolerate any more indecency in my presence. I keep a dungeon ready for such things, and I can always find space if necessary."

Adina sighed, "Sister, I didn't come here to argue with you or to start a fight. I came to speak with you about what we need to do—what we *have* to do, if we want any hope of standing up against Belgarin's armies."

"Oh?" Isabelle asked, "and who is this *we* you speak of sister? There has been much talk of my army but none of your own. Oh, but that's right. You don't *have* an army any longer, do you? And what is it you think you know, *dear sister,* that my general, knowledgeable as he is in the art and tactics of war, does not?"

"I will tell you what I know," Adina said, "Belgarin is coming— whether today or tomorrow, I don't know, but make no mistake, he *is* coming. When he does, he will bring an army much larger than your own, an army experienced in warfare, and he will not stop until he is the only royal left to claim the throne."

The general grunted, "An army of peasants, no doubt, that barely know which end of the sword to hold."

"If I may," the scholar, Mirmanon said, "I think that it must be agreed, princess, that Belgarin's army *is* coming. The recent past leaves little doubt to his desires and the acts he is willing to commit to bring those desires to fruition. My question, then, is, what do you believe should be done about it?"

Adina nodded to the man gratefully, "I'm glad you ask, sir. I propose that the only possible option," she said, turning back to the queen, "is to ally with Ellemont, to combine your army with his own."

The general laughed, "Preposterous. You would have us combine forces with that ... that *mole?* Would have us sully our ranks with men smelling of damp and earth from burrowing into their mountain home like rodents?"

"That *mole* you speak of," Adina said, "is of royal blood. Shares blood, in fact, with your *queen.* I think you'd do well to remember that, general."

The old scholar, though, was nodding. "Even so, princess, as you say, Prince Ellemont's army is smaller than my queen's. If your numbers are right, and I've no reason to doubt them, then we would still be outnumbered."

Adina nodded, "Yes, historian, it's true. However, there are people at work, even now, trying to gather the forces of Avarest. If they are successful, we may have an army of a size close enough to rival Belgarin's own."

The young captain snorted then winced in pain, touching his bandaged nose gently, "Everyone knows that Avarest is a city of thugs and prostitutes. What do you intend, princess? That we will defeat Belgarin's army with such a force?"

"I confess," the general said, "I must agree with our—" he paused to grin, "injured captain. We do not have the time, alas, to let the prostitutes do their work on Belgarin's army and hope that they all catch the rot."

"It is an idea that could very well bear fruit," the old scholar said, ignoring the disgusted looks of the other two men. "Avarest and its surrounding environs, it is known, are more populated, by far, than any of the other royal kingdoms. If they were to be armed and made ready for war—"

"And what does an old man know of *war?*" The general sneered.

"I think, perhaps," the old man said with a humble shrug, "I may have read a book or two on the topic."

"*Books,*" the general mocked, "how very useful."

"I would have your thoughts, sister," Adina said.

They all paused then, glancing at the queen, and Adina knotted her fists underneath the table. *Please, Isabelle,* she prayed, *do not be foolish.*

"I do not enjoy the idea," the queen said, "of coupling my armies with Ellemont's own, sister. He is of royal blood, but there is no question that he is craven. I doubt, seriously, if he would even accept, should I make such an offer."

"But we have to *try*," Adina said, "surely, you see that. I'll go myself, if you wish."

The queen frowned in thought. Then, finally, "We must consider this further," she said. "It is late, and I am tired. It has, after all, been a very busy day. Guards," she said, motioning, "show my sister and her companions back to their rooms."

"Isabelle," Adina began, "there's no ti—"

"*Enough,* sister," The queen said. "I have heard your arguments, but *Isabelle* not *Adina* is queen in Isalla. Now, my men will see you back to your rooms." She glanced at the young captain with disgust then turned to the general, "General Vander, if you might be so kind as to remain, I have a few things which I would like to discuss."

The man smiled, bowing his head low, "I live to serve, my queen."

"Forgive me, Majesty," the scholar said, "but I, too, have some few matters regarding the princess's idea that I would like to discuss with you."

The queen sighed, "Very well. The rest of you may leave."

CHAPTER THIRTY-FOUR

The four of them sat gathered in Adina's rooms once more, their expressions troubled. "The general is a fool," Adina said, "as is the captain. I'm glad you broke his nose, Aaron. Both men could do with a lot more than that."

"I was thinking along those lines myself," Aaron said.

"Of course, you can't do anything," Adina said, meeting his eyes, "we are already not in my sister's good graces. We can't afford to anger her any further."

"Don't worry," Aaron said, smiling, "She said she'd send for us tomorrow. I can't get into too much trouble in a day."

Leomin grinned "Don't sell yourself short, Mr. Envelar. We all here know that your skill is unsurpassed when it comes to making friends." His expression grew more serious then, thoughtful, "Mirmanon." He shook his head, "Truly, it is incredible to meet such a wise man in person."

"Yes," Adina said, frowning, "let us just hope that he is able to make my sister see reason. No matter what that fool of a general says, Belgarin's army will hardly slow down as it tramples my sister's into the dust if they meet in the open. It would be a slaughter."

Aaron nodded slowly, "The man is stupid, but I wonder if even he can be *that* stupid. Pretty armor or not, he has to understand that Isabelle's army stands no chance against Belgarin's."

"What are you saying?" Adina said, "Do you think that ... what, he's somehow in league with Belgarin?"

Aaron shrugged, "I don't know what I think, princess. But a general—fool or not—has to know better than to take on a force many times his own's size in a pitched battle with any expectation of winning. My father taught me that numbers aren't everything in a war, but five men with swords will take one man with a sword pretty much ten times out of ten. It seems strange to me that a man of the general's rank doesn't know that."

Adina considered that, frowning, "It isn't as if Belgarin hasn't used inside agents before. It's what happened to my kingdom." She nodded, "The next time we speak with Isabelle, perhaps we'll have to raise the possibility. And, however tomorrow goes, I think it would be wise for us to dig a little deeper into the general, if we can. If the man is indeed working for Belgarin, we will need to find proof of it. I do not think that my sister will choose a cold bed without reason."

They talked on for a while longer, but there really was little else to say and soon Leomin and Owen went to their own rooms in search of what sleep they could find. Aaron was at the door heading to his own when Adina spoke. "Aaron."

"Yes, princess?" He asked, turning back.

She grinned mischievously, "I think you can call me Adina. Anyway, be careful, will you? That captain was staring blades at you during the meeting."

Aaron smiled, "I'm always careful, Adina. And don't worry—I won't get in trouble." He gave her a wink and left.

CHAPTER THIRTY-FIVE

Aaron dreamed that he was running through Avarest, his home, being chased by something. He never got a good look at it, but heard it, *felt* it, and knew that each time he turned a corner, should he look back, he would see it, this terrible, monstrous thing, but he would not turn, *could* not, for the dream, like all dreams, had its own rules, its own design. So he ran on, his breath ragged in his chest, each step feeling as if he was pushing against a strong current of water.

His friends were in the dream: Adina, May, Leomin, Gryle, and all the rest, but every time he drew close to one, shouting for help, they'd change. Their forms would shift and melt into shadow until that's all they were, darkness given form and function, and soon they too were pursuing him, an army of creatures from the darkness and of it.

He jerked awake with a gasp, somehow knowing someone was in his room. He leapt to the side of the bed away from the door, had a confused moment when he looked for his sword only to realize the guards still had it, then he glanced up, expecting to see the young captain, Francis, his blade drawn. The captain, however, was nowhere to be seen. Instead, four soldiers stood before him, silver breastplates over their fine white uniforms, and—about this much, at least, he'd been right—swords clutched in their fists.

"What the fuck?" He said, remembering that he'd told Adina he wasn't going to get into any trouble. Well, trouble had a way of finding a man when he least expected it—his life had taught him as much, and he cursed himself silently for forgetting. He crouched low into a fighting stance, his hands at his sides, ready.

"Please, Mr. Envelar," one of the soldiers said, and Aaron realized with a start that it was Brandon Gant, the old sergeant's easy smile nowhere in evidence now, "don't make this any harder than it has to be."

"Make what any harder?" Aaron said, his gaze darting between the four men.

The sergeant grunted, "You'd have me believe you don't know."

"What I know," Aaron said, "is that I was in the middle of having one of the world's most fucked up nightmares and, normally, I would have been happy to have been wakened from it but, just now, I'm a little unsure. If you'd wanted to have breakfast together, sergeant, all you had to do was ask."

The sergeant smiled sadly, "Ah, Mr. Envelar, I do wish that I could believe you had nothing to do with it—I truly do. But, you see, there are witnesses. Witnesses that saw your man skulking from the old man's chambers."

"My man? Brandon, what in the name of the gods are you talking about?"

The older man sighed, "The Parnen, Aaron."

"Hold on," Aaron said, rubbing at his temples, "let me get this right. You're saying someone was killed and, what? Leomin was seen *skulking* away? Brandon, you saw the man; he's got bells in his hair for fuck's sake. That man's never skulked a day in his life."

Brandon shrugged, "It's the word the witness used. Anyway, it doesn't matter, Aaron. He was seen leaving."

"Okay," Aaron said, his mind racing, "let me take a guess. Was the witness Captain Francis, by chance?"

Brandon grunted, "You're right there and believe me, Aaron, my thoughts ran much the same as yours no doubt are now. Problem is, there were *three* witnesses. The captain, General Vander, and a cleaning woman. They all say they saw the same thing—your friend with blood on his clothes, a knife in his hand. We already checked his room, got him held down below in the dungeons. Aaron, we found him naked, the bloody clothes tossed under his bed, along with a knife."

"Under the bed?" Aaron said, "Brandon, are you kiddin' me? Did Leomin strike you as simple? He's going to murder someone then come back and hide the evidence under the damned bed? He was framed—had to been. I know Leomin, and the man can be a right pain in the ass sometimes, but he's no murderer."

"The door was locked from the inside, Aaron. The only other option is that the real killer somehow went into the Parnen's room while he was sleeping, managed not to wake him while he hid the bloody rags and the blade under the bed Leomin was *sleeping* in, and then this same culprit managed to latch the door from the inside while he was leaving."

Aaron thought a moment, looking for some other possibility. *Co, any ideas?*

Something's happened, Co said, *I ... I don't know, Aaron.*

Great. "Well. Shit. Will there be a hearing? I could speak on the man's behalf—I've known Leomin for a while now. Listen, Brandon, give me a day. I'll look into it; I can guarantee you that whatever happened, Leomin didn't kill anybody."

"You don't understand, Aaron," the sergeant said, wincing, "it's worse than that. The captain and the general ... well, they're incensed at the idea that one of the queen's guests murdered one of her closest advisors. The same guest that you, Adina, and your friend Owen came with."

Aaron shook his head, running a hand through his hair, "You're going to arrest all of us."

The sergeant nodded, "Those are my orders. Except for your friend, Owen, that is. Seems he abandoned the rest of you in the night. We've men out searching for him, but they've been gone a while now and no one seems to have seen him. It's as if he vanished, like a ghost."

"Like a ghost."

The older man shrugged, reaching his hand out with a pair of manacles in it. "I'm gonna ask you to come peacefully, Aaron. If you did this, then you're not the type of man I had you pegged for, and if you didn't, then it isn't going to do you any favors to fight it. The truth will out—it always does."

"Yeah," Aaron said, "I've heard that. Of course, I've also seen men executed for crimes they never committed, so where does that leave us?"

The old sergeant gave a weary sigh, "I don't know. But I'll tell you, Aaron—you've got skill. Maybe you manage to take down one or two of us before we cut you down, but, to be honest, I doubt it. You standing there no shirt on, weaponless, and the four of us fully armored and armed. Aaron, don't throw your life away—not now."

"Brandon," Aaron said, almost desperate now, "look, what of Adina? You said you knew her when she was a child. Lock me up, if you have to—the gods know it won't be the first time I've seen the inside of a cell. A man in my line of work, well, if he doesn't get hauled in from time to time, he's not very good at his job. But *Adina?* Tell me, sergeant. Tell me you're not going to lock up the little girl that was always nice to you. Tell me you're not gonna sit by while she's executed."

The sergeant cleared his throat, a shamed look coming across his face. Then, in another moment, it was gone, replaced by an angry frown. "I don't appreciate words said in good faith being thrown back at me like that, Mr. Envelar. I said them from one man of the sword to another. Besides, the general and the captain didn't say anything about any executions."

"Oh, don't treat me like a fucking idiot, Brandon," Aaron said, "they might not have said it, but that's only because they don't have to. You and I both know how something like this ends."

Brandon shook his head slowly, "Maybe most times, but you come with me peacefully Aaron, I promise I won't rest until I'm certain of the truth. Not until I find out for sure what happened, and you've got my word I'll make sure the guilty party pays."

"That'll be a comfort, I'm sure, while I'm lying in my grave." He considered it then, looking at the four men arrayed before him. The sergeant wasn't far wrong. Alone? One, maybe two. With Co's help, he thought maybe he could take all four, but he wouldn't be able to do it without bloodshed. Men would have to die, if he wanted to stay out of the dungeons. The thought turned his stomach and that in itself was strange. It wasn't as if he hadn't killed before and for a lot less. If he let these men have their way, he'd be imprisoned sure, but so would Leomin. So would Adina. But if he didn't, if he fought, there were no guarantees; maybe he could take the men. But if not, there'd be no doubt of his guilt then, would there? No doubt of Leomin's or Adina's either, come to that. Even that wasn't the real problem though. With his bond with the

Virtue, he'd done some amazing things, and he was pretty sure he had some more in him. But if he did it, if he drew on that power, there would be blood and a lot of it. Innocent blood.

"To the Fields with it," Aaron said, stepping forward and offering his arms to the man. "Let's just fucking get it done then."

"Thank you, Aaron," the older man said, "and you have my word."

"Words mean little to a dead man," Aaron said as the sergeant latched the manacles on each of his wrists, following it up with two more around his ankles. Brandon did his work in silence then two of the guards took up position in front of Aaron, Brandon and the other behind. "Oh yeah," Aaron said as they led him out the door, "who died?"

***

More guards were waiting with Adina and Leomin in the hall, along with the smiling captain. "Are you okay?" Aaron asked Adina as the guards pushed the three of them together and moved to encircle them.

Adina nodded slowly, still groggy with sleep, "I'm fine, Aaron, but … what's happening?"

"Well," Aaron said, "I guess I might have lied to you, princess. Seems I've gotten into trouble, after all."

He glanced at the Parnen and saw the man's scalp was bloody, a crimson stain marring one side of his face. "Captain?"

Leomin turned to him, and it seemed to Aaron that he had a hard time focusing. His mouth, too, had been gagged, but he managed a drunken nod.

"Gag him as well," the captain said, his face alight with cruel joy.

One of the guards pulled out a kerchief and started forward. "Is that really necessary, captain?" Brandon said, "his feet and wrists are bound. He can't cause us much trouble with his mouth."

"Do not forget yourself, *sergeant*," Francis said with a sneer, "there is only one captain here. Now, unless you wish to be chained up beside this bastard and the rest of the lot, you'd best keep your mouth shut."

"Maybe you could cover my ears too," Aaron said, "at least then, I won't have to hear your fucking bitching and moaning you pompous little bastard."

The captain's face went a dark shade of red. "*Hold him,*" he growled and two guards stepped forward, grabbing Aaron's arms. He could have struggled, but there wasn't really any point, not with his arms and legs chained as they were. Once the guards had a good hold, the captain stepped forward and struck Aaron in the stomach with a gauntleted fist.

The air left him in a whoosh, and the guards released him enough so that he fell to his knees, gasping for air. "You ... hit like a bitch." Aaron managed.

"Bitch am I?" The captain asked, then a fist struck Aaron in the side of the face and stars exploded in his vision. "*Bastard, am I?*" The voice asked, but Aaron's thoughts were muddied, confused, and it seemed to him that the voice came from far, far away. He heard someone screaming, thought maybe it was Adina, but he couldn't be sure. "How about you listen to this bitching and moaning?" the voice said. Something heavy struck Aaron in the back of the head, and he knew nothing more.

CHAPTER THIRTY-SIX

Hands touched his face, and Aaron shouted in panic, waving his arms in an effort to get them away from him. "Aaron, it's okay, it's me!"

A woman's voice, one he recognized. "Adina?" He asked, holding a hand to his head and the side of his face, feeling dried blood beneath his fingers. His thoughts were fragmented, confused things, and with the pain he felt in the side of his face and his head—awful, terrible pain—he couldn't seem to put them into any logical order. "Gods be good, did someone hit me with a smith's hammer?"

"Not ... far off," a new voice said, and Aaron turned to see the Parnen captain, dried blood still coating the side of his face.

I've done what I could, Aaron, Co said, her voice sounding strained, *but I can do no more for the pain. I'm sorry.*

It's alright, Co, he thought back, *thanks for what you've done. Something I learned a long time ago. Life's pain—you learn to live with it or you die. I'll manage.*

"No permanent damage, at least," Leomin said, his white-teethed smile not managing to hide his own obvious agony, "you'll keep your looks, though whether that's a blessing or not, I'm sure I can't say."

"Oh, gods, Aaron," Adina said, her fingers soft against his face, "I'm so sorry."

"For what?" Aaron managed, "I'm the one can't keep his damn mouth shut."

Aaron felt gingerly at the back of his head and saw that someone—Adina, he was sure—had wrapped cloth around his head. He thought of Captain Francis, of the cruel smile on his face, visible in its pettiness despite the bandage across his nose. *A bandaged head, a bandaged nose. Oh, what a pair we make.* He sat up, wincing, and put his back against the wall, glancing around. The light was poor—almost nonexistent—the only illumination coming from a sputtering torch somewhere further down the hall, but it was enough to see that they had all been thrown into a dungeon with hard-packed dirt for a floor and stones for walls. "And here I'd been hoping for a nice inn, maybe a palace," he said.

"What's that, Aaron?" Adina asked.

He shook his head, "Nothing. How long have I been out? How long have we been here?"

"An hour," Adina said, "maybe two, but *why* are we even here? They didn't tell me anything."

Aaron glanced at Leomin who appeared as curious as the princess. "They think Leomin here is a murderer and since he came with us...."

"A *murderer?*" Adina said. "That's ridiculous!"

"That's what I said," Aaron said, still staring at Leomin who watched Aaron with a shocked look of confusion on his face—if the man was faking, he was doing a damned good job. "Thing is, they've got witnesses—three of them."

"Three witnesses?" Adina said, turning to Leomin, "but how?"

Leomin shook his head, his eyes wide, "Mr. Envelar, I swear—"

"Oh, come off it, Leomin," Aaron said, "I know you didn't kill anybody. Point is, *they* don't. Someone's set out to put us in a spot, and they've done a damn fine job."

Leomin gave a ragged sigh of relief, as if he'd expected Aaron and Adina to accuse him. "Thank you, Mr. Envelar. May I ask, however, who I murdered?"

Aaron sighed, glancing at the two of them, both of them staring questions him. "The old man, Mirmanon. Brandon told me somebody killed him while he was asleep." Actually, from what the sergeant had said—as much as what he'd not said—Aaron got the idea that it had been a whole lot worse than that. Brandon had no doubt seen some things in his past, his a profession that made a man well acquainted with blood, but even he seemed to pale when recounting it. The scholar hadn't just been killed—he'd been butchered.

They both gasped in surprise. For a few moments neither spoke, and Aaron let the silence linger, giving them each a chance to come to terms with it.

"That's horrible," Adina said finally, "Who would kill such a kindly old man?"

"Not just a man," the Parnen said, and Aaron thought he could see tears gathering in the man's eyes, "A genius. One of the wisest men of our age."

Aaron shrugged, "It gets worse. According to Brandon, three witnesses saw you," he said, looking to Leomin, "walk out of Mirmanon's bed chamber with blood on your clothes, a bloody knife in your hand. Give it a day, there'll be twelve people swearing they were sittin' in the room having a whiskey when you walked in and cut the man's throat."

"But ... that's ridiculous," Adina said, "Mirmanon was the only one on our side. What possible reason would we have to harm him?"

Aaron raised an eyebrow at her, and her eyes went wide with realization. "They think we're here working for Belgarin."

"It's likely," Aaron agreed, "I mean, consider, princess. We made no attempt to hide that we'd come from Baresh—the very city and kingdom your brother has just taken over and, if I'm not mistaken, weren't you allied with Eladen before his assassination?"

"Yes," Adina said, "but what...." She paused again, then brought a hand to her face, "gods we look guilty."

Aaron nodded. "The thing I don't understand, Brandon said there were three witnesses. The captain, the general—apparently they were having words or measuring cocks outside in the hallway for all I know—and a servant, cleaning the place. I can see why the captain and the general were lying, but a cleaning lady?" He shrugged, "Only thing I can figure, they must have bought her off or threatened her. Still, that's risky." He shook his head, "I just don't know. Seems like a lot of risk only to get another witness they don't really need. I mean, let's face it, the two of them managing to agree on something would be enough to convince damn near anybody it was the truth."

Adina shook her head, "Something's still not right. Aaron, I *know* Isabelle. She can be petty and immature, sure, but she's also vain. She believes that, due to her royal blood, she deserves to be treated differently, and I share that same blood. She wouldn't have me thrown in this dungeon, I know it. And once I get a chance to talk to her, I'm sure that I can get her to release you," she said to Aaron. "And don't you worry, Leomin," she said, turning to the Parnen captain, "we'll get to the bottom of this."

Aaron frowned, "You're right. The queen wouldn't let her own sister be thrown in the dungeon—her vanity wouldn't allow it. Then why...." He cut off as a troubling thought came to him. Brandon had said that the captain and general had ordered them arrested. He'd never mentioned the queen at all. What if, whoever framed them, had never been trying to get them all executed. Whoever it was, surely they knew that Adina, a princess, wouldn't long sit in her sister's dungeon. Why, then, go through all the trouble of having them all arrested? The captain and the general were in on it that was almost certain. Either that or they'd been fooled somehow and the figure leaving the scholar's chambers truly had looked like Leomin.

Aaron was mulling over this, trying to figure out what exactly was going, when he heard the sound of footsteps further down the hall. Someone grabbed one of the torches from their bracket, and orange light and black shadow shifted on the walls like something alive as the person drew closer. Who would it be? Vander, come to gloat? Or Francis, come to take what revenge he could? That, to Aaron, seemed the most likely. The man didn't strike him as the type to take embarrassment well.

"Get behind me," he said to Adina as he rose to his feet, shaking his head in an effort to clear his blurry vision. The footsteps drew nearer, and Aaron tensed in expectation. Then the figure carrying the torch stepped into view, and Aaron grunted in surprise. "Brandon?" He said, wincing and holding his hands up in an effort to block the light from his dark-accustomed eyes, "Is that you?"

"It's me," the sergeant said, "just thought I'd come to check on you all. I'm glad to see you up and about, Mr. Envelar. What the captain did ... it wasn't necessary. I'm sorry for that."

"No need for you to apologize," Aaron said, "I'll get an apology from the captain himself, next time I see him."

"Tell me," Adina said, stepping forward, "does my sister know that you've locked us in here? That you've locked her own *blood* in the dungeon?"

The sergeant's face showed a pained look, "Forgive me, princess, but the queen hasn't been feeling well since last night. The healers have examined her and seem to think it must have been something she ate. They assure me she'll be okay," he added hurriedly, glancing at Adina, "but we haven't been able to speak with her about the ... current situation."

"So you took it upon yourself to throw us in the dungeon anyway, without your queen's consent? Brandon, you know me. Surely you must understand that we did not do this."

The sergeant shook his head, "Not myself, princess, the captain. In the event of a crime within the palace, the captain of the palace guard is the ruling authority until the queen decides what is to be done. And since she's indisposed...."

"Francis gets to decide what to do with us."

"Nothing untoward, princess, I assure you," the sergeant said, "he can only keep you here until the queen is feeling better. He cannot hold trial, nor choose a punishment. And as soon as the queen is well, I 'm sure we will figure the truth out." He glanced at Leomin, still sitting, his hands draped on his knees, "whatever that may be."

Realization struck Aaron like a hammer blow, and he smacked a hand against his forehead, "*Of course.* I'm a fool."

"What do you mean, Aaron?" Adina said, stepping forward.

"Don't you get it, princess?" He said, his thoughts racing now, "whoever is behind this never *meant* for us to be executed. They meant for us to be *out of the way.* Like, say, *in a damned dungeon.* Whatever their plan is, I'd bet my life it's going to happen today."

The sergeant frowned, stepping closer to the cell, "What are you talking about?"

Aaron shook his head, frustrated that it had taken him so long to figure it out. "We've been framed, sergeant." The man started to speak, but Aaron held a hand up, "just for the sake of argument, let's say we *were* framed, alright?"

"Go on," the sergeant said reluctantly.

"Thank you," Aaron said, "you see, whoever did this has to know that Adina won't be kept in a dungeon, not for long. They knew that, should the queen hear of it, she would take her out, want to speak with her. Imprison her in a room maybe, with guards, but throwing someone of royal blood, her own sister in a dungeon?" He shook his head, "Not a chance. And now, coincidentally, the queen ends up sick ... tell me, Brandon, what do the healers believe did it?"

The sergeant frowned, "They're not sure. They said the food might not have been fully cooked."

"And did anyone else eat that food? The queen doesn't seem to me like the type of person who likes to eat alone."

"Yes," the sergeant said, his frown growing deeper, "as I understand it, she dined with General Vander last night."

"And is he sick?"

"No..." the sergeant hesitated then shook his head, "it doesn't mean anything, Aaron. It could have been anything she ate yesterday and even if she *did* get sick because of that meal, it doesn't mean the general was behind it."

"No," Aaron said, biting back a curse, "it doesn't." Whoever had set them up, they'd done a thorough job. The bastards. Another thought struck him, "Sergeant, in my room you told me that there were three witnesses. Is that right?"

The older man nodded, "Yes."

"The general, the captain, and another."

"A cleaning lady."

"That's right. And, this cleaning lady, is she new, maybe? Only just started working at the castle?"

The sergeant shook his head, "That's where you're wrong, Aaron. I've already spoken to Castellan Gregor, and he assured me that Matilda—the cleaning woman—has worked for the castle for years. One of his best, he said."

Aaron cursed, running a hand through his hair in frustration. "And you spoke to her, this Matilda?"

The sergeant frowned again, "No. I sent some men to find her, to get a statement from her on exactly what she saw, but no one seems to know where she is; she's supposed to be cleaning the west wing of the castle, but the guards and other cleaning staff say they haven't seen her."

Aaron banged his hand against the cell, "There it is. And if they do find her, Brandon, I'd bet just about anything they won't find her alive."

"You think she's been killed too?" Brandon asked, "Why would anyone kill a cleaning woman?"

"Because she's not *needed* anymore, Brandon. Her job wasn't to testify in any trial, her job was only ever to be another voice during the confusion, another reason for you to round up Leomin and the rest of us. To make sure we were put *here.*" His eyes went wide, another realization dawning on him, "These people," he said, "they're not looking for a trial at all, Brandon. They're looking to get us out of the way while they do whatever they're planning." *Which makes us loose ends that need to be tied up.*

"Look, Aaron," The sergeant said, "it's a good story, I'll grant you, but that's all it is. A story. I can't let you all out because of some wild idea you had, and I certainly can't take it to the queen— not in her condition. The captain is guarding her personally, along with some of his handpicked men."

"That I don't doubt," Aaron said. "Listen, Brandon, I don't expect you to let us out—you've no way of knowing we're telling the truth, I understand that. But you need to check on the queen. *Personally.*"

The sergeant nodded at that, his expression troubled. He started way, but Aaron thrust a hand out, catching hold of the sleeve of his tunic. "Sergeant," he said, glancing back at Leomin and Adina, "there's just one more thing...."

CHAPTER THIRTY-SEVEN

"Ma'am?"

May turned, startled to see Nissa, a slight, pretty girl who sometimes sang at the club standing in front of her desk, the girl's eyes wide and nervous. *And how long has she been here, I wonder?* She'd been so caught up in thinking of how it would go, of what words she could use to make Grinner and Hale see reason that she hadn't even heard the door open.

"Relax, girl," May said, speaking to herself as much as she was the young singer. "They'll listen. They have to, and they wouldn't be fool enough to start trouble here, anyway." *At least I don't think they would be but who can tell with men such as those?*

The girl nodded, but her expression remained strained, anxious. "Yes ma'am. Celes sent me. She told me to tell you it's time."

"So soon?" May asked, a chill rushing up her back.

"Yes ma'am."

May took a deep slow breath to steady herself. Well, it wasn't as if she had really expected them to wait until morning anyway. Men such as these conducted their business at night, in the shadows. "Very well," May said, forcing a confidence into her tone that she didn't feel. She stood, pausing in front of the full length mirror hung on the wall, studying herself. She stared at her face, her eyes, not liking the anxiety she could see in them, telling herself she had to stay calm, relaxed. Fear drew such men as these like honey to bees.

"Ma'am?" The singer asked, "what if they say no?"

May took another deep breath, staring at the mirror until the confident, no nonsense club owner was looking back at her then she turned to see the girl biting her nails. "They won't say no," she said. *And anyway,* she thought, *saying no is not the worst thing they could do, girl. Nowhere close.* "Now, why don't you go up to one of the rooms and lie down for a bit? You look like you could use some rest."

The girl breathed a sigh of relief but then paused, "I ... ma'am, that is, Celes told me to stay with—"

May waved a hand, "Never mind what Celes said, girl. Just go and get some rest—everything will be fine."

She waited until the girl was gone through the door then glanced back at the mirror, smoothing the green dress she wore. "Everything will be fine," she said to the woman looking back at her from inside the glass, but judging by her expression, the woman had her doubts.

***

May was sitting in the club's main room with Celes when they came in. She'd sent the chamberlain, Gryle, out with Balen, ostensibly to speak with Festa about staying in Avarest, should they need him. The truth, of course, was that the first mate was a kind, clever man, but with his gruff, direct way of speaking, she didn't think he was built for meetings like this, and the fussy, nervous chamberlain less so.

Grinner came in first, followed by his latest bodyguard—a massive, nearly seven-foot tall man that had to duck to make it under the door's frame. A giant of a man with a rugged, hero's face that looked like he would have been more at home swinging a massive axe on a battlefield, soaked in the blood of his enemies, than anywhere near what could even loosely be considered polite society.

Grinner himself was an older, unassuming man, dressed in a simple robe that a priest might wear. A humble, simple appearance never mind the fact he was one of the richest people in Avarest if not the richest. He favored May with a grandfatherly smile as he walked over and had a seat at the circular table near May and Celes, his bodyguard taking up a stance behind him, his massive forearms folded across his chest.

"May," Grinner said, bowing his head of long silver hair and speaking in a cultured, educated voice that was surprisingly soft, "I must admit, I was surprised to receive your invitation. I had thought we were not on the best of terms since our last ... interaction."

"By which," May said, smiling, "you mean when your men tried to rob and kill Silent?"

The old man sighed, shrugging in a 'what can you do?' sort of way. "Not my men anymore, I assure you. No one's men, in fact. Still, you must admit that Mr. Envelar is not the easiest individual to get along with. The man has a penchant for ... disruptiveness. I wonder, is he here, now? I think there are a few words I would like to say to him."

"Disruptiveness, is it?" May said, "as I heard it, he quite disrupted your last bodyguard. Gregory, wasn't it?"

The cool façade Grinner had been affecting changed then, and he frowned, anger dancing in his eyes. "Well, is he here or isn't he?"

"Sadly no," May said, "any words you have for Aaron, you must leave with me, and I'll be sure that he gets them. He is away from the city, just now."

The old man nodded, his mask of calm back in place once more, "Unfortunate," he said, "but, then, I am a patient man."

May was just about to speak to that veiled threat when the door opened again, and they all turned to see Hale making his way into the club, a casual smile on his face. Hale was a big man with wide shoulders and a gut to match. He'd once been a street tough, one of the best, until, years ago, he'd decided that there wasn't much point in taking orders from his boss when he could just kill him and take his place instead—which he had.

He was a big, brute of a man with knuckles the size of walnuts and ears that were little more than fleshy lumps on the side of his head. Looking at him, people would have thought him some dumb street tough with a mind capable of little more than finding new ways to cause pain. Unfortunately, they would have been wrong. "Well, hello there, my lovelies," he said, glancing at the people gathered at the table as he made his way to a chair and sat, the wood creaking dangerously under him as he did. He leaned back, as casual as a man in his own house. "May," he said, "woman, you don't mind me sayin' you're lookin' just about as lovely as ever."

May smiled, "Hale," she said, nodding her head, "thank you and thanks for coming."

"Ah, well," he said, in his loud, deep voice, "I wouldn't have missed it for the world, lady bell, not the world." He smiled at Grinner seated across from him, "Grinner. How's things fare with you?"

Grinner was not grinning now, studying the man with hate in his eyes. "They go well enough, Hale. Yourself?"

"Ah, I get by," the big man said, "I get by. And what about the big fucker behind you there?" He said, waving a meaty hand at Grinner's bodyguard, "he your nurse maid, make sure you don't trip and fall in your old age?"

Grinner's eyes narrowed, about to say something, but May held up a hand and spoke before he could, "Gentlemen. I thank you both for coming. I know that it took a certain degree of trust to come, and I am thankful for it."

"Ah, shit," Hale said, shrugging his massive shoulders, "I didn't have much else to do. Anyway, May, when I heard my good friend Grinner was gonna be here?" He smiled widely, "Well, how could I refuse an invitation such as that? Matter of fact, I brought a little welcome party along with me." He leaned back in his chair, put two fingers in his mouth, and gave a loud, ear-splitting whistle, a smug smile on his face.

Nothing happened and, after a moment, he frowned, trying the whistle again. "I'm afraid," May said, "that you could whistle until you were blue in the face, Hale. I don't think your men will be coming just now."

The smile on the big man's face turned to a scowl as he glanced at May, "My men—"

"Are fine and well," May said, "although, it *is* possible that a few of them might have a headache, come the morning. But, then," she said, her own eyes narrowing, "that is a small price to pay for men that would bring violence to a truce meeting."

The big man studied her for several seconds then abruptly he gave a loud, bellowing laugh and sat back. "My, but I do love me a strong woman. Still, you'll have to forgive me for tryin', lovely. I just couldn't resist."

May nodded, "I had expected as much. Thought it best to save you from yourself."

"Just so," the man said laughing, "Just so."

"Why am I not surprised?" The older man, Grinner said. "I had expected as much from a thug like yourself, Hale."

"Is that so?" May asked, "I wonder, Grinner, is that why you brought your own men? Oh, don't look so surprised; you've been glancing at that door so much you're liable to have a sore neck in the morning. Sadly, I'm afraid your men won't be able to attend us either, for the time being. They are all quite ... tied up."

Hale bellowed another round of laughter in the air, and Grinner frowned—the man really did a lot of that for one with a name as he had—then snapped the fingers of one hand. "Malcolm," he said.

The big man stationed behind him took a step forward, and May held up a finger. "Just a moment, Mal. That is what your mother calls you, isn't it? Mal? A sweet lady, truly, though, if her food is as good as my men tell me, they'll all come back fat and useless."

The big man froze, his eyes going wide. "My mother—"

"Is well, young Malcolm," May said, "and will remain so, I hope. What do you hope?"

The big man took a step back, his hands up in front of him, "Uh ... yes ma'am, please don't hurt my mother."

May smiled, "Handsome and polite too. Your mother must be very proud," she said, "and I wouldn't worry, Malcolm. Your mother will be just fine. As," she said, turning to study Grinner and Hale both, "will we all."

The two crime lords stared at her for several seconds, stunned, and May smiled. Good. Stunned was good. Keep them off balance, keep them guessing. "My, but I love me a woman takes charge," Hale said finally, "Surely, I do."

"But ... how?" Grinner said, "My men—"

"It wasn't an easy thing," May said, nodding, "had to rent out the whole street, in fact. I knew you'd both bring them along, hide them somewhere or another with instructions to come when you called or after a certain amount of time."

"That," Grinner said, scowling, "must have cost you greatly."

May favored him with her best smile, "Not so great as you might think, Grinner. In fact, when they heard that you would both be coming, they damned near offered to pay me."

The big man, Hale, gave a bark of laughter at that. "Alright, woman, alright. You've got us here, powerless. What is it you want?"

"Not powerless," May said, "not you two. You both are many things but never that. That, after all, is why I brought you here. Now, I take it that you are aware of the situation regarding Belgarin?"

The two crime lords scowled at that. On whatever other things they might disagree, neither relished the idea of someone coming in and taking over, uprooting all of the long standing bribes and contracts they had with those in authority, threatening their business and their profits. "Aye," Hale said, "I know of the bastard well enough. Fucker's been taking over kingdoms left and right."

"Yes," Grinner said, "so he has. Still, I don't see what that has to do with us, May."

May smiled, leaning forward and studying the two men. "That's alright, because I'll tell you. Come on, gentlemen. Let's have a talk."

CHAPTER THIRTY-EIGHT

Aaron wasn't able to get any sleep or rest, pacing back and forth in the small area of the cell, his nerves taut, the clink and rattle of his manacles a metallic measure of his anxiety. He didn't know all of what was going on, but he knew enough, and that was what bothered him the most. Knowing there was a problem but being stuck in this cage, waiting for the men to come finish the job. They would come, that he was sure. He'd spent a lifetime dealing with criminals, understood pretty well the way their minds worked—when they worked at all, anyway. He knew that such men would decide the best thing would be for Aaron, Adina, and Leomin to end up dead. He'd lived around criminals all his life, and he knew them well enough to know that their solution to most any problem was murder. Man sleeps with your wife? Kill him. Man owes you money? Kill him. Man bumps you while walking in the street? Well, he knew enough to say that criminals were predictable.

He knew they were coming, but he didn't know if he would be ready when they did. His head still hurt, his stomach too. Already, there was a big bruise on his side where the captain had hit him. He was wondering, mostly, how many they'd send—two or three, he thought, no more than that. They'd be going up against an unarmed man, after all, one who had only recently gotten his ass beat pretty thoroughly. They most likely expected him to be curled up in a ball of pain, whimpering and praying that the world would forget about him, at least for a while. Truth was, without Co and the bond keeping back the worst of it, he probably would have been.

I don't like this, Aaron, Co said, *sitting around and waiting for them to come. There's got to be something we can do.*

We've done everything we can, firefly, he said, *unless you think maybe you can magic that cell door open?*

No.

Maybe give me the strength to break it off its hinges?

I'm not the Virtue of Strength, Co said.

Right, right. Well, maybe we can just have a heart to heart with the door, what do you think? Let it know how important it is, it opens up.

How you can make jokes at a time like this, while you're waiting to die, I'm sure I don't know.

Times like these are the best times for jokes, firefly. Besides, everybody's always waiting to die; it's the jokes and the laughter make the wait bearable.

The sound of footsteps came from the other end of the hall, and he froze, listening. Only one set—surprising but not unduly so. After all, they thought they'd be dealing with a severely wounded man. Still, he smiled, twisting his neck first one way then the other, trying to work what stiffness out of it that he could. He thought he was as ready as he would be, ready to pounce the moment the man opened the door, but he froze as he saw the figure walk into view holding a torch.

"Sergeant?" He said, surprised.

The older man nodded, "It is. I thought it was wrong, Aaron, what the captain did, so I spoke with the queen about it; she's agreed to have a private audience with you."

Aaron frowned, "With me? Not her sister?"

The older man shrugged, "I just follow orders. Besides," he said, looking past Aaron into the cell where two covered forms lay on either side of the floor. "Might as well let the princess and your friend get some sleep."

Aaron started to ask the man what in the name of the gods he was talking about but something told him to keep his mouth shut and go along, at least for now. "Yeah, well," he said, "I guess you're right. But," he frowned, looking down the hall, "where are the other guards? Seemed to me, you all used just about the whole army to bring us down here the first time."

The sergeant barked a laugh, louder and somehow more jarring than the laugh Aaron had heard him make before, "Yeah, well, most of the men are training or sleeping. I'll tell you, your visit here has done this much—there's men you could barely get off their asses long enough to watch the gates without falling asleep out there practicing with their blades now, convinced that Belgarin and his men are hiding out in the fields somewhere. Anyway, I thought it would be better to bring you to the queen without involving the captain—he's not a big fan of yours, in case you hadn't noticed. Besides, you couldn't do too much, not with those manacles on your wrists and ankles, even if you did plan on causing me any trouble. You don't, do you?"

Aaron frowned, studying the man, something troubling him, but he couldn't quite put his finger on what it was.

"Everything alright, Mr. Envelar?" The sergeant said, leaning in as if to see him better in the poor light.

"I'm fine," Aaron said, pushing the feeling aside for the moment, "and no, sergeant, I won't be any trouble."

The older man nodded, running a hand over his salt and pepper beard, "That's fine, that's fine. Now, stand back, will ya?" He said, bringing the cell keys out of his pocket and winking, "I don't want you getting any ideas."

Aaron did as he was told, taking several steps back but remaining in front of the two recumbent forms lying in the shadows covered by the blankets the sergeant had brought earlier. The sergeant tried several keys on the ring in the door before finally finding the one he was looking for and opening it. "Damn things," he said, shaking his head, "never can keep them straight."

"Well," Aaron said, following the man out into the hall and studying his back while he closed the door and latched it, "you've got a lot on your mind, I guess."

"Don't I just?" The sergeant said, finishing and tucking the keys back into his tunic. "Alright, this way."

He led the way, and Aaron followed him up a flight of stairs and out of the dungeon, wincing as the sunlight coming in through the castle windows lanced into his eyes. Brandon nodded at the two guards stationed at the dungeon's entrance and moved past without saying a word, Aaron in tow.

The sergeant didn't speak as they made their way through the castle, and Aaron's mind raced, knowing something wasn't right but having a hard time trying to figure out what that something was. "The queen knows we're coming?" He asked.

Brandon led him around a turn in the hallway past two more guards, "Of course."

Aaron nodded, "Guess she's got some guards in her room waiting, in case I, I dunno, go crazy and start trying to murder everybody."

The sergeant laughed but didn't say anything else, leading him further through the castle. Aaron tried to quest out with his bond with Co, to get an idea of what the man was feeling, what he was thinking, but it was as if he'd run into a wall. For some reason, he could sense nothing of the sergeant's thoughts or intent. Soon, they came to an intersection in the halls, and Brandon hesitated for a moment before going down the left path. They'd only walked a short distance down it when he paused, smacking his head, "Gods, what am I thinking?" He laughed, "It's this way." He turned back the way they'd come, and Aaron followed, alarm bells ringing in his mind now.

Aaron followed the sergeant up several flights of circular stairs, the walls so close together that he almost had to walk sideways to keep from bumping his shoulders into them. Instead of going to the top of the stairs, as Aaron had expected, the sergeant led him up two flights before stepping off and continuing on.

Aaron had only met the queen, Isabelle, the day before, but he knew enough to know that the woman's vanity would have demanded that her quarters be situated at the center of the castle, no doubt as high as possible so that, from time to time, she could look out a window, down on all those that she ruled, putting those that she saw as figuratively beneath her beneath her in truth.

Guards were present here, but not at such regular intervals as they had been on the bottom floor, nor as common as Aaron would have thought they'd be on the floor which housed the queen's own quarters. The sergeant led him past the main hallway onto one of the side ones, glancing back at him, "Surely," Aaron said, "the queen's rooms are on the main concourse."

"What?" The sergeant said, glancing back, "Oh, right. This is a shortcut. I thought it best we avoid as many people as possible—wouldn't want the captain or one of his men trying to keep you from getting to the queen, would we?"

Aaron glanced around and noted that no guards were visible on this hallway. He frowned at the man's back, following him a few more steps before he spoke again. "Well," he said, forcing his voice to sound casual, almost bored, "I guess it's a good sign, the queen asking you to come get me instead of the captain or the general. Of course, young Francis seems to have fallen somewhat out of favor in the queen's eyes. Who knows, sergeant. You might just get lucky, get a promotion to that captain spot."

The sergeant nodded without turning, "We can hope so, can't we?"

Aaron's eyes narrowed at the man's response, and he took a few quick steps forward, wincing at the clink and rattle of his manacles as he did, "Hey, sergeant?"

The man turned, his mouth open to speak, but before he got the chance, Aaron slammed his head into the man's face with as much momentum as his manacles would allow. The man—not the sergeant, Aaron knew that without question now—cried out in surprise and pain, stumbling backward, stunned from the unexpected blow. Before he had a chance to recover himself, Aaron grabbed hold of the chain between his two wrists and slung it at the side of the man's face with all his strength. The steel links struck hard, leaving a path of bloody, ripped skin, and the sergeant cried out again, wobbling on his feet, but not falling.

Aaron brought the length of chain back and hit the man across the other side of the face, and he heard the crack of something—the man's cheekbone, most likely—giving way. The man gave a grunt of pain, but still refused to drop. If anything, he looked as if he was recovering, his feet getting steadier beneath him. *Fucker won't go down*, Aaron thought, amazed. Knowing that if the man recovered, he'd be in trouble, he lunged forward, jerked the man's sword out of his scabbard and brought it to the sergeant's throat.

The sergeant, fully recovered now, stared back at him, and though the man's face was a bloody ruin, he smiled, his teeth stained crimson. "Aaron, why would you do that? You understand the kind of trouble you're in, don't you? Striking a sergeant in the queen's army?"

"I don't know who you are," Aaron said, panting from the exertion, feeling more tired and worn out than the man acted, never mind what his face looked like, "I don't know *what* you are, but you're not Sergeant Gant."

The thing smiled wider, impossibly wide, it seemed to Aaron, "What gave it away?"

"Forget that," Aaron said, holding the sword steadily on the man's neck, "if you so much as move, I'll put this blade through your throat." The thing's smile stayed well in place, apparently unconcerned about the length of steel at its neck.

Aaron, Co said, *whatever it is, it isn't human, not anymore, at least.*

Aaron grunted, staring at the cracked and misshapen sergeant's face, his broken nose. Any normal man would have been screaming in agony from such wounds, but the man only stood there, staring at Aaron with that arrogant smile as if it was all a game.

"Tough bastard aren't you?" Aaron said, "well, being tough's all good, but unless you want to be a dead bastard, you'll hand me those keys you're carrying."

The thing reached into the pocket of its tunic, its hand coming out with the key ring, "These, do you mean?" It said, and Aaron noticed that the thing's voice had changed. It didn't sound like the sergeant at all, now, sounded like someone else. A voice he didn't think he'd heard before, but one that sounded familiar anyway. "Sure, take them," he said, and when Aaron reached out a hand the thing that wasn't the sergeant threw them at him instead. Aaron recoiled, surprised by the movement, trying to catch them with his free hand by instinct, his instinct forgetting that his free hand just happened to be chained to his sword hand and the sudden movement pulled on his wrist, tugging the blade away from the thing's throat.

The imposter took a step back, screaming for all he was worth, "*Guards, to me!*"

"*Damnit,*" Aaron hissed as the halls suddenly rang with shouts and the sound of men running.

The sergeant gave him another bloody smile, "Oh, Aaron," it said, "You really should have just come along, like I asked. I would have made your passing as painless as possible. Now, well ... I do not think the men who come will be so kind. Still, you always *have* had to do things your own way, haven't you?"

Aaron felt a cold shiver run up his spine at that strange, alien voice coming from the sergeant's mouth. "What *are* you?"

The man started to answer but suddenly he looked behind Aaron, his face a mask of pain and terror, "Thank the gods," he said, "this man is an escaped prisoner, trying to assassinate the queen."

Aaron glanced behind him to see two guards coming forward. *Shit. Any ideas, Co?*

Um ... the Virtue said, *run?*

Aaron glanced back and saw that two more guards had approached behind the sergeant, the man now hobbling and holding his face as if overcome by pain. A quick look showed Aaron that there were no doors to run into between him and the guards on either side of the hallway. *Thanks a lot, firefly,* he thought. "Listen," he said to the guards, knowing it was a waste of his time even as he did it but having no other options, "that isn't your sergeant," pointing a finger at the wounded man. "It might look like your sergeant, but I promise you—"

"That's enough out of you, bastard," one of the guards spat. "You'll pay for hurting the sergeant." Aaron moved so that his sides were facing each group of men, trying his best to keep his eye on both at once as they inched forward, their own blades drawn.

He watched them coming closer, knowing it was hopeless. One against four, his wrists and ankles manacled? Sure, he was still holding the keys, but somehow he doubted the guards would just stand by and watch while he unfastened the manacles at his ankles and wrists. "You have to listen to me," He said, glancing at the thing pretending to be Sergeant Gant, seeing that it had taken a couple of steps back so that it was behind the guards. Its expression was still pained, but he could see the dark amusement in its eyes. "This ... *thing* is not your sergeant."

The guards ignored him and suddenly one was rushing forward, swinging his sword in a fatal arc. Aaron batted the blade aside with his own then charged his shoulder into his attacker sending him stumbling backward into his companion.

"*Wait,*" Aaron said, turning to the two guards behind him who'd used the opportunity to move closer so that they were nearly within striking distance, "just fucking *wait.* Look, I *know* it doesn't make any sense—"

"*Wait!*" A hoarse shout came from further down the hall, and Aaron turned with the guards to see the real sergeant Brandon Gant shuffling toward them, one arm clasped around his bloody stomach, the other using the wall for support and leaving a bloody trail along its length to mark his passage. "That ..." he said, clearly struggling to stay upright let alone speak, "is not me. The thing jumped me in the hall, fucker stabbed me. Aaron's telling the truth."

"Sergeant?" One of the guards asked, he and his companions shooting nervous glances between the real sergeant, holding an arm over his bloody stomach, and the impostor.

"It's a trick," the impostor said, "this ... man, whoever he is, is in on it. Cut him down men, while you can."

The guards hesitated unsure, and the imposter shouted, "*Now,* damnit!

The authority in his voice was enough to make the guards' heads snap back around, and they began moving toward Aaron, one breaking off to make his way toward the wounded sergeant, his blade in front of him. "Wilhelm?" The real Sergeant Gant said, "That you? Look, lad, it's me, alright? Remember, what was it, two seasons past, when your girl, Bella, came down with the flux and you didn't have the coin to take her to a healer? Who was it, Wilhelm, lent you the money you needed to get her seen to?"

The guard that had been moving toward the sergeant came to an abrupt stop, his eyes going wide. "You did."

The wounded sergeant nodded weakly, leaning heavily on the wall and looking past Wilhelm. "And you, Dale, you know me. You're the worst card player I've ever seen—always callin' on a draw ain't got a chance of hittin'."

"Sarge?" One of the other guards, presumably Dale, asked. "Hold on," he said to the others, "That's him. That's the sergeant alright, now—"

He cut off at a growl of frustration from the imposter, something not quite human about it. *"Fools,"* he said, "You should have done what I told you—now you're all dead men."

They were still staring at the imposter when, suddenly, his flesh began to heal before their eyes. His cracked face reformed, reshaping itself to its original look, and the gashes on his face, caused by the chains, began to shrink. It was all done in an instant, and when it was finished, the only proof that Aaron had attacked the man at all was the blood still covering his features. Blood but no wounds.

Gods be good, what is he? Aaron thought.

Aaron, Co said, her voice panicked, *it's Carlyle, it has to be.*

Carlyle? Aaron thought, unable to take his eyes away from the unmarked flesh of the imposter's face. *Another brother, is it?*

"What the fuck?" One of the guards asked, managing to find his voice and pulling Aaron away from his thoughts.

"What are you?" Another of the guards said, his voice high and frightened.

The thing that was not the sergeant tilted its head at an impossible angle and smiled that too-wide smile again. "Me?" It asked, "I'm complicated."

Then Aaron watched in shock as the creature's arms began to grow and lengthen at its sides, the hands transforming into sharp spikes of flesh at the end. It bellowed a scream of rage and pain, and suddenly four more arm-like appendages erupted from its sides, ripping the shirt it wore into tatters. It screamed again and six spiked appendages shot forward, impossibly long, lancing toward Aaron and the others.

Aaron lunged desperately to the side, hacking at the impossibly long limb that would have impaled him had he not moved, chopping it clean through with his blade. The limb severed easily enough, flying across the room in a shower of blood that splashed on Aaron's face and clothes. Then, more on instinct than conscious thought, he spun and threw his sword, impaling another limb that had been shooting toward the wounded sergeant and pinning it to the wall.

He shot a look back at the creature, ready to defend himself against another attack and cursing himself for throwing his sword—what a fool move *that* had been—but the creature was only standing there. Its form was still manlike but there was no question that it wasn't a man, not now. Six spikes protruded from the creature's body, the one Aaron had cut, the one he'd pinned against the wall, and four others. He followed their lengths and saw that each of the four guards had been impaled, the men struggling weakly as they died.

"What the fuck?" He said. The thing smiled at him again and, in the blink of an eye, the protrusions of flesh retracted in a blur of motion and then it was only the man standing there once more, his shirt in tatters where the flesh spikes had ripped their way out of his body.

"You should have gone peacefully, Aaron," the creature said, starting toward him down the hall, a confident swagger in its step, but Aaron could see that it seemed winded, at least, as if it had just run several miles. "Now, there will be pain." It grinned, "Great, terrible pain."

Aaron glanced over at the sergeant only to see that the man had apparently passed out, though from pain, blood loss, or plain fear, Aaron couldn't say, and he couldn't have blamed him either way. "What do you want, you bastard?" Aaron said, looking at the four dead guards lying in the hallway.

"Want?" The creature asked, taking its time moving forward, in no rush, knowing that it was going to win, that it could do nothing else. "I want the world to burn, Aaron Envelar. Until nothing is left of it but ash and memory, until the memory itself fades. I want the only sounds in the world to be the sounds of women weeping for their husbands, their children, until even their cries grow silent and still and there is only the darkness. *That* is what I want."

Aaron dashed to one of the dead guards and snatched the sword from the corpse's hand. He held it in front of him, forcing his breathing to slow and fighting down the panic that bucked in his chest like something alive. "I was hoping you'd say gold. A woman, maybe. True the whole skin spikes thing might throw them off, but you'd be surprised what a professional is prepared to accept, assuming you've got the money for it."

The thing grinned, shifting its shoulders backward, so that its arms hung down at an angle to the floor behind it. Then its arms blurred, becoming spikes that dragged the ground behind it as it stalked closer. "You are amusing, Mr. Envelar, I'll grant you that. I have always thought so, for years now. It's too bad that I have to kill you, but you have something that belongs to me, and I will have it back."

Aaron raised an eyebrow, pointing his sword at the piece of flesh lying on the ground where he'd sliced it off from the first attack, "You mean that? Take it—the gods know I don't want it."

"Not that, Mr. Envelar," it said, "something else. Something ... *magic*. Tell me," it said, cocking its head to the side in that unnatural way, "which of the Seven do you possess?"

Aaron felt his skin grow cold, "Seven?"

The thing spread its mouth in a silent laugh, "There is really no need to dissemble, Mr. Envelar. I know you have it; I've known for some time now, and don't worry, you need not tell me. I will find out soon enough."

It took another step toward him then paused at the sound of armored feet approaching at a jog. A lot of them. *"Damned nuisances,"* it hissed then it turned and fled down the hall, impossibly fast.

Aaron cursed, kneeling by Brandon and shaking him. The sergeant's eyes opened, though with a great effort, and it took them several moments to focus on Aaron. "Mr. Envelar?" He said in a voice little more than a whisper, "is that you?"

"It's me," Aaron said, "look, are you okay? I need to get that thing, stop it before it hurts anyone else."

"Can you?" The sergeant asked, meeting Aaron's eyes.

Aaron shook his head slowly, bending to use the keys on the manacles at his ankles and then his wrists, "I don't know. I don't think so. Still, I have to try. Will you be alright?"

The sergeant nodded, "Go, then. I'll explain to my men what's happened—they'll fetch me a healer, and I'll be along as soon as I might."

Aaron nodded, throwing the last of the manacles aside and rising, "Alright. I'd say it's been a pleasure, sergeant, but...." He glanced around the room at the dead men and shrugged, starting away.

"Mr. Envelar," the sergeant said, causing him to turn. "May the gods be with you."

Aaron grunted, "That'd be a first. Still," he winked, "at this point, I'll take all the help I can get."

CHAPTER THIRTY-NINE

He raced down the hallway after the creature, pushing his battered, exhausted body to its limits and then beyond them. *Co,* he thought, glad to not have the need to speak—not sure if he'd have been able to, with his breath heaving in his chest—*what can you tell me about this thing?*

Carlyle, the Virtue said, her voice full of worry and something like hate, *his was the task of channeling the Virtue of Adaptability, according to Caltriss it was the second most important virtue of all—second only to compassion.*

Damn, firefly, he thought, *vain much?*

He said it not me, you ignorant ba—

Alright, alright, Aaron said, turning a corner just in time to catch sight of the thing take a left at the next intersection, *that's nice, good history lesson. Can you tell me anything else, anything useful, maybe?*

Adaptability, Caltriss said, was a commander's ability to change to suit his circumstances, to give himself the best chance of victory.

Oh, well this fucker changes alright, Aaron shot back, thinking of the way the creature's flesh had erupted in spikes, impaling the guards. Any fool with the sense the gods gave him would be running the other way, but, then, he'd been called a lot of things in his life and smart had never been one of them.

Aaron, the Virtue said, her voice full of warning and worry, *such a one as has bonded Carlyle ... he will not be easily slain.*

Tell me something I don't know, Aaron thought, remembering the way the creature's face had healed in an instant. A cleaning lady was in the hall, frozen looking after the way the creature had gone, her eyes wide and skin pale, and Aaron was forced to dodge around her as he turned down another corner. He was gaining on the creature now, twenty strides away, no more, and it turned back, bearing the teeth in its too wide mouth at him even as its arms changed again, this time becoming similar in form, if not size, to hooks fishermen might use to catch fish.

It was approaching the end of the hall—an end with no hall on either side, only a large stained glass window. Aaron came to a panting stop, knowing he'd need strength and energy left to fight the creature, once it realized it had nowhere to go but through him. Instead, it didn't so much as slow, leaping out the window, its clawed arms behind it. Stained glass shattered and flew out into empty space in a cacophony of sound, and Aaron stared after it, slack jawed. "You've got to be kidding me."

He crept toward the window, peered out, and was immediately overcome by a sense of vertigo. He'd known that they were high up, but he hadn't realized just how high, the houses and shops beneath him like little more than a child's toy village, the streets populated by people the size of ants going on about their daily lives. He squinted his eyes, trying to see if he could make out anything of the creature's shattered form below but saw nothing.

Dreading what he was going to see, Aaron leaned out of the window and looked up to see the creature using its hooked arms as climbing instruments, working its way further up the castle to what appeared to be a balcony jutting out near the top. "Shit." Aaron said. "It doesn't exactly take a genius to know who that belongs to."

It's the queen," Co said, *Aaron he's going to try to kill the queen.*

"Yeah," Aaron said, still looking up at the creature making steady progress up the castle wall, apparently oblivious that it hung out over nothing and that one slip would send it plummeting hundreds of feet below. "Yeah," he said, swallowing, "it looks that way."

Well? Co said when he didn't move, *what are you going to do?*

Aaron considered then finally spat out the window, "One of the dumbest things I've ever done, I guess." He said. He started to slide his sword in its sheath at his back only to remember that this wasn't his sword at all, his sword—as well as its sheath—having been taken by the guards when he entered the castle. "I'd bet they'd regret that right about now, if they were here to see this."

But no one is here, Aaron.

"I know, damnit. So I'm the only one regretting it." He tossed the sword to the ground. True, if he made it to the top, he would be forced to face the thing without a weapon—not exactly an appealing thought. Of course, the thing was he'd have to *make* it to the top first, and he'd need his hands and his feet free—shit, would have taken two more hands, if he could get them—to have any hope of making the climb. "Alright then," he said, more to himself than to Co, "it's just climbing, that's all. You've climbed before."

He glanced down at the ground again, swallowing hard. Sure, he'd climbed. But only high enough so that falling *might* kill him. Two stories or so. This high up, a man would have enough time to ask himself some very pointed questions, should he fall. The only bright side was that maybe, just maybe, he wouldn't have time to answer them.

Aaron—

I know, I know, he snapped, *I'm going.* He grabbed hold of a couple of protruding stones to the side of the window and then, cursing himself for a fool, jumped. There was a stomach lurching, heart wrenching, wild-eyed scared as shit moment when his feet were touching nothing but air. He breathed a heavy sigh of relief when they hit the castle, and he managed to get a toe hold on the stones.

What I was going to say, the Virtue said, *was that you could have taken the stairs.*

Aaron laughed then, and if it sounded a bit wild, a bit like a scream, then that was understandable, given the circumstances. "Sure," he grunted, moving his right foot up then reaching another stone with his left, "and I'm sure all the guards would be fine, letting me go, letting some stranger head toward their queen's quarters."

Oh. Right. Because a few men with swords are way worse than this. I don't know what I was thinking.

Aaron grunted. *You know, firefly,* he thought, *you can be a real pain in the ass. Anyway,* he glanced up at the man or whatever it was, scaling the wall above him, *he's doing it.*

Well, he also has hooks for hands and apparently heals nearly instantly. But, hey, you're doing great.

Aaron frowned at that but didn't answer, focusing on pulling himself up one handhold at a time. Luckily, there was enough separation in the stones that had been used in the castle's construction that handholds were easy enough to find. A fact he was thankful for as he didn't relish the idea of having to backtrack to try to find another path. As far as he was concerned, the only thing worse than climbing away from the ground, in this instance, would be climbing toward it. Both likely meant death, but climbing up, at least he didn't have to stare at it—knew it was somewhere far below him, sure, but that was manageable. Something a man could stand. At least, that was what he told himself as he grabbed another handhold and another, forcing himself on faster, trying to gain ground on the creature.

The wind, this high, was a fierce, cruel creature with a mind of its own, cutting through his clothes and skin, making his fingers numb, and reaching out hands of air to try to rip him free of where he clung. He gritted his teeth and pressed on, grabbing the next stone only to have it come loose in his right hand. He swung left, wincing at the pressure on the fingers of his left hand, and the stone hurtled past him, missing his head by inches. He let out a cry of surprise and fear and for a terrifying moment, he couldn't seem to get a hold with his right hand. Then, finally, he managed to grasp a stone that didn't give, and he stared down at the ground far below, swallowing hard. *Salen's Bell,* he thought, *if someone was standing down there, they've just had a really shitty day.*

He glanced up at the creature, but it was moving on, apparently oblivious of his pursuit. The one good thing about the wind—it blocked out any sound of pursuit.

Particularly any womanish screams of terror, the Virtue said.

Yeah, Aaron said through gritted teeth, starting up again, *not the mood I'm trying to set—hey, and thanks so much for chiming in, lightning bug. Not all of us can fly.*

The creature reached the balcony in another few minutes, climbing up over the railing and disappearing above. *Shit.* Aaron pressed on, forcing himself to reckless speeds and wondering how exactly it was he managed to get into these kinds of messes.

It's a rare skill, Co supplied.

Just like being a person without a body, Aaron thought back, as he planted his foot on a stone, crouched low, and leapt up, knowing that if he wasted anytime the queen would be dead, and he'd have done this whole thing for nothing. "Well," he said, gasping, as he set himself for a moment after catching some handholds. "That went well."

It will, Co said, *until it doesn't. Try not to die, Aaron. You have no idea how tedious it is having to explain to someone what I am and what the bond means. I'd really rather not do it again, not so soon.*

Aaron grunted, leaping upward again and catching another handhold. "Yeah," he gasped, his arms burning with strain, "I can see how that'd be really inconvenient for you. Tell you what, for you, I'll do my best not to end up splattered on the cobbles somewhere below us."

He kept on in this way for another minute or two and finally reached the balcony, his arms burning, his fingers numb from the biting cold, but not so numb that he couldn't feel the sharp ache in them when he forced them to straighten out. He heard screams from inside as he was pulling himself over the balcony's railing and saw that the balcony door had been broken in. Straining with effort, he managed to leverage his body over the railing and tumbled to the balcony floor, landing in a gasping, shivering heap. He closed his eyes for a moment, trying to steady his breathing and get his racing heart under control.

Another scream came from within, and Aaron lurched to his feet, moving toward the balcony's broken door, all too aware of the fact that he had no weapon. No weapon and, what was worse, no plan. His dad had once told him that not having a plan was, nine times out of ten, the reason why men died in battle.

Aaron leaned in the doorway, glancing inside. The inner door to the queen's chamber had been thrown open and two guards lay dead or dying inside the room's entrance, gaping holes through their chests, and he was pretty sure he knew what caused them, having seen it recently. The creature stood over the queen's bed, staring at her, that grizzly smile on its face. The queen gaped at the creature, her eyes impossibly wide in her pale, sickly face. Even as Aaron watched, the creature's arms finished reverting from those long, spiked appendages to normal, human arms. Aaron glanced at the guards lying dead on the floor, their swords drawn but no blood on them. *They never stood a chance. Salen's Fields, but what am I doing up here.*

Being a hero, Co said, *you can do it, Aaron. We can do it.*

Heroes die, firefly, he thought back. *It's what they do best. How many stories you heard of heroes and the amazing things they've done only to find out they live next door? None. Heroes die, Co. It's what they do.*

He considered it then, really considered it. He could let whatever was going to happen—and there was no real question about what that was—happen then leave. The castle, the city. Shit, the country, if he had to. The thing was a demon or something worse, but apparently even demons couldn't fly. Well. Probably couldn't fly. He could sit here on the balcony and let it do what it had come to do—he damn sure wasn't climbing back down, that wasn't even a question—and then leave.

But what would Adina think? He started to snap back at the Virtue until he realized that it hadn't been her speaking it all but his own thoughts. And anyway, what *would* she think, knowing that he'd stood and watched her sister die, knowing that he'd let this thing—whatever it was—get away. And, thinking bigger for a second, what would happen should the queen die? Would the creature take its place? He thought that the most likely as it had shown it was capable of taking a man's form. And, once it had, how long before it hunted down Adina and Leomin? They were loose ends waiting to be tied.

The creature was making its way leisurely to one of the guards now, reaching for the dead man's sword. *Damnit,* he thought, *it's suicide to go in. You know that.* But, to his surprise, he found himself going in anyway, not just going either but running, sprinting directly at the creature with every bit of speed he could muster.

The thing, whatever it was, didn't turn until the last moment and by then it was too late for it to react. Aaron barreled into it, sent it hurtling across the room to slam against the wall and, barely slowing, scooped up the sword from where it had slipped from the thing's hands. He lunged forward, stabbing the thing in the stomach before it had gathered its wits.

The creature screamed in surprise and pain, its hands going to the steel piercing it. *"There,"* Aaron said, panting, "Got you, you fucker."

The creature's scream grew quiet and quieter, then they changed. Not screams at all now but laughter as the creature studied him with that mad grin. Gritting his teeth, Aaron forced the sword up, straining with the effort as it tore through the creature's internal organs, but the thing only laughed louder. Then, with a speed Aaron didn't expect, it swung an arm at him, the hand becoming something that looked similar to a smith's hammer. He lunged to the side, barely managing to avoid getting struck in the face. Still, he did not dodge the blow completely, and it hit him in the shoulder with shocking force sending him flying across the room in a roll to fetch up against the room's ornate writing desk with a painful thud.

He shook his head to clear the dizziness that had settled there, groaning in pain, and glanced up to see the creature pulling the sword out of its stomach, the damage healing even as it did. "Oh, Aaron," it said, "you have caused me more pain than most, that I'll grant you. Oh yes," it said, as if to answer a question he'd never asked, "I do feel pain. I have felt more pain in my life than you could possibly imagine. More pain than a dozen men, more pain than thousands. The difference, Aaron, is that I do not die. I will never die." It finished pulling the sword out by the blade. Then it glanced at the queen, still staring at it, frozen with shock and fear. Smiling, it grabbed the sword by the handle and started toward her.

Aaron winced, grunting with pain. Each breath was an agony, and he was pretty sure a few of his ribs were cracked, if not broken altogether. "What *are* you? *Who* are you?" He managed.

The creature paused, glancing at him. "Oh, Aaron," it said, "now, you're hurting my feelings. Don't you know me? Even after all this time?" It shifted before his eyes, becoming Owen, the mad grin on his old friend's face strange and alien. "I'm your best friend, Aaron," it said, "don't you remember me?" It changed again, Owen still but this time Owen as he was as a child. Small and frail, the blood slicked blade huge and unwieldy in his hands. "I'm *me,*

Aaron," it said. "I always have been. You've known me since you were a child—though, I confess, I was not a child myself. Or, at least, in appearance only. You see, Aaron, I have lived for millennia. I have watched whole family trees wither and die and pass on to time only to be forgotten. *What* am I, you ask? I am eternity, Aaron Envelar. I am everything and everyone. "

"No," Aaron said, shaking his head at the sight of his childhood friend, the one who'd taken a beating for him, who'd rubbed ointment on his wounds after the headmaster's attentions, standing there with that mad, bloody grin. "You're not Owen. You can't be."

"Can't I?" The thing asked, feeling its nose. "Broken, wasn't it, Aaron? Broken by my father—a drunk," he said, his voice childlike and scared, "he beat me, Aaron. Me and my mom until my mom left and there was only him. Only him and the beatings and nothing else. Only the pain and the beatings and the few moments in between. You *do* remember my nose, don't you Aaron? The story I told you? The way you understood my pain, the way you comforted me when I could no longer hold back the tears. Don't you remember?"

"You're not him, you bastard!" Aaron shouted, anger flooding him, "You *can't be him!*"

"Oh, but I can," the creature said, "and I have, Aaron. I have been thousands of people at thousands of times," and as he spoke, his body shifted from one visage to the next in such succession that Aaron thought he would go mad. Now, a short, balding man Aaron didn't recognize, now a young woman with aristocratic features, an old man, a fat woman, a thin child, all looking down on Aaron, all with that same bloody, cruel grin, and the blade in their hand.

It went on for thirty seconds, a minute, and in that time Aaron saw a hundred different people, a hundred different souls. Men and women and children who had died, maybe, so that this creature could take their place, or who'd never existed at all, yet still he felt the loss of them. Finally, when he thought he could stand no more, the creature settled on an image.

"I was your friend," the woman's mouth spoke, "rubbing ointment into your flesh, feeling the sting of the headmaster's switch. I was the servant," it said, gesturing at itself, its form that of a heavy-set, middle aged woman with a confused, scared expression on her face, "who witnessed your Leomin as he killed the old man." It's grin widened, staring at Aaron and there was madness there, dancing in its eyes, "I was Leomin," it said as its flesh changed and suddenly the Parnen captain was staring back at him, "as he dug the knife into the old fool's throat, and oh, the blood, Aaron, the blood that gushed from that wound. I was all of these, and I was more. I was the man," he said, shifting to another form now, that of a man in his twenties, his muscles lean and well maintained, his stance the stance of a man trained to kill, "I was the man, Aaron," it said, "who *killed your parents*. Who watched their blood seep from their bodies and pool at my feet. The man who stood in the darkness and watched a young child creep down the stairs, scared of the darkness and what it might hold, the youth who seemed to know what he would find even before he found it, but went on anyway. I was there, watching as the youth screamed and cried and held their dead bodies to him as if by the degree of his love he might perform some miracle of rebirth. But he did not, Aaron. You do remember don't you, Aaron?"

Aaron screamed then, and Co screamed with him, their voices a brutal melody. Old rage and old pain mixing together in those screams, and there was power in them, such emotion that the room itself seemed to shake. The creature winced, seeming uneasy for the first time as it witnessed the outpouring of grief and fury, watching warily until it was done, until Aaron's head slumped to his chest, and he wept, his face buried in his hands, the man becoming the child he'd once been, and then it smiled. "Yes," it hissed, "yes, Aaron. I have been a murderer, and I have been a saint," it said, shifting to an old man in a priest's clothes. "I have been evil, and I have been good and all the things between. I will tell you my name, Aaron Envelar," it said, "so that you might know it as you die, might know it and despair."

It changed again then to the figure of a man of what appeared to be thirty to forty years. A man who would have been handsome if not for the worry that creased his brow, for the envy and jealousy that danced in his eyes. "Once, a long, long time ago, I was called Boyce Kevlane."

There was another scream then, but this time it wasn't Aaron's but Co's, the Virtue's shriek one of betrayal and pain beyond mortal imagining, and it tore into Aaron's mind like glass, so that he bent over, his hands tearing at his hair, wild and unknowing in his pain.

Co ... he thought, each word an impossible effort, *you're ... killing me.*

Abruptly, the scream began to lessen, subsiding into terrible, heartbreaking whimpers of a child abandoned in the darkness by those who had been meant to love it. "Yes, child," The creature said, "it is me. Do not fret, for we will be together again soon. The vessel," he said, meeting Aaron's eyes, "is insufficient to your power. Come to me, and we will rule everything until it burns and there will be nothing left to rule. You understand, don't you? It is the greatest gift of compassion we can give them. They live only to hurt, to lie and betray, to regret and mourn. To age and to die and to watch all their loved ones die with them. It is a gift, little one."

The Virtue suddenly appeared a few feet between Aaron and the creature, the normally calm magenta a raging storm of light and shadow. "You would kill them. All of them." The Virtue said, but whether she disapproved or not, Aaron could not tell, for her voice was flat and without emotion.

The creature nodded, smiling its bloody grin, "I would kill them all and put an end to their pain, little one."

"You do not understand them, Boyce Kevlane. Teacher and master. You have forgotten what it is to be one of them."

"*Have I?*" He hissed. "I have forgotten *nothing.* Do you not think I remember watching Caltriss, my best friend? Oh, and how they all loved him. His people, even his enemies. I, myself, loved him more than any other. Do you think I don't remember that, little one? Do you think I don't remember that spell? I knew the laws, the words, yet his spell was greater than any I might conjure. His was a spell of *being,* a spell which was not cast and could not be ended but with his death. Do you think I do not remember the way she would look at him and *only* him? All the while too caught up in the spell to even *see* me? To even know that I existed beyond the ways in which I served him? Too enthralled to ever see me as a man with a man's needs and wants, a man's *love?*"

"You speak of Elisandra," Co said, still in that strange, alien voice, so different than the one Aaron had come to know.

"*Yes,*" the creature hissed, "I speak of her. I loved her, and I coveted her. And I told Caltriss the spell would fail, that it *had* to fail. We were not ready, *I* was not ready, yet he insisted. I told him it would be the death of him. I warned him. 'Boyce,' he told me, 'all men die. But men who are not willing to sacrifice everything for those they love, for others, never live.' He told me the spell would work. He told me everything would be okay, and *I believed him. Don't you understand, I believed him, and I lost everything! I lost the man and the woman both!*"

"The barbarians," Co said, "they ... were not kind."

The creature screamed then, and if Aaron's pain was old, this thing's was ancient, a pain beyond understanding, beyond reckoning, and beyond cure. "As my body lay broken and battered on the ground near the castle, broken, but *not dead,* they came. They came with their axes and their swords, their fire and their desire, and as I lay there, I heard her, little one. I heard her scream. I heard her beg. Even from that distance, even though she was at the top of the castle, and I lie broken at its bottom, *I heard her.*"

His eyes danced with madness as he stared at Co floating in the air in front of him, "They knew me when they found me alive, student. They knew me, and they rejoiced, and they gifted me such pain as you cannot fathom, yet the physical agony was nothing compared to what those screams had wrought. For years, they gave me the gift of pain only to watch me heal again. I tried to kill myself, dozens, hundreds of times," it said, laughing wildly, "but *I cannot die.* I am *eternal.* I am *a god.*"

"The Virtue of Adaptability," Co said and now there was something in her tone now that Aaron recognized. Compassion, "it would not let you die."

The thing chuckled then, but there was no humor in it, only madness. Only darkness. "The barbarians died, eventually," it said, "as barbarians will. As *all* men will, if but given time. And, I decided, her screams still fresh in my ears, the years having done nothing to dampen their sound, that I *would* do as Caltriss had wished. I *would* gather the Seven Virtues together, to create something beyond all mortal reckoning. Beyond even the reckoning of the gods. Caltriss had wanted to save the world of men, but I will burn it. I will watch them die and feast on their blood and their sadness until there is nothing left. Men die—it is the way of things."

He motioned to her with his hand, "Come with me, little one. Too long have we been apart. We will do this together. Once this queen of theirs is dead, I will take her place, and we will see that the whole of this world falls beneath the sword. It is a mercy. It *is* compassion."

Co did not speak for some time, and Aaron watched her, feeling empty and broken and finding that he didn't much care what way she chose. Before him was the author of some of his greatest happiness and his greatest sadness, and he could do nothing about either. He never could.

"There is one thing you do not understand, Kevlane," the Virtue said, finally, "for all your wisdom, for all your learning, you have never understood it."

"Oh?" He said, his eyes narrowing, "and what's that?"

"Without sadness," The Virtue said, "there is no joy. Without pain and suffering, there can be no relief, no true pleasure. It is not their end that defines humans, Kevlane. It never has been. It is their journey. Beauty is found among the dross, is *created* among the dross. And not just beauty but power. When a starving mother gives up what little food she has to nurture and feed her child, *that* is beauty, Kevlane. True beauty, is not found in appearance but in *purpose*. There is beauty in sadness, as there must be. Beauty in pain and, yes, even in death, for death is not the story, nor is it even the ending of the story. Death is only the proof that the story was. The journey, the life, the pain, the heartache and heart break, *these* are the story. A man is not defined by the substance or the manner of his death but by the chronicles of his life. Even anger has its beauty for *just* anger is the blaze of a flame in the darkness, the flowering of petals in the desert. *Life* is beauty, Kevlane. You did not understand this then, and you do not understand it now. To want something you cannot have, to *need* it, is not suffering; it is to be human. You do not see it, even now. But you will. You will be made to."

With that, the Virtue flew toward Aaron and, in another moment, vanished inside of him. Aaron barely noticed. He felt drained, empty. A wineskin burst apart in the sun, ragged and of no use. He knew, now, who had killed his parents, knew the identity of the man on whom he'd sworn to have his revenge. The man stood only a short distance away, sneering now. His best friend, his parents' murderer. And he could do nothing.

Aaron, the Virtue said, *you have to get up.*

"It makes no difference," the man, Boyce Kevlane said, walking slowly toward them, "I will have you nonetheless, little one. There are ways to make you bond with me and no other."

Aaron, get up!

Aaron stared at the man drawing closer, watched him raising his sword in anticipation, but he did nothing. He was hurt, physically and emotionally both, and it seemed that the easiest thing would be for it to end. One more death, his own, and he need not worry anymore.

Aaron, he killed your parents. Remember.

And he did. A memory coming to him that was not a memory at all but a moment relived. He came down the stairs, holding his breath whether at fear of being caught or fear of what he might find, he hadn't been sure of then, and he was not sure of it now. Each step down the stairs seeming to take an eternity and flash by in an instant both at the same time, him needing to know but not wanting to see and then, too soon, he was at the bottom and his fears were not fears now but truth. Truth lying before him in pools of blood. Truth and despair. His mother, always so kind, his father who he'd always thought the strongest, smartest man he'd ever known. A man who knew difference between right and wrong and held to it, no matter what. But how could he be smart, how could his actions be right, if they led to this?

Death is not the story. He wasn't sure if those words were spoken by the Virtue or by some voice inside of himself, but there was a quiet strength in them. A true strength. Still, he did not stir, looking up at the man now, raising the sword above his head, ready to end it. And why would he fight that? There would be worse things than an ending. *Death is not the ending.*

Refusing to feel is not the answer, Aaron. It never is. You must move now. Would you not fight for your parents' memory? Would you not fight for Adina? For you know what he will do once he's finished here. Adina, Leomin, May and the rest ... all of those who you call friends. He would take them from you, Aaron. Take them as he took your parents.

"Goodbye, Aaron Envelar," the man said, grinning that cruel grin.

"*No.*" Aaron hadn't been aware he was going to speak until he did and with that denial, that rejection, a fire kindled in the ashes of his soul, growing and growing, fed by all the suffering which he had endured over the years. The loss of his parents, the abuse he suffered and was made to watch others suffer at the orphanage, the loss of his friend, the loss of himself. All of it fuel, feeding the fire until it was blazing inside of him, its heat so intense that he arched his back against it. "*No!*" He screamed.

The man took a step back at the power in Aaron's voice, at the strength in it. Then, hissing, he swung his stolen sword at Aaron in a vicious arc, but Aaron was no longer there and the blade bit deep into the wood of the desk.

Aaron flowed to the side of the blow, and the thing was still trying to get the blade out when he was on it, striking it once, twice, in rapid succession in the face, screaming his rage and defiance and still the anger built, an all-consuming tide of it, growing and growing, and his fists struck like hammers, the man's face twisting and cracking beneath them. There was pain and blood in his knuckles, but Aaron ignored it, hitting the man again and again, the creature, surprised and in pain, releasing the sword and stumbling back until it was against the wall.

Aaron ripped the sword free of the desk with a bestial growl and was on him before he could recover, hacking and hacking at him, the blade carving great chunks of flesh that came free in showers of blood, and the creature screamed again. Each scream was more fuel for the fire that raged inside, Aaron, and although the blaze was great and terrible, it did not consume, did not take him over, as it had the other times, because now he knew. He understood. *Beauty is created among the dross. Things must die so that others may grow. People are not their own stories, they are all one story. And the story is never truly over.* He hated the creature before him, true, the man who had taken so much from him, but he pitied it more, and with that knowledge the anger burning in him shifted, not a blaze any longer, wild and uncontrollable, but a blade of fire, sharp and hot and precise. Something that could be wielded. Controlled.

Several spikes of flesh shot from the creature, threatening to impale him, but Aaron felt them coming even before he saw them, reacting before they appeared, stepping to one side as they came and hacking them away. The creature swung one of its arms at him, the fist taking the shape of a hammer as it had before, but Aaron was ready for it this time, and he jumped back, the appendage passing in front of his face so closely that he could feel the wind from it. He took a moment to get control of his ragged breathing, and the creature, bleeding from dozens of cuts and stabs, many of which should have been fatal, was breathing hard itself, but smiling, too. "Fool," it croaked, its voice hoarse and full of pain, "I cannot die."

"Why me?" Aaron said, "Why my parents?"

The creature only grinned then, and Aaron stepped forward, hacking off one of its hands. It came free in a spurt of blood, and the creature screamed.

"*Why me?*"

The thing's scream abruptly cut off and it looked at the bloody stump as if fascinated by it, a thoughtful expression on the man's face. "Why you?" It said, looking back at him, "is it really so hard for you to understand, Aaron? It's because of who your father was, because of *what* he was. I'd say ask him," it grinned, "if you could."

"What do you *mean,* damnit? Because he was the general of Prince Eladen's army?"

The thing spat a mouthful of blood, bearing its crimson teeth. "I care nothing for Eladen, no more than that he was a vessel for one of the little ones. My interest with him ended there. No, Aaron Envelar, your father did not die because of the prince. He died because of a choice, one he made long before you were ever born."

"What choice?"

The creature smiled wider. "It would have been so neat, don't you see? So clean. You would have been found in the queen's chambers, dead, and the queen, oh she would have been terrified, of course, but alive. Or, at least," it winked, "someone that *looked* like the queen. I had meant, of course, not to be in such a rush—it generally is not my way, I assure you—but that fool Belgarin sends his army despite my orders. A thorn in my side, but one that will be dealt with as soon as I'm finished here."

"What *choice?*" Aaron repeated.

"Your friends, of course, the Parnen and the princess," the creature said as if he hadn't spoken, "well, they *had* to die, Aaron. Surely, you see that. They couldn't be left alive—they would ask too many questions. No," it said, "it is better that they are dead." It said the last with a grin, preparing to savor his reaction.

Aaron smiled back, "Sorry to disappoint you, friend, but Adina and Leomin are alive and well. The men you sent though ... I do not expect you'll hear from them again."

The creature's eyes drew down in a scowl then it howled, and though its visage was one of a man, the sound that issued from its throat was like that of some raging beast. It charged him with a speed that was shocking, its arms forming into spikes in front of it and had he not been prepared for it, Aaron would have been skewered. As it was, he stepped to the side, sliding his sword through the thing's throat but didn't completely manage to avoid its onward rush, its shoulder clipping him and sending him rolling backward. He rolled end over end until he finally came to an abrupt and jarring halt against the balcony's railing.

He grunted, shaking his head to clear it and looked up to see the creature standing framed in the door to the balcony, watching him with eyes filled with rage as it pulled the sword from its throat in a spurt of blood. It tried to speak, but the wound in its throat had not yet healed, and all that came out were wet, wheezing sounds.

It charged him, holding the sword in what was a normal arm once more and striking down at him where he lay. Aaron leapt up, inside of the thing's reach and grabbed the front of its tunic, rolling onto his back, bringing the creature with him, and kicking both legs into its stomach with all the momentum the roll gave him. The creature gave a scream and then it went tumbling over the railing.

Wincing, Aaron stretched his neck, one hand on his injured ribs as he lurched to his feet. He glanced over the railing and saw the creature hanging there by one hand that had transformed into a hook and latched onto the balcony's railing. Even as Aaron watched, it was lifting itself up, still smiling that bloody, mad grin. It tried to speak, but the wound in its throat had not closed yet—it seemed to Aaron that the healing it did slowed with each wound it was forced to mend—and it didn't matter anyway. Aaron knew well enough what it would say.

By the time he shuffled back to the railing with the discarded sword, the creature had managed to get its other arm around the railing and was working its way up. "What choice did my father make?" He said.

The creature stared up at him, the hole in its throat healed. "I will destroy everything you care about. I will find your woman, and I will carve such pain into her body—"

The blade went through the creature's wrist smooth, and its words dissolved into guttural grunts of pain and rage as it struggled to cling on with its remaining hand. "What choice?"

What little of a man remained in the thing was gone now, and it hissed and spat and chomped its teeth at him. "Maybe you can't die," Aaron said, shrugging and immediately regretting it for the pain that lanced through his chest, "I don't know one way or the other. But it seems to me, you're healing slower now. Have you noticed?"

The creature stopped and stared at him, frozen, its eyes going wide, then the blade cut down on the other wrist, and Aaron watched the thing fall into space. It struck the roof of a building far below, fell through it, and he lost sight of it as the ceiling collapsed.

There was a sound behind him, and Aaron turned to see the young captain Francis rushing in, his blade at the ready. "Guards come quickly! Someone tries to murder the queen!"

Aaron frowned, his eyes narrowing and stepped back through the balcony door to stand in the room facing the captain. "Strange," Aaron said, "that you would think someone was going to murder your queen, captain. Why is that, I wonder?"

"What?" The captain said, just noticing him, "I don't ... *you.* Why are you—"

"Alive, captain?" Aaron said, "Is that what you were going to ask? I'm supposed to be dead, right? Supposed to be lying here on the ground, and you were what, exactly? Supposed to take credit for killing me, for saving the queen? Only, it wouldn't have *been* the queen anymore, would it, captain? It would have been your master."

The captain glanced between the queen who stared at him with wide eyes back to Aaron. "I don't ... Your Majesty," he stammered, "this man ... this man—"

"This *man*," Isabelle said, her anger helping her to finally find her voice, "saved my life while the captain of my own guards plotted to take it. You will be executed, captain, your lands and title taken from you and your family, if there are any unlucky enough to be claimed as such. You and your name will be disgraced."

"You fat bitch," the captain said, and then he was rushing toward the bed, but Aaron, having seen it coming as the queen spoke, intercepted him halfway, charging his shoulder into the man and sending him hurtling against the wall. The captain grunted with pain and steadied himself, his blade still in his hand, "Alright, you common bastard," he said, "this will be no show this time, and I will kill you for my entertainment, and my entertainment alone. I will show you what true skill is."

The man came forward in a rush, his sword leading, swinging it in a wild, furious arc. Aaron knocked the blade aside almost casually then slammed the hilt of his own borrowed blade into the captain's nose, crushing it again and ruining whatever work the healers had done. The man fell to his knees, screaming in high-pitched, keening wails. Aaron brought the sword up and then down again, the hilt hammering into the captain's temple and the screams abruptly cut off as the man's body went limp and crumpled to the ground.

"Sorry," he said, glancing at the queen, "just couldn't take that screaming."

He looked up at the sound of approaching boots to see several guards pouring into the room. "Damnit," he said, "you guys have a knack for showing up at the perfect time."

They filed into the room without saying a word, six of them in total, spreading out along the edges of the room, their blades drawn. "Stand down," a familiar voice came, and Aaron saw Sergeant Brandon Gant limping into the room, a makeshift bandage wrapped around his middle. "Thank the gods," the man breathed, "Your Majesty, are you okay?"

The queen swallowed hard, visibly taking a moment to master her emotions, then she glanced at where Captain Francis lay in a pile on the floor, still unconscious. "Captain," she said, turning back to Brandon, and the older man's only reaction was to raise an eyebrow, "Have some of your men take this filth to the dungeon."

The sergeant nodded, "Of course, Your Majesty," he said, bowing his head. He motioned two men forward and they lifted the unconscious captain up between them and started away. "Go with them," he said to two more, "make sure he doesn't wake up and cause any trouble."

"*Yes sir,*" the men said in unison and then they too were gone, disappearing through the doorway.

"You were right, by the way," the new captain said, turning to Aaron, "four men came to assassinate your friends. Imagine my surprise when one of them was the general himself."

"*General Vander?*" The queen said, shocked.

The captain nodded, "I'm afraid so, my queen. General Vander is a traitor."

"What about Adina and Leomin?" Aaron said.

The sergeant smiled at him, "The princess and the Parnen are both alive and well, Mr. Envelar. Thanks to you."

Aaron breathed a heavy sigh of relief, sinking down to sit on the floor, his back against the wall. He realized he was still holding the borrowed blade, its edges coated with blood and dropped it. "Not me, serg—I'm sorry, *captain.* You did what I asked when you didn't have to and because of that they're alive. Thank you. If there's anything you ever need in the future, I'm your man."

"Well," the older man said, smiling wider now as he glanced at the queen, "there might just be one thing."

CHAPTER FORTY

"Come on, damnit!" Aaron shouted, "*Move your feet! You there, what was that?* Yeah, you," he said as the soldier who'd just been knocked down turned to him in question, "you're not chopping wood, man, you're fighting for your life. I see another wild swing, you're doing laps, you hear me?"

"Yes sir," the soldier said, getting back up and facing off with his opponent again. Aaron sighed, stretching in a vain effort to loosen the bandages that had been wrapped thickly around his chest. Seemed to him that the damned healers had decided Kevlane hadn't done a thorough enough job and planned to kill him by squeezing his insides to mush.

The bandages are to help you heal, Co said, and though he couldn't see her eyes, and although she didn't even *have* eyes, as far as he knew, he could hear her rolling them in her voice.

An easy thing to say when you're not the one that can't draw a breath, firefly. "Circles, damnit, stop moving back and forth like you're on some kind of damn game board. Move in circles!"

"*Yes sir,*" several of the soldiers shouted in unison before promptly going back to being game pieces.

"Maybe I should have been more specific when I said I'd help you any way I could," Aaron said, glancing sidelong where Captain Gant stood beside him.

The older man grinned, rubbing at the salt and pepper stubble on his chin, "Maybe," he said, then he glanced back at the hundreds of troops engaged in their practice duels. "Do you think they'll be ready?"

"To chop trees, maybe," Aaron said. "*You there, Bastion!*"

A thickly muscled youth of no more than nineteen years held up a hand to his winded opponent, turning to Aaron, "Sir?"

"Good foot work," Aaron said, and the young man grinned wide, "now, stop holding that sword like you're a virgin latched on to his first tit. *Gently,* Bastion, hold it *gently.* So gentle that, if it was a woman, her virtue would be gone before she knew it was being taken, you understand?"

"Yes sir," the youth said, still grinning, "just like a woman!" Then he went back to battering his weary opponent.

"According to the scouts we sent," the captain said, "Belgarin's army still hasn't left Baresh. We've still some time, it seems."

"Good," Aaron said, "maybe by the time they get here, some of these men will be able to swing their swords without dropping them. It'll be entertaining to watch, anyway, though I'm not sure for who."

"Ah," The captain said, looking past Aaron, "it seems you've someone that wishes to speak with you." He winked, "I'll come back."

Aaron turned to see Adina standing not far away and made his way to her. "General," she said, smiling widely, and Aaron groaned.

"Don't remind me, please. My *father* was a general. I'm a sellsword that knows how to make people bleed and little else."

"I'm no strategist," Adina said, still smiling, "but it seems to me that making people bleed is part of the requirement for winning a war."

She was beautiful standing there, as always, the sun shining in her dark hair, the dusty riding leathers she wore doing nothing to diminish her beauty. "How comes the training of the horsemen?"

"Well," Adina said, wincing, "they all know what a horse is now. At least, I'm fairly sure."

Aaron grunted a laugh, "It's a start, anyway."

"And you?" Adina said, glancing at the soldiers in their dusty leathers, watching the dance of their practice swords as men struggled against their opponents. "You know," she said, "they look different, out of those white uniforms and golden cloaks."

"Yeah," Aaron said, nodding, "they almost look like soldiers."

"We received word from Ellemont this morning."

"And?"

She turned to meet his eyes, "He agreed to meet with us."

"Well. It's a start," Aaron said again. "And what of Leomin? I haven't seen him in a day or two."

"Not many have, from what I gather," Adina said, smiling ruefully, "there also just so happen to be some young noblewomen that seemed to have vanished right around the same time."

Aaron groaned, "Gods, we'll find the man shacked up in one of those rooms or another," he said, glancing at the castle behind them.

"I suspect you're right," Adina said, "but, then, it might take some time. It's a big castle."

He sighed, "Right. And Owen?"

Adina frowned, "Still no sign. The men all have his description, anyway."

Aaron grunted, "For whatever that's worth. The man changes faces like I change clothes. More really."

She sniffed, "I noticed."

He grinned at her, and she pretended to fight him as he pulled her close and kissed her, feeling the best he'd felt in a long time. There was a lot of blood and pain and death coming their way— but, then, there always was. For now, the day was cool, the sun was warm, and she was with him. "I love you, you know."

"I know," she said, grinning, "Now, how much longer do you think it will be before you're finished here?"

Aaron let her loose of his embrace and glanced back at the training soldiers. "I don't know. Couple of hours, maybe, before they break to eat." He turned back, "Why?"

"Well," she said, grinning, that mischievous glint in her eyes that he'd come to know—and love. "I was just wondering. It's a big castle, after all."

Aaron couldn't help the grin that spread across his face, "*Sergeant Wendell!*" He yelled without looking away from her.

A man who'd been marching between the lines of fighting men, correcting them, ran to where Aaron and Adina stood, "Yes sir, general. Is the general too weary to eat and needs me to hand feed him again, sir?" He said, giving a grin that stretched the scar running diagonally across his face.

Aaron had discovered the man a few days after taking over as the army's general. A gruff, irreverent bastard that had been consigned to the most menial tasks Vander could find. Not pretty enough, Aaron guessed. As for his irreverence, Aaron found it refreshing. An ugly bastard, no doubt, but a good man. A good sergeant. And one that knew how to use a blade and command soldiers. "Nah, I just like to see a man with a dog's face run, always wonder if you're gonna go down on all fours or not."

The man's grin grew wider at that, and Aaron grunted. "Sergeant, I've got matters to attend at the castle, and I'll need you to take over."

"You mean," the sergeant said, "you got tired of standin' there holdin' that piece of ground down, and you want I should do everything, like always?"

Aaron grinned at Adina before looking back at the man. "Something like that, sergeant."

He grabbed Adina's hand and started leading her toward the castle in the distance when the sound of shouting and clapping erupted behind them. Aaron winced, refusing to turn as he led Adina on. Cheering. The bastards were *cheering*.

THE END

BOOK TWO
OF
THE SEVEN VIRTUES

BY JACOB PEPPERS

I hope you enjoyed visiting with Aaron, Adina, and the others again in *A Sellsword's Wrath*. To stay up to date on the next release and hear about other great promotions and giveaways, sign up to my mailing list at www.jacobpeppersauthor.com.

For a limited time, you will also receive a FREE copy of *The Silent Blade,* the prequel novella to The Seven Virtues, when you sign up!

Thanks for reading *A Sellsword's Wrath.* You can continue your journey with Aaron and the others by picking up your copy of *A Sellsword's Resolve,* the third book in The Seven Virtues series.

If you enjoyed the book, I'd really appreciate you taking a moment to leave an honest review—as any author can tell you, they are a big help.

If you want to reach out, you can email me at JacobPeppersauthor@gmail.com or visit my website at www.jacobpeppersauthor.com

Note from the Author

Well, dear reader, we've come to the end again. I hope you've enjoyed spending some more time with Aaron, Adina and the others. I also hope you were as surprised by some of the book's revelations as I was. As always, the book you've read would be much worse (picture a dozen wadded up page 1's, and you won't be far off; also, they'd probably be on fire) without the help of several people, so I'd like to take this opportunity to thank them now.

Thank you to my wife, Andrea, who sacrifices a lot so that I can sit around in house shoes and make things up. Thanks to my mom, dad, and brothers who never complain that nearly every conversation we have starts with me talking about people and places that aren't strictly real. Thank you also to my newborn son, Gabriel. I'm not sure how he helped with the book, but I'm sure he did and, anyway, he makes sure I get my exercise. What can I say? The little guy keeps me on my toes.

Thank you to all of those beta readers who took the time out of their busy schedules to share this dream with me for a time—the book is better for it. A very special thank you to Morris. Above and beyond, sir. Above and beyond.

And the final thanks? Well, I've saved that for you, dear reader. If it's been slightly gummed, I apologize. Gabriel tried to run off with it, but he's a baby and doesn't know any better, so I ask that you forgive him. Anyway, he didn't make it far. You see, he can't run yet. Or walk. Take it from me though, he's got the intense stare mastered. He reminds me of it every time I consider putting him down to work on my next book.

I am glad you took the time to visit with Aaron and the others. Aaron probably won't say it—truth is, he can be a bit of a jerk—so I'll say it for him. Thanks. And until next time,

I hope you find some wonderful worlds to explore,

Jacob Peppers

About the Author

Jacob Peppers lives in Georgia with his wife, his newborn son, Gabriel, and three dogs. He is an avid reader and writer and when he's not exploring the worlds of others, he's creating his own. His short fiction has been published in various markets, and his short story, "The Lies of Autumn," was a finalist for the 2013 Eric Hoffer Award for Short Prose.

Printed in Great Britain
by Amazon